The Regency *Season*

SCANDALOUS AWAKENING

ELIZABETH BEACON

MILLS & BOON

Published in Great Britain 2018
By Mills & Boon, an imprint of HarperCollins*Publishers*
1 London Bridge Street, London, SE1 9GF

THE REGENCY SEASON: SCANDALOUS AWAKENING © 2018
Harlequin Books S.A.

The Viscount's Frozen Heart © 2014 Elizabeth Beacon
The Marquis's Awakening © 2014 Elizabeth Beacon

ISBN: 978-0-263-93152-5

52-0218

Our policy is to use papers that are natural, renewable and recyclable products and made from wood grown in sustainable forests.
The logging and manufacturing processes conform to the legal environmental regulations of the country of origin.

Printed and bound by
CPI Group (UK) Ltd, Croydon, CR0 4YY

THE VISCOUNT'S FROZEN HEART

The Regency Season

August 2017

September 2017

October 2017

November 2017

December 2017

January 2018

February 2018

March 2018

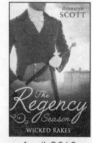
April 2018

May 2018

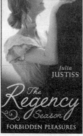
June 2018

July 2018

Elizabeth Beacon lives in the beautiful English West Country, and is finally putting her insatiable curiosity about the past to good use. Over the years Elizabeth has worked in her family's horticultural business, become a mature student, qualified as an English teacher, worked as a secretary and, briefly, tried to be a civil servant. She is now happily ensconced behind her computer, when not trying to exhaust her bouncy rescue dog with as many walks as the Inexhaustible Lurcher can finagle. Elizabeth can't bring herself to call researching the wonderfully diverse, scandalous Regency period and creating charismatic heroes and feisty heroines work, and she is waiting for someone to find out how much fun she is having and tell her to stop it.

Chapter One

Luke Winterley, Viscount Farenze, turned to help his daughter down from the carriage and watched Eve eye the fine house nestled into the rolling Wiltshire hillside like a jewel bedded on winter-pale green velvet.

'If only I had remembered Farenze Lodge was this beautiful I'd have teased you to bring me here a long time ago, Papa. I do recall Aunt Virginia giving me a sugarplum after I fell down the steps and cut my knee as a little tot, but that's about all,' she said and he had to smother a pang of guilt as he handed Eve's small but formidable maid from the carriage before answering, since he had kept Eve away so he wouldn't have to spend any more time here than necessary.

'No wonder that event stuck in your memory, but, yes, it *is* a very fine house,' Luke said with the second look the Palladian villa's neat elegance always deserved.

He had to brace himself for the empty feel of it without the last Viscountess Farenze here to make it a home, though. It was his duty to see Eve didn't feel the loss of her great-great-aunt even more acutely here, despite his own sorrow and frustration, and the less anyone knew about that second, rough-edged emotion and how hard it always bit him under this roof, the better.

'It doesn't seem anywhere near as vast to me now as it did back then,' Eve said, as determined to be cheerful for him as he was for her.

'No, it was built as a home, for all its grace and classical proportions,' he replied rather absently. It was currently home to a full complement of grieving staff and one very inconvenient housekeeper.

The mere thought of Mrs Chloe Wheaton waiting inside this serenely lovely house made him want to groan out loud, but somehow he kept silent and smothered another pang of guilt that he was about to make her homeless. He couldn't live under the same roof as Chloe Wheaton, yet still he felt this urgent need to see her again, if only to find out if she was as bitterly overwound by ten years of avoiding each other as he was.

'Virginia and Virgil liked their comfort, although I'm sure she would have done her best to love Darkmere if he really wanted to live there. Luckily he was always far happier in the home they made together here,' he told his daughter.

Somehow he must distract himself from Mrs Chloe Wheaton's presence here one more time, or he would end up wanting her almost beyond reason again. She was a widow with a young daughter. He had no right to long for her with this nagging, nonsensical ache whenever they were in the same county, let alone the same house.

'I don't remember your Uncle Virgil, Papa, but he looks far too rakish and cynical in that portrait of him in the gallery at home to fall deep in love with anyone, however lovely Aunt Virginia must have been sixty years ago.'

'Ah, but that was painted before they met and Virginia was a woman of character as well as an exotic beauty if *her* portraits are to be believed. I thought them the most deeply devoted couple I ever encountered and I'm far more of a cynic than Virgil ever was,' he said with a smile that went awry as he missed them both for the first time now Virginia had joined her beloved the other side of eternity.

'I'm not so sure you're as hard-headed as you think, Papa, but this is a fine house and it certainly *feels* as if it's been done with love.'

'I know what you mean,' Luke said with a brooding glance at the lovely place.

Unlike his predecessor, he loved Darkmere Castle and the stark beauty of its airy, windswept setting, but could see the attraction of having a smaller, more modern dwelling to retreat to on an ice-cold January afternoon like this one. He would need to spend part of the year here if he was to make sure it remained the gracious and elegant home Virgil and Virginia had always intended it to be. He cast a brooding glance at the lush parkland and rolling hills around him and decided most men would think him a fool or a liar if he said it was a mixed blessing. Yes, Mrs Chloe Wheaton would have to leave if he was to live here for very long, for both their sakes.

Even as he reaffirmed the rightness of his decision he saw a slender feminine figure come to stand below one of the half-lowered blinds at the long window of

Virginia's bedchamber to see who had arrived. Luke felt his heart jar, then race on at the double when the youthful housekeeper of Farenze Lodge visibly flinched under his fierce scrutiny. She met it with a proud lift of her chin and an icy composure he could only envy.

He couldn't swear under his breath with Eve standing so close she could hear every syllable, yet a clutch of unwanted need tightened its hot claw in his gut while he gazed back with furious hunger. It seemed my Lord Farenze wanted the dratted woman as hotly as ever and he still couldn't have her.

He's here, whispered the siren voice of unreason as Chloe glared at her bugbear and did her best to ignore it. *He's come back to you at last*, it whispered yearningly and she wished she could silence it for ever. It sprang back to life like some annoying spectre, refusing to be banished to outer darkness whenever she tried to pretend Lord Farenze was a gruff and disagreeable gentleman she could forget when she left for good. Since Virginia became so ill they lost hope of her survival, the thought of the viscount's arrival to mourn his beloved great-aunt only added to her desolation.

Yet she still felt a charge crackle in the air when he set foot on the straw-muffled gravel. Chloe knew who the latest arrival at Farenze Lodge was by some misplaced instinct, so why was she standing here staring at him like an idiot? Lord Farenze quirked a haughty eyebrow as if to ask why she had the right to stare? He was master of Farenze Lodge and so much more and she was only the housekeeper. Her inner fool was so hungry it kept her gazing at him even after she'd made it clear she wasn't going to shrink and tremble at the sight of him.

'Imbecile,' she muttered to herself.

He looked dominant, vigorous and cross-grained as ever. She could see that his crow-black hair was untouched by silver and too long for fashion when he mockingly swept off his hat and gave her an almost bow; dark brows drawn sharply above eyes she knew were nothing like the simple grey they looked from here. Close up they were complex as he was; silver grey and would-be icy, but with hints of well-hidden poetry and passion in the rays of gold and green at the centre of his clear irises. She wondered if such feelings would die if a man refused to admit he had them long enough.

Recalling a time when he'd almost swept them both to disaster on a raging tide of wanting and needing, she did her best to pretend her shiver was for the cold day and this dark time in both their lives, not the memory of a Luke Winterley nobody else at Farenze Lodge would recognise in the chilly lord on the gravel sweep below. The besotted, angry girl of a decade ago longed for him like a lost puppy, but mature Mrs Wheaton shuddered at the idea of succumbing to the fire and false promise of a younger, more vulnerable Lord Farenze and knew she had been right to say no to him.

'Who is it, my dear?' Culdrose, her late mistress's elderly dresser, asked from her seat by the vast and luxurious bed.

'Lord Farenze, Cully,' Chloe said with an unwary sigh and almost felt the older woman's gaze focusing on her back.

'And very good time he's made then, but why call him "imbecile" when he got here as fast as he could?'

'You have sharp ears, Cully. I wasn't talking about Lord Farenze,' Chloe said and promised herself she'd break free of his compelling gaze any moment now.

'I may have white hair, but my wits haven't gone a-begging. His lordship is a fine man, as any woman with two good eyes in her head can see. You'll only be a fool if you lose your wits over him.'

'I shall not,' Chloe murmured and turned away with a dignified nod she hoped told him: *I have seen you, my lord. I will avoid you like the plague from now on, so kindly return the compliment.*

What was so special about the woman his toes tingled and his innards burned at even the sight of her from afar? Luke told himself to be relieved when she broke that long gaze into each other's eyes across yards of icy January air. He didn't want more reminders of how close to disaster he once walked with her. Feeling ruffled and torn by feelings he didn't want to think about right now, he did his best to let the frigid breeze cool his inner beast and shivered at the idea of how cold it would be to ruin a good woman's reputation and mire her little girl's prospects with scandal.

He was six and thirty, not a green boy with every second thought of the female sex and an incessant urge to mate. If she could turn away with such cool disdain, he would get through this without begging for her glorious body in his bed. She was an upper servant; he recalled the fate of such women whose lovers wanted them so badly that they married beneath them out of desperation and shuddered. He might not like her much just now, but he couldn't wish such a fate on a woman he respected for her strength of character, even if it got confoundedly in the way of the pleasure they could have had in each other if she wasn't so sternly armoured against it.

'I wonder how it feels to love someone as deeply as Virginia did,' Eve mused and jarred Luke back to here and now. His heartbeat leapt into a panicky race at the idea his daughter had inherited her mother's ridiculous romantic notions.

'Painful and dangerous, I should imagine,' he replied brusquely.

'Now I think it could be wondrous and exhilarating to love the right person and have them love you back, Papa.'

'Your mother would have agreed with you, time after time,' he cautioned and shuddered at the memory of his wife falling in 'love' again and again as soon as she decided her young husband wasn't her ideal after all.

Sometimes traces of Pamela's pettish outbursts shook him if Eve pouted mulishly, or flounced out of the room in a headlong temper, but his Eve was too kind-hearted to treat a man as if he had no more feelings than a block of wood. He often wondered how such a loving child came from such an ill-starred marriage.

'Please choose someone worthy of you when you marry, Eve,' he cautioned. 'Don't accept the first beau to say he loves you one day and someone else the next.'

'I'm not an idiot, Papa, and you'll end up a lonely old cynic when I do find a fine man to spend my life with if you're not careful.'

'I want you settled before I find a suitable wife.'

Eve grimaced and rolled her eyes. 'Suitable?' she echoed dubiously. 'Aunt Virginia would hate to hear you speak so. It sounds as if you're expecting to choose a wife from an emporium and have her delivered to the church on an appropriate day for a wedding, complete with her bridal attire and a suite of attendants.'

'Although you're an impertinent young miss, I have to admit Virginia wasn't happy with the idea,' Luke said, his last conversation with his great-aunt by marriage running through his mind a little too vividly for comfort.

'You only married That Fool because your father and stepmother threw her at your head and it seemed a good idea at the time,' Virginia raged when he unwarily set out his plan to remarry as soon as Eve was settled. 'If you wed a "suitable" young lady, at least have the decency to fall in love with a mistress.'

Virginia had given a weary sigh when he smiled cynically at the very idea of loving a female he must marry to beget an heir.

'No,' she argued with herself. 'Don't. No woman deserves to marry the cold fish you think you are, then watch you love a hussy instead. You're a passionate man under all the starch and to-hell-with-you manner and another marriage like the last one will break you. Please don't imagine you'll be lucky enough to breed a sweet child on a ninny twice in one lifetime— no man deserves to be that fortunate.'

'I'm not a lovable man,' Luke said gruffly. His mistress's enthusiasm told him he was a good enough lover, but lust wasn't love.

'Then your Eve and I secretly hate you, do we?' Virginia argued. 'And your staff and tenants loathe you behind your back as well, I suppose? Obviously they only put up with you brooding and barking at them because you pay well enough and don't burn their cottages down for fun, or prey on their womenfolk when you feel the urge to rut. You married an empty-headed flirt who dedicated her life to falling in love with any rogue she took a fancy to when she had a good and handsome husband, but it wasn't your fault, Luke. Your father knew he was dying and persuaded you to marry far too young, and how lucky for that harridan he wed after your mother died that Pamela birthed a daughter, then ran off with the first rogue who would have her.'

'Lucky for me as well. I love Eve dearly,' he had said stiffly.

'Yes, yes I know, and James will be your heir if needs be. But he needs to be his own man instead and your second trip up the aisle will be a bigger disaster than the first if you only intend to wed a "suitable" wife,' she warned a little too seriously for comfort.

'If I thought James would manage the Winterley interests with half the dedication he puts into carousing, curricle racing and gambling, he could have it all with my blessing. If I were leaving my downtrodden tenants in safe hands when I meet my maker, there would be no need for me to remarry.'

'Safer than either of you think, but James can't spend his life waiting to step into your shoes; he deserves better.'

'Does he indeed?' Luke had replied harshly, wondering if even Virginia had any idea how deep the rift between them ran.

'Papa?' Eve prompted now and he wondered how Chloe Wheaton stepping into that window shot his concentration into the ether.

'I should have made you stay home, Eve. For all Virginia wanted nobody to mourn her, her household loved her too much to carry on as if nothing has happened.'

'This is real life, not a pretty fairy story, Papa,' his daughter chided as if she were an adult and he the sixteen-year-old.

'Then I suppose we'd better get on with facing this place without Virginia to welcome us, since you would come.'

'Yes, I would. I loved her too.'

'And she adored you from the day she laid eyes on the squalling brat you were back then, my Eve. It was beyond the rest of us at the time why she should, since you were screaming like a banshee about some new teeth we were all having trouble with at the time. Virginia spent three months at Darkmere every summer until you were old enough for us to meet her in Brighton for sea air and shopping, so you must know she loved you back, considering she couldn't abide the place.'

'I do,' she said and looked so bereft he wanted to hug her, then send her back to Darkmere straight away, but he knew she was right—his daughter was almost an adult. He must let her make her own decisions, even if they went against his instincts to guard her from anything that might hurt her. 'Why didn't we come here instead when I was young, Papa?' she asked. 'You never stay at Farenze Lodge for more than a few days, yet you seem to love it almost as much as Darkmere.'

'It's easier not to,' Luke replied carefully.

Easier for him, since it was either that or stay here and make Chloe Wheaton his mistress by stoking this fire between them until she gave in instead of dousing it as best he could by avoiding her. The lady had had some very pithy things to say when he was driven to suggest it years ago and it would have been a long siege, but something told him it would have succeeded in the end.

So how *would* it feel to love and be loved? Impossible; intolerable even and he didn't love the woman and she certainly didn't love him. He would wait a year or two and find his suitable wife once Eve had decided her own future. A pretty and biddable young widow or some sweet-natured, overlooked spinster lady he could marry for an heir would suit him very well. Even as he reaffirmed that sensible plan with his rational mind the image of a very different Mrs Chloe Winterley from the sad-eyed female he'd just seen drifted into his head and made him bite back a virulent curse.

The first summer day she strolled into his life she looked warm and open as well as ridiculously young and stunningly beautiful. That version of Chloe Wheaton jarred something into life inside him he'd thought he was far too cynical and weary to feel by the time he was six and twenty. Luke frowned now as he had then, because people who felt that vividly got hurt. He hadn't wanted that lovely, ardent young creature with her red-gold locks escaping the bands she'd tried to confine them to end up narrowed and disappointed as he was, yet the woman he had just seen was nothing like the warm and irresistible girl he thought he'd met that day.

Somehow he had made himself leave her to swing her bonnet by its strings as she walked home to whatever well-to-do family she hailed from with impossible dreams in her heart he'd only wished he could make come true. No, he was too embittered and shop-soiled for such a hopeful young lady, he'd decided regretfully, even as he met her astonishing violet eyes and only just prevented himself falling headlong into them as if that was where he belonged. Riding away from her was one of the hardest things he'd ever had to do, but he'd been disillusioned about her even sooner than he had about Pamela.

Only a couple of hours later he found out the girl was Virginia's new companion and supposed housekeeper, on the way back from visiting her baby daughter at nurse. A widow who claimed to be two and twenty and looked a young eighteen. Virginia had reassured him she was as well aware of the tallness of Mrs Chloe Wheaton's story, but she hadn't had so much fun in years. So what could he do about an encroaching so-called widow when Virginia did indeed seem almost as full of life again at last as she had been when her beloved Virgil was still alive?

Her furious rejection of his offer of a *carte blanche* ten years ago still rang in his ears as if she'd denounced him an arrogant and repellent rake only yesterday. If she still felt the same hellish tension that roared through him whenever he set eyes on her, she had learnt to hide it very well. Seeing her drawn and exhausted hadn't helped *him* ignore it so regally though. Instead it laid a line of fellow feeling between them to see her so grief-stricken and he didn't want to share anything with Mrs Chloe Wheaton.

Luke shook his head and thanked heaven he was wearing a long greatcoat to conceal how eagerly his body ignored his stern orders not to want the housekeeper as he turned his gaze away from the now empty windows and silently cursed himself for being such a fool.

Chapter Two

'Who was that, Papa?' Eve asked.

'Whom do you mean?' he asked stiffly, like a school-boy caught out in a blatant lie, he decided, as he wondered what sort of blundering beast the wretched woman would turn him into next.

'The lady at the window.'

'A maid on the alert for mourners?'

'She looked more like the housekeeper, although if so she looked very young for such a responsible role.'

'She is,' Luke replied grimly. 'She must have been in the schoolroom when she met Wheaton.'

'Who on earth is Wheaton? The January air seems to have addled your brain instead of sharpening it as you claimed it would when you left us to count church spires and grey mares while you rode most of the way here, Papa.'

'I thought you two had enough schemes to hatch out for who was to do what and when after we got here to keep you occupied for a sennight.'

'Slander; we're not at all managing, are we, Bran?' Eve quizzed her diminutive one time-nurse and now ladies' maid.

'Even if we was, we'd be well and truly talked to a standstill by now,' Eve's unlikely personal dragon answered with a sharp look that told Luke she understood his latest battle of wills with Chloe Wheaton even if his innocent daughter didn't.

'Well, now we're here you will have too many people to talk to rather than too few,' he warned as they climbed the shallow steps.

The hatchment over the door was a stark reminder why they were here and Luke felt the wrongness of this place without the lady who had loved and lived here for so long to bid him welcome. He sighed and told himself the next few days would pass and life would go relentlessly on, whatever he had to say about it.

'Miss Winterley is with his lordship,' Chloe remarked as she turned from the window and only wished she dared avoid the master of the house a little longer.

'No doubt she had to plague Master Luke something relentless to make that happen. Very protective he is; a good father and a fine man, whatever that stepmother of his says.'

'I imagine he takes little very notice of her,' Chloe said absently.

Having been on the wrong end of his protective nature herself, ten years of enduring his distrust stung more sharply than it should. He was probably surprised she hadn't run off with Virginia's jewellery or the housekeeping money long ago.

'That woman made the poor lad's life a misery. I can't understand to this day why Mr Oswald married her. Mr Oakham overheard her telling Mr James to do all he could to blacken Mr Luke's name now the family are here to put the "old besom in her grave", as the nasty-minded old crow put it. Lady Virginia wouldn't have her over the threshold if she was alive to say her nay, but Master Luke was always too kind-hearted for his own good and no doubt he'll let her stay.'

'I'm sure Mrs Winterley will behave herself now his lordship is here, whatever she might say to her son. She seems in awe of Lord Farenze and I've heard he controls her purse strings.'

'Then I hope he gives her short shrift one day; she deserves no better.'

'I don't want any more tension and upset, so please don't put something noxious in her soup, Cully. She might never leave if she fancied herself too ill to travel and think how awful it might be if she once got her feet under the table.'

'She'll leave fast enough if I put a purge in her coffee, and good riddance.'

'No, wait out the week and most of the mourners will go home and leave you all in peace,' Chloe urged, trying not to wonder where she would be by then.

'I suppose so,' Culdrose agreed reluctantly, 'but it's hard to stay silent when we loved her ladyship dearly. I won't have her name blackened now she's not here to stand up for herself.'

'Nobody would do so at her funeral. It would be disrespectful and heartless.'

Culdrose sniffed loudly; 'I still caught the woman sneaking about her ladyship's boudoir yesterday. Searching through her letters and personal things she was as if she had every right to do what she liked here.

It's as well we locked Lady Virginia's treasures away in the strongroom after Oakham caught that Miss Carbottle taking her ladyship's diamond brooch as a keepsake, or so she said. Keepsake indeed, she's no better than a jackdaw.'

'She does have a habit of taking anything pretty or shiny that's lying about. Her sister always brings it back, but I'm glad you spared her the embarrassment. Now I must go down and greet Miss Winterley as she is the new mistress of the house. Promise you won't make things worse between Mrs Winterley and the staff than they already are though, Cully?'

'You know it's my way to let my feelings out with them I trust to keep their counsel, so I don't say aught I shouldn't in front of the quality. Miss Eve being mistress of this house until his lordship marries again won't go down well with Mrs Winterley though, you mark my words.'

'So noted,' Chloe said and went downstairs to do her duty.

Stupid to feel as if a knife had been stabbed in her heart at mention of Lord Farenze remarrying, as he must to beget an heir. Best not to think where she would go next until the mourners left either. Lord Farenze wouldn't keep her on and she couldn't stay even if he wanted her to, but there *was* a deal of work before she could walk away with her last duty to her late mistress done.

Luke signalled at the waiting footman to close the doors behind them against the icy easterly wind and missed Virginia's imperious command to come on in do, lest she expire in the howling gale he was letting in.

'Thank you, Oakham,' he said, seeing the butler had set chairs near the blazing fire and offered hot toddies to Eve and Bran to stave off the cold. 'I would wish you a good day, but we both know there is no such thing right now.'

'Indeed not, my lord,' the elderly manservant replied with a sad shake of his head that said more than words.

Even over the mild stir of activity Luke caught the sound of Mrs Wheaton's inky skirts and disapproving petticoats as she descended the grand staircase and tried to pretend neither of them were really here. *So, she steeled herself to meet the new master of the house, did she?* Luke admired her courage even as he wished it would fail her and his senses sprang to attention. Even in buttoned-up mourning array she was hauntingly lovely, but close to she looked even more drawn and weary. Feelings that seemed far more dangerous than simple desire kicked him in the gut and he wished her a hundred miles away more fervently than ever.

'Good day, Mrs Wheaton,' he greeted her woodenly. 'Please show my daughter and her maid to their rooms, then see their luggage is sent up.'

'Good afternoon, my lord; Miss Winterley,' she replied with an almost respectful curtsey in his direction.

'Good afternoon, Mrs Wheaton,' Eve said with a smile that seemed to relax the stubborn woman's air of tightly wound tension. 'I've heard so much about you. Great-Aunt Virginia was always full of your daughter's quaint sayings and doings when she was a babe and she sounds a bright and lively girl now she's at school.'

'By "bright and lively" folks usually mean a limb of Satan, into every piece of mischief she can find. If the girl is anything like you were at that age, Miss Eve, Mrs Wheaton has my sympathy. I could fill a book with the things you got up to when you were a child,' Bran said dourly.

Luke concluded Bran liked Mrs Wheaton for some reason and, whatever the facts of Eve's birth, Mrs Brandy Brown was the closest thing to a mother his Eve had. He was grateful to the diminutive dragon for loving his daughter fiercely after losing her husband, then her own babe soon after birth, but he wished Bran would show her usual distrust of any servant likely to look down their noses at such a unique ex-nurse and ladies' maid. The last thing he needed was closer contacts between his family and the Wheatons, but, if she diverted Eve from her grief, he supposed he would have to endure it.

'My Verity is on pins to meet you, Miss Winterley, and Lady Virginia told her lots of exotic tales about the castle you live in and the wild Border Reivers who once fought over it. As my daughter persuaded her teachers I need her to come home, she will be here as soon as a carriage can be spared to fetch her,' Chloe said ruefully.

A smile softened her generous mouth and lit her violet-blue eyes to depths of enchantment that would make a poet quiver with excitement when she talked of her only child. Even Luke's workaday imagination wanted to go on the rampage when a red-gold curl escaped her black-trimmed housekeeper's lace bonnet and threatened to curl about her heart-shaped face. Given freedom, her rebellious auburn locks would kiss her forehead with escaped fronds of red-gold fire. Or maybe they would lie in loose ringlets down the refined line of her long neck and on to white shoulders revealed by a gown cut to show off her womanly charms... Poetry be damned, the woman was a temptation to pure sin and never mind the romantic sighing of buffle-headed dreamers who ought to wake up to the realities of life.

'She's probably right,' Eve was insisting softly and Luke had to rack his brains to recall who *she* was and what she was right about. 'Papa would have it I should stay in Northumberland and sit out Aunt Virginia's funeral, but that would only make me miss her more. Your daughter has lost a good friend, Mrs Wheaton.'

'And you are a wise young lady, Miss Winterley.'

'Oh, I doubt that, but you must call me Eve, ma'am.'

'I can hardly do that if you insist on calling me so and it would be considered sadly coming in a housekeeper to address you by your given name.'

'Then will you do so when we are private together? And I think we could resort to my rooms and send for tea now, don't you? We must discuss how best to go on over the next few days and I'd rather not be Miss Winterley-ed all the time we're doing it.'

Listening to his remarkable daughter do what he couldn't and coax Chloe Wheaton upstairs to join her for tea and some gentle gossip, Luke sighed and met Oakham's eyes in a manly admission: they didn't understand the restorative power of tea or small talk and probably never would.

'I have refilled the decanters in the library, my lord, or I could bring some of his late lordship's best Canary wine to your room. I believe Mr Sleeford and his father-in-law are currently occupying the billiard room.'

Taking the warning in that impassive observation,

Luke murmured his thanks and made his way up the nearest branch of the elegant double stairway. He entered the suite of rooms Virginia had insisted he took over as the one-day master of the house a year after Great-Uncle Virgil died and was glad Mrs Wheaton had ordered fires lit in all three rooms against his eventual arrival.

He was grateful for the warmth and sanctuary the suite promised him tonight, despite his reluctance to use it at first. With so many people gathering for his great-aunt's funeral he must savour any peace he could get over the next few days.

As they sipped tea and discussed arrangements for the household over the next few days, Chloe wondered why Miss Evelina Winterley hadn't been permitted to stay here during the decade Chloe had lived here. Lord Farenze and his daughter always joined Lady Virginia in Brighton or Ramsgate for several weeks every summer, but his visits to Farenze Lodge were so fleeting he rarely stayed so much as a night, let alone long enough to uproot his daughter and bring her with him. Fury flashed through her as the familiar notion *she* was the reason he had kept Eve away until now fitted neatly into her mind.

It was true that scandalised whispers spread through the neighbourhood when she first came here as Virginia's companion-housekeeper, with a baby daughter and no visible husband all those years ago. If only they knew, she decided bleakly, weariness threatening to overcome her once more. She fought it off by using her anger with the new master of the house to stiffen her backbone, for she might be about to leave this place, but she intended to do it with dignity intact.

'Lady Virginia told me I would like you if I ever had the chance, Mrs Wheaton, and I feel I know you already,' Eve Winterley said as she refilled a teacup and passed it to her maid without even needing to ask if she would like seconds after their long journey.

Such closeness between mistress and maid should not surprise her, she supposed, but Chloe recalled Lord Farenze's attitude to those he considered beneath him and contrasted it with his daughter's more liberal one. Reluctantly she decided it spoke well of him that he was so relaxed about Mrs Brown's role in his daughter's life, then did her best to forget him for a few blissful moments.

'And I'm very glad to meet you, Miss Winterley, even at this sad time.'

'You will miss Lady Virginia as badly as any of us after being her friend and companion for so long,' Eve said sincerely and for a long moment all three women sat thinking about how odd their lives felt without that vivid presence. 'Although this is a beautiful house, Papa has never coveted it. He always said the Lodge was Aunt Virginia's home and wouldn't hear of her moving out of it when Uncle Virgil died. It's quite lovely, don't you think?' Eve asked with a guileless look Chloe didn't quite trust.

'Exquisite,' she said carefully.

'No wonder Aunt Virginia couldn't bear to leave when Uncle Virgil died, although I believe Papa was very worried about her when rumours went about she had run mad with grief, wasn't he, Bran?'

'Indeed he was, the poor lady.'

'Papa says he wondered if she should still live here for her own sake then, but she couldn't abide Darkmere and refused to set foot in our house in Kent. Papa could hardly evict Mrs Winterley from the Dower House there, so he let the subject drop when Virginia bought the house in Hill Street and we all went on very much as we were, or so I'm told, since I was but a babe in arms at the time and don't remember.'

'Her ladyship thought the Kentish house old and dreary and she said most of the chimneys smoked, so I doubt she would have wanted to live there, even if the Dower House was vacant,' Chloe said, hoping her dislike of Mrs Oswald Winterley didn't show.

She wouldn't want to live within a day's drive of the lady herself, given the choice, and, as Mrs Winterley reluctantly resided in the Haslett Hall dower house, instead of the fashionable London town house she thought Luke Winterley owed her, for some reason nobody else could fathom, Virginia had avoided Haslett Hall like the plague.

'Papa had several chimney stacks rebuilt when he took over the Farenze estates, so I doubt any smoke now. He won't have climbing boys used in any of our houses and if the sweep says they're too small or crooked to use brushes on, he has the stacks rebuilt until they can be done that way without sending those poor little boys up into the dark to choke or get stuck.'

'My little brother was put up chimneys when hardly old enough to walk and he didn't live to see his tenth birthday. His lordship's a good man,' Mrs Brandy Brown insisted and Eve Winterley agreed then watched Chloe with expectant eyes.

'To oppose such a practice he must be,' she said as tactfully as she could and tried to pretend he meant no more to her than any good man would.

Liar, a more truthful inner Chloe prodded her uncomfortably, but somehow she would make it true. Ten years ago she had longed for gruff and embittered Luke, Lord Farenze, with every fibre of her being. At seventeen she'd been little more than a wilful, embittered child though; it took her daughter's dependence on her to force her to grow up and realise she couldn't have what she wanted and keep her self-respect.

Chloe sighed at the familiar tug of hot warmth she'd felt at first sight of the viscount in possession even today. No, it didn't matter. Whatever she felt changed nothing. She only had to keep out of his way and stamp on any wayward desires left over from that heady time for a few more days then she would be free of him.

Yet this infernal tiredness was dragging at her like a pall and threatened to spin her back into dreams of forbidden things if she let her control slip. First there would be the old fantasy of the Chloe she should be—if life was fair. A charming, alluring lady who could win, and hold, the passionate devotion of gruff Lord Farenze as they danced off into a rosy future. An image of him; his expression impossibly tender as he made it clear how desperately he longed for her with every fibre of his cynical being, shimmered like a mirage.

Horrified, she snapped her nodding head upright and righted her empty teacup before it slipped from her slack grip and shattered. *Oh, heavens, had she mut-*

tered any of that out loud? She met compassion instead of horror when she plucked up the courage to meet her new friend's eyes, so perhaps not.

'I hope you don't mind me saying so, Mrs Wheaton, but you need a nap,' Mrs Brandy Brown told her.

Chloe shivered at the thought of nightmare-haunted snatches of sleep she'd had since her beloved mistress died. 'You must know how long a woman can go without sleep from your experience when Miss Evelina was a baby, Mrs Brown,' she forced herself to say instead of admitting the turmoil had awoken old memories that haunted her dreams until she avoided her bed as if it was stuffed with thistles.

'Aye, some nights the poor little mite cried as if her heart was broken and it was all I could do not to join her,' the tiny, forceful little woman agreed with a rueful, loving look for the girl who seemed so equable nowadays it seemed hard to believe.

'I know exactly what you mean,' Chloe said with a picture of her own struggles to calm a restless and furious baby when Verity was teething, or ill, or just plain fretful and she felt about as useful as a tailor's dummy, making her very glad those times were over for both their sakes.

'His lordship used to put his little miss into a pack on his shoulders and carry her for miles over the moors until she slept at long last. I'd stay behind, telling myself they were quite safe and he could see like a cat in the dark and knows the paths across his land like the back of his hand until I fell asleep too, whether I wanted to or not. You had to cope with all that on your own and run this great house at the same time. It sounds as if you got through it stoutly enough all these years, but we're here now, so at least you can have a rest when you need one,' Bran told her with an earnest nod that disarmed Chloe and made her wonder if it might be bliss to lay her burdens down and do as she was bid after all.

'Indeed you must, Mrs Wheaton,' Eve told her with some of her father's authority sitting quaintly on her slender shoulders. 'Sleep is the last thing on *my* mind after hours shut up in that stuffy carriage dozing because there was nothing else to do—how about you, Bran?'

She gave the comfortable bed in the slip of a room the other side of the dressing room, reserved for a maid if her mistress wanted one close, a significant look and her maid nodded her approval of the unspoken idea. It looked just right for an afternoon nap if Chloe did happen to be as bone weary as she obviously looked.

'I had a nice doze on the way to Bath this morning, as you know very well, Miss Eve, since you've been twitting me about it ever since.'

'How disrespectful of me, but I think we should wrap ourselves up in cloaks and shawls to walk in that pretty Winter Garden I saw from the window on the half-landing. I'd like to stretch my legs and it would do us good to air our wits before it gets dark. Nobody will disturb you if I order them to leave our unpacking until we return, Mrs Wheaton, and Bran and I will soon have everything arranged when we get back. I can be very finicky about the disposal of my things when occasion demands and nobody will interfere.'

'She can indeed, Mrs Wheaton,' Bran agreed smugly and Chloe felt weariness weigh down as she wondered if she dare risk her dreams for once.

'You would wake me the moment you came back in?' she asked and heard her own words slur with tiredness, as if she'd been fighting it so long it now had to win.

Lord Farenze was here to shoulder the responsibility of the estate and the ageing staff and she would rather sleep than think about him.

'If you can sleep through madam here ordering me about, you're a better woman than I am,' Bran said, then followed her young mistress from the room.

Chloe barely managed to slip off her shoes, unhook her gown and slip out of it before falling fast asleep the moment her head hit the pillow.

'Lasted as best she could until help came, if you ask me,' Bran observed softly as soon as she and her young mistress were finally clear of the house unseen and able to speak freely.

'Poor lady,' Eve replied carefully.

'Aye, she seems like one to me as well,' Bran mused and met Eve's speculative gaze with a thoughtful frown.

Bran did not believe a fairytale lay behind whatever made a lady become a housekeeper. Even if a story started out with garlands of roses and fairy dust, it rarely ended so in the stark light of day in Brandy Brown's experience.

Chapter Three

Luke waited until his valet accompanied a footman upstairs, his luggage borne along as carefully as the crown jewels, before quitting his private sitting room with an exasperated sigh. He wondered why he'd employed such an exacting valet; he was old enough to dress himself and could tie a necktie that wouldn't scare the horses. In a year or so he'd have to present a neat appearance for Eve's début and his wife-hunting campaign, though, and it had seemed a sensible enough idea at the time. Right now he'd welcome a tramp across the countryside, or a long ride on a swift horse to banish his blue devils, but wealth, power and a title came at a cost so he ignored the urge to escape.

Hearing his stepmother's sharp voice in the drawing room and the rumble of male ones from the billiard room, Luke tried to find some peace in the library. Virginia's godson, the Marquis of Mantaigne, was ensconced in a comfortable chair by the fire, but Luke gave a sigh of relief. The air of world-weary cynicism Tom wore like a suit of armour drove women wild with desire for some odd reason, but he was good company and a loyal friend.

'Tom, you rascal,' he said, managing a genuine smile and a sincere manly handshake even on this sad day. 'When did you get here?'

'This morning—you must have travelled in my dust.'

'You only had to come from Derbyshire and there was more mud than dust.'

'How unobservant of me,' Tom drawled.

'Don't try to hoodwink me that you're too idle to take an interest in what's about you, Tom. I know you too well to be taken in by the air of cynicism you use to keep the world at bay. Just tell me who has come here to gladden our heavy hearts and your estimate of how long I'll be forced to house them for, there's a good fellow.'

'Whoever told you I'm a good fellow clearly needs disillusioning.'

'I don't pay much heed to the opinions of others when it comes to my real friends, my lord Marquis,' Luke said and accepted the glass of fine burgundy his friend poured out of the decanter at his side with an almost smile.

Feeling more relaxed after the mellowing effect of the very finest wine and a shrewd and succinct summary of his assembled guests from Tom Banburgh, Luke left him to his solitude and the burgundy and avoided the groups in the billiard room and drawing room to go up and re-assure himself Eve and Bran were settling in after the trials and discomfort of their long journey.

Chloe felt weighed down by sleep when she managed to blink her heavy eyes open and tried to gauge how long she'd been lost to the world. For a moment she had no idea where she was and had to force her eyes open to stop herself sinking under the weight of sleep beckoning her back like a siren. Virginia would probably be the first to order her to get up and face the world, so she blinked several times and did her best to banish the huge waves of sleep trying to drag her under again.

Even an upper servant could enjoy the luxury of a long stretch, so she yawned and extended her legs fully against the fine cotton sheets of Brandy Brown's narrow bed, then reached her hands high above her head so her arms could feel the pull and strength of youth in them. She shook her head so the auburn locks tumbled down in a tangle it would take far too long to tease out when she'd already wasted goodness knew how long asleep when she should be up and doing.

'Bran?' a deep masculine voice questioned from the other side of the slightly open door and Chloe felt her heartbeat speed up like a greyhound after a rabbit. 'You can't be asleep because I saw you in the garden not five minutes ago. Where's Eve and why is her luggage still cluttering up her bedroom?'

If she wasn't in her shift with her hair falling down her back, she could call out a brusque answer and he would go away. Would that serve anyway? If she sounded assured and awake enough, he might go away rather than risk being discovered here with a female servant in the middle of a winter afternoon?

'Mrs Brown is taking the air with your daughter, Lord Farenze,' she managed to call out as if she was busy and didn't have time for answering questions.

A stiff moment of shocked silence and she could almost feel him flinch at the sound of her voice a room and a half away. Unfortunately, she didn't hear him walking away though. *Yet did she really want him to?* As usual her inner Chloe chose the worst moment to stage a revolution. She told her to be quiet and get back in her cage and stop there. She *did* want him to leave and sat up in the neat little tent bed, holding every muscle and sinew tense and still in the hope he would go. Something about the silence on the other side of the door told her he was still there, but a woman could always hope.

'Why the devil are you unpacking Eve's things when one of the maids could do it if Bran is busy?'

'I…' She ground to a halt and told herself if she hadn't slept so deeply and so stupidly in the middle of a working day she might be able to find an answer that would satisfy him somewhere in her befuddled brain.

'Cat got your tongue?' he growled and was that really a thread of laughter in his deep voice?

Impossible—Lord Farenze and Mrs Wheaton had nothing to laugh about. There was no level of intimacy to put a hint of smoky amusement in his voice. She'd imagined it and now her inner Chloe was busy imagining more than she ought to all over again. Such as how it might feel to wake up in his bed with her mind misted with sleep and loving, then share the closeness of lovers with him as he teased her back to full awareness of where she was, and who she was with, in his own unique fashion.

'No, it's still in perfect working order,' she managed to reply as if she was merely too busy to argue with him.

'Then come out here and talk to me face to face; I refuse to hold a conversation through inches of fine mahogany.'

'I can't, I'm far too busy today, my lord,' she managed and heard the note of panic in her voice as she sensed him stepping closer to the door in question and about to discover her sitting here in a state of scandalous disarray.

'No doubt but, since I'm master here now, you must deal with me sooner or later. Far better to get the plans we must make for the next few days out of the way as soon as possible and rub along as best we can, rather than skirt round the subject all week and send the staff spinning about in opposite directions between us.'

He sounded as reluctant to have that discussion as she was, so why couldn't he put it off until he was rested from his journey and she was back in her buttoned-up gown with her wretched hair wound safely under a neat cap and hidden away with feral Chloe, who so badly wanted to respond to him in every way a woman could?

'Very well, my lord, I will meet you downstairs as soon as I have finished here,' she said and heard the waver of uncertainty in her own voice.

Her reluctance to confront him with the memory of sitting here half-naked and all he could have been to her, if everything was different, wobbled in her too breathy voice. She didn't dare stir in case he heard the rustle of crisply laundered sheets and realised she was in bed. Sitting frozen and speechless, she gasped in horror when he finally lost patience and thrust the door open.

Time seemed to stretch and waver as he strode into the little room then stopped dead, as if a wicked witch's spell had frozen him in his tracks. He stood staring hungrily back at her and how could she fool herself everything that could have been between them was dead now?

He should turn and walk away of course; leave her to blush and squirm and be furious with herself for giving in to exhaustion and his daughter's urgings to rest. He didn't, though, and it was there in his eyes, the might be. Not a never, but a might be; a dangerous chance of more between master and servant than there ought to be.

A detached part of her seemed to be looking down on them; speculating how two rational human beings could look so much like codfish and still stare rapt into each other's eyes as if they'd longed for the sight of the other all unguarded for the years they'd been apart. The rest couldn't even find the presence of mind to squirm down in her bed and hide her disarray.

Now he looked like all the robber barons who founded his mighty dynasty rolled into one as he stood stock still, so vividly present he seemed to suck the air out of the room along with her common sense. *Like a very well-dressed statue of a warrior prince*, that annoying wanton Chloe remarked, *would he was a little less still and a lot less well dressed*. 'Be quiet!' she whispered, then covered her mouth. She couldn't believe she was arguing with her wicked inner self with *him* in the room. Perhaps she really was going mad?

A wistful hope she might wake up and find she'd dreamt him made the tension drain out of her muscles for all of half a minute. Nobody could dream muscular, powerful, intimidating Lord Farenze when he was all too present. He was a living, breathing human being, staring at her as if being torn by a raging tumult of contrary emotions as well. There just wasn't enough dreaming in the world to conjure up a man like him, here, locked in this particular moment with her.

'I didn't say a word,' he managed in a rusty voice that sounded forced out.

'Not you.'

'You have a lover hidden under the bed?' he barked as if he thought her everything a woman shouldn't be if she wanted to retain her self-respect.

His hot eyes dwelt on her wildly flushed cheeks, shocked and hazy eyes and the tumble of hot gold curls she knew were in nearly as big a tangle as her tongue.

'No room,' he mused more softly and let his gaze explore the little room as if he'd never seen one like it before and saw the exposed space under the high little bed with what looked suspiciously like satisfaction, 'nor a second door for a coward to escape through if he was in danger of being found and the closet's not big enough.'

'I don't have a lover.'

Now she sounded like an outraged stage heroine and Chloe thought it as well he couldn't see her toes curling under the bedclothes. His black brows rose and a smile of cynical appreciation she assured herself she would like to slap off his face kicked up his mouth and made him look nigh irresistible for a breathless moment.

'Any man who saw you thus would be your slave as soon as he could persuade you into his eager arms. Say the word and we'll adjourn to my own lonely and echoing suite along the hallway,' he offered half-seriously.

'Never, never, never,' she shot back at him, spine rigid and chin high.

He couldn't know she burned for his touch. Even the tips of her toes seared her with a need to be kissed and seduced that made a lie of her conviction there could never be anything between them, after she'd angrily informed him she would rather die than become his mistress ten years ago.

And he just stood there; let his complex grey gaze play over her as if she had been arranged here especially for his pleasure. He wanted her, the need in his complicated eyes was as real as the hot rush of heat between her legs. She clamped them together under the sheets then instantly regretted it as the movement drew his attention to the fact her breasts had rounded and peaked under the inadequate fine lawn chemise.

'Oh, come now, ma'am,' he gritted, as if her denial made him angry as finding her half-naked in Bran's bed when she should be working had not. 'We have a decade worth of wanting on the slate between us. Sooner or later we'll have an accounting.'

'No, there isn't and, no, we won't,' she informed him as furiously as she could when sitting here nearly naked.

She could hardly thrust the bedclothes aside and run away when her legs would refuse to carry her and where would she run to without scandalising half the household and any guests who happened to be standing about with their mouths open?

'I may be a fool, Mrs Wheaton, but not such a one I'm prepared to pretend to you that passion couldn't break us, if we let it. It might do us both less harm if we admit its existence,' he said sombrely and their eyes met.

Chloe almost said the words in her head—*Why not try it and see?* There it was again, her wicked inner self, whispering sinfully in her ears and offering lures she thought she'd cut off in their heady prime a decade ago. She squirmed and made herself be glad even the sleep still clouding her brain hadn't let her speak that impossible invitation aloud.

Wasn't it exactly the sort of rash remark that landed her and her twin sister Daphne in the suds in their younger days? Chloe clamped cold fetters on her wilder self at the reminder how it came about she was sitting here glaring at her new employer like a hungry she-wolf. If she was careful enough, they could go back to stiffly avoiding each other until she left.

'It might not do that much harm to *you*,' she muttered crossly and folded her bare arms across her chest; because she couldn't endure him standing there knowing how much she wanted him.

'I shouldn't be too sure about that,' he rasped as his hot gaze now dwelt on the exposed upper slopes of her breasts, Chloe looked down to see she'd only made them look fuller and even more rounded by seeking to hide her tight, need-peaked nipples from his fascinated gaze. 'I've always known you could be my ruin,' he murmured, looking ready to resign himself to it if he could climb into this narrow bed and make use of every tight inch of space it would leave him to seduce her until she screamed for him with a sombre house party of guests a mere misplaced call away.

'No, never!' she croaked and almost gave in to the urge to scissor her legs together to deny the hot need and frustration grinding at the heart of her.

He was here; not some fevered fantasy she had woken up with, as she so often had in the first days, weeks and years after he left Farenze Lodge as if the devil himself was riding on his shoulders. Until today she thought she'd banished that folly to outer darkness along with him and now she knew better.

'If things were different, I could make you eat those words with one kiss and you know it,' he said grimly.

'They're not though, are they?' she whispered and almost sobbed at the years of regret she'd betrayed with those stark words. 'Please leave me be, my lord. I should never have slept when there is so much to do and it won't happen again, I assure you.'

'Nonsense,' he said gruffly. 'When I first laid eyes on you today I thought you looked as if you might break if you didn't bend soon. You're too thin and look as if you haven't slept or eaten properly in weeks.'

'I can't sleep and food seems to choke me at times,' she admitted reluctantly.

'Go on like this and you'll make yourself ill. Do that to yourself if you must, but how can you risk shocking your daughter with your wan appearance when she sees you? She must be struggling to come to terms with losing Virginia, close as I know they had become to each other while she was growing up.'

'Yes, she was heartbroken,' Chloe said heavily, remembering how it felt to hold her sobbing daughter whilst she cried as if her poor heart might break the day Chloe had Lady Virginia's coachman drive her to Bath so she could tell Verity Lady Virginia was dead.

'So eat something,' he demanded.

'I have, at regular intervals.'

'Then eat more and go to bed and sleep properly tonight, instead of pacing the corridors like a ghost and making the night watchman think he's being haunted.'

His voice was brusque, but there was what looked

like genuine concern in his eyes as he inspected her face. His well-hidden kindness touched her as she couldn't let herself be touched by her employer. She rubbed her eyes self-consciously, pushed an annoying curl behind her ear and tried not to gaze back at him as if she might adore him, if things were different.

'I must look like something the cat brought in,' she muttered unwarily.

The wretched man stared at her with a glint of humour and something they'd both declared forbidden in the depths of those grey-, gold- and green-rayed eyes of his. She wanted to fall into them and never land on solid ground again for a long moment.

'You must know you're beautiful,' he said wryly, almost as if talking to himself and being overheard by the wide-eyed sceptic in front of him.

She shook her head in hasty denial and tried not to love the fact he thought so.

'But you're still too thin,' he insisted, 'and you have shadows under your eyes a Gothic heroine would envy.'

'Well, she'd be welcome to them,' she said unwarily and the quirk of humour kicking up his fascinating mouth became a true smile.

There was all the warmth and hope and unwary fellow feeling in them that had nearly carried them over the precipice a decade ago. Chloe felt them both balance on the edge of the inevitable again. It felt terrible and utterly desirable, as if even their thoughts were cursed to curl up together and purr with delight at being reunited.

He reached out a long finger, as if he wanted to physically brush the shadows away from her eyes. She felt the whisper of his almost touch on her skin and gasped with hope and fear at how much she wanted it. She slicked parched lips with her tongue and watched him hesitate, had the sense of a strong man fighting what he knew was wrong, yet he was still drawn on by what felt so strong between them it could overrule everything, if they let it. There was curiosity and impatience in his eyes, before he blanked them and my Lord Farenze was himself again; remote, self-assured and cynical and as distant from the housekeeper of Farenze Lodge as ever.

'Eve and Bran are coming,' he warned her huskily.

Chloe strained her senses to catch a hint of whatever sound or instinct told him they were about to be rescued from folly, whether they wanted to be or not.

'Pretend I never came in here. Act as if you woke up the moment they asked what I'm doing here,' he whispered.

Chapter Four

Lost for words again, Chloe nodded, then burrowed her face into the pillows and drew the bedclothes over her chilled shoulders. At least pretending to be fuzzy with sleep would give her time to pull wanton Chloe into line and forget he'd been here as best she could. If she proved as obedient to the curb as his rampant side, she had nothing to worry about.

'Bah!' she muttered crossly into the pillow, 'just bah, my Lord Farenze!'

No danger he might hear her. He was back through the door and nearly closing it again before she could slide down the bed and cover her now-shivering body. Nobody else would ever know he'd found her here, heavy-eyed with sleep and wanton desire.

She heard Miss Winterley express surprise at her father's presence in an over-loud voice meant to warn Chloe not to start awake and betray herself and felt a hard flush of shame burn her cheeks at the thought she knew of Luke Winterley's presence all too well. She felt it in every fibre of her being and the man was Miss Winterley's father, for goodness' sake.

'You took my book,' he replied and if his excuse sounded lame and defensive, it might explain what he was doing here better than a smoother lie, designed to cover something clandestine and shocking.

'And there are none downstairs in the famously well-stocked library Aunt Virginia and Uncle Virgil amassed between them?' Eve asked, as if she knew very well her father had really stumbled on the housekeeper enjoying a nap in the wrong place at entirely the wrong time, but how could she?

'Not the one I was reading before you stole it,' he said grumpily.

'And now *I* am reading it, so you would be stealing it from me. I can't believe you to need distraction so badly, especially in the midst of a house party you must play host to, that you need to barge into my bedchamber when I am not there and try to repossess part of your library, Papa. I'm not even going to think about the list of tasks awaiting you here that you reeled off as an excuse for not being able to spend much time greeting neighbours who call to express their condolences.'

'I didn't know then how much distraction I'd need,' he muttered darkly.

Chloe's eyes stung at the sound of him so gruffly sheepish it opened up a host of new temptations inside her. She didn't want to love him and screwed her eyes shut in denial of any tears tempted to come further.

'Don't be such a cross old bear, Papa,' Eve told him and Chloe could hear the rustle of her skirts as she marched up and hugged her father.

Wrong to envy Eve such ease with her father, that

ability to breach the chilly touch-me-not air he normally carried about with him like a shield.

'I'll try not to be, my she-cub, but there will be reasons aplenty for me to growl over the next few days.'

'Aye,' Brandy Brown added from what sounded like a position just inside the room, 'you'll need the patience of a saint before the vultures fly off at last.'

'They're not all vultures, Bran,' Eve chided.

'We don't know them well enough to judge what they are yet, my lamb,' her maid said cynically and Chloe decided there was no need to worry about Eve Winterley with such a formidable protector at her side, as well as a father who would clearly walk through fire to keep his beloved daughter safe.

'I know Lord Mantaigne and Great-Uncle Giles perfectly well and even Uncle James isn't as savage and sarcastic as he used to be. Aunt Virginia was always trying to persuade him to live a steadier life, so perhaps he will turn over a new leaf in her honour.'

'And I'm a Dutchman,' Chloe thought she heard Lord Farenze mutter darkly and wondered what divided the half-brothers so deeply, so alike in colouring and stature as they were, yet as sharply distant with each other as two siblings could be without openly declaring war.

'No, what you are is a curmudgeon, Papa, so I can't imagine why you're worrying about reading a book you seem very familiar with when you have your brother nearby to argue with once more. I dare say if you start now you could have Uncle James simmering nicely by dinner and ready to call you out the moment Aunt Virginia's funeral is over.'

'Thank you, minx, the gossips have plenty to say already, without a brotherly feud or a family riot breaking out. I'm not sure I should have let you read *Tom Jones* after all, it seems to have given you some odd ideas.'

'There's a copy in the study, if you truly want to take up where you left off,' Eve called after the sound of her father's retreating footsteps and surely it was wrong of Chloe to wish he wouldn't go at the same time as she longed to be up and away and pretend he hardly impinged on her thoughts, let alone her wildest dreams? 'Virginia told me where all her warm novels were in the event of my ever having to be bored here in her absence. It's all right, Papa, she told me anything she and Uncle Virgil locked away was far too warm for a young lady to read and I really can't think why the tabbies make such a fuss about Mr Fielding's splendid book.'

'Don't get caught with it, then, and it's probably best if you don't admit to reading it in polite company. I won't have you labelled fast before you're even out.'

'Of course not and stop being such a worrywart, I'll be so painfully good over the next few weeks you will hardly recognise me.'

The only reply Chloe heard was a distant masculine humph then Eve ordered her maid to shut the outer door before hastily pushing open the one to the bedroom where Chloe was sitting up in bed, feeling flustered and confused.

'That was close,' Eve confided with an impish smile.

'We should have locked the door,' Bran told them. 'Imagine if his lordship had opened it and found you lying here asleep, Mrs Wheaton.'

'Yes, only imagine,' Chloe echoed hollowly and used

her artistic shudder as an excuse to spring out of bed and start setting herself to rights.

'I'll help,' Bran said as Chloe then tried to struggle into her gown and wrestle with her rebellious curls at the same time. 'Button yourself up and I'll comb out your hair and dress it for you, although it seems a crying shame to screw it into a knot and hide it under that thing when it's so beautiful. There's many a fine lady as would give her eye teeth for hair half as thick and full of life.'

'It's wild and unruly and people get entirely the wrong impression of me if I allow it to show. Anyway, I'm nearly thirty years of age and a respectable widow, not a dewy-eyed débutante.'

'You don't look much older than one right now,' Bran observed as her eyes met Chloe's in the square of mirror above the diminutive washstand.

'I can't afford dreams,' Chloe murmured.

'Neither of us can, but it don't stop us 'avin' 'em, do it?'

'What do you dream of, Mrs Brown?'

'A fine man for my girl; one who'll love her as she is and not try to make her into a society missus without a good word to say to anyone but a lord.'

'I can't see him doing that, whoever he might be.'

'Can't you, ma'am? Then you've been a lucky woman up to now.'

'Maybe I have at that,' Chloe admitted and suppressed a shudder at the thought of all the ways in which a man might mould his wife.

'His lordship now, he's a man as would let a woman be herself and love her all the more for it, if you know what I mean?' Bran said as she finished pinning Chloe's wild mane back in place, then eyed the cap with disfavour before fitting it over her handiwork with a sigh.

'He doesn't strike me as a man on the lookout for love,' Chloe argued.

'Ah, well, there's what a man *says* he wants then there's what he really does want. They don't always meet in the middle, until the right woman comes along and changes his mind.'

'If I understood all that I might argue, but since I don't and dinner will be served in a little over an hour, neither of us has enough time for riddles,' Chloe said with a last glance in the mirror to make sure she was correct and subdued again.

'Just as well, since we'll never agree about his lordship.'

'Maybe not,' Chloe said distractedly and, picking up her keys, clipped them back on her belt and with a word of breathless thanks fled the room.

Luke stumped back downstairs to the study and cursed as rampant need roiled inside him. This wasn't some unique enchantment; he was tired and it was too long since he'd visited his mistress. Forcing the pace on a long journey had left him weary and less in control of himself and his masculine appetites than usual. Combine tiredness and grief with Mrs Wheaton's exhaustion and Eve's kind heart and trouble looked inevitable with hindsight, but at least it hadn't led to catastrophe.

He bit out another fearsome curse at his painful arousal over the mere thought of Chloe Wheaton sitting up in that neat little bed, looking at him as if every fantasy he'd ever had of her as his lover was about to come true, before she awoke fully and recalled who they were. Of course he'd wanted her since she was painfully young and hauntingly beautiful, with a tiny dependent child. He felt the familiar dragging heat of frustrated desire, as if his senses were soaked in need of the woman and refused to give her up, however hard he told them they must.

On some level he'd known she was there even when he saw the inner door slightly ajar and Eve's baggage piled on the Aubusson carpet, as if the footmen had been told to leave it there and depart in order not to disturb Chloe Wheaton while Bran and Eve took a stroll about the Winter Garden. He wished they hadn't done what he couldn't and ordered the woman to bed for an hour or so.

Eve had a heart big enough to sacrifice her comfort for a woman she barely knew, because the housekeeper looked so breakable. How could he be anything but proud of such a daughter, even if he wished she'd left well alone? Eve had done the right thing, but now he wanted to run upstairs and throw the pig-headed Mrs Wheaton over his shoulders and tell the world to go hang and do the wrong one.

If he was not to avoid Farenze Lodge as if he hated it for another decade she had to leave , but he must find a place where her skills were valued and her fine figure and spellbinding violet eyes ignored. Did convents have housekeepers? Luke forced his hands to unclench at the idea of her being leered at by her employer's husband, or some gangling oaf of a son, and decided to keep a stern eye on Mrs Wheaton's next household from afar.

Yes, he should have trusted his instincts, but curiosity, or something even more dangerous, led him to open that door. Once he had, he could no more bow coolly and leave than stop breathing. Even now the scent of her seemed to linger in the air. It was only the lavender in the big bowls Virginia always insisted on having about to sweeten the air in winter-closed rooms.

He suspected Chloe had lavender water used on the last rinse of her linen and that was why he couldn't seem to get her out of his head. The rest of that exotic scent he associated with her was probably lingering aroma of a spicy moth bag or two, deployed to stop the industrious creatures chewing through her mourning attire. So it was a mix of simple strewing herbs, cinnamon, orris and perhaps cloves, but the memory fogged his senses, reminding him how tempted he'd been to kiss the fine creamy skin at the base of her elegant throat and find out if she tasted as exotically artless as she smelt.

Confound it, he hadn't kissed her and could still savour the taste of her on his tongue. He ran it over his lips and the memory of her doing the same took fire and wrenched a tortured groan from him. After a decade of avoidance and abstinence he *still* wanted her, wanted her more than at first sight and now they were both mature adults and better designed for mischief.

The waif was a woman and he'd been wrong about the figure under that deplorable gown—Chloe the woman was nothing like the skinny girl she'd once been. She was slender, yes, probably too much so after forgetting to eat for grief and worry. What there was of her was sweetly curved, though, and her skin looked so silken and perfect he could imagine the feel of those full high breasts of hers against his palms. He held up his hands as if convicting them of a heinous crime for flexing on thin air as if they knew what they wanted better than the rest of him did. His other senses were betraying him, so why shouldn't touch join the turncoat army?

Because somehow he had to resist what he and Chloe Wheaton might be to each other, he supposed with a heavy sigh. For a decade he'd done his best to stay away; he'd seen the desperation in her eyes; the hunger for the love Virginia had to offer a pair of homeless waifs. So he'd taken her rebuff to heart.

Easy enough to make a holiday of visits to Brighton so Virginia and Eve could enjoy one another's company. He had even endured a few weeks in London each spring so they could eat ices at Gunter's and visit Astley's Amphitheatre and there was no more noble fatherly sacrifice when Darkmere was the finest place to be in the spring.

He suspected Virginia knew why he avoided the Lodge, but she didn't say a word because she knew as well as he did that it was as impossible for Lord Farenze to do aught but ruin a housekeeper. The polite world would laugh at him and sneer at her if he tried to make anything of Chloe Wheaton *but* his mistress.

'There you are,' Tom Banburgh remarked from the doorway and he welcomed the interruption, didn't he?

'There's no fooling you, is there?'

'I can go away again until you're in a better humour if you like, but I thought misery might like some company.'

'Devil take it, I'm not miserable.'

'Face like thunder.'

Luke stopped himself pacing up and down like a general before a crucial battle and took the filled glass Tom was holding out to him for the second time today. He took a sip of the finest cognac Virginia always kept for a favoured few and felt a little better after all.

'I miss her so much, Tom,' he finally admitted the lesser of two evils.

'How could you not? I expect Virginia saved you from the tender mercies of your family when she could. She certainly rescued me from my unloving guardian when I was a scrubby boy nobody else cared enough to worry about.'

'True, and she was always taking in waifs and strays. Seems a shame she couldn't give Virgil children when she was born to be a mother.'

'And this remark is coming from a man who would be a mere mister today if she had? You're either a saint or a liar, my friend.'

'I'm neither and you know as well as I do a title can't change the beat of a man's heart or make him any happier.'

'I really wouldn't know,' Tom said indifferently and Luke reminded himself his friend had been a marquis since he was five years old.

'Well, I do,' he argued, 'and mine hasn't bought me any great joy.'

'That's because you hadn't much left in you when you acquired it, Luke,' Tom said sagely.

Luke wondered if anyone else would get away with saying some of the things Mantaigne came out with so blithely without being called out. 'And you have no memory of being without one, so are necessarily full of fun and laughter, I suppose?'

'Going a bit far, but I never saw the point in being gloomy. I'll go on trying to laugh at the world even now, because Virginia wouldn't want long faces and a grand carry on over her departure from this vale of tears.'

'True, and we both know she missed my great-uncle as if someone had lopped off an arm or a leg after Virgil died.'

'Aye, and if there *is* a heaven at least they're in it together again.'

'Since it clearly wouldn't be so for one without the other, you must be right.'

'Makes you wonder though, don't it?' Tom said.

'No, love is still a myth for the rest of us.'

Luke gave his friend a long hard look before deciding he was the one obsessed with love and lovers and in danger of tripping over his own tongue. Not that he felt anything like love for Chloe Wheaton.

'Thing about myths is a lot of people believe them,' Tom said with a long look at Luke that left him puzzled and fidgety.

Was he being warned not to lightly charm the object of his desires? He could imagine nobody *less* likely to fall in love with him than aloof and sceptical Mrs Chloe Wheaton. Then he recalled the sight of her disarmed by sleep and a hundred times more vulnerable and wondered all over again.

'I don't,' he muttered half to himself.

'You could have been cut straight out of the pages of a Gothic tale and pasted into a young girl's scrapbook of fantasies you look so close to the little darlings' ideal of a heroic villain.'

'What nonsense have you been feeding yourself this afternoon, man—a three-decker novel from the yellow press, perhaps? Or are you already three parts cast away?' Luke asked incredulously.

'Neither, but you don't have the faintest idea, do you?'

'Faintest idea of what?'

'That your long and dusky locks, brooding frowns and touch-me-not air are sure to drive the débutantes insane with longing at their first sight of you across a crowded ballroom. The moment you stand among a London rout glaring at any boy brave enough to dance with your Eve, the little darlings will start swooning by rote for the lack of space to do it all at once in comfort.'

Luke felt himself pale at the very idea, so no wonder Tom laughed. 'Why?' he asked hollowly. 'I'll be old enough to be their father.'

'As are all those dark and brooding villains out of the Gothic novels they devour by the yard, I suppose. Who knows what flights of the imagination such silly chits are capable of dreaming up between them, but you'll be a prime target for them and their ambitious mamas if you set foot in London without a viscountess at your side.'

'I wasn't going to worry about one of those until Eve is safely wed.'

'Leave Eve to find her husband when she's ready, man; you owe her that for enduring life with a hermit like you all these years.'

Luke shook his head, but was Mantaigne right? He

couldn't see much attraction in a beetle-browed countenance and raven's wing black hair he only kept overlong because he had no patience with constant visits from a barber or his new valet's fussing and primping. When it came to his features, he'd just been relieved Eve had escaped the Winterley Roman nose and put down the occasional appreciative feminine stare as a penchant for his acres and title. Marriage to Pamela Verdoyne had cured him of vanity and he wondered if she'd done him such a great favour if he was about to blunder into the ballrooms of the *ton* unprepared.

'I won't have Eve endure a stepmother like mine,' he said with a shudder.

'That's in your hands,' Tom said with a shrug.

'What is this, some sort of conspiracy to marry me off?'

'That takes more than one person, my lord, and I'm not a matchmaker.'

'So Virginia, you and my own dear, sweet scheming Eve don't make a set?'

'Not through prior agreement, but all three of us can't be wrong.'

'Yes, you can—by Heaven you're more wrong in triplicate than alone.'

Tom merely raised his eyebrows and looked sceptical before calmly helping himself to another glass of cognac.

'Did Virginia put you up to this?' Luke asked suspiciously.

'Don't you think I've a mind of my own and the sense to see what you won't yourself? If she wasn't dead, I could strangle that spoilt witch you wed so hastily,

Luke; she married you for your expectations, then rejected you for so-called love, as if it was your fault she was born vain, empty-headed and contrary.'

'I should never have agreed to marry her,' Luke said with a shrug, recalling the long and bitter rows of his marriage with a shudder that sent him back to the brandy decanter for a second glass before he'd quite taken in the fact he'd drunk the first.

'Your father and wicked stepmother should take the blame for pushing such a paltry marriage on an infatuated lad. You're not a boy now, though, and you badly need a wife, my friend, at least you do if you're to avoid being ruthlessly pursued through every ballroom in London by a pack of ninnies when Eve makes her début.'

'Shouldn't you be more concerned with securing your own succession, since you're the last of the Banburghs and I have a younger brother?'

'The Banburghs can go hang as far as I'm concerned, but it's not good for James to be in limbo, never sure if he's to be your heir or only the "what if tragedy struck?" spare Winterley male. He's bored and restless and probably lonely and who knows what he gets up to when our backs are turned?'

'You know very well he'd never confide in me,' Luke said and let himself feel how much it hurt that his brother hated him, even if he had cause to hate him back.

'Left to himself, he would have followed you about like a stray puppy when you were younger.'

Luke gave a snort of derision at the idea of elegant and sophisticated James Winterley following anyone slavishly, let alone his despised elder brother. 'That particular apple never fell far from the tree,' he said darkly, even as the laziness of the cliché made him wonder if he wasn't guilty of prejudice himself.

'And you think his lot so much better than your own?' Tom persisted impatiently.

'Whatever I think, let's postpone feeling sorry for James because his mother loved him and hated me for another day, shall we?'

'Don't leave it too late to remedy,' Tom warned with a steady look that made Luke wonder if he didn't know more about James's dark and tangled affairs than he was letting on. 'I'm going off to bother my valet and idle away an hour until dinner. Who knows, maybe we'll have a pleasant and peaceful evening against all the odds,' his friend said before he sauntered from the room.

'Slim enough chance of anything of the kind under this roof,' Luke muttered grumpily and finished his brandy before going upstairs.

Chapter Five

The January twilight was already all but over when Luke stumped up the elegant staircase. He rang for the bath he needed as soon as he reached his bedchamber and heard hot water carried in within minutes, so there was no excuse to sack the housekeeper on the spot and end this torture. As he relaxed into the tub images of the dratted woman slid slyly into his head.

Why her? Why was it Chloe Wheaton he seemed doomed to want every time he set eyes on her? She was a fine-looking woman, despite the deplorable gowns and concealing cap, but he'd met other fine-looking women and some of them diamonds of the first water. No other woman on this fair earth could get him in a stew of frustrated yearning with one distrustful glance and how he wished it otherwise.

If only it was merely the thought of a fine female body in his bed that made him want her so badly. He ached with the frustration of not having her as his lover. There was something unique about her that even ten years of trying couldn't expunge from his senses. He recalled a fateful day that summer when they first met;

he'd come upon her playing with her little girl in the woods above the house and just stood and watched where neither could see him.

At last the heat of the day drained the child's energy and Chloe had sung softly to calm her, then rocked little Verity to sleep in her arms. Luke recalled envy eating at him like acid as he wanted such love and tenderness for the babes they could bring into the world together, if only everything was different.

Instead it had been Wheaton who recklessly married a schoolgirl and got a baby on her, or so she had once told him. Luke felt his fists tighten at the thought of Wheaton exposing the woman he was supposed to love to such a hard, narrow life as she'd had to lead since.

He had been about to turn away when the June sunlight picked out the trail of tears on Chloe's face as she gazed down at her sleeping babe. Even now he felt the jar of it as his heart thudded at the memory. Back then he had had to clamp down on the need to stride over to her and take her in his arms so hard he discovered afterwards he'd clenched his fists until the blood flowed.

He left the next day, all his wild schemes for somehow making it easier for her to be his mistress by getting her to act the quietly respectable wife, whose reclusive husband sailed the seven seas, then wanted no company but hers whenever he was home, shattered. He couldn't do that to her, or little Verity or any other babies they might make between them. It was a half-life and he couldn't offer her so little.

Curse it; he wouldn't let passion waft him along as if he had no free will now either. Yet when he conjured a picture of his late wife ranting at him that he was a stern, unlovable stick to correct his obsession, the fantasy of his great-aunt's housekeeper naked and eager in the great bed next door blotted her out. Luke felt heat roar through him at the very idea and the physical evidence of his arousal with nothing between him and civilisation made him a fool.

Chloe only had to be in the same county for him to want her and from the moment he saw her at Virginia's window today he'd barely been able to conceal his ridiculous state from the world. Idiot body! Hadn't marriage taught it anything at all?

His response to Pamela's challenge to his manhood when she refused to let him bed her again after they returned from their bride trip slotted into his memory and reminded him how easy it was to need a woman without liking her. He relived his distaste at himself and his wife when she enjoyed his furious promise to seduce her into taking him until she screamed for more as she never had during his gentle lovemaking. The fulfilment of that vow excited her and left him at odds with himself.

Their marriage limped on for six months, Pamela blowing hot and cold as Luke grew sick of her and himself. How typical that she announced her pregnancy the day she finally left him. Her letter from her sister's London address saying she'd been brought to bed of a daughter and he'd better come and get her arrived on his twentieth birthday. To this day Luke couldn't recall the journey and it took Eve to blast through his rage as the real innocent in the whole wretched business.

'You're welcome to the squalling brat,' his wife had shouted when he dodged past her to reach the attic where, the butler informed him, his daughter had been banished for crying a little too loudly. Pamela scurried after him; 'Pushing it out nigh killed me and I never want to see it again.'

'Don't you feel the need to raise a heroine in your own tawdry image?'

'Not one of your get, not that I'm sure she *is* yours. You're not the only Winterley ready to rut like a hog,' she said smugly.

His bellow of fury woke the baby and made her furious nurse run out of the bare attic bedroom he wouldn't wish on a foundling to upbraid them.

'If you two 'ave a mite of pity in your black hearts, you'll be quiet,' she barked in a hoarse voice that sounded as if its skinny owner spent most of her years on this earth bellowing to be heard and had worn it out in the process.

A smile replaced Luke's frown as he recalled his shock at being addressed so sharply by a tiny female who looked as if she'd dashed in off the street to feed his child out of the kindness of her weary heart. She hardly reached his elbow and her face had the wizened yet somehow ageless look of one used to hardship since birth.

'Whose get is she then?' he'd asked his wife more quietly, as the furious girl-woman was still barring his way like a flea-bitten terrier confronting an angry bear.

'Oh, she's a Winterley all right; which is probably why I can't endure to have her near me.'

'Then she's mine.'

'There are other vultures crouched in the branches

of your family tree, hoping their seed will carry off the family honours under your long nose, Luke Winterley.'

It wasn't the unlikely idea of his already ailing father laying hands on his wife that made Luke feel as if the finest Toledo blade had sliced into his heart. A terrible possibility dawned as he stood there and mentally crossed all his male relatives off the list but one. His stepmother resented the fact he was heir to the Farenze titles and always had done her best to make the half-brothers hate each other. Luke thought a gruff affection bound him and James even so, until that moment.

Would even Pamela stoop to seduce a seventeen-year-old boy? Yes, he'd decided with bitter sickness threatening to choke him. To take a twisted revenge on Luke for marrying her without adoring her slavishly she would, and enjoy every moment of her betrayal. Young enough to hurt to his very soul, he felt as if sharing a city with her a moment longer would surely suffocate him.

'Bring the child, we're leaving,' he'd snapped at the street urchin wet-nurse.

'Not 'til I'm sure she's better off with you than the ragman,' she said, appearing at the nursery door with Eve wrapped in a worn shawl that had to be her own since Pamela wouldn't even give it to her maid.

'Why didn't I think of that?' Pamela said spitefully.

'How can you say such terrible things, dearest?' her sister, Alexandra, Lady Derneley, protested faintly from behind her. 'She's your own dear baby.'

'I'd prefer to house a ferret or a weasel than that squalling brat. Has James visited me once while I was fat and lumbering like a cow because of a *girl* they got on me between them? You know he hasn't, Lexie; he promised undying devotion when he seduced me behind his brother's back and look how long it lasted. I'd hate her for ruining my figure, then chasing dear Blasedon away with her wailing and whining, even if she wasn't a Winterley. I'll be happy never to set eyes on the whelp again as long as I live, she can go to hell along with him and the sooner the better.'

Lady Derneley turned chalk white as her little sister's true nature hit home and fainted to avoid it.

'To hell with *you*, you unnatural bitch,' Luke roared.

'To 'ell with both of you,' the street urchin's voice somehow rose above the uproar. 'This poor babe ain't 'ad time to do wrong, whatever the rest of you 'ave been up to and you be quiet,' she ordered Pamela, who gaped at her open-mouthed. 'If you've a spot of pity use it on an 'elpless mite who din't ask to come into this world instead of yourself for once. Mister, you can take us both away from 'ere afore the poor little thing dies of cold and 'unger, or missus 'ere murders 'er while I'm asleep, never mind if you're 'er pa or no.'

It was then Luke made the life-transforming error of looking at the tiny little being in the girl's bony arms and realised she was right. Almost as frightened by the quiet as by the shouting, the baby screwed her tiny face up to wail her woes to the world. He put out a finger, more by instinct than in hope his touch would soothe her. Eve paused, opened her eyes wide and seemed to focus on him as if she'd been waiting for him to come since the day she was born. She made him her father, whatever the facts, by latching on to his finger and refusing to let go.

Somehow he managed to hide that fact while convincing Pamela he would stop her allowance and sue for divorce, instead of legal separation, if word got out Eve might not be his. The journey to Darkmere with Eve and Brandy Brown in tow was a nightmare he shuddered to think of now, but they all survived it somehow and Eve grew up free of a mother who hated her for being a Winterley.

Luke made himself ignore news of Pamela cavorting round any bits of the Continent free of revolutionary wars with a succession of lovers. He didn't care if the generous allowance he paid her kept her and her latest love in luxury and when news of his wife's death reached Darkmere three years later he hadn't enough hypocrisy left to mourn.

Now Lord Farenze might seem harsh and indifferent as the moors in sight of his castle towards the wider world, but he truly loved his daughter. A sneaky voice whispered it was safe to love Eve. If remembering his wife kept Chloe Wheaton and the danger of feeling more than he ought to for her at arm's length, then he would dwell on the last time he let a woman walk into his life and rearrange it for however long it took to put him off the idea.

Resolved to do so often over the next few days, he was dressed before he found out dinner had been put back an hour. Eve *had* been informed, however, and was discussing which black gown was better suited to the occasion with Chloe and Bran. He could see little difference and left the room as if the devil was on his tail as soon as he saw the housekeeper lurking in the darkest corner of the room. Feeling thoroughly out of sorts with the world, Luke went downstairs like a guest arriving too early for a party.

* * *

Chloe was consulting Cook about the number of entrées Mrs Winterley thought fashionable to serve at dinner and agreeing this wasn't the time for excess, even if they could find half-a-dozen more dishes at the drop of a hat, when the sound of a late arrival surprised them all. The terse announcement she was needed outside made her scurry in the head groom's wake to the stable yard.

'Verity, oh, my love!' she cried as she saw her daughter blink against the flare of the stable lads' lanterns when she stepped down from the coach.

'Oh, Mama, I'm so glad to see you,' Verity said with a wobbly smile that made Chloe want to cry, instead she hugged her as if they'd been parted for months.

'But how did this come about?' Chloe asked as Lord Farenze's coachman nodded tersely at her and she could only marvel at his endurance.

'His lordship ordered it soon as he heard little miss here was waiting to come home,' Birtkin said as if he drove all the way to Bath and back after enduring the long drive here from Northumberland at least once a week.

'I'm very grateful to you,' she replied with a warm smile of gratitude.

'Not my doing, ma'am, you should thank his lordship,' Birtkin mumbled as if trying to reclaim his dour reputation.

'You and your men were the ones who drove through twilight, then darkness, on Verity's behalf, so I'm grateful to you, whether you like it or not.'

'We was doing our duty, ma'am.'

'I will stop saying thank you, since it seems to trouble you, but I'll ask Cook to send plenty of the food left from feeding his lordship's guests to the servants' hall for dinner. You and your men need good food and some cheer on such a night.'

'My thanks, ma'am, we'll settle the beasts and see we're clean and tidy before we comes in.'

'See that you do,' Chloe said and led Verity into the house.

She could afford time away from her duties; Oakham would supervise the dining room while Cook organised the footmen behind the scenes with dire threats of retribution if they dropped even a teaspoon of her food.

'I should scold you for telling your teachers I need you here when I wanted to spare you this, my love, but I'm far too pleased to see you for that,' she said as she urged Verity upstairs, guessing she'd slept very little since the day Chloe made that sad trip to Bath to tell her daughter Lady Virginia was dead. 'But now you are here you must go straight to bed,'

'Oh, Mama, why? I'm not in the least bit tired.'

'I can see that, but I suppose you will just have to humour me, now you have got your way in everything else,' Chloe said with a wry smile.

How hard it was not to spoil this wilful, clever little conundrum of hers and how right Virginia had been to insist Verity went to Miss Thibett's very good school. Her daughter needed to learn the self-discipline and all the other disciplines that Miss Thibett considered made up a well-rounded human being who happened to have been born female. Chloe and her sister had never had a governess, let alone gone to school, and look where that lack of any learning but what they happened to light on in their maternal grandfather's long-neglected library landed them.

Verity's room was in the nursery wing the late Lord and Lady Farenze had built in hope of a family of their own, then used for other people's children, such as Verity and Lord Mantaigne and the current master of the house and his half-brother when they were boys. Chloe had been sleeping within call of Lady Virginia's room and she didn't want to move back and risk Verity hearing the terrifying nightmares that were plaguing her again.

When Verity was a baby her night terrors had returned again and again and Chloe had been glad to be up here where nobody else could hear. Her daughter would no longer sleep through any screams and shouts Chloe let out though and she wished there was a way of stopping them. She suppressed a weary sigh at the very thought of trying to relax and pretend all was well on the eve of Virginia's funeral with Viscount Farenze sleeping under the same roof.

'I'm still in the Triangle room; you will remember where I am if you wake up and want me, won't you, love?' she asked as she helped Verity undress.

'Very well, Mama, but I won't,' her child said as she held up her arms to accept her nightgown being slipped over her head as if she was much younger than the self-sufficient young lady she was now. 'I'm so glad to be home I know I shall sleep well tonight. Can I really eat supper in bed?'

'I'll be hurt if you don't, I had to coax the cook to make it for you and she is very busy,' Chloe said.

She undid the plaits constraining Verity's unruly

golden hair and brushed it as gently as she could while her daughter tried to do justice to the chicken soup, dainty sandwich and apple flummery brought up by the shy little scullery maid.

'There, I think that's all the knots out at last,' Chloe murmured as she began to re-plait it into a thick tail in a ritual that reminded her poignantly of doing so for her sister at Verity's age.

'I do love you, Mama,' Verity assured her with sleepy seriousness. 'I shall always miss Lady Virginia, but you're my mother and I won't let you leave me,' she said so seriously Chloe knew she was feeling the loss of her best and oldest friend in this world even more deeply than a mother had to hope she would.

'I can't imagine anything nicer than being with you as long as you need me and becoming a sad charge on you when I am old and grey and a little bit disgraceful, love,' she said with a deliberately comical grimace. 'For now it's time you went to sleep and I made sure all is ready when the family and guests retire as well.'

'Goodnight then, Mama,' Verity murmured sleepily as Chloe pulled the covers up and checked the nightlight was safe.

'Goodnight, my darling,' Chloe said softly and Verity fell fast asleep as soon as her head hit the pillow.

Taking the tray and her own candle, Chloe allowed herself a long look at her sleeping child before returning to her duties. This was what her life was truly about. Verity's arrival was a timely reminder why she was housekeeper at Farenze Lodge and would be one somewhere else for as long as Verity needed her to be. She refused to consider the day her daughter left school to a world where a young lady with a mother who worked for a living might find her a liability. By then she might be able to afford the cottage by the sea she'd promised herself when even housekeepers with daughters to raise alone needed dreams to distract them from harsh reality.

'I wished to thank you, Lord Farenze,' the cool voice he'd been doing his best not to hear in his head all evening informed Luke when he sought a few moments' peace and quiet in the library after dinner.

'Did you? I doubt it,' he replied dourly.

'You believe me so ill mannered I wouldn't say a simple "thank you" that you ordered my daughter to be fetched from school tonight?' Chloe Wheaton asked and surely that wasn't hurt in her necessarily soft tones as they murmured in the corridor where anyone might overhear them?

'I wasn't casting aspersions on your manners, but on your pride, madam,' he said shortly, secretly shocked he was being so disagreeable yet not quite able to stop himself being so somehow.

'You believe housekeepers are not entitled to that commodity, my lord?'

'I believe *you* have a superfluity of it, entitled or not.'

'How revolutionary of me,' she said blandly and turned to go, presumably before she said something she regretted.

'Stop, I'm sorry. That was ill-mannered of me and now I owe you another apology,' he said and grasped her hand to stop her leaving then felt as if he'd been struck down by lightning from the mere feel of her bare wrist under his hand.

'You owe me nothing,' she said stiffly and glared at him before wrenching her hand away then stalking off as if she could imagine nothing more repulsive.

He entered the study he still considered the domain of his predecessor and glared moodily into the fire. Just when he had been feeling calmer and altogether more able to resist the charms of women who clearly didn't like him, she loomed out of the semi-darkness to throw him into turmoil. It wasn't as if it cost *him* anything to order Virginia's coachman to fetch the housekeeper's daughter. Her manners were better than his today and he only just muffled an impatient groan when someone else loomed out of the shadows to disturb his evening.

'What is it, man?' he demanded as he met his own coachman's sharp gaze.

'Just thought you ought to know, m'lord,' the man said stoically.

'Know what?'

'I drove the carriage to Bath and back.'

Luke cursed as he would never dream of doing in front of a lady and felt no better. 'What the devil for? I ordered Binns out, as you drove here from Northumberland.'

'He don't see well in the dark,' Josiah admitted uncomfortably and Luke wondered if the old coachman could see much at all. Josiah wasn't a man to betray any man's secrets lightly, though, and Luke sensed there was more to come.

'It's high time I pensioned him off, he must be nigh seventy,' he said anyway.

'Likely a bit more if you ask me, but that ain't what I came to tell you.'

'What was it then? That you're a disobedient ruffian who should be abed rather than dashing about the countryside? The head groom could have gone, man, he's no top sawyer, but even he could keep Lady Virginia's ancient team up to their bridles.'

'I knew it would be black dark long before they could stumble home, so I ordered the bays harnessed instead. I couldn't have Miss Verity careering about the country with a whipster holding the reins.'

Luke struggled to be fair. Chloe would hate him if her precious child was involved in a carriage accident because he had an urge to please her and he deserved censure for not thinking his impulsive scheme out better, not Josiah.

'You did the right thing,' he conceded reluctantly. 'I should have told you to wait until morning for all the difference it will make.'

'The little wench was that happy to know she wasn't forgotten I'd go twice as far in the dark to see her face light up when she realised I was there to fetch her home.'

Since he was about to evict her from that home, Luke felt the goad of his own weakness bite. 'Then what *did* you want to say?' he asked brusquely.

'That we was followed back,' Josiah told him with a straight look that told his master there was no point saying he might have imagined it.

'Who by and why the devil would anyone trail *you* home?'

'Don't know, m'lord, all I cared about was if he had a gun and if we was about to be held up.'

'Why didn't you inform the authorities in Bath?'

'Because he wasn't nowhere in sight when I got there.

Nearly caught us up about a mile this side of Bath, then stayed on our tail all the way back.'

'Why didn't you challenge him then?'

'Because he never got close enough to answer me, nor take a clean shot. I drove as fast as I dared and Miss Verity thought it was a great lark to go like the devil was on our tail.'

'She's well plucked?'

'Game for any lark going if you ask me,' Josiah agreed with a grin that told Luke to be glad Eve was five or six years older than Verity Wheaton, or they might set the countryside by the ears with misdeeds.

'Do your best to keep an eye on her over the next few days for me then, Josh. I don't like the idea of anyone wasting time in such a fashion and he's more likely to have a grudge against me than a child from a Bath seminary, but it won't hurt to make sure the girl's kept safe. We've trouble enough without the girl tumbling into more.'

'You think she's like Miss Eve was at her age, m'lord?'

'Very like from the sound of things. You know as well as I do what mischief a reckless girl can find if left to her own devices too often.'

'Aye, well, girls will be girls,' the coachman said with a reminiscent grin. 'I'll keep an eye on her when she's out, or get young Seth to if I'm busy. When she's in the house you're far better placed to keep watch over her than me, my lord.'

Josiah's tone was so bland Luke wondered if the old villain knew how much he needed to avoid the girl's mother over the next few days. He truly hoped not.

'Oakham will tell me if anyone breathes on her the

wrong way,' Luke informed his childhood ally in the hope he'd stop making bricks without straw.

'Then we don't need to worry ourselves, do we?'

'I'd still like to know who our curious stranger is, though,' Luke mused and at least it gave him a problem to consider for the rest of the evening, instead of wondering how he'd get through the next days and weeks without disaster befalling himself and Mrs Chloe Wheaton.

Chapter Six

When the household was settled at last, Chloe made her weary way to Lady Farenze's bedchamber ready to take over the night vigil from Culdrose. She braced herself to try to appear as awake and cheerful as any of them could be tonight. She couldn't let the elderly maid know she felt tired to the bone, even after her ill-advised nap this afternoon.

Especially not after that; she shuddered at the very idea of what she might have given away in those un-guarded moments while she gazed into Lord Farenze's hot grey eyes like a besotted schoolgirl. At the time a strange sort of exhilaration had buoyed her up, as if a wicked part of her was whispering she should stop fighting and give in to fiery attraction. Except he was a lord and she an upper servant and in a few weeks they would part, never to meet again.

The notion of such heady freedom stretching ahead of her made it an effort to set one foot in front of the other. The notion of all those empty years to come without even the occasional sight of him pressed down

on her like a ton weight. She stopped outside the door
to put on a suitably serene expression before she met
Cully's shrewd gaze, then walked in.

'Oh, there you are, my dear. There's no need for you
to stay with her ladyship tonight,' the elderly maid said
with a nod to the other side of the bed where the new
master of the house sat. 'Master Luke won't hear of
anyone else keeping vigil.'

'No, I won't,' he said in a flatly emotionless voice
that told her there was no point arguing.

'Quite right too,' Cully said with an approving nod.
'You need a good night's sleep and no argument, Mrs
Wheaton. If you spend one more day trying to fit a
month's worth of work into twenty-four hours, you'll
collapse. Your little miss is home now and we don't
want her more upset than she is already.'

'Aye, go to bed,' Lord Farenze barked from the most
heavily shadowed corner of the room.

'Very well,' she said, knowing she couldn't argue
in front of Culdrose and turned to go before the temptation to do it anyway overtook her.

'See she drinks one of your noxious potions and
really does sleep, Cully,' she heard Lord Farenze say
when she'd almost shut the door behind her. 'I wouldn't
put it past the confounded woman to steal in here if I
fall asleep to take your place, so she can boast she sat
by her employer day and night when she applies for
her next post.'

As if she would be so mercenary. Arrogant, unfeeling wretch—he would never believe she had loved
wonderful, complicated Lady Virginia Winterley very
deeply. He was always on the lookout for a base mo-

tive, a different sin to visit on her, as if she might have sprouted horns and a tail when he wasn't looking.

'Now then, Master Luke, you're being unjust. That girl loved her ladyship and would have done almost anything for her.'

'Except go away,' he raised his voice just enough to grumble so she couldn't fail to hear him.

Chloe flinched and wondered how he knew she couldn't bring herself to leave when Lady Virginia breathed her last, before he got here. Bracing herself against the fact he wanted her gone, she made herself walk away noisily enough to let him know he could say whatever he liked and she didn't care.

Back in her room, she wished it as many rooms as possible from where Lord Farenze was taking the last vigil at his great-aunt's side. To be within call if her mistress needed her, Chloe was using an odd little bed-chamber over the grand gallery that only unimportant guests were ever given, because the high ceiling of the room below meant the floor of this one was raised on a minor staircase with three other cramped chambers. It had been convenient to stay close to Lady Virginia's lofty suite, until now. So why hadn't she moved back to her modest room a floor up and at the back of the house as soon as Lord Farenze had set foot in Farenze Lodge? She hadn't known Verity would be home then and marvelled at herself for being so foolish as to stay within shouting distance of the state rooms now.

It was too late to change even if Verity hadn't ar-rived so much in need of a good night's sleep, so she yawned and hoped for a dreamless sleep against the odds. She had more to disturb her than ever, but after a soft tap came on the door, Cully opened it a half-inch on her invitation to enter.

'Are you decent, dear?' she whispered.

'Aye,' Chloe admitted with a half-smile at herself in the dimly visible mirror that said it was as well nobody could see into her head. 'Come in, Cully.'

'His lordship says you're to drink this down and I'm to stay until you do,' her old friend told her sternly.

Chloe sniffed the fumes coming from the steaming mug she held out and caught a hint of camomile, a waft of cinnamon and some honey to sweeten it all and decided there was nothing in it to worry her, even if such a mild concoction was unlikely to make her sleep soundly tonight.

'Very well,' she said with a resigned shrug. She knew that resolute expression of Cully's of old and didn't feel like a battle to resist her at the moment.

'I'll sit here until you're finished then go to bed myself. My lady is in safe hands and would be the first to tell us to get to bed and show some sense.'

'I know, but you're the last person I need to tell how hard it is to be sensible at a time like this,' Chloe said with a sigh as she paused her drinking and earned a frown. 'If I drink any faster, I'll choke,' she excused herself.

'I suppose so, but his lordship is right. You look as if a strong gust of wind could blow you into next week.'

'Kind of him,' Chloe retorted ruefully.

'He *is* a kind man, child, if only you would see it. You two bring out the worst in each another, but Master Luke was a good-hearted, gallant lad before that silly girl nagged and flouted him until he hardly knew which way was up any more.'

'He's hardly a lad now, or very gallant.'

'No, he's a man nowadays and a fine-looking one at that.'

Chloe distrusted the sly glance her old friend was shooting her. Cully knew her a little too well, after ten years of service in the same house. So, if the elderly ladies' maid knew she was deeply attracted to her gallant lad, who else might have their suspicions she wouldn't leave Farenze Lodge as heart-whole as a sober and respectable housekeeper should?

Chloe shook her head and carefully ignored that truth as she swallowed the last of Cully's brew. She felt as if she was back in the nursery herself when Cully unpinned her tightly bound locks and gently combed them out, but the deft touch soothed her as the potion hadn't yet managed to.

'There, is that better?' Cully asked as she brushed Chloe's heavy locks into a burnished red-gold mass.

'Aye,' Chloe admitted with a long sigh. 'You're very good at your job, Cully,' she murmured when she felt the silken thickness gathered into the elderly maid's hand and separated into three as Cully began a loose plait.

'And you have beautiful hair, Mrs Chloe,' the maid told her with a hint of sternness in her voice. 'A good many ladies would give their eye-teeth for such a colour and it's so fine and thick they would be green with envy if they ever saw it. You shouldn't screw it into such a tight knot. It's not good for it and small wonder if you have the headache after going about with all those pins skewered into it all day.'

'If I don't, it keeps trying to escape.'

'And a very good thing if it succeeded, if you ask me,' she thought she heard Cully mumble under her breath, but looking up she found the older woman was looking back at her in the mirror with such a look of bland innocence she told herself she must have been mistaken. 'There you are, you're all ready for bed and make sure you stay there till you're rested in the morning. Martha Lange's quite capable of getting breakfast cooked without you there to tell her how to coddle an egg and that head housemaid you set such store by can set the maids to work for once.'

'Yes, Miss Culdrose, ma'am,' Chloe said with a mock salute and was brusquely told not to be impudent before Cully wished her a dignified goodnight and went off to spend a full night in her own bed for the first time in weeks as well.

At first it was the most wonderful dream. Chloe shifted under the smooth linen sheets to murmur approval in her sleep. Luke was here, kissing her and doing all the things she had longed for him to do all these years. She had sent him away and told him she could imagine nothing more humiliating than being his mistress all those years ago, but she'd lied. In her unchecked fantasy he was indeed Luke and not Lord Farenze and he kissed her as if the next beat of his heart depended on her kissing him back.

She writhed against her hot pillow and keened a protest as a dash of reality beat in and she knew the hands running over her excited curves in the heat of the night were her own and not the firm, male touch her body truly longed for, as if it had found its ideal long ago and had no intention of letting the idea of him go, ever.

She wanted him, wanted him here and now and in her bed, in her. Even in her deepest sleep, her cheeks flushed with even more heat at the very thought of such emphatic possession as she knew his would be. Then the part of her that longed for him all the time she was trying to forget took over and wrenched that spectre lover back into her bed. He followed her impatient hands with kisses, tracked merciless trails of slick heat over her sensitised skin, pressed questing fingertips into the places she most wanted them to explore and she gasped in pleasure, at last.

In her dreams he was hers as surely as she was his, so why wake up to cold reality? Her unconscious self conspired with her inner wanton to revel in their heat and closeness and her body tingled and writhed and strove for something more against the heavy bedclothes and the depths of the long night. *He's here!* The words seemed to have been whispered, as if he truly was with her in every way there was between lovers. Doubt invaded even her imaginary idyll as soon as she felt they were not alone in this dream of fulfilment she had given herself, though.

Even as her phantom lover reared over her to feast his hungry mouth on her waiting lips and sink his mighty, roused body blissfully into her longing depths to complete them as lovers, she heard a voice from beyond the grave whisper, 'No, no, don't let him love you like that. Never love a man, Chloe. Look where love got me. Push him out of your heart, keep him out of your body and never, *ever* let yourself love him,' it ended on a wail, as pain took a deeper hold and the pale ghost sliced a dead and icy hand down on dream Luke's warm neck and he vanished like smoke on the wind.

Chloe's dreams landed her back into a cold, wind-swept wreck of a house high on the moors where no-body went unless they had to and even then they came away crossing themselves as if they'd met the devil at the back door. She writhed against the cooling sheets in terrified protest as images flashed through her sleep like the torn black of mourning weeds, weathered to faded shreds of their midnight prime.

There was blood, so much blood, and Chloe began to whimper in her sleep. The unending awfulness of the time and tragedy of that forsaken place bit into her. However hard she tried to clean the gore up she couldn't wash it away and into her terrifying dream flashed images of a fragile young woman laid out pale and cold on the narrow, mean bed as love leeched out of that wretched house and grief rolled in to replace it like the dense cloud hanging over the wintry moor.

Then she was back to the following December day, winds beating savage and remorseless on the tiny win-dows until even the stout shutters shivered and shifted against the threat of it as if they might break open. The younger Chloe wept and over the roar of the wind came the relentless slash of rain, beating on the narrow win-dows as if it wanted to drown every last breath of life in this place where only wind and rain should rule and people didn't belong.

Now she desperately needed Luke and he wasn't

there. He faded and forsook her when she drifted back to a time when there was no Luke to tempt and tantalise her, only a howling and an empty stretch of pain inside that seemed to go on for ever. Then the storm softened and grew less with every breath and instead of tempest outside there was one within determined to give her no peace. A howl rose high and demanding as the child she'd done her best to forget refused to be comforted, or to sleep when there was no solace to be had here. The baby's enraged cries beat louder and louder on her poor ears until they filled her whole world. Young Chloe wanted it to die, too, if that would make it stop. The woman she became wanted to shake the girl so she forgot her selfish woe and got on with the life that came out of all that pain.

'No, don't take her with you!' she woke screaming and shot upright in the bed, trembling and sobbing. The coils of that terrible dream still wrapped round her, she began to rock as she tried to fight her way back to now and tell herself it wasn't true.

'Whatever is it? Who frightened you?' a gruff demand came out of the night as the door creaked open and she hadn't breath enough to reassure anyone she was perfectly all right, let alone him. 'What the devil is it?' Lord Farenze barked.

He pushed the door to behind himself and set his candle in the nightstick to peer more closely at the tousled wreckage of her once neat bed and the shivering wild woman staring back at him with all the terrors of the night in her eyes.

Some detached part of her knew she was behaving like a ninny, but she couldn't wave away the terror that still made her heartbeat race and her breath gasp between parched lips as if she had just finished running a mile in her dreams.

Luke was glad he had sense left to listen for the sound of anyone else stirring, not sure if he was glad or sorry when he didn't hear it. His daughter and Bran were too weary from their journey to wake easily and nobody else was within earshot.

'A dream,' she finally managed to gasp as if even that cost her dear.

'I never heard one like it then, even in Eve's wildest nightmares,' he said and did what he'd wanted the moment she looked up at him with terror in her eyes; took her in his arms and dared the devil to do his worst.

'Cry it out,' he encouraged, feeling helpless against the fear still ruling her.

Eve was about six years old when some fool told her the truth about her mother's death, dashed to oblivion at the bottom of a mountain road after a wild race to some would-be poet's latest party only a fool would embark on in winter. He spared a moment from the feel of Chloe shivering in his arms to be glad Eve was over her night horrors and now slept soundly of a night.

For a long moment Chloe felt stiff and resistant in his arms then, with a great heartfelt sigh, she squirmed closer with a ragged sob she tried to stifle against his shoulder, as if she wasn't allowed the luxury of tears. No storm of feminine hysterics could disarm him more. He could feel the shudders that still racked her body and the hand he rubbed across her slender back was meant to comfort. She stilled as if remembering who he was, then seemed unable to fight the security of another being close enough to push away her nightmares. Giving in to her need for human contact for once, she moulded herself against him so intimately her head rested on his shoulder and he felt the impact of her closeness through several layers of fine tailoring.

Feminine heat cindered all the distance he'd tried to put between them. The scent of warm, frightened woman teased his nose along with stray wisps of fiery gold hair that escaped the heavy plait down her back. She shivered and he reassembled the sense to recall it was January. Wrapping her in the bedcover, he murmured a promise not to leave her as he crossed to the fireplace and set his candle to the fire laid there. He must have words with her in the morning about why, when every other chamber on this floor had a fire to warm it, hers was as cold as charity.

Once flames were licking about the pine cones and sea coal, he went to the bed and picked her up, bedcover and all. It said much for her emotional state that she let him and still seemed to be staring sightlessly into some dire fate with horror in her wide eyes. He carried her to an old-fashioned chair banished from a more important bedchamber. *You might as well sleep in a lumber room,* Luke silently chided the shivering woman, then sat down with her in his arms, covering and all.

Despite a half-hearted shake of her head she clearly didn't want him to go. She tucked a slender foot into his side to warm it when the bedcover slipped and it felt more intimate than a week of passionate lovemaking in another woman's bed. *Steady*, he ordered his inner fool; *she doesn't see you as a rampant male, but a source of comfort. You could be anyone.*

'If you refuse to cry it out, at least tell me what frightened you,' he urged and felt her squirm in protest at the thought of giving so much of her inner life away. He fought his predictable male response to the slide of supple feminine curves against his over-eager body and hoped she was too deep in shock to notice. 'No? Then I'll puzzle it out for myself, shall I?' he suggested softly against the ear she hadn't snuggled into his shoulder and felt her flinch.

She shook her head a fraction in denial and he heard her breath hitch, as if she wanted to scold him for bad-mannered prying into her private life, but couldn't quite manage it, so she wriggled even closer instead.

'I presume my arrival roused a fine nest of vipers in your clever, contrary head to upset you so deeply,' he murmured into that tempting ear and thought she managed a muffled 'no' to deny it. 'I don't think I'm unduly vain to suspect I'm the reason you dreamt so vividly,' he persisted.

'No,' she protested more distinctly, so he knew he was right.

Although they had sworn never to kiss or long for each other again on a night of almost love they had shared a decade ago, this unwanted; ill-starred connection between them refused to die.

'Yes, madam, you did,' he persisted, 'you very likely cause yourself to dream even more vividly by denying this feeling between us so fervently when you're awake. So that explains why you dreamt, but not what.

Not even the way we don't want to feel about each other explains *why* you scream out in your sleep, then look as if all the devils of hell are on your heels the moment you wake.'

Chapter Seven

That was it then; the frustrated desire of ten years finally said and in the open. Luke waited for Chloe's reply, resigned to the fact she mattered to him more than either of them wanted to admit—except he just had.

'I've had nightmares night after night since Virginia died,' she admitted as if living with them was better than feeling something unique for him.

'Why?'

The story behind her arrival must be even more painful than he'd thought. Luke willed his hands not to fist when he thought of the rogue who got a child on her, then left her to cope alone. Back then he'd told himself it was best not to know her story when he felt so damned guilty she was trying to build a respectable life and he wanted to ruin her more thoroughly than the rake who found her first.

'Do you think you're the only one to see love as a disaster?' she demanded, but he knew a diversionary tactic when he heard one.

'I thought you adored your reckless, headlong husband and regretted every minute of your life you must live without him? That's what you told me when you whistled my dishonourable proposals down the wind.'

'And you *believed* me?'

'You were very convincing.'

'Of course I was; it was a dishonourable proposal.'

'Surely you didn't expect me to offer marriage?' he demanded unwarily.

She stiffened as if about to jump up and glare at him with her usual armed disapproval. 'No,' she admitted with a sigh instead. She must be too comfortable or too much in need of human comfort to push him away, but she sat up in his arms and stared into the fire instead. 'I learnt not to expect much of anyone the day Verity was born. There was nobody left to care what became of us.'

'Then she was truly a posthumous child?' he asked gently, wanting to know about the man who left her with child, but feeling he was intruding on girlish dreams that might feel very private even if they'd rapidly turned into nightmares.

'Yes, Verity only had me.'

The admission was bleak and he bit back his frustration at having to prise information out of her like a miner hewing coal. 'Could neither family help you?'

'No,' she denied as if it hurt even now.

Luke felt she had a storm of emotions behind the calm she was forcing herself to hold as if her life depended on it. They seemed so much nearer the surface now he wanted to take the heavy weight off her shoulders, then put her world right. He wanted to protect her so badly, yet she insisted on shutting him out.

This contrary, complicated woman was making him a stranger to himself.

'Did you ask them?'

'Not then,' she bit out and somehow he managed to stifle a curse that she still wouldn't let him into her true past or trust him with her real self.

'Had they refused earlier?'

'It was a runaway match,' she said so blankly he suspected she was telling him a well-rehearsed version of what might be the truth, but didn't feel like it.

'They might be glad to meet their grandchild now.'

'I'd walk barefoot across Britain or beg in the streets before I let them near her.'

It sounded as if unforgivable things had been said or done when she was so painfully young, alone and vulnerable. Fury burnt in his gut that anyone could treat a young girl so harshly that she never wanted to see them again. Conscience whispered he'd treated her pretty appallingly himself by offering *carte blanche* to such a youthful widow with a tiny child to consider.

Shame joined fury then; it wasn't Chloe's fault his wife smashed a young man's dreams to powder, or that he was too wrapped up in not hurting to risk having any more. The revelation that he truly cared for this woman as he never had for Pamela, even before they married and hurt each other so much, overtook him with the force of a natural disaster. It felt as if the real Luke Winterley had woken from hibernation. He flexed powerful muscles against an almost physical ache and wished he'd go back to sleep.

'I'm not saying you should,' he managed to say as he gathered up the threads of their not-quite conversation and reminded himself he was rated a very fine whip by the sporting set and ought to be able to do this a lot better.

'I wouldn't do it if you did,' she said scornfully.

'And I couldn't ask you to do something that went so strongly against the grain. We mean too much to each other for that; like it or not.'

'I'm sure you underestimate our will-power, Lord Farenze,' she said icily, as if not ready to make a similar leap into the dark.

'Maybe I do. I still intend to find out why you were driven to take this job to keep yourself and your daughter out of the poor house.'

'Then how dared you use me as entertainment for an idle moment?'

Luke felt oddly wounded she thought so little of him, but he couldn't leave her to lie sleepless or tumble back into night terrors.

'I would not dream of it and we're talking about you and your daughter, not my many and varied shortcomings.'

'No, we're not. Please go to bed and leave me to watch by Virginia one last time, my lord. You must sleep if you're going to be chief mourner at your great-aunt's funeral. I have had my fill of sleeping for now and really don't want to experience that nightmare again tonight.'

Luke opened his mouth to deny he felt the least need to rest, but a huge yawn stopped him. 'I'm not a nodding infant,' he insisted brusquely afterwards.

'No, you're a stubborn man who rode here as fast as coach and horses could go in order to be in time for your great-aunt's funeral. What good you will be for that if you're nodding over your duties is beyond me, but I'm only the housekeeper, so who am I to tell you not to be a fool?'

'It never stopped you in the past,' he muttered crossly.

'Oh, just go to bed, my lord. As a mere woman, I'm not required to put in an appearance until after you return from church tomorrow, so I can sleep in the morning. You owe it to Lady Virginia to be properly awake and aware for her last rites.'

Luke saw the logic of her words, but couldn't let go his duty to care for all those who lived under one of his roofs. His housekeeper would be heavy eyed and weary tomorrow if he did as she suggested. The idea of her keeping watch when he should be the one to hold his loved ones safe also made him feel as if he was less of a man, foolish though that might be.

Still, it seemed as if she preferred waking to sleeping and didn't that betray how haunted and disturbing her nightmares truly were? He longed to offer her simple comfort and scout her demons, so she might sleep sweetly and wake without the shadows under her remarkable eyes. Folly to find it touching that she appeared to care he was tired, despite the dagger-look she shot him, as if he'd made her another dishonourable offer.

'How can I let you take on a duty rightly belonging to me?' he said clumsily.

'Mere servant as I am?' she bit out furiously.

Luke wondered if he'd imagined her burrowing so desperately into his arms when he came to this room to find out why she was shouting in her sleep and why his tongue always tied itself in knots when he was with her.

'No, because you have done more for my great-aunt than anyone had a right to ask you; not that I'm suggesting you can't withstand every tempest life throws at you, so don't bite my nose off,' he argued and wondered why his temper wasn't rising to her barbed comments this time.

He was weary to his very bones, but he knew she was trying to get him out of here before heat and awareness flared back to life. In some ways he knew her so well it hurt, in others she felt as much of a mystery to him as she was the first day he laid eyes on his great-aunt's new companion–housekeeper and felt his world tilt on its axis for a terrifying moment.

'If you watch for an hour or so, I will lie on the bed in the Lord's Chamber with the connecting door open. It's been locked since Virgil died and nobody will recall it's there at a time like this. That way you won't be alone and I'll feel more of a man.'

She looked unconvinced, but eventually nodded and seemed prepared to accept a compromise to end this uncomfortable intimacy. 'I loved Lady Virginia too much in life to be frightened now she's with her Virgil again at last. I'll miss her all my days, but she wouldn't want to live without him any longer than she had to. So please take yourself off whilst I dress, my lord.'

'Very well, my lady,' he said with a bow he might give to the equal in rank she suddenly sounded.

'Exasperating man,' she muttered as he left the room to wait in the cramped little corridor over the nobly proportioned room below.

Out in the dark, Luke fought a battle between physical tiredness and feelings he didn't want to examine. He'd wanted to stay in that neglected room and feel her sleep in his arms. It shocked him to feel so much for the contrary mixture of a woman Chloe had grown into. He'd tried to convince himself for years only his daughter was allowed under his guard and into his heart, but right now it looked like a battle lost.

'What are you doing here?' she demanded in a fierce whisper as she came out of her room and nearly cannoned into him in the gloom.

'Waiting for you,' he managed suavely.

He saw something in the depths of her dark eyes when her candle wavered in her shaking hands that said he wasn't the only one fighting his feelings tonight. He forced himself not to grin like a triumphant boy.

'Well, don't,' she said crossly.

He raised his eyebrows and let some of the passion he felt for her show as their eyes met.

'Verity is ten years old, my lord, and has a right to all I am. I won't accept a lover when my daughter would be harmed by association, so waiting for me to do so will only waste your time and energy you need for the obligations ahead of you.'

'I'm here to escort you to Virginia's bedchamber.'

'Where I don't belong,' she said to herself as much as him.

'Where you will be doing me a favour I should not permit, considering you're so tired yourself,' he corrected.

'I didn't ride all the way from Northumberland in the depths of winter.'

'And I wasn't here to nurse Virginia through her last illness, but if we're not to be caught in a tryst and forced into wedlock, Mrs Wheaton, it's about time we quit this draughty corridor and got on with all that needs doing.'

Chloe sniffed a very expressive sniff of reproach, yet something else lurked behind her coolly composed look. The thought of what Virginia would make of them standing here like a pair of star-crossed lovers unwilling to say goodnight hung unspoken in the air between them and made him flinch.

His beloved but infuriating great-aunt would be planning their wedding before one more late and reluctant January dawn had passed. Virginia usually opposed misalliances and a viscount and a housekeeper were one of those many times over, but something told him she would have been delighted if they ever found the courage to defy convention and wed. So what did Virginia know about the woman he didn't?

'I am going to sit with my beloved late employer and friend and you are going to sleep, my lord, and that is all,' Chloe said sternly and he let her lead the way while he struggled with puzzlement and weariness and did as he was bid for once in his life.

The next morning was bright and frosty with a sky as clear and delicate a blue as the flower of a mountain harebell. Chloe finished drying her hair by the fire Lord Farenze had ordered to be lit in her room and told herself she hadn't really needed the bath he ordered after she spent half the night nodding in a comfortable chair in the late viscountess's bedchamber. Even so, it felt good to be clean and new vitality sparked through her along with the crackle of electricity in her heavy auburn hair. She really ought to have it cut, but it had been easier and cheaper to let it grow so ridiculously long she could sit on it when it hung down her back.

It seemed wrong she should feel vital and alive, today of all days, and she looked at the frosty scene outside the window and let herself be sad Virginia wasn't here to see the rolling hillsides wrapped in sparkling crystal, or the dark bare branches of the trees in the wood that couldn't quite hide the brave snowdrops flowering in the sheltered hollows. She almost heard the words as if Virginia put them straight in her heart.

Don't mourn me, Chloe; after sixteen years without my love we'll never be apart again.

If she took that last piece of advice she could glory in the morning and forget the future until the funeral was over and the will read. Impatient of the last damp strand of hair, she wound it into the heavy knot she usually confined it to, but left out some of the pins that would have screwed it back from her face and made it possible to wear the all-enveloping housekeeper's bonnet she'd bought herself behind Virginia's back.

Today she'd restricted herself to the frivolous piece of lawn and lace her late mistress had reluctantly allowed became a companion and let herself be the girl who shared Virginia's lonelier years again. She recalled her employer saying she wanted bright faces about her, not a death's head got up to fright babies when Verity took one look at her mama in her first all-enveloping cap and burst into tears.

Mrs Winterley would send her a hard-eyed glare for being a housekeeper got up as a lady today, but Chloe owed Virginia one last glimpse of the light-hearted girl she would have had her be, if she could spoil her and Verity as she wanted. There would be little enough cause to be anyone but her mature and sensible self once she took a post in another household.

She tiptoed down the secondary staircase the architect ordered for less important visitors lodged in her corridor of this grand house and wondered who she was being quiet for. Lord Farenze was up and being his usual lordly self, Miss Eve Winterley was downstairs and Verity had begged to be allowed an early morning ride with the grooms, before anyone else was awake to forbid it on this solemn day.

'Mr Filkin says horses need exercise whatever the day brings and I might as well help with the ponies as lie a-bed fretting,' she reported when she came in to ask if she could go and change into her habit.

'Be sure to come back by the nursery stairs though, love. I doubt his lordship's stepmama would approve of you careering about the countryside today.'

'She's an old misery and his lordship won't listen to her,' Verity claimed confidently and Chloe wondered how Luke Winterley had made such a favourable impression on her daughter in such a short time.

She felt beleaguered; the indoor staff adored him; the stable boys and grooms were always full of tales about his horsemanship and now Verity appeared very ready to admire him as well. He sounded as if he'd been reckless and outrageously lucky to live through most of the incidents she'd heard related and she frowned and wondered what manner of man he'd be now if he hadn't made such a disastrous early marriage. A happy one, she decided gloomily.

She snatched up the old cloak she kept in the flower room and stepped out into the winter sunshine to escape the house and her duties for a few precious moments. How unworthy of her to find the idea of Lord Farenze happily wed and content with his wife depressing, rather than wishing him better luck next time.

'Dratted man,' she muttered under her breath as she marched towards the Winter Garden. 'Why does he have to disturb me so deeply?' she asked the statue of some god among the frost-rimed box and the few brave winter flowers hiding their heads under frozen leaves this morning. 'For years he pretends I don't exist, now he's back and I'm wasting time dreaming about him all over again.'

The statue stared into the parkland as if silently slumbering winter trees made more sense than she did and Chloe suppressed a childish urge to kick him.

'Men!' she informed it, glad nobody could hear her. 'You vex women with your ridiculous arguments, pretend logic and stupid longings, then you swat us aside like annoying insects and walk away. How the devil does the contrary great idiot expect me to carry on as if nothing happened now? Does he think we can act as if he never saw me sitting in that bed staring at him like a besotted schoolgirl or came to rescue me from my nightmares? Oh, I'm sorry, you're a man, aren't you? Or at least you would be if you were real. Then you'd huff and puff like the rest of them and drive us all mad before you stamped off to roam about the country shooting innocent animals or riding your poor horses into the ground until you felt better.'

'He might do, if he wasn't made of stone,' Luke Winterley's deep voice said from far too close for comfort and Chloe refused to turn round and blush at being caught talking to a piece of stone. 'Otherwise you would probably be quite right, of course.'

'You should still be asleep,' she told him crossly.

'Lucky I'm not then, for this would be the oddest dream I've ever had,' he told her with a lazy grin.

She wanted to walk into his arms and kiss him good morning so badly she had to swing away and march down the nearest path away from him to stop herself doing exactly that.

'What are you doing?' he asked, following and putting out a hand to prevent her walking straight into a sacking-shrouded potted plant the gardeners had wrapped up for winter.

'I'm counting to a hundred,' she told him between clenched teeth.

'Isn't it supposed to be ten?'

'With you ten is never enough.'

'Oh dear, that bad, am I?'

'Worse,' she bit out.

She would *not* turn round at the warm rumble of his laughter; refused to feel warmed and soothed into good humour because she'd amused him at this saddest of times. Half of her might want to be in his arms so badly she could almost feel his warmth and strength wrapping her up again; more than half if she was honest, but dishonesty was safer.

'Leave me be, my lord.'

'No, you spend far too much time alone already,' he said impatiently, as if it was her fault her role in his household demanded a certain aloofness of her.

'And you shut yourself up in that northern fortress of yours years ago and did your best to pretend the rest of the world doesn't exist, so you have no room to talk.'

'We're lone souls with much in common then, but I didn't walk away from the danger we posed each other then in order to take advantage of you today.'

'I'm sure you're a man of infinite honour, my lord.'

'No, but I fight my demons as best I can; something you should consider before you provoke me again, madam.'

'*I* provoke *you*?'

'Yes, you should have the sense to realise you're always in acute danger when I'm about, Mrs Wheaton, yet you seem determined to court it.'

'You're the one with a large house, acres of garden and an entire estate to avoid *me* in. I don't see how you can berate me for taking a brief walk within hailing distance of the house? In your shoes I could use my freedom to simply walk away.'

'Marching about in front of the windows of a room you know I always work in when I'm at Farenze Lodge is *not* disturbing me then? Did I not give you fair warning this could happen if you teased me instead of avoiding me like the plague?,' he rasped and tugged her into his arms as if she'd driven him to it.

'Let me go, you barbarian,' she snapped, but he lowered his head and met her eyes with a storm of fury and need in his that mirrored the argument raging between her heart and head and making her feel recklessly susceptible to his nearness.

'Stop me,' he demanded gruffly, so close she felt a warm whisper on her skin.

Chapter Eight

Chloe knew Lord Farenze would leave her alone if she breathed *no* or flinched away. Yet she couldn't say it, or take that step back. His mouth on hers was gentle as a plea and she waited for him to remember he was kissing the housekeeper and retreat in horror. She had to breathe at last and he followed the winter air into her mouth as if he was starving for her. Heat flooded every inch of her body and mind as his lips and tongue explored her mouth in sensual wonder.

Needs she had fought for so long clamoured and fidgeted to let a decade of frustration and loneliness go. She swayed into his arms and opened her mouth even as sensible Chloe whispered she was a fool. Somehow the slight shake in his touch freed some last curb on her conscience and she felt him test her narrow waist, banding her closer to the difference and heat of him, narrow flanked and broad shouldered as he was against her curves and unable to conceal how badly he wanted, no, needed her.

Intrigued by such wild heat, despite the frigid January air and this saddest of days, she felt every pore and whisper come uniquely alive to him. Senses sharpened as if they'd slept since that last kiss so long ago. She wanted to strip off her tight tan gloves and feel this exceptional man under her naked touch. Doing her best to add the soft covering to her senses instead, she brushed a finger along his high cheekbone and wherever he felt the butterfly touch of fine leather on taut skin a flush of hard colour tracked her fingers. Shocked by her own boldness, she rose on tiptoe and rested her hands on his broad shoulders so she could watch him more closely, more intimately. For these few seconds outside time he was hers and she was his.

His coat was frost chilly where they'd had no contact, yet where their bodies strove to meld no cold could reach them. They had an antidote to winter and who would guess so much heat was pent up between gruff Lord Farenze and his coolly composed housekeeper?

He moved his hands up from her waist to cup a shamefully hot and responsive breast under her layers of winter disguise and the sweet novelty of his long-remembered touch, real again on her eager body, made her heart leap and her stomach fall into that familiar burning longing only he could stir in her. She gave a low moan as need ground at her insides like hot knives and heated her inner core with impossible promises.

Shocked by her own need of him, she pulled back far enough to watch him and hotly unanswerable questions flashed into his grey gaze and echoed her own. He'd focused too much formidable attention on her at last, given too much away to snatch it back and pretend they were nothing to each other, hadn't he? This was the real Luke Winterley, the passionate man behind

Lord Farenze's cold exterior and reclusive reputation. She felt too much for that man and she was opening her mouth to ask questions neither of them wanted to know when the return of the riding party sounded on the clear air and let Chloe's real life back in with a sickening thump and a deep breath of icy January air. She tugged free of Lord Farenze's arms and faced him with all she shouldn't feel in her eyes.

'I can't,' she gasped. 'Neither of us can,' she told him sadly, then hurried off towards the stable yard and her beloved daughter before Luke could argue.

'I quite agree, Mrs Wheaton,' Luke muttered to the January air. 'So what the devil have you done to me this time, my conundrum-in-petticoats?'

No point trying to sit and work on the letters of sympathy and solutions to estate matters now. All he'd see out of the window now was an image of himself, tangled so tight in kissing Virginia's protégé he'd forgotten where, when and what they were. He couldn't settle for the ordeal ahead and hardly knew how to live in his own skin without Chloe to remake him every time he set eyes on her.

The very thought of her as she was just now set his pulses jumping and his manhood rigid with need. Yet she was Virginia's housekeeper-cum-companion; a lady already burned by the chilling harshness the world showed those who fell from grace; a woman who'd wed recklessly, then found herself alone with a babe to support when she should have been in the schoolroom herself.

Recalling her list of activities for crass males, Luke wished he *could* ask for a hack to be saddled and ride for hours to avoid longing for more unsuitable meetings with the Farenze Lodge housekeeper. No, there could be no more of those and it was high time he turned his mind to the sad and solemn occasion ahead of him.

If he'd had his way they would celebrate Virginia's long life and the fact she was reunited with her beloved Virgil, instead of mourning the passing she had begun to long for of late. Instead, he was chief mourner at a solemn funeral and must hide his grief as best he could for the sake of those who looked to him as head of the family and master of the house and estate.

His great-uncle's will left his wife only a lifetime tenure on the house they had built so lovingly between them with ultimate ownership going to Luke. He'd been too wound up in baby Eve and playing down the chaos Pamela had raised on the Continent when Virgil died to take much notice, but lately he'd tried to discuss the future of Farenze Lodge with Virginia and got nowhere even faster than usual.

'Virgil left you this house and estate to save me having people constantly badgering me to leave it elsewhere,' Virginia told him.

'But why me?' he asked. 'James might change if he had an estate of his own. You have told me he needs to be his own man.'

'Let me worry about James,' she said mysteriously, 'you're the only man we wanted living here after us, Luke. You love and understand it as we did, so enjoy it as a holiday from that grim barrack you live in most of the year. You can retreat here when the rigours of Darkmere become too great for your wife.'

'I don't have a wife, nor shall I until Eve is wed,'

he replied, meeting her level gaze steadily to show her he meant it and there was no point scheming to pair him off with some hopeful young lady she might have handy before then.

'One day you'll have to take that armour off and learn to be happy,' she had replied with a knowing smile he didn't want to question, so he shrugged and accepted their decision, since he could hardly do otherwise now the deed was done.

And now the whole world seemed to be conspiring against his long-held plan to find a convenient wife once Eve was old enough to marry. Virginia, Eve and even Tom Banburgh seemed to think he ought to wed for something warmer than mere convenience and surely they were all wrong?

'There you are, m'lord,' Josiah Birtkin's bass voice rumbled at him from the doorway leading from the gardens to the stableyard and Luke swore at himself for getting distracted from all he had to cope with today.

'So it would seem,' he replied mildly enough.

'Thought you should know,' Josiah went on as if words had a tax on them.

'Know what?'

'Cross said they was followed back from the gallops just now.'

'Why on earth would anyone follow a schoolgirl?' Luke mused.

'Don't know, m'lord.'

'Have you any idea who it was?'

'No, he stayed well back. Cross thought it was his fancy to start with.'

Luke frowned even more darkly at the thought of

Chloe's daughter as quarry. 'It makes no sense,' he muttered and Josiah shrugged as if nothing his fellow humans did made much of that. 'Where is he now?' Luke asked, resolving to confront the rogue and demand what he was about.

'Rode off when they got back to the paddocks, and, since he managed to look as if he was on his way somewhere else, nobody thought to challenge him.'

'And you saw him close up, I hope?'

'No, he was some way off by the time Cross mentioned him and had his hat pulled down over his eyes and a scarf over his mouth.'

'It's a cold day and a traveller might cover up against it, I suppose.'

And why trail a schoolgirl back to Farenze Lodge when a few casual questions would reveal her mother was only housekeeper here? And why would Verity Wheaton's location matter to anyone but her mother, after all the years when nobody outside the household took any notice of either of them?

'His beast had some Arab in him though, m'lord, and if the man wasn't dressed like a farmer I'd have to call him a gentleman.'

'Keep a lookout for him and I'll have the watch doubled at night. If Miss Wheaton or my daughter ride out again, please make sure you or Seth stay with them and go armed, Josh, just in case,' Luke ordered with a frown. 'Be discreet about it; the fewer people who know the better since I don't want panic breaking out, or the man scared off before we find out what he's up to.'

'Trust me not to blab,' Josiah said, looking offended anyone might think he could, let alone Luke who'd known him since he was set on his first pony at Dark-mere while still in short coats.

'Aye, of course I do,' Luke said with a wry grin and sent him back to the stables with orders to keep an eye on those who came and went on what would be a busy day for them all.

Luke intended to catch the man haunting Verity Wheaton and challenge him, so why was a prickle of apprehension sliding down his spine like ice water? He didn't know the girl, had only set eyes on her a few times since she was a baby. Yet Eve had taken to her instantly and Chloe adored her, so how could he not be furious at any man who might try to harm or bother the child?

He would feel so about any girl, he reassured him-self, and it was probably true, given the appalling haz-ards that could stalk a child as distinctive as Verity Wheaton. She had her own version of the striking col-ouring he found so irresistible in her mother. Her hair was closer to blonde and her eyes a paler blue than her mother's stormy ones, but they shared the same fine-boned build and heart-shaped faces; the same fierce intelligence as well, he suspected, and some of the mother's stubborn will and pride had been passed on to her child, if Verity's determination to be with her mother at this sad time was any indication.

Luke frowned and decided he must make time to ask Chloe about Verity's father sooner than he wanted to. Until then he'd trust Josiah's sharp eyes and Eve's com-pany as well as his own vigilance to keep the child safe while her mother was managing his house and seemed barely to have time to eat, let alone sleep soundly.

* * *

A few hours later Chloe and the maids stopped work and wrapped themselves up in shawls and mittens before going out on the balustrade roof to watch the funeral cortège wind its way towards the church where the fifth Viscount Farenze was buried. The sombre procession went in and out of sight as it crossed the park and Chloe wished she could attend the service. As she was a female and a housekeeper with a house to prepare for cold and sorry mourners to return to, she bowed her head and recited the Twenty-Third Psalm and the Lord's Prayer in memory of their beloved mistress and silently wished her ladyship Godspeed with all her heart.

When that was done they watched with tears in their eyes when the horses were taken out of their harness so the male servants and estate workers could drag the sombre rig the last stretch to the church instead. Chloe nearly sobbed as unguardedly as the maids at the sight of such love and devotion to a wonderful woman. She took a deep breath instead and handed out snowy squares of soft cotton and salvaged linen to those who had forgotten their handkerchiefs and hugged Verity close as they said a private goodbye to Lady Virginia.

They stayed in the chilly winter sunshine until a crush of nobility and gentry left the tiny church while the tomb was opened inside and Virginia's closest family and friends saw her laid beside her beloved Virgil. Only then did Chloe order the staff downstairs to get Farenze Lodge ready for the mourners' return and all the rituals of this solemn winter day.

Bran's militant look at her former charge told Chloe she wanted her ewe lamb out of the frigid January air as urgently as she did Verity, but at that moment a robin began to sing as if its life depended on it from the top of an old holly tree nearby. Neither of them could bring themselves to scold the girls for avoiding the ladies who were gathered about the fire in the grand drawing room sighing and reading their prayerbooks after that. They went downstairs with the echo of that joyful song in their ears, a last serenade to a woman who had always lived life so richly and loved so well.

'I'm glad Lady Virginia made it clear she didn't want a grand formal fuss when she died. Miss Eve will miss her too much to want to play hostess to half the county as if she'd only lost her pet canary, with her being as close to her ladyship as she always was,' Bran observed to Chloe over tea in the housekeeper's room several hours later.

'She did it very well, but she's too young to endure much more formality today and Lady Virginia's real friends know it. By leaving as soon as they decently could they took the rest with them by sheer force of will, which is why they were Lady Virginia's friends in the first place, I suppose,' Chloe replied as she eased her aching feet on to the footstool and blessed the comfort of a fire of her own. The demands of the last few hours seemed to crowd in all over again and she wondered if she'd forgotten some small but vital detail. 'I thought Lady Bunting and the Squire and his wife would never leave, though.'

'And I wondered if that dratted Mrs Winterley would ever stop eating,' Bran said with a grimace.

'But, Bran, "in a well-regulated household there

would be more sugar in the plum cake and less salt in the cheese scones",' Chloe parodied the lady wickedly. 'That didn't prevent Mrs Winterley eating vast quantities of both while telling anyone who would listen how prostrated she was by grief.'

'Fat old hypocrite,' Bran said as she lay back in her chair and closed her eyes.

'I can't argue, although I know I should,' Chloe replied as the warmth of the room and her own deep weariness tugged at her conviction she still had a deal to do before she dared try to sleep again. 'You're a bad influence on me, Bran,' she said drowsily.

'Someone needed to be,' her new friend declared and opened her shrewd eyes as if she'd only been pretending to be half-asleep. 'It's high time you learnt to live again, young woman,' she said, as if she could see into Chloe's heart and all the bitter memories she didn't want to face.

'I could say the same about you.'

'I did all the living and loving I ever shall with a man before Miss Eve was born. My Joe is buried at sea on the other side of the world and I'll have no other, but you deserve better than life seems to have handed you so far.'

'No, I don't,' Chloe said shortly, even as a picture of Luke Winterley flitted into her mind, laughing and at ease as nature intended him to be and murmured, *But aren't I better than you imagined in your wildest dreams before you met me?*

'Then perhaps he does,' Bran said.

Chloe's heartbeat had accelerated at the thought of him and the way all the longings she wished she could kill shivered through her body whenever the wretched man was in the same room. It must have shown in her eyes.

'He needs more than I can give,' Chloe said and closed her eyes again in the hope it might put paid to such a painful topic of conversation. All her normal defences felt so weak it was as if her emotions were about to spill over in a disastrous flood. 'More tea?' she asked with a brightness they both knew was false and Bran nodded obligingly and let the painful topic of Mrs Wheaton's feelings for her noble master drop, with a look that said this wasn't the time for an argument, but her new friend would have to confront those feelings sooner or later.

Chloe was glad Mrs Winterley and the other ladies favoured the state rooms as the early January dusk began to darken the skies outside and most of the gentlemen congregated in the billiard room. They couldn't divert themselves with a game on such a day ,but seemed comforted by the idea that Virginia would have told them to forget such flummery and get on with it and most of them were avoiding the drawing room and the low-voiced gossip that was all the ladies could indulge in as dusk came down on this solemn day.

It seemed a good time to place the little vase of snowdrops someone had snatched a moment to gather earlier and she had only now found time to arrange with a few sprigs of wintersweet. The gardeners always forced as many spring flowers as they could to bloom early, since Virginia delighted in the bravest of the spring ones to remind them winter wouldn't last for ever.

Sooner or later she would have to stop behaving as if

Virginia might walk into a room and exclaim at such a simple luxury and ask about a gardener's elderly mother, or perhaps his wife being close to her time, when one of them came to hand the flowers over. Chloe thought it a shame to kill off Virginia's routine and make her loss even harder to bear. She did her best not to make things worse than they must already feel when the speechless, grief-stricken head gardener came to the door with this tribute to his employer and old friend and simply nodded her sincere thanks and told him how beautiful and hopeful they seemed in the depths of winter.

'Oh, heavens! I didn't see you there, my lord, but why on earth are you sitting in the dark?' she gasped now, shocked when he rose from the chair by the window where Virginia often sat to catch the best light for her book.

'Because I enjoy sitting in the dark?' he replied wryly, but she heard the flat weariness in his voice and somehow couldn't make herself walk away.

'I doubt it,' she said as her eyes grew accustomed to the gloom and instinct warned her to plunk the vase down and leave.

'You're right,' he said gruffly and she wondered if he didn't want her to see tears in his supposedly steely gaze when he turned his head away.

'How gratifying for me; good evening, my lord.'

'No, stay,' he asked, again in that rough voice as if he couldn't find the energy to smooth it into any sort of gentlemanly restraint right now.

'You know I can't,' she murmured as she sank on to the chair closest to his and folded her hands to stop them reaching to him as if by right.

'Don't speak of "can't" today.'

'I have to,' she argued, gripping her fingers more tightly together to stop them soothing his lean cheek, or ruffling the stern discipline he'd imposed on his unruly raven locks in his great-aunt's honour.

'Virginia wasn't a great one for rules and conventions,' he replied with tension in his voice that said he wanted human contact, too, even if he hadn't moved since she sat down.

'I imagine she was as determined not to be confined by them as a young woman as she was when I knew her.'

'She was a rogue, or so her sisters said before she outlived them all,' he said with such pride and love for his late great-aunt by marriage in his voice Chloe felt herself melting from the inside out.

'So many people loved her for it that it makes you wonder if being correct and ever ready to criticise, as I remember her sisters being when I first came here, is the way to live a good life after all. They used to visit and sniff and carp at her for simply having me and Verity in the house, let alone employing me as her companion-housekeeper.'

Chloe shifted uncomfortably in her seat as she recalled he'd been almost as critical once he found out about that act of kindness himself, but perhaps he'd decided this wasn't the day to have too good a memory.

'I think when she and Virgil wed, Virginia gave up scandalising society one way, so she was determined to find as many ways of confounding its prejudices in other ones as she could.'

'You think of me as one of her rebellions, then?'

'Perhaps at first—later even I could see that you and your daughter were more to her than a whim to infuriate her sisters and any stuffy neighbours she wanted to annoy. She needed you almost as much as you did her. She would have been an excellent mother and would have doted on any grandchildren who followed in her children's footsteps.'

'Instead she was a wonderful friend and mentor to me and so many others society would like to turn its collective nose up at and ignore.'

'You were not a charity cases, but a good and dear friend to her; allow me that much insight today, even if we must pretend to be enemies again tomorrow.'

'I know, I am sorry,' she said softly.

He smiled at her unguarded apology and they sat in companionable silence for a few wonderful moments, as if they understood each other too well to need words.

'Virginia was the product of another age,' he finally said with a sigh, 'but even she wouldn't have been quite so eager to break the rules if she knew it would reflect back on her progeny.'

'No, I suppose she didn't have a daughter of her own to make those rules real for her. It colours everything when your own reputation affects another's whole life so drastically,' Chloe agreed with a hearty sigh of her own.

'As those girls of ours both changed our lives?'

'Yes.'

'Sooner or later we must talk about it,' he warned.

'No, your daughter is your business; mine is hers and mine alone. We have nothing to discuss, my lord.'

'Yet we must talk about it all the same,' he said as implacably as he could, when he sounded as if grief and weariness were weighing him down too heavily to face a confrontation now.

'Not if I can help it we won't,' she muttered under her breath, but he heard her in the intimate gloom of the dark room. Only a glow from the banked-down fire was left to show them their thoughts and feelings now the light had faded, but when he wanted to he could read her like a book.

'Do you remember the day we first met?' he asked sneakily.

All of a sudden the gloom of a January dusk was gone and they were bathed in summer heat again, her most disreputable bonnet was hanging down her back and his bright, curious gaze sharpened on this new phenomenon tramping her way up his great-aunt's drive.

She had just paid a visit to her little daughter at the wet-nurse's neat cottage on the Farenze Lodge Estate and she was buoyed up by the hope Verity was finally going to be big enough to come home with her next week. The world seemed a light and happy place that fateful summer day, then she had looked up and met a pair of complicated masculine grey eyes and a fluttery feeling of excitement joined the hope that was rekindling in her after a long winter.

'Where are you going to, my pretty maid?' he'd asked as lightly as if he hadn't a care in the world, for once in his too-responsible life, either.

'I'm off to London to see the Queen,' she'd said, suddenly as giddy as a girl as she tossed her fiery gold curls out of her eyes and refused to regret they were wild and tumbling down her back for once.

'Can I come?' he'd said and that was it, her heart had opened to him. Dark-haired, smiling Viscount Farenze's eyes promised her impossible things as they met as the equals they should have been and were no more.

'Too well,' she admitted sombrely now, the memory of all they should have been to each other in her eyes as she stared into the fire to avoid his.

There were no pictures of unattainable castles in Spain hidden in the complex depths of it. She'd spent ten years convincing that hopeful girl there could be nothing between Viscount Farenze and Verity Wheaton's mother, so how could there be?

'If only things had been different for us, then and now,' she added regretfully and thought she heard a gruff groan, hastily suppressed, at the thought of what could have been, without their daughters and their duty to make it impossible.

'It's time we stopped pretending we're nothing to each other, Mrs Wheaton.'

'No, it's our best protection. My Verity and your Eve will always make it impossible for us to be other than master and servant and you know it. Now, if you'll excuse me, it's been a long day and you must be weary and eager to have it over and done with,' she said with a would-be humble nod.

She could only just see his shadowed face and his white shirt and collar and stark black necktie through the deepening darkness. A lot of her longed for the right to move closer; feel cool linen and hot man under her spread palms; offer him comfort nobody else could give on this sorry day and take some in return. It was a right she'd relinquished the day Verity was born, so she hid her hands in her midnight skirts and waited for the words of dismissal that would set them free of this fiery frustration, for now.

Chapter Nine

'I *am* tired,' Luke Winterley admitted with a sigh, as if it was a weakness he was rightly ashamed of, and tenderness for his manly conviction she had no right to feel threatened to undermine her aloofness.

'Despite your attempts to prove otherwise, you are only human, my lord. You need a proper night's sleep after your hard and hasty journey, last night's vigil and all you have had to endure today,' Chloe replied.

'I haven't enjoyed one of those under this roof from the first day I set eyes on you,' he snapped, as if she was an idiot to suggest he might now.

She'd offered him the only warmth and understanding she decently could and he'd thrown it back at her as if it revolted him, drat the man, but he could stand apart from the rest of humanity with her blessing. 'I will get back to my duties,' she said, snatching back the hand she hadn't known she'd stretched out as if he'd scalded it.

'Before God, woman, I could shake you until your teeth rattle,' he gritted between what sounded like clenched teeth.

'Because I speak sense and keep a cool head? If so, you're a fool.'

'Then let's see how idiotic I can be, shall we? Then maybe next time you will take a warning in the spirit it is meant,' he said in a husky voice and sounded so brusque her mouth twisted in a wobbly smile.

He was my Lord Farenze at his most bearlike and made her feel emotions no other man had ever stirred. Her fingers itched to test his athlete's body and fallen-angel features; to curl themselves into that overlong raven mane of his and tug him down to meet her mouth with his kiss; to discover anew he was as addictive to the touch as to the rest of her senses.

Temptation made her senses flex, stretch and luxuriate in the promise of him. How familiar and seductive and dangerous it was. To be part of something with him was almost as irresistible as the physical fact of him and his ill humour at not being able to freeze her out of his life as he clearly wanted to. Heat flashed through her like sheet lightning; her breathing went shallow as her heartbeat raced and she leaned towards him to…

No! Her body was as wrong now as it was ten years ago. She'd felt such yearning need to be passionately loved back then it was little wonder bitter, guarded, dashingly handsome Lord Farenze unleashed wild dreams in her that ought to be dead and done with. He still could, simply by being here, but her world could never be well lost for love. She had a daughter who must come before him, and her, and everything else in Chloe's life.

Anything that smirched Chloe's reputation would make Verity less in the eyes of the world. Yet every time she fought this battle it was harder, as if this darling bear of a man was wound so tight into her senses she would never be free of the feel and look and touch of him, that faint scent of masculine cologne and Luke Winterley. All of him, gruff and smooth, tender and sharp, was caught into her heart so securely that she only had to scent that cologne to be aware of him as a lover until her dying day.

No, she must win her battle one last time and then she would be free of temptation for ever. The thought of never seeing him again made tears sting her eyes. How could she not pity herself all the long years with not even the sight of him ahead? A voice whispered, *Giving in to what you both need won't hurt this once*, but it lied.

Never to see him again, never to feel him and his mighty body respond to her after they threw caution to the four winds and indulged in the unimaginable luxury of loving for one short night? Verity had been enough to make her step back and say no before and must keep being so, because one night would never be enough.

'No, my lord, we could make a fine pair of fools of each other together, but I've worked hard to be the respectable woman I am now, despite the gossip and doubts you and so many others had when I came here with a babe in my arms. I can't give in to improper advances from so-called gentlemen like you and waste all that effort now,' she said with a careless smile meant to lessen the tension.

'Do you think me such a rake I might take what isn't freely given?' he demanded, refusing to let her joke them out of something that really wasn't funny. 'I have never chased the maids or tried to sneak kisses from a poor governess who can't fight back and I never will,' he snapped and marched over to glare at the glowing fire as if he couldn't endure being so close any longer.

'I'm sure you're all that's noble, but you're the one who has always insisted I'm in danger of causing gossip and scandal by staying here.'

'You're not a servant,' he snapped.

'Try telling that to your guests, or indeed to the other servants.'

'We both know you've been masquerading as a companion, or a housekeeper, or whatever act you and Virginia settled on to fool the world with. If you were truly born to be even an upper servant, I wouldn't have come near you other than as your employer, but you make it open season for me to hunt down the truth and force you to face it. No, wait and hear me out, woman, I must know who you truly are, before someone else finds you out and we must marry to right your good name.'

'I'd never ask such a sacrifice and stop sorting through my life to divert yourself from your grief. Or is that too much for a housekeeper to ask of a lord?'

Despising herself for the wobble in her voice, Chloe felt a terrible weariness weigh her down. Resolving to resist him until she rode down the drive for the last time on the carrier's cart with all her luggage was sapping her strength, as even the disturbed nights and dark days they'd suffered here of late had not been able to do. It felt as if a cloud of feathers were falling on her as his concerned voice came and went over the beat of her suddenly thundering heart.

'I'm not sure, but sit down before you fall over,' he

barked as he dashed over to scoop her up before she could do exactly that.

After last night she knew how seductive it felt to let someone care for her, to feel his gentle touch on her forehead and lean into his powerful masculine body while she regained her own strength after the weary days while Virginia lay dying. She was tempted to let go and simply allow him to hold the world at bay for her for once.

'I'm quite all right,' she murmured, willing away the faint that would make her weak with the very last man in the world she should be weak with.

'Of course, you're so well you snatch sleep in half-hour parcels and nearly faint from grief and whatever else you're worrying about rather than confide in me. I can see how robust you are, Mrs Wheaton. Rude health is written all over your ashen face and painted under your shadowed eyes.'

'Why not make me feel worse and tell me how hag-gish I look?' she asked, as if her appearance mattered when her whole world was falling apart once more.

Somehow it did though, when he was the one look-ing at her. Chloe enjoyed the luxury of meeting his gaze, once he was satisfied she could sit up without his help and he crouched down in front of her so she didn't have to crane her neck. It felt as intimate as when he held her in his arms and did his best to scout her demons last night.

'Can't you see that I need to help you?' he ground out as if it hurt to admit it. 'Whatever we can or can't be to one another, I can't let you wander off into the wide world alone, as if it doesn't matter a jot to me what hap-pens after you leave here.'

'I won't *be* alone,' she protested, his gruff sincerity tugging at her resolution.

'Virginia told me she has set aside a sum to cover your daughter's education and a small income to fall back on if she ever needs it. She wouldn't leave you to worry yourself to flinders by keeping that secret, so will you be returning to your family now you don't need to support your daughter?'

'There's nobody to go back to,' she admitted.

'Then you have no family?'

'None who cares what becomes of me or Verity,' she said wearily.

'Someone is damnably curious about your daughter then. Birtkin thought the coach was followed back from Bath,' he said.

Chloe frowned at the idea, then dismissed it as foolish. Her father was dead and her brothers wouldn't bother to track her down, let alone Verity.

'My family would take no interest in us, even if they knew where we were,' she said.

'Tell me who they are and I'll make them take one,' he said with such arrogant determination she only just managed to stop herself reaching up to kiss him.

'They are as dead to me as I am to them,' she said, finding she couldn't sit and let him confuse her secrets out of her any longer. Her turn to march up and down the room now, her faintness forgotten. 'And I will never go where my daughter is not welcome,' she told him when her circuit brought them close again.

'Then she *is* a love child?' he asked with surprising gentleness, and no judgement in his voice, as he stopped her by standing in front of her and making it impossible to go on without brushing against his muscular strength in the shadows.

Chloe ached to avoid his question by taking that step, but Verity and all the reasons why not forbade it. She hugged herself defensively instead, not sure if she was keeping hurt out or the pain of denying them in. 'I don't know,' she said unwarily, so agitated by the hurt of forever denying them each other that the truth slipped out unguarded. 'No, that's wrong, of course I know. I know only too well,' she said too loudly.

'She's not yours, is she?' he said with all the implications of that fact dawning in his now furious gaze. '*Is* she?' he demanded harshly, as if lying to him was a bigger sin than bearing Verity out of wedlock, as he'd always half-suspected she had done, would have been.

'Yes,' she insisted and it was true. 'Verity is *my* daughter.'

'And I'm the Archbishop of Canterbury,' he scoffed.

She shrugged and turned to stare sightlessly out of the window, looking from almost darkness into even more of it, as she tried to ignore the furious male presence at her back. Instead of all-too-real Lucius Winterley, she saw a dark mirror image of him in the shining panes in front of her.

Even the small amount of light in the room made a sharp contrast to the darkness outside and their reflection showed her a plain and pale female of very little account and the mighty man she could have had in her life, if she didn't have a child to put before everyone else. He was brooding and intense and utterly unforgettable; the shadow image of the man she didn't want to love. Nobody would ever need to search their memory to remind themselves if Lord Farenze was at a certain event; he was someone you couldn't ignore even when you wanted to.

'I don't care who *you* are, Verity's my daughter,' she lied.

'As Eve is Bran's daughter in every way but fact, I know Verity is yours,' he said with that new gentleness in his voice. 'You took on even more than Bran when you accepted Verity as your own, for whatever reason you felt you must.'

'There *was* no choice. She is my child.'

'Don't take me for a flat any longer. I've been one for the ten years I stayed away from you for her benefit as well as your own. Now I see why there was such fury in your eyes when you first told me to take my dishonourable intentions straight to hell all those years ago, such a steely need in you to keep you and your child safe at whatever cost. I suppose going back home would mean admitting you'd failed.'

'No, there is no going back. Verity would have been left on the doorstep of the nearest foundling hospital on a bitter night like this one if I let them get their hands on her. If I even wanted to go back now, they would find a way to rid themselves of her the moment I took my eyes off them,' she told him, the defiance, hurt and grief she'd felt after their reception of the fact Verity had survived her rough birth sounding harsh in her voice at that terrible truth.

'I doubt they would have brought themselves to carry out such an inhuman scheme, whatever threats were made in the heat of the moment,' he said as if she had taken Verity and stolen away on some childish whim.

'Exposing unwanted babies to the elements, given even the slim chance they might be found and raised to some sort of life by the parish, is an everyday sin in a world that despises tiny children for the mistakes of their parents,' she said bitterly. 'So, yes, they refuted her as coldly as an unwanted kitten and would have dealt with her as lightly if I had let them,' she said, refusing to spare him when she had all the details of Verity's terrible beginning etched on her memory, to live with for the rest of her life as best she could.

'Why did her mother sit by and let you take her babe?' he prompted so gently she let the information past her numb lips before her mind could leap in and argue he should not know so much about them.

'Her mother was my twin sister and she died in childbed,' she told him, the sorrow of it heavy in her heart, memory so vivid it could have happened yesterday.

He knew so much she hadn't wanted anyone to know now, at least until Verity was old enough to hear the truth. She wondered if that day would ever come when all it could bring her was sadness at the fact Daphne refused to name the father of her child, even as she lay dying.

'The other half of you,' Luke said, as if he knew the bond of twins was tighter than that between ordinary siblings.

'We weren't identical,' she said with a wobbly smile as she recalled the many differences between herself and Daphne, despite that shared birthday. 'I can't tell you how shocked everyone was when it was the quiet and angelic twin who threatened to disgrace the family name, not the one they always predicted would come to a bad end. From the day we were born Daphne was the sweet little angel to my devil, although she was as capable of mischief as I was. We argued and fought like cat and dog at times in private and she sometimes let me take the blame for our sins because I looked as if I deserved it. I supposed one of us might as well be punished as both.'

'And yet you truly shared your sins about equally?'

'More or less,' she admitted cautiously.

'You were the dog with the bad name being hanged for it, were you not?' he asked as if he already knew she'd taken curses and blows for her sister more often than for herself, because somehow she needed the good opinion of others far less than her sister had done.

'What if I was? We had each other and precious little attention from anyone but our nurse after our mother died. Daphne made it up to me by bringing food and books when they were forbidden me, or thinking up a new adventure to distract us from my latest punishment. I wasn't a saint and we were both heedless and unruly. I expect the aunts were right to say we were a sad burden to them and our brothers are much older than us. They blamed us for our mother's death, although Mama didn't die until we were five, so that's about as logical as blaming Verity for whatever sins Daphne committed. Oh, don't look at me like that, I'm not so innocent I don't know she had a lover, but I never caught her out in an assignation, saw a love note passed to her, or overheard a furtive greeting to give me a clue who he was.'

Hearing herself saying far too much again, Chloe forced her mind back into the present and glared at him for luring her into a past she still found it hard to revisit.

'What of your father?' he asked blandly, as if they

were engaged in polite conversation instead of talking about the upending of her young life.

'What of him?' she said, wondering how different hers and Daphne's lives might have been if their father loved them half as much as Luke did his daughter.

'Where was he in all this?'

'Away. He used to claim he couldn't abide the sight of us because we were such a painful reminder of our mother, but I found out later he'd installed a mistress in his town house before she was even cold in her grave. Whatever the truth, he spent his time in London or Brighton, or at his main seat in Northamptonshire where his daughters were not permitted to join him. Until we threatened to bring such disgrace on him even he couldn't ignore us, we rarely saw him from one year to the next.'

'What did he do when he recalled the twin daughters he'd left to raise themselves as best they could?'

Oh, but he was good at this, Chloe decided, even as she heard herself answer as if nothing stood between her ears and her tongue. 'He came back,' she said with a shudder. She hugged herself even tighter to ward off the terrible day of his return.

'I suppose he would have to, once your sister was with child.'

She rounded on him to rage at his insensitivity, but he bewildered her before the words could leave her mouth by stripping off his viscount-warmed superfine coat and wrapping her in the heat of his body by proxy.

'You'll be cold,' she protested even as she snuggled into the seductive smoothness of the silk lining and warmth of him and breathed in the unique scent of clean man and lemon water and sandalwood.

'I'm a tough northerner, don't forget,' he argued with a wry smile.

How could she *not* want him when he stood there, so completely masculine and would-be cynical, and made her heart turn over with wanting this unique man in her life? In his shirtsleeves it was impossible to ignore the width of his shoulders and the lean strength of his mature body. She could imagine him at twenty, the young husband of a silly little débutante without the sense to see what a fine man she'd wed, and wondered how they would have gone on if they had met when she was young and impulsive and silly and married each other instead.

Impossible, Chloe; he's almost nine years older than you are and was a father and a widower before you left the schoolroom, she chided herself, yet she couldn't get the idea out of her head that, if he'd only waited for her to grow up, everything could be so different for them now. At six and twenty to her seventeen and steady as the rock his northern eyrie stood upon, he would have been steadfast as granite when Daphne's loneliness and need for love and approval brought the world tumbling down on the Thessaly twins. A pipe dream, she dismissed that fantasy of love and marriage with him, and did her best to see them as others would. She shivered again at the thought of the sneers and jeers that would greet the revelation they'd been closeted in this room so long and only talked of past sins, not committed a whole pack of new ones.

'Come closer to the fire,' he urged gently at the sight of her apparently still feeling as cold as charity.

He couldn't know it was the temptation of him that made her seek occupation for her hands, lest they reached for him. In his pristine white linen shirt, with that simply elegant black-silk waistcoat outlining his narrow waist so emphatically by the glow of the fire he had stirred into stronger life for her, he was temptation incarnate.

How she longed to wrap her arms about him and be held until the pain and grief abated. She told herself it was nothing more than the concern he would feel for any girl left so alone that was softening his hawk-like features. He had a young daughter and felt for her plight when she faced such a stark choice between her old life and Verity's death.

More than likely he would have opted to rescue Daphne if he'd met them in their hour of need. She was appalled by the jealousy that blazed through her at the idea of him in thrall to her sister's angelic blonde looks and easy smiles. Apparently there *was* something that could make her hate her sister for being so lovely and needy after all, or rather *someone*.

Chloe felt ashamed that Luke Winterley meant more to her than her twin had done. Until she met Verity's furious gaze the first time and became a mother, despite the facts, this man could have meant more to her than any man should to a girl of such notoriously rackety lineage as hers.

Chapter Ten

'Do you think that just once during our acquaintance you could be sensible and come here to get yourself properly warm, Mrs Wheaton?' he barked in fine Lord Farenze style and set her rocking world back on an even keel. It felt so familiar, his lord-of-all-I-survey guise, that she came back to the present and found she liked it a lot better than the past that had haunted her for so long, despite not being able to be more to him in it than she already was.

'I should give your coat back and leave,' she managed with a weak smile for the man now glowering at her with such impatient concern he could break her heart.

'Flim-flam,' he asserted with a wave of his hand that dismissed convention and the rules of master and servant as if they didn't exist. 'The important thing is for me to know who you really are, so I can make your idiot of a father realise what he's done and put it right. He should at least grant you an income so you may bring up your niece as the lady you truly are, instead of standing by with his hands in his pockets. Virginia may have relieved him of the need to provide for his grandchild, but he has a duty to his remaining daughter, whether he likes it or not.'

'He proved my sister and I were dead to him when he sent us to the remotest place he could think of so she could have Verity alone and unseen. Anyway, I saw a notice of his death in the papers over a year ago, so even you can't harry him to do his duty in his grave, Lord Farenze.'

'Luke,' he corrected impatiently and how she wished she *could* call him so. 'If the rogue was alive, it would be, "Behave as a gentleman should or else", and think himself lucky he was my senior so it was not, "Before I kill you with my bare hands,"' he said, the gruff rumble of his voice coming to her as much by feeling as sound.

'Thank you.'

She couldn't help the wobble in her voice as she tried to find words to say how it felt to know he cared. She'd lost so much she could have had if fate was kinder, but told herself Verity outweighed it all. Chloe knew her youthful choices would not have been wise if she had made her début in society.

She would have scandalised the *ton* with her wild ways and headlong temper, but she was banished to a remote farm with her pregnant sister before either of them had been properly noticed by the polite world and saved them the task of disapproving of her. According to her father and the aunts, one twin could not be introduced to society without the absence of the other being remarked. She wondered how they accounted for the disappearance of both Thessaly twins, but doubted anyone recalled their existence now.

'I don't want pity,' she made herself add.

'Should I pity a slip of a girl who refused to turn away from a helpless infant because a killer told her to? Or be furious you were forced to renounce all you should have had before you could grasp it? If I heard this sorry tale at second hand I might pity you, I suppose, but as it is I can't offer you aught but my respect for your courage, as well as my lack of surprise at finding out you're as stubborn with everyone else as you have always been towards me.'

'Thank you, I think. Your family and friends must be gathered in the drawing room by now, though, and wondering where you are, so I suggest we abandon this topic and get on with the business of the day. You have more pressing matters to deal with than a weary housekeeper with a sad past,' she said as she did her best to renounce the fairytale of him admiring her.

'Eve is my family and I only have one true friend staying here to concern myself with,' he informed her dourly.

'I have a ten-year-old daughter and my reputation to guard,' she replied and it seemed to jar him out of his king-in-his-own-country frame of mind.

'We both know that's not true now,' he said as he crossed the room to loom over her instead of walking away, as she told herself she wanted him to.

'Verity is my niece and not my daughter in the strictest sense of the word, but you knowing the truth changes none of it.'

'Does it not?' he swung round and demanded, direct and passionate as she had always suspected he was under the icy self-control he tried to fool the world with. 'Is that truly all the difference you make between the "us" of today and of yesterday, Mrs Wheaton? Today I know you have never loved a man so wildly you had to bear his child alone when you were barely out of the schoolroom; never gave yourself wholly and completely to another man's passion and need and haste for complete possession of you, one lover to another. If you think that's nothing, I'm as mistaken in you as I was ten years ago, or yesterday afternoon when I saw you sad-eyed and pale at the loss of my great-aunt and your home of ten years and wanted you so urgently across all that frost and stone I've burnt like hot iron for you from then to now.'

Chloe stood dumbstruck and searched her mind for some phrase that could turn them back to lord and upper servant and came up blank.

'Cat got your tongue?' he mocked her silence.

She struggled against the weary impatience in his voice as he waited for her to produce a glib excuse. 'No,' she said quietly, 'you leave me nothing to say.'

'Not even, "No, never even look at me again with all this in our heads to remind us of what you just admitted?" Can't you even bring yourself to deny it as you have since we first met and longed for each other as lovers?'

'No, it's as true for me as you say it is for you. From the first moment I set eyes on you and let myself regret for a second I must put Verity before my own wants and needs. Her existence makes sure I can't be what we both want.'

'My mistress?' he insisted ruthlessly, as if he must get the words out of her to repay the weary frustration of a decade.

'Yes,' she admitted at last, as polite lying was impossible today.

'I could have seduced you back then if I'd persisted, but I didn't.'

'Oh well done, Lord Farenze, how very noble of you,' she forced herself to half-sneer and half-praise him, as if his chilly, and true, résumé didn't hurt.

'Luke,' he corrected as if determined she should learn a name she could never use. She found him cruel for that and let her glare tell him so.

'I didn't seduce you because you were so young and vulnerable and it would lessen us both too much. You have no right to reproach me; we both know I would have ruined a virgin if I'd ignored my scruples. Back then I had a young daughter to raise on my own as well and I wanted her to respect her father when she was old enough to know what the world said. I couldn't face her with you on my conscience when that day came,' he insisted as if it was important she understand he had his own version of her impossible situation to struggle against.

'Don't you know half the world already thinks me an unnatural monster whose coldness drove his poor vulnerable little wife to ruin herself with every buck and roué in town?' he went on as if finally willing to open himself up to someone and why did it have to be her, when she was still bound hand and foot by the decision she'd made on another cold and starry January night all those years ago?

'That was before I somehow forced her to flee with half a dozen of them to the Continent in an attempt to avoid my terrible lack of wrath towards them for taking her away, of course,' he said, as if mocking himself was his way of protecting the young man he had been from the humiliation his wife had heaped on him. 'What would the rest of the world think of a rogue who seduced his great-aunt's housekeeper when she was doing her best to bring up a child alone?'

'I'm amazed you care a snap of your fingers for such fools,' she said simply. What else was there to say about those who couldn't see his wife must have been insane to whistle a husband such as Luke Winterley down the wind?

'I try not to, but I do have a daughter to consider.'

'Only introduce me to them and I'll say it for you.'

'I wouldn't dare,' he said as if he admired the wild spirit that had been raging for release for so long, rather than condemning it as unfeminine and graceless as her aunts had always done.

'No, they would be sadly offended to be harangued by Mrs Wheaton or Lady Chloe...' She stuttered to a halt as she realised where her unwary tongue was about to take her.

'What a day for revelations this is almost proving to be,' he said as smoothly as if he'd never raged and prodded and challenged her and had stumbled on this latest truth by pure accident.

'You accused me of being a lady in disguise at the outset of this unsuitable conversation, if you recall?' she reminded him crossly.

'So I did. Maybe I have the instincts of a gentleman after all and we should be proud of them.'

'And perhaps we should not,' she returned, reluctantly unwrapping herself from the warmth of his coat and handing it back to him with a haughty look meant to put him in his place. If he wanted Lady Chloe to make a brief return to his world, who was she to deny him the dubious pleasure of her acquaintance?

He grinned like an unrepentant schoolboy as he shrugged back into it and made a show of appreciating the scent of her on it, as she had more secretly when he put it round her with the heat and spice of him still lingering on the fine cloth. 'Have you never wanted to kick over the traces with me as dearly as you wanted your next breath then, Lady Chloe?' he invited as if it was even a possibility, with ten years of not doing so between them.

'Mrs Wheaton has no right to when she has a child to bring up and the kindness your great-aunt granted her when she needed it most to live up to.'

'And yet she wants to?'

The lie formed in her mind, but somehow she couldn't bring herself to say it. Instead she met his eyes with her pride and ten years of isolation hot in them. 'Yet she still says *No*, to both of us,' she said as coolly as she was able.

'And I say, *Not yet, but soon*,' he told her as if, because he willed it so, it would be in the end.

'Only in your dreams, my lord,' she argued, but how she longed to be his dream. No, it would be a nightmare if they succumbed to the sensual passion raw under the aloof politeness lord and housekeeper had tried to maintain.

'Don't promise more of those, Lady Chloe. You haunt mine and have done far too long,' he warned her with a look that would have burned his way out of an ice house, if they were careless enough to get trapped in one.

'I'm not Lady Chloe now and wish you good evening, Lord Farenze. Your dinner awaits and I regret I am unable to join you for a delightful evening of housekeeper-baiting tonight,' she managed to tell him, before sailing out of the room as if her dignity and secrets were all intact.

She was amazed to find only half an hour had passed since she found him in the dark and nobody seemed to have noticed they'd been together far too long.

Luke stared at the space Lady Chloe Whoever-she-was had occupied and forced himself not to shout out a plea for her to stay. The revelations he'd drawn from her like a barber-surgeon pulling teeth left him feeling raw and furious on her behalf, but the essentials hadn't changed. He'd always known she was gently born, but couldn't help wondering now which nobleman had managed to mislay twin daughters without a scandal he would have heard about even at Darkmere.

Apparently he urgently wanted to bed a noble virgin and couldn't do so with an iota of honour unless he actually married her. He wondered if he dared take such a wife without loving her with every fibre of his being. Chloe and her sister were left to grow up wild as ponies on a moor, so she wasn't just a virgin, but pitchforked from schoolroom to motherhood without much pause, or any idea how her beauty and bravery could tear a man's soul until he was a danger to himself and her.

Now her innocence loomed between them instead of the mythical Mr Wheaton, he ought to be glad he'd listened to his conscience years ago and walked away from the unfledged girl she'd really been back then.

Luke ran a distracted hand through his dark hair and went back to pacing like a restless wolf. He frowned at the bookshelf where a *Peerage* sat, tempting him to track down any earl or above with twin daughters. He doubted she was in a rational enough state when she told her sad tale to lie to him and who would expect a Lady Chloe to pose as an upper servant in order to save her baby niece from the poorhouse?

It astonished him two such beauties could disappear from any local society without a great many questions being asked. Either their father was a powerful man, or such a reprobate nobody expected good of him. Luke paced on, clenching his fists against a need to lash out at whoever should pay for the isolation and terror Chloe endured after refusing to abandon her dead sister's child.

Unable to bring himself to smash Virginia's personal treasures to relieve the frustration roiling in his gut, he snatched up his empty brandy glass and dashed it into the fireplace instead. Feeling not much better, he marvelled at himself for expecting he would. A day's headlong ride on a half-broken stallion, or a long bout with one of the professional pugilists at Gentleman Jackson's Boxing Saloon might take the edge off it, but a broken glass wasn't going to lessen his urge to wrench a dead man from his grave and dance on his corpse.

Breathing deeply to calm himself, he reminded himself he'd lived through an appalling marriage and humiliating legal separation without breaking up furniture or violating graveyards. Then he'd thought Pamela had done everything she could to test his temper to the edge of insanity. Now he knew otherwise and what wrenched most was the fact Chloe thought it was her fault for some ridiculous reason.

Could she have stopped her perfidious twin sneaking out to meet a lover and getting pregnant in the first place? No—it was obvious to him Daphne expected to dance her way through life, laying blame for her sins on her sister's shoulders before she flitted off to make more. The last one killed her and left Chloe more grief and worry than any young girl should carry alone. Even the pleasure of begetting a lover's child was denied his Chloe and he cursed the unworthy curl of satisfaction in his gut at the thought no man had touched the woman he wanted so badly it was a chronic ache of need that never quite went away, however many miles he put between them.

With a wry twist of a smile it was as well he couldn't see for the tenderness it might show, he decided he was in danger of making her a plaster saint. Nothing could be further from the truth of stubborn, defiant, contrary Lady Chloe—warrior and termagant.

If her life had been different she would be as famous, or notorious, by now as Virginia was before she wed her last husband. Luke recalled the portrait his Uncle Virgil had commissioned of his wife in all her splendour after their wedding and mentally put Chloe in silks and satins, let them drop from her glorious white shoulders so her firm high breasts were only half-covered and desire boiled at even the thought of her lounging on the sofa in the Blue Saloon, not quite wearing a scandalously revealing evening gown for his exclusive pleasure.

If posterity wanted an image of *his* viscountess to envy him by, it would have to make do with one of Chloe sternly buttoned to the neck. No hot-eyed young artist was going to glimpse *his* lady in such a state of sensual abandon, ever. He gasped at the place his imagination had taken him to then froze as every cell in his body locked on that revolutionary idea. His mind might want to scream a panicked negative, but the rest of him was very happy with the notion of spending the rest of its life with an extraordinary woman.

He couldn't ask her to marry him simply because she was Lady Chloe and not humble Mrs Wheaton. Whatever his eager senses had to say, he'd promised himself never to marry for what Pamela called 'love' and why else would he wed Verity Wheaton's supposed mama? Yet he couldn't ask her to live in a quietly scandalous neighbourhood in London either; forever on the wrong side of every town and village he chose to inhabit for the rest of his life. The idea of never seeing her again, of living life as if he'd never met and wanted her so achingly hurt like hell.

Left with the conclusion he couldn't let her walk away, or be his mistress even if she would consent, that left marriage or the madhouse.

'What a confounded tangle,' he grumbled aloud, a frown pleating his dark brows until he knew he must look the very picture of forbidding Lord Winter he knew the wags of the *ton* had christened him last time he glowered at them across a London ballroom in Virginia's wake.

He cursed fluently as he marched up and down the library as if he might find an answer in a shadowy corner. If he was reckless enough to ask the woman to wed him, she'd lead him a dog's life. Passion driven and beguiled by her enchantress's body, fiery hair and the infinite mystery in her blue-violet eyes, he might forget himself in idiocy for a while, but what use was such a besotted idiot to his daughter and all the others who depended on him?

For a moment he nearly fell into the fantasy, but it was too much like Pamela's constant pursuit of 'love' for him to stay there long. He shuddered at the idea of need turning to hatred as it had between him and Pamela when their youthful delight in each other wore off, when the honeymoon was over and he couldn't spend every waking moment pandering to his new wife's whims any longer. He should restore Lady Chloe to her family, then find that convenient viscountess he'd promised himself as soon as Eve was ready to find her own path through life.

Fool, he told himself, then bent to coax the dying fire back to life, *your life will be cold and dark as this room if you let her go*. He shuddered at the very idea and a faint waft of Chloe's unique scent beguiled him anew as he savoured the knowledge she'd shared his jacket as if it was one intimacy she couldn't resist. Dash it, he didn't want to live without her and he needed a wife. Somehow he'd persuade her to marry him and they'd live every day as it came. Each of them would feel as bleak as the January night closing in outside without her, so what did he have to lose?

* * *

'Now the preliminary part of Lady Virginia's will has been read, we can get to the main business,' Mr Poulson, senior partner of Poulson, Scott, Poulson and Peters informed his audience with the flair of a masterly performer the following afternoon.

Chloe pictured him putting on matinee performances of the wise family lawyer in libraries up and down the land and wondered why she was still here when the rest of the servants had been dismissed after hearing their late mistress had not forgotten them.

She eyed the assembled gentlemen and wondered what they thought of Virginia's housekeeper being included in such an exclusive gathering. Mr James Winterley, the Marquis of Mantaigne, Lords Farenze and Leckhampton had every right to be here, so she exchanged glances with the only other misfit, a seemingly nondescript young man she judged to be in his late twenties.

The stranger looked a modest professional man of middling rank, until his cool gaze made you to take a second look. He was a shrewd gentleman, she concluded, wondering why Mr Poulson needed his junior partner here to assist with Virginia's estate even so. Mr Peters smiled faintly to admit his senior was pacing his speech for dramatic effect and Chloe wondered why she'd thought him nondescript.

She gave a faint nod to admit they were the outsiders and felt Lord Farenze's glare as if it might burn her through the pristine white-lace bonnet she'd put on this morning, now Virginia was no longer here to forbid it. Never mind respecting her late employer's wish she should dress as befitted a valued companion; she needed all the camouflage she could get after admitting too much about herself to him last night.

Chapter Eleven

'Get on with it, man,' Lord Leckhampton, Virginia's old friend and one time suitor urged querulously, 'we haven't time or inclination for an oration.'

'I need to be on my way before night draws in, I suppose,' Mr Poulson said with a frown that told them a master craftsman was being told to botch a job as if he was a mere day labourer.

'Not at all, Poulson, you must stay,' Lord Farenze said with a hard look at Chloe to order she confirm his hospitality.

'Your bedchambers are prepared and we have a footman very happy to act as valet for the evening, gentlemen,' she agreed, hoping Carrant hadn't scorched their linen in his eagerness to take up a career as a gentleman's gentleman.

'You are very kind, Lord Farenze, ma'am,' Mr Poulson said with a seated bow Chloe thought old fashioned and charming, even if Lord Leckhampton snorted as if heckling a fine performance. 'But to proceed, since it *is* a complicated document and needs some explanation—Lady Virginia leaves the residue of her fortune to Miss Winterley, but her ladyship made a series of unusual bequests to all of you...' He paused to gauge the effect of his words.

'Don't need a penny of her blessed money,' Lord Leckhampton said.

'Just as well, my lord. Her ladyship left you the contents of all the bins in her late husband's inner wine cellar,' the little lawyer told him and Chloe saw an impish smile on the elderly peer's face.

'That's Virgil's finest burgundy and the best cognac. God bless her. I'll think of them both whenever I tap a bottle,' he said and blinked determinedly. 'Dare say you don't need me any more, then?' he said with much harrumphing and a pretend cough into a black-bordered handkerchief.

'If these other beneficiaries refuse to take up their parts of the estate, you are to administer Miss Winterley's fortune until she marries or attains the age of five and twenty, my lord, but if you wish to leave, no more of this unusual document purports to you,' Mr Poulson replied.

'Good, good, something in my eye, y'know?' Lord Leckhampton said and left the room to come to terms with that proof of Virginia's deep affection.

'Now, Mrs Wheaton and gentlemen, we come to the core of her ladyship's will and most eccentric it is as well, but it was what she wanted. Lady Virginia has left a series of letters to be delivered to four people one by one. The first letter is to be handed over today, the second when that first gentleman has fulfilled his request from Lady Virginia or handed it back to the trustee and so on, until the last letter has been given out. Each stage of these tasks is to take no more than three months of your time and, on completion of the quarter of the year allotted to it, the next task will begin. I trust you understand so far?'

'Dashed if I do,' James Winterley said with a glance at Chloe that told them he would not come out with such a mild expletive if she wasn't here.

'Lady Virginia thought we needed to keep out of mischief, Jimmy,' Lord Mantaigne said with a careless shrug.

'I'm a busy man,' Lord Farenze muttered grumpily and Chloe wondered if that was the reason her late mentor demanded he spend three months not being the viscount in possession.

'Hence a provision her ladyship made for the time each of you will spend on your allotted task,' the lawyer replied smoothly. 'Peters here will be available so each of you can put his talents to good use in turn. In your case, Lord Farenze, perhaps he could turn land agent so you can concentrate your energies elsewhere. My junior partner has accomplishments I cannot always approve of, but he recently assisted the Duke of Dettingham with a series of confidential investigations as well as managing to bring the perpetrators of the Berfield outrage to justice.'

'You must be very unpopular in certain quarters, Peters,' Lord Mantaigne observed with a gleam of respect behind his easy smile.

'Only if they know about me,' he said with a long look at his senior partner that made the little lawyer shift in his chair.

'I'm sure no whisper of it will leave this room,' Mr

Poulson blustered, but from his blush was conscious he'd let himself be carried away by a desire to impress.

Chloe flushed under the combined gazes of four interested gentlemen. 'Of course I shall not reveal a word,' she promised, wondering why she was here again.

'Which brings us to your role, Mrs Wheaton,' the lawyer said as if he'd read her mind. He pushed his eyeglasses up his nose and glared at the parchment in front of him as if will-power alone might change the words on it.

'Lady Virginia left you her personal jewellery not already covered by bequests to family or friends and all her personal effects not likewise left elsewhere.'

Chloe allowed herself an audible sigh while she fought the urge to weep over such a magnificent gift. As a housekeeper she could never wear the exquisite pieces designed for a famous beauty in her scandalous prime, or use the delicately wrought *objets d'art* Virginia's lord delighted in showering his love with, but owning them meant so much.

'How kind and generous of her,' she said, puzzled why she'd been allowed to hear so much before being told this, then dismissed.

'Stay, Mrs Wheaton, I am not done,' Mr Poulson said and she sank back into her chair and looked quizzically back at him. 'There is a gatekeeper for this odd affair of one gentleman, then the next, taking up Lady Virginia's quests. That person controls the allotted monies and letters for the next twelve months and will receive a generous stipend in return. I am to tell you that you have the role and must not argue.'

'Me?' Chloe managed faintly.

'If you would take a look at this part of the document and confirm your true identity?' he asked and Chloe sat open-mouthed.

'How did she know?' she managed to mutter numbly.

'Your confirmation, if you please?' he prompted, pointing to a passage in the closely written script that said Lady Virginia's housekeeper-cum- companion was the Lady Chloe Bethany Thessaly, eldest daughter of the seventh Earl of Crowdale and late of Carraway Court in the county of Devon.

Numbly she nodded, then realised that wasn't enough for the law. 'Yes, that is my name,' she affirmed and raised her chin, 'What else did her ladyship tell you?' she let herself ask.

'Only that she had been very slow at putting two and two together and couldn't imagine where her wits had got off to. Indeed, who knows what she knew and didn't know about any one of us? I should not like to hazard a guess.'

'Do either of you intend telling me who has been housekeeper here for the last decade?' Lord Farenze demanded crossly.

'Not now,' she said.

'Later, then,' he promised, or was it a threat?

'Who is the lucky recipient of Virginia's first bomb-shell?' Lord Mantaigne drawled.

Chloe was beginning to see past his assumption of lazy indifference and sensed he was both diverting attention from her and adjusting his own expectations in case he must start Virginia's year of imposing her will on her favourite gentlemen.

'Lord Farenze is first on Lady Virginia's list, but

he is at liberty to delay his task until later if he needs time to settle his affairs,' Mr Poulson said with a glint of what looked like humour in his eyes.

'I have no need; what is my so-called quest to be?' Luke demanded and Chloe let tenderness quirk her lips into a betraying smile at the scepticism in his deep voice that he could be anyone's hero.

Luckily the rest of them were watching him as if not quite certain if they were sharing a room with a primed incendiary or an occasionally uncivil nobleman.

'You forget I'm not in charge of that part of the instructions, my lord. No doubt Mrs Wheaton will inform you of your task, once she has read Lady Virginia's letter to her and understands her own role in this business a little better.'

If I ever do, Chloe added under her breath, trying to shrug off the feeling too many powerful males were focused on her as she tried not to squirm in her seat.

'It might prove difficult to maintain a disguise with us happy band of adventurers to keep in order, Mrs Wheaton,' Mr James Winterley cautioned with a wry smile she found rather charming when she caught echoes of his elder brother in his grey-green eyes.

'Nevertheless, I am Mrs Wheaton for now and ask you all to respect my privacy,' she made herself reply steadily, dread of the scandal if she made her true identity public making her shudder.

'Am I never to know?' Lord Farenze asked, frowning as he bent to stir the fire into a blaze.

'If it ever seems safe for me to be other than a housekeeper, you will be among the first to know, my lord,' she said briskly. 'Now could I have my letter?'

The little lawyer bowed respectfully. 'Here you are, ma'am,' he said gently, offering the sealed letter as if it was a crown jewel. 'I'm told this will cover the most salient points and expect any details can be discussed later.'

'There's one you managed to skirt round,' Luke said with a long hard look Chloe admired the man for not flinching under.

'My lord?'

'Who is your fourth Knight of the Round Table, or do you intend keeping him secret until we spot some fool dashing about searching for dragons to slay for my late great-aunt's heavenly amusement?'

'I fear I cannot tell you who he is at the moment.'

'Say you won't rather and why not for heaven's sake?'

'Because I don't know myself,' the lawyer said.

Chloe thought he was telling the truth, but given Mr Poulson's acting skills it was difficult to tell.

'Then it will be impossible to recruit him to Virginia's happy band of heroes.'

'I was given four envelopes, my lord. Three have your names on and they will be handed to Mrs Wheaton when she asks for them. Lady Virginia included one with a question mark on and told me Mrs Wheaton will tell me who is to have it when she has instructions to begin his part of the task. You will be the first to have that secret in your keeping, ma'am, and I'm sorry to hand you so much responsibility,' Mr Poulson said with a frown of what looked genuine concern.

'Lady Virginia would never leave me with a task I couldn't carry out.'

'She did insist you would succeed in any venture you set your mind to,' he admitted.

Lord Mantaigne laughed, then smiled wryly to invite her not to take offence. 'I suspect that's a tactful way of saying you're stubborn as a mule and sharp as a knife, Mrs Wheaton,' he said with a knowing nod at Lord Farenze's thunderous frown.

'If I was that clever, I wouldn't be working as housekeeper here, Lord Mantaigne,' she told him with a repressive frown, but he let his smile stretch into a mocking grin and shook his head.

'Nobody found out you were here though, did they?' he said as if that was an achievement in itself. Chloe supposed it was and held her head a little higher.

'Never mind fawning on her, man, let Mrs Wheaton read Virginia's letter so I can get this fiasco over and get back to everything else I should be worrying about instead,' Lord Farenze grumbled, but his eyes met Chloe's with a myriad of complex emotions under the cool control he was trying to show the rest of the world.

'And the sooner I read my letter, the sooner you can have yours, my lord.'

'Eager to be rid of me?' he murmured as he rose to walk past her, indicating to the others it was time to let her and Mr Poulson begin this rackety affair.

'Of course,' she said with eyebrows raised as if it was obvious.

'Liar,' he whispered so intimately she felt his tongue flick shockingly into the intricate curls of her ear before he stood watching with all sorts of threats and promises in his darkened grey gaze.

'I know,' she let herself mouth once he'd finally left the room with his half-brother, his best friend and the mysterious Mr Peters in his wake.

'I shall leave you to read this missive, Lady Chloe,' Mr Poulson said with one of his best bland looks. 'I trust you will not be disturbed.'

'Little chance of that,' Chloe muttered as the echo of the door softly closing behind the little lawyer died and she eyed the thick packet dubiously.

No point sitting here and hoping the whole business would go away if she avoided it long enough. She broke the familiar seal of Virgil and Virginia's entwined initials and peered at the closely written missive, half-longing for and half-dreading whatever her late employer had to say to her.

'Dearest girl...' it began, in Virginia's familiar, elegant hand and tears blurred Chloe's eyes until she forced them back and made herself concentrate on what her late employer and friend had to say, instead of missing her so deeply a gulf yawned inside her that would never be filled.

You have become the daughter of my heart, or perhaps I should call you my granddaughter as you are so much younger than I am. I never could give my Virgil a child, but with you and Verity in the house these last few years it has felt as if he approved of your presence here. Would he was truly here to play great-grandfather to your daughter, for he would have delighted in her quickness and mischief even more than I have done.

Chloe blinked and stared blankly out of the window for several minutes until she had control of her emotions and could carry on reading.

I knew you were born to a higher sphere than the country vicarage you admitted to when you first came to the Lodge. Since I disliked all the other candidates the agency sent me, I overlooked the fact you were clearly lying and settled down to be amused by you and your babe, when Verity came back from the wet nurse. That really was a give-away, by the way, my darling Chloe, since you would never let your child be nursed by another woman unless you had no milk yourself and you certainly didn't have any of that, now did you?

Again Chloe had to stop reading with a shake of her head at the turmoil her late employer's words sent racing in her head. She'd suspected Virginia had doubts about her made-up ancestry at times, but never Verity's.

You have been very wary about giving me the smallest clue to your true identity and it wasn't until I took notice of a tale Lady Tiverley whispered to me a few months ago about Rupert Thessaly's outrageous brood that I realised who you really are. Now, if I happened to be a good woman, I would have delved deeper there and then and found a way to force your brother to admit he and his father and that milksop brother of his conspired to throw his own flesh and blood to the dogs three times over, then make restitution

*to his surviving sister and niece. I fear I am not
that noble and have come to love you and your
supposed child far too much to find the idea of
living without you at all comfortable, so I managed not to see how I was compounding damage
already done to you both for as long as I could.*

*During the last few weeks I have come to re-
alise how deep an injury I did you by not doing
or saying anything to restore you to your true
place in life. I love you and my great-nephew
as far as I am capable of loving anyone, but apparently I love myself more than both of you. I
can see you shaking your head and refusing to
believe Luke has anything to do with you even
now, my dear, but take a deeper look into your
stubborn heart and I pray you'll see there what
you two have ignored far too long.*

Since Chloe was shaking her head at the very moment her late employer accused her of being stubborn,
she stared round the room as if her wraith might be
watching. If Virginia was born in another age to poorer
parents, she might have been accused of witchcraft,
she decided with a shudder. Dare she look hard at her
feelings for Luke Winterley? Something told her she
might have to soon, but for now she had the distraction
of Virginia's letter to shake her head over instead. Not
that it did much good, since every other word seemed
to be of him.

*If you ever do decide to lay down that stout
armour of yours and consider what you and*

dear Luke could be to one another, please forget the petty details and seize your happiness at last, my dear Chloe. It is for your brothers and the Thessaly connection to talk their way out of what they did, or didn't do, by leaving you to raise your sister's child as your own. Such things have been managed well enough in other noble families for centuries. Since it sounds as if you two girls were left to more or less bring yourselves up, such neglect was sure to end in trouble.

I hope your brothers have spent the last ten years feeling deeply ashamed of themselves after you proved better and stronger than either of them, but somehow I doubt it. You have a tender conscience and a good heart, Chloe, and the rest of the Thessaly family were ready to commit murder by leaving poor Verity on a freezing doorstep well away from their own nest. I'm quite sure they would have done so if you hadn't stolen away like a thief in the night as well.

Penelope Tiverley is a sad rattle-pate, but she was your sister's godmother and I'm sure she has told her tale to nobody else. She only wanted to ease her conscience by telling her mother's old friend how uneasy she felt about the affair. My years seem to bring confidences, whether I want them or not, and please don't think the story is common currency in society. I know it is not so and have kept the promise I made Penelope not to repeat it. Given she did

*not see who was under her nose, I doubt you
were ever close to your sister's godmother, but
I wish your mama had picked one for you who
might have helped when you had to disappear.*

Chloe impatiently undid the strap that held her fussy
cap in place then threw the constricting thing into a dark
corner and rubbed her temples against the headache it
had caused. She looked ruefully at a red-gold curl escaping from her tight chignon and wondered if its colour
explained the differences between her and her angeli-
cally blonde twin sister. Even her mother must have decided Daphne needed a sweet-natured godmother and
Chloe could make do with a chilly and puritanical distant cousin, who disowned her as godless and ungov-
ernable long before she walked away from Carraway
Court with Verity in her arms.

Chapter Twelve

Chloe reminded herself of Virginia's opening words and decided she had been given the best godparent ever born and felt as if her mentor's hand stroked her fiery curls for a moment to confirm her true place in Virginia's heart.

So there it is, child. I confess my part in you being misplaced for so many years, not so much from your family, who don't deserve you, but from wider society. I am a wretched old sinner and the more I knew you, the less I wanted to live without you and Verity. Now I sense my race is almost run, and about time too, so don't you dare mourn and mope over me, my girl. I have set my conscience to consider my sins a little more seriously than I quite like of late and will do my best to atone for the worst of them. It has to start with you and darling Luke, because I have finally realised why he avoids Farenze Lodge as if it were a noxious pest house. That selfish little cat he wed convinced him he was a heartless monster because he wouldn't fawn on her, but I was wilfully blind to his feelings for you for too long.

How very much I wish I had used the brains God gave me sooner, dear Chloe. Of course Luke is attracted to my beautiful young companion housekeeper and won't let himself stay more than a couple of days in this house I love because you live here as well and he's an honourable fool. Don't shake your head again and wonder if I've gone senile. Look deep into your heart and his before you risk breaking them both. I suspect Luke also thought both your daughters would suffer if he made an unequal marriage. The poor darling clearly has no idea you're his equal and possibly superior in rank. Legend has it the Thessalys were princes in Byzantium before they landed in England and settled for being warlords instead.

Chloe did shake her head this time, not because Virginia raised the mirage of love binding her and Lord Farenze together, but because she knew the Thessalys were descended from a Barbary pirate who captured, then fell in love with, the widow of a crusader, on her way back home to claim her husband's lands before the king could seize them. Apparently the lady captivated her captor, married him, then brought him home and set that legend about to baffle those who might take Crowdale from them. Chloe was torn between pride in her adventurous ancestor and doubt the Winterleys would consider it a wonderful connection if they knew. Descent from a pair of bold adventurers and a long line of gamblers, opportunists and downright thieves wasn't much to boast about.

Anyway, that is all by the by—I have been a wilful fool about you and Luke for far too long. Lately I have taken the chance to observe the two of you on his fleeting visits to Farenze Lodge and believe you are as besotted with him as he is with you, even if you don't yet know it. It would be a far darker sin to turn away love than to leap straight into the joy of it. Age comes on far too soon, so grasp your youth and beauty and reach for the happiness you deserve. I beg you not to fail yourself and Verity by letting the sins of others stand between you and a man truly worthy of you. Society would accept Verity as your adopted child, if Luke does the same. He is a truly noble man, so please don't hurt him even more than his wretched wife managed to during that ill-fated marriage of theirs, dear Chloe.

By now you will know there are more things to put right than this, even if this tangle concerns me most, but I beg you not to refuse the role I allotted you. I am forcing your hand and making you reveal things to my great-nephew you would rather keep secret, but those things need to be out in the open.

Chloe gasped and found out she was nowhere near as strong as she hoped when it came to Luke knowing the full details of her ancestry. She tried not to notice how sadly her hand shook when she took up Lady Virginia's letter again to read the last page.

Stubborn independence is all very well, but it's terribly lonely and for you I fear it might also be dangerous. Your brother Crowdale has fallen into bad company since he inherited, so be wary if he pretends repentance and wants to take you and Verity home. Please don't push Luke away when he comes to ask you about yourself, as he must once he's reads the letter beginning my year of wonders. I hope and pray it will *be wonderful. There are four wrongs I must see righted and thank God I was granted time to realise they cannot stay quietly wrong for ever.*

So there we are. I trust you to do your best to make sure my sins of omission are put right. You are a better woman than I ever was, my love, and you have a fine mind to go with that soft heart. Remember Luke is nothing like the harsh recluse he would have the world believe and look how he loves and indulges his daughter if you doubt me. If the worst comes to the worst, at least you now have a year's grace to decide what you want to do, but I hope and pray you will reach for a better future and a fine man instead.

Goodbye, my dear, live well and be happy; nobody deserves a blissfully argumentative marriage more than you and my stubborn great-nephew.

Chloe let the letter drop into her lap and stared out of the nearest window, surprised to see twilight outside when she hadn't noticed she was straining to read the last few words of Virginia's letter. She wondered how she was supposed to face Lord Farenze with this epistle in mind and decided the best thing to do was to give him his letter and leave him to read it.

'Here is your task from Lady Virginia, my lord,' Chloe told Luke, her composure so brittle he wondered if she might shatter if he breathed too hard.

Luke left it in her outstretched hand and waited for her to meet his eyes with a challenge in her own—ah, that was better. There was his Chloe, furious and ready to fight the world with any weapon she could lay hands on if it threatened those she loved. Somewhere along the long line they'd walked towards each other these last ten years he'd come to know her, despite his resolution never to expect more than hot passion and a few nights of mutual pleasure from any woman when he found out what Pamela had done for 'love'.

'I suspect my great-aunt of plotting to push us together as well, Mrs Not-Wheaton, but so far I've barely seen you,' he said, holding her eyes and wishing she would trust him.

'Read your letter,' she said with a resigned gesture that might be designed to show off her long-fingered hands and elegant wrists, if she wasn't his contrary Chloe and convinced there was nothing worth showing.

'Stay,' he ordered, wrapping her slender capable hand in his own larger paw and pulling her down on to the elegant little sofa by the fire they had stared into last night. 'You're half-frozen,' he reproached as he rubbed her chilled fingers to get some warmth back into them.

'Never mind me; you must read your letter. It's my job to make sure you do, don't you see?' she asked and the blank look in her eyes tore at his heart.

'Just this once I think we can let duty go hang, don't you? Sit with me, Chloe, let someone take care of you for once in your life.'

'I don't want to be a cause you champion because nobody else will.'

'Apart from our daughters; my late great-aunt and Mantaigne, I suppose? I thought Tom was too idle to bother with anyone but himself these days, then he ups and tells me I should look after you properly before another man leaps in and does it for me. Even my self-absorbed brother wants to make sure you come out of this odd affair unharmed and I thought Poulson was going to adopt you himself if you refused Virginia's original offer of employment for the coming year.'

'That's very kind in all of them.'

'I tell you people around you have come to care for you and you call them kind? You must always be the one who gives, must you not?'

'It's what mothers do,' she said with a shrug.

'And fathers,' he said and decided, since he had her hands locked in his, he might as well put his free arm about her stiff shoulders and offer her some of his warmth and maybe more, if she would only let him.

'I'm not your daughter,' she argued with a militant stir in his embrace he gloated didn't go far enough to shake him off.

'Does it feel as if I look on you as other than a fully mature woman totally unrelated to me, Mrs Wheaton?' he asked and let the heat of her next to him run under his skin like wildfire wherever their bodies touched, despite her bombazine armour and that truly absurd cap she had jammed back on her head any old how.

'Um, no,' she admitted and he waited for a militant objection.

She surprised him by sighing deeply, then snuggling into his embrace as if she'd needed him to hold her all day. Something like triumph roared through him, but caution came in its wake. She was looking for comfort. Only yesterday they had buried the woman who had given her security, shelter and love these last ten years, while the rest of the world turned its back on her and twiddled its thumbs.

Perhaps his friend Mantaigne could have offered her a broad shoulder to lean on and share some human warmth with on a dark day and been just as welcome. Grief and injustice had ruled her life for too long and the world must seem out of kilter to her now Virginia wasn't here to keep it at arm's length. Maybe wily old Poulson would have done equally well to offer comfort, or even, Heaven forbid, his brother James?

He would have wanted to kill every one of them if he'd found them sitting in his place like petrified granite, trying to give what she wanted and not what he needed so badly it hurt. Except for the extraordinary fact they would probably offer comfort and no more, whether from male stupidity or fear of him he wasn't quite sure. He seemed the only one deeply aware of her beauty and potential for passion, but he lusted after her so rampantly it made up for them. He squirmed in his seat to shift her so she wouldn't be terrified by the evidence, fully awake and roaring for satisfaction as it was when she was in the same room, let alone in his arms.

'I don't want a stand-in father,' she murmured and he could hardly believe his ears.

'Good, I want you so badly I can't remember my own name,' he admitted with shaken acceptance she was looking at him as if the sky might fall on her head.

'Kiss me, you idiot,' she ordered.

'Willingly, my lady,' he agreed with a sense of inevitability in his heart and did it anyway.

To leash his inner beast he framed her face with his hands, noting the contrast of pale feminine skin with his calloused hands—he was so impatient of wearing gloves he often rode without them. Her lashes swept down to hide her thoughts from his fascinated gaze so he studied them instead. Tipped with fiery gold, they were darker than her hair and ridiculously long, almost sweeping down to touch high cheekbones he wanted to explore in the finest, most intimate detail.

No good, he was making himself more outrageously male rather than less so by lingering over every detail of her face like a miser. She was a lovely woman; not a secret cache of inanimate gold. He sighed a whisper of intent against her pert nose and felt the precipice they were walking narrow under his feet and still couldn't make himself draw back from the brink. He gloated over the perfection of her rosy lips before he met the slick softness of them with a gasp of awe and they stepped off the cliff together and who knew where they would land?

Let me not hurt or shock her, his inner lover begged as she seemed to have to remind herself to breathe under the onslaught he was holding so carefully under control. *Let her be caught up by this endless storm of wanting too much to fear it.*

'Delicious,' he heard himself whisper as if testing a fine wine and a flush of mortification almost burned away the one of fierce arousal already scorching his cheeks. *Idiot,* he chided himself and heard the word slip from his lips as he held a little away from her tender mouth and sucked breath into his aching lungs. Somehow he had to stop himself plunging into her shy welcome like a boorish great bull.

'If I'm one, you are too,' she informed him crossly and so close he felt the movement against his aching mouth and her breath on the tongue he used to slick moisture on to his dry lips.

'Not you, me,' he managed to rasp and heard her chuckle, felt her chuckle and it threatened to turn him completely feral.

'My idiot,' she argued, sounding nearly as ambushed by need as he felt. 'Kiss me properly then, you great fool. I won't break.'

'No, but I might,' he breathed and did exactly what they both wanted until he could hardly remember his own name for wanting Chloe Wheaton with every fibre of his being.

Chloe tumbled into mysteries that had been beyond her wildest imaginings even after their first, disastrous kisses all those years ago. Not even longing for him so badly it hurt had prepared her for this. Her wildest fantasies; dreamt of and half-recalled with a blush when she woke, hadn't said how it felt to be kissed so deeply by this unique man. Those wild dreams, she supposed now, were brought on by lack of *this*. Lack of him; Luke Winterley; the only man she would ever love. It jarred through her in a long, hot shudder as he used touch and taste to fit them closer, strove for unity deeper than flesh on flesh. It opened up huge chances for pain as well as promises, added the feel of falling through vastness, tumbling into loving him as if her life might depend on it, to the already novel feeling of walking on fire.

He was the *one*—her Luke; her love. Of course it didn't hurt, his mouth on hers, his gentle, fascinated touch as he padded sensitive fingers through her loosened hair as if he loved the feel of it and when had he done that?

Her mouth kicked up in a smile even as he teased her lips apart. The rogue had more seduction in his fingertips than a hardened rake had in his whole armoury. He'd disposed of her hairpins so neatly she hadn't even spared a breath to ask why he'd let her heavy hair hang loose down her back and now seemed to adore the heavy weight of it against his skin. The thick mass felt wild and undone, just like her.

The hand he hadn't kept free to weave her ever deeper into his spell, learning her features by touch, was smoothing her back through the waves and weight of it. The bane of her younger life was being gloated over by her lover; a shiver of joy slid through her as he reminded them both he liked her carroty hair far more than she'd ever dreamt a man could, but he also adored her eager mouth and had work for it.

Oh, never mind her hair, he'd thrust the tip of his tongue into her mouth as if asking if he could. Chloe gasped in a breath and opened on an unmistakable *yes*. He would be a fool not to read surrender in every inch of her and she spared a thought to chide herself for that, before he cindered it by deepening his kiss. This was *him*, the man she had longed for and lingered over in her head for so long passion and need and love stuttered down her supple spine and warmed her toes. *Yes* wound a little tighter, she wriggled closer so she lay against the cushions and felt him shift to follow her down with a smile of satisfaction he read on her lips. She used her freed hand to pull him after her and still his hot, deep kiss never hesitated on her willing mouth.

Wasn't it amazing what ten years of trying to live without a man she'd cried for far too often could do? Fire shot through her everywhere they touched and she found out how to shiver with sensual heat in mid-winter. Still he held himself away to shield her from the full force of his arousal. *Bless the man; doesn't he know his rampant need makes me melt from the inside out?* If he wanted her this much, it must be possible to play with fire, now she had the lick of it deep inside her to remind her there was more to making love than kissing.

A snatch of uncertainty nibbled at her conscience, but she loved the tightly muscled fact of his powerful torso tensing under her hands, as if he felt her touch and wanted to take her deeper. All the reasons she couldn't loose her gown or rip off his neckcloth and push away his snugly tailored coat to insinuate herself closer screamed in her head. She tried to ignore it as every inch of hot satin-smooth skin over hard muscle fascinated her; for a precious few moments he was her Luke.

She wanted to be naked with him, was almost ready to find allure enough and even some feminine enchantment she hadn't recognised in herself until today. All the reasons that couldn't be were stronger now; Verity was full of life and promise and must soon dream as a young girl should, without her hopes being smashed before she had time to grasp the bright promise of all life might give her.

Meanwhile Luke was kissing his way along the pared-down curve of Chloe's jaw, as if it was uniquely fascinating to feel his mouth there. *Ah, just one more minute,* she promised her inner woman as her breasts seemed to swell and kick up against the buttons of his waistcoat and the leashed strength of him, begging for release from the demure gown and very correct corset she'd imposed on them for some reason that eluded her right now. Somehow her nipples felt as if they had a life of their own, needs they hadn't fully told her about until this moment and now they were hard and tight and begging to be satisfied.

Under their disguise they pouted and longed, then made her sigh when she shifted against the cool silk and jet of his black waistcoat, fine buttons and him, then felt them tighten even more. Far better with his bare skin over taut muscle to writhe against her, her wildest instincts whispered sneakily. Chloe moaned at the very idea and almost wished it hadn't sprung into her head that to feel his fingers explore her might go beyond pleasure into something desperate and driven and even needier.

Maybe he read her mind because he rolled a little closer, lay half over her and she felt those wanton breasts of hers bloom with satisfaction against a hard wall of muscle and her almost painfully hard nipples tightened even more mercilessly. He raised his head to look down at her with so much in his eyes she had to blink and decided there was no point trying to hide her arousal from him. She held his hot grey eyes with steady acceptance they wanted each other more than she'd known a man and woman could. No use guarding herself from him any longer, no point pretending he was only a man just like any other. Luke was *the* man; the only one who could build a universe for her; spin stars and planets into the sky, and if only this world was different, go on doing so for the rest of their lives until it was vast and beautiful and all theirs to explore together.

'I want you so much,' she murmured as reason slammed back into his dear grey eyes and she finally saw his beloved northern skies, clear cool moorland air and the full depth of his fine mind and loving heart in them.

'You know I'm on fire for you,' he muttered, endearingly gruff about the fact, so explicit now even she could hardly help but know it.

'I want it all with you, Luke Winterley, everything a mature woman can share with a very well-grown and mature man,' she murmured with dreams in her eyes and far too much love in her heart to hide it from him. He'd awoken a wicked sensuality she hadn't even known she was capable of until now and it whispered of endless delight and satisfaction to be had, if they were not who they were.

'But?' he whispered and the knowledge there was always a 'but' for them was deep in the clear depths and complex shadows of his gaze.

'You know why,' she said with Verity's secrets misting her gaze with tears.

'Aye, I do,' he acknowledged roughly, as if saying so hurt.

'Not because of you,' she said as if that might make it right.

'Yes, because I'm me,' he argued and it nearly broke something in her when he levered himself away to put distance between them. 'If I wasn't a titled aristocrat with more houses than a one man can decently live in, you would give yourself to me heart and soul, Lady Chloe Whoever-You-Are. If I could offer you decent obscurity and a full heart, you would marry me and be my love for the rest of our lives, but because I'm Farenze and will be until the day I die, you won't see what we could be.'

'Oh, I see,' she argued shakily, 'but I won't do. You don't believe in love and swore to marry again only for convenience. In your wildest dreams you could never describe me as convenient.'

Chapter Thirteen

'Marry me anyway,' Luke asked, stubbornness in his intent eyes.

'You don't even know who I am,' Chloe objected even as joy sang in her heart and a flock of butterflies seemed to take up permanent residence in her fluttering stomach, then fly lower to whisper of delights unmapped and infinitely pleasurable.

'I know you're Chloe; Verity's aunt and mother in all but giving birth to her. I know you would give everything for someone you love, let alone your sister's child, a girl you love deeply for her own sake. I'd be a fool to try and part you from her. How can I not want that for our children, Chloe? How can you refuse it to the red-headed, mule-tempered brats we could have between us, if only you would let go of your pride and allow them to live?'

'Who I am would come back to bite you and our black-haired, dark-eyed wild things, the ones we can't make because of me,' she argued sadly, feeling the air chill between them. They sat upright on the graceful little seduction of a *chaise*, designed for two lovers to while away a long winter evening together.

'Don't I deserve to even know why not, Chloe?'

Of course he did, even though he would know she was right as soon as she told him. She had no reason to prolong the sweet moment when she might reach out and grab her wildest dreams, if only she loved him less.

She delved in the pocket no fashionable lady would have permitted to spoil the line of her high-waisted gown and silently held out the letter, addressed in Virginia's elegant sloping hand to *Lady Chloe Thessaly*.

Watching him read those three damning words, she waited to see all she dreaded cloud his face and make him frown with revulsion, but there was only mild interest in his eyes. Hadn't he heard her family name under all the notoriety her father and brother heaped on the title until it stank like three-week-old fish?

'My father was Lord Crowdale,' she made herself admit.

'Mine was a fool, but it doesn't prevent us marrying,' he insisted.

She was shocked into meeting his gaze and saw anger deep in the silver-and-gold-rayed irises and clear black pupils; besotted Chloe mused how she might lose herself in such complication for hours on end, if only she dared and he'd let her.

'Don't you realise what a scandal my resurrection from whatever early death they made up to account for losing two daughters would be? Far better for Verity to remain the daughter of an obscure housekeeper who might or might not have been widowed tragically young. Nobody will care enough to argue the birth of a girl of the middling sort as they would about Lady Daphne Thessaly's child.'

'And you would narrow all her choices to that? Being a nondescript girl of the middling sort? Oh, no, Lady Chloe Thessaly, you can't make a nonentity out of a girl who carries all the promise of being as inconveniently beautiful as Virginia once was. Haven't you noticed she has the fine bones, character and colouring that will take the world by storm in a few years' time? Foolish of you if you haven't, but as the child of a mere housekeeper she is going to have a terrible time without a father to protect her from the storm her looks and grace will bring down on both of you as soon as she's old enough to attract the wolves to your door.'

'I…' Chloe ground to a halt and wondered if he was right.

'Yes, you…?' he insisted mercilessly, temper now sparking in his grey eyes and knitting his brows in a formidable frown.

It made her want to love him even more. His fury was part on Verity's behalf and part because he seemed, wonder of wonders, to want to be her daughter's father.

'I can't simply change my mind and say yes because it suits me to have a noble husband, that wouldn't be right.'

'Oh, Chloe,' he said on a choke of unwilling laughter that chased the thunder clouds from his stormy gaze. 'My Chloe,' he said as if nothing would ever change that fact, whatever she did to argue him out of it, 'I would say never change, but I'm not quite sure I could mean it when you're keeping us apart with such idiocies. I promise to cherish your daughter as if she is truly my Eve's little sister. Please accept me and admit we'll never stop wanting each other this side of the grave. I vow I'll do my best to track down your Verity's father and make him honour his obligations towards her, if he still lives. She is a Thessaly when all is said and done, Chloe, and that means something to me, if only because you are one too.'

Chloe would have argued, but he shook his head.

'No, don't insist on reeling off a list of your father's and now your brothers' sins to blight both your lives with. Yours is still an old and loyal name and the title was won by better men than the current holder or your father. Thessaly women have defended castles and led soldiers in their husbands' absence; tramped across battlefields to find loved ones and guarded fortunes so their sons wouldn't have to go to the devil in their father's footsteps. Stay in hiding and you will oblige your brothers even more than you have already by staying away, as well as robbing your Verity of her heritage and all the fierce warrior ladies she has a right to know about.'

'No,' she denied. 'How can you sit there and condemn me for doing what was right? Are you accusing me of being less than all those rash and outrageous Thessaly women, because I ran instead of letting them put Verity out to freeze to death in the depths of winter?'

'I don't need to, you've done it to yourself,' he said so quietly she stopped in mid-rage and stared up at him with her mouth open. 'And now you're doing it to me and both our daughters as well,' he added ruthlessly.

'No, whatever happens they will be safe from harm.'

'That's not true, Chloe. Unjust as it may be, they could still suffer for the sins of their fathers,' he said bleakly and how could he call himself a sinner when he had been so desperately young when he became a father himself?

A boy of twenty seemed unlikely to have a pocketful of sins to carry around, let alone the vast burden he looked as if he had on his shoulders as he said it with a heavy sigh that spoke of mysteries and secrets she wasn't sure she even wanted to think about right now.

'And their mothers?' she said, thinking of Daphne dying in agony as she strove desperately to give her child life. 'Birthing them ought to wipe out all of them in one blow,' she said with a shudder.

'Would that it did,' he rasped as memory seemed to suck him back into the past as well. 'Not that your sister had time to bank many sins in her short life,' he added, as if forcing himself to slam the door on whatever his wife had done before she met her end in a carriage accident in a far-off country, too many miles and years away from her husband and daughter to matter in their lives any more by then.

'No, and I refuse to believe Daphne died as a punishment for what she did to bring Verity into the world. I can't pretend many wouldn't say that was so, then go on to blame Verity for being born the wrong side of the blanket. We must think of her, Luke. I might not like it, but there's no point pretending the world won't point the finger and speculate endlessly who her father is if the truth comes out,' she said gently, his name openly on her lips for the first time and would it wasn't to find another way of saying no to him. How she wished for the right to squirm back into his arms and forget the past in loving him now.

'Aye,' he said with a heavy sigh, 'so it might, but if we have each other it won't touch us. That's what I've learnt from being Eve's father and you need to learn it as well. As long as there is love and strength inside our home the evil and pettiness outside can only touch us if we let it.'

'You can't stay shut away in that bleak castle of yours for ever though, my lord,' she half-teased and half-warned him, wondering how he would cope with the fuss and attention of Eve's début in a couple of years' time, if he had a stepdaughter with no apparent father and a wife who had sensationally returned from the dead with an orphaned niece at her side to make them all a seven-day wonder.

'It's not enough any more, thanks to you,' he said dourly.

'There's no need to sound quite so cross about it.'

'Why not? I was almost happy living with what I could have if I didn't think too hard about what I truly wanted, until I learnt to hope. You're the one who taught me, Chloe, so do you really think you have any right to take it away from us now I've learnt the trick of it at last?'

'I'm not sure.'

'Then be sure, be so certain you could carve it into rock and display it in the Strand, Lady Chloe Thessaly, because until you can, I won't give up.'

'Can you imagine it in the announcement, my lord? Lady Chloe Thessaly, whom the world thought dead a decade ago, is to marry Viscount Farenze, who deserves our profound sympathy.'

'And can you imagine what the world had to say about me and mine when my wife dragged my name through every muddy puddle she could find and the odd boggy swamp or two along the way? I don't care what they say; the people who matter to me will know the truth and those who don't can do as they please. It's of no consequence to me what the wider world thinks.'

'But it is to me.'

'That is your cross to bear, don't make it mine as well.'

She met the challenge in his straight gaze once again and nodded to admit it was a problem she must worry at until she knew if she could accept such notoriety for them all or not. Wasn't it asking too much of any man to take her and Verity on, but could she and Luke endure *not* to take that risk? Could she live without him; wait every day to read of his marriage to another woman; the birth of his children and not hers? Wouldn't it drive her mad to stay in her narrow little existence as housekeeper in some house she didn't want to learn like she knew this one and long uselessly and bitterly for my Lord Farenze for the rest of her life?

'I have a set of tasks to carry out, whatever you and I could be, Lord Farenze,' she reminded him and rose to her feet.

'So Lady Chloe Thessaly puts her disguise back on to be Mrs Wheaton again. I'd be more impressed by that if you didn't look so thoroughly kissed and rumpled, madam. I suggest you rearrange the housekeeper if you want her to be taken seriously,' he said with a look that admitted he was being harsh. 'Go on then, leave me with Virginia's missive to soothe my pride. Rebuild your defences for me to knock down again, because I will find the weak points in them and tear them away.'

Not sure if it was a threat or a promise, she shook her head and felt the unfamiliar weight of her hair about her shoulders with a distracted frown. 'I'm sorry,' she said numbly then gathered up her scattered hairpins and discarded cap. The words *I love you* almost got on to her tongue and into the evening air, but it would be unfair to say it and walk away, so she bit her lip and went.

'Read your letter,' she'd said. Luke opened his last missive from Virginia with less reverence than he would have half an hour ago, then held it unseeingly instead of reading.

How could he take in Virginia's words as if nothing much had happened? Impossible to let her words glide into meaning now, instead of dancing across the page as if written in code. All he could think of was *her*—Lady Chloe Thessaly; Mrs Wheaton; the woman who kissed him like a heated dream. The dream he'd refused to have for so long.

He wondered what life would be like if he wasn't a coward. Pamela had treated him like a wooden effigy without feelings, but why had he let her spoil so much that could be good and right about his life once she was no more than a bitter memory? If he'd forced his way through Chloe's barriers when she was young and wild and daring, they could have been happy together for years.

Instead of seizing the happiness he could have, he'd clung to his wrongs. Pamela said he was a cold-hearted martinet, so he'd become one—not with his daughter, but to the world outside the castle walls. He was nineteen when he made that disastrous marriage, twenty when Pamela taunted him with what she'd done and walked away. His hands fisted involuntarily, but he made himself open them, then laid Virginia's precious last letter aside until he was fit to read it again.

It had come to him when he kissed Chloe that his future felt right with her in it and those wasted years weighed heavy. He might have had Chloe at his side, could have seen his second wife flourish and flower as their closeness grew, if he wasn't such a fool. Even when she eyed him hungrily as a half-starved wildcat at a banquet ten years ago, he had not taken his advantage.

He'd been such a *boy*, that unformed youth Pamela took in lieu of the rich, titled and sophisticated man of the world she'd really wanted. The hurting youth she made of him went on lashing out every time his precious isolation was in danger. It really was high time he grew up, he decided, with a wry smile to admit to himself that he'd left it a little late.

'Nothing ventured, nothing gained,' he told the small and exquisite marriage portrait of Virginia and Virgil that hung in their favourite room, 'and any other cliché I can think of to get me where you two sat so smugly contented with each other all those years ago.'

For a moment it seemed as if the lovers took their love-locked gazes off each other, focused on him with mocking approval and whispered, 'About time.'

'Must be more tired than I thought,' he muttered as he blinked and looked again.

No, they were as they'd always been, so absorbed

in each other he could imagine the exasperated artist demanding they look outwards and let him do what he was here for time after time, until he gave up and painted what he saw instead of what they did. Of course they were still lost in each other's eyes, every idea in their heads focused on one another, painted lovers caught in an endless moment of loving and wanting each other.

'A trick of the firelight,' he assured himself and his great-uncle and aunt's painted likenesses, then bent down to light a taper from the glowing fire to light a branch of candles. 'You'll have to do better than that if it wasn't,' he told the oblivious lovers, glad Chloe had closed the door behind her so there was no risk of being overheard talking to a picture.

'She might not have me anyway,' he argued with a stretched canvas and a few layers of expensive paint. 'Little wonder if she's curious about what she missed and responds to me like a man's wildest fantasy. Maybe she wants to know what her sister risked so much for.'

He could feel a huge gap opening up inside him at the very idea he might love Lady Chloe and she could not love him back. He shook his head to try to reason it away, or accept the full echoing emptiness of that future.

'You could give me a clue,' he told the youthful image of Virginia with so little of her attention on the world beyond her lover's gaze.

It seemed to his tired mind Virgil spoke this time, 'You did tell the boy to read that letter, not use it to line his hat with, didn't you, love?'

Since he'd be a fool not to, he did as he might have been bid, if his conversation with two dead lovers wasn't impossible.

'Lady Farenze was very specific, my lord,' the portly little lawyer said a few minutes later and took off his spectacles to peer at Luke with apparently mild eyes. 'We went over her will in minute detail six months ago and I can confirm that her ladyship was of sound mind and very clear about her wishes.'

'I dare say, but this scheme of hers is ridiculous. No, it's beyond ridiculous. You must find a way to set this part of Lady Virginia's will aside and allow me administer the estate instead of Lady Chloe.'

'Lady Virginia was very specific—either the whole of her will is proved and enacted or none of it. Naturally you will receive this house and the Farenze Lodge Estate under the terms of your great-uncle's will, but the rest of the provisions of her ladyship's will must be rendered null and void. Her personal fortune will then go to her blood kin as her legal heirs. By the time it has been fought over and split between all the DeMayes and the Revereux family entitled to a share it will do little good to anyone, but if you fight this document, that is what must happen.'

Luke swore as he paced the room angrily, raging at the devil over the few words Virginia left him to fume over echoing about in his head.

Darling Luke,
Your task for the next few months is to track
down Verity Thessaly's father. I only wish for

*your happiness, my dear boy, but I suggest you
start out by visiting Crowdale's Scottish estates
to look for clues to the man's identity.*
All my love,
Great-Aunt Virginia

Chapter Fourteen

So that was his last letter from Virginia; a couple of lines and a cryptic reference? Now he was supposed to do what Chloe least wanted him to do—dig into her sister's past as carelessly as if excavating potatoes. Curse it; he'd always thought Virginia loved him, despite his faults and managing ways. Now she'd left him an impossible task and expected him to be happy at the end of it. Chloe would curse him up hill and down dale, then refuse to have anything more to do with him if he found out her sister had cavorted with a married man to beget her child.

How could he not suspect Verity's father was an adulterer when he'd abandoned a seventeen-year-old girl to carry his bastard alone? If so, the damned rogue would have left no trace of himself in Daphne Thessaly's life, except the unarguable fact of his child and who could prove one way or the other who her father was on the strength of hearsay and rumours? If Chloe didn't get the truth from her sister, it couldn't be uncovered when Lady Daphne Thessaly was ten years in her grave.

'What if I can't do it?' he barked at Poulson when he came to a halt.

'What if you cannot do what, my lord?'

Luke sought a reason for that confusion and found it in the challenge he'd offered to Virginia's will and her damnable scheming.

'This ludicrous quest I've been given,' he snapped impatiently.

'Oh, that's simple enough. Then you must inform Lady Chloe you are not willing to carry out your task and she will subtract a quarter of the sum put aside to purchase a manor and estate for Mr James Winterley at the end of the twelve months, if enough of you complete your quests, and forward it to the Prince Regent.'

'That's devilish,' he ground out, Virginia was giving with one hand and taking away with the other.

'Perhaps the word ingenious describes it better, my lord.'

'However you look at it, my great-aunt has me tied up so tight I'm surprised I'm not screaming. I'd give a great deal to see my brother decently occupied and financially independent of me. Happy is probably beyond him, but at least he deserves a chance to prove me wrong. James won't accept a penny from me to set himself up in a new life, but such a bequest could change his life.'

'Mr Winterley might surprise himself and everyone else if he had the means to do so,' Mr Poulson suggested as if he thought there were hidden depths to one of the most notorious rakes of the *ton* as well as Tom Mantaigne. The lawyer shook his head as that idea played through it and he realised how much looking it demanded. 'If he was better occupied, it would divert his resentment from your inheritance of the family lands and titles.'

'What a fine prospect you do dangle before me,' Luke said, wondering why James's dislike still hurt after all these years of mutual distrust, 'but it still begs the question whether I can do what Virginia asked me to.'

'Lady Virginia had more faith in you than you do in yourself, Lord Farenze.'

'I assume you don't know what she asked, unless you managed to undo this letter and reseal it without leaving a single trace, Poulson, so pray don't imagine you understand the task she set me until I come back and admit it can't be done.'

'I'm sure you won't do that, Lord Farenze,' the lawyer said with a smile Luke didn't trust one bit.

The man eyed the legal documents he'd been working on to transfer the estate and various other pieces of property to their new owners, as if he could imagine nothing finer than burying himself in wheretofors and howsoevers until dinnertime and Luke sighed impatiently, then left him to it.

By the time Chloe left the library it was nearly dinner time and she was soon caught up in the rush and urgency when Cook burned her hand and the cook maid dropped a pint of cream on the kitchen floor. She felt a sadly neglectful mother by the time the family and their guests were all served and the kitchen was calm again and she was free to make her way upstairs to spend a few minutes with her daughter.

'There you are, Mama,' Verity exclaimed, looking up from the much-crossed and amended first attempt at an essay her headteacher had set her. 'I was never more pleased to see you in my life,' she admitted with a quaintly adult shrug and mischief in her bright blue eyes.

'Because I am an exceptionally wonderful mother, or because you need help with whatever fiendish task Miss Thibett set you this time, my love?'

'Both, of course,' Verity said and Chloe wondered if her father had been a charmer as well—if so, it seemed little wonder poor Daphne had found him irresistible.

'What have you been afflicted with, then?'

'It's geography, Mama,' Verity said tragically, as if she had been asked to visit Hades and report on the scenery.

'Oh, dear me, that's certainly not your best subject,' Chloe sympathised and wished she had more than a scratch education. 'There must be some clue in one of Lady Virginia's books or on one of the globes.'

'I can't find the Silk Road on a globe,' Verity said with a pout that told Chloe she hadn't tried very hard.

It was a trait that reminded Chloe of Daphne and, whilst she would always defend her sister fiercely if anyone else criticised her, she refused to let Verity grow up with the same belief she only needed to cry or bat her eyelashes to get unpleasant tasks done for her.

'Then you will find it in the new atlas Lady Virginia purchased last year for times like this. Once you have a list of the countries it passes through you can look up the history and trade it carries in the books the last Lord Farenze collected about the more exotic corners of the world. You should be grateful to have such knowledge at your fingertips so you can answer your headmistress's questions when you return to school next week.'

'Oh, Mama, must I?'

'Yes, Verity, you must.'

'I thought you might help me. It would be so much more interesting than wading through a lot of dry-as-dust philosophising about the savage ways of peoples those dreary old travellers considered less civilised than their own kind on my own.'

'You must have been looking in the wrong ones. Find a book by someone who loved exploring new places and meeting new people and read what he has to say instead of some person who probably never went to the places he wrote about. There must be writings like that in such a collection. Lady Virginia's husband doesn't sound the sort of man who was happy to be bored witless every time he picked up a book.'

'Then I must plough through every book in the library to find out a few facts that will satisfy Miss Thibett I didn't idle my time away this week?'

Chloe was tempted to snap an easy reply and go back to her housekeeping accounts. She knew an unsaid question about where her daughter now fitted into the world lay under her Verity's fit of the sullens and she must set aside her not-very-tempting household accounts to deal with it.

'You need an occupation, my love. Miss Thibett is a wise woman who knows far more about life than you do and she knows Lady Virginia stood in the place of a family for both of us. That is why she let you come home to say farewell to her ladyship. I was wrong to try to shield you from the pain of loss, my love, and your headmistress was right to let you grieve for the person who meant so much to you.'

Suddenly her daughter wasn't a young lady, or the

mischievous urchin who had torn about on her pony and worried her mama with daring exploits until Lady Virginia offered to send her to school. Chloe tried not to let her own tears flow as Verity turned into her arms to be comforted.

'I miss her so much, Mama,' she wailed and wept at long last.

'I know you do, my darling,' Chloe whispered into the springing gold curls making their escape bid from Verity's fast-unravelling plait. 'You have every right to cry at the loss of such a good friend. Lady Virginia loved you very dearly and I know how deeply you loved her back.'

For a while Verity wept as if her heart might break and Chloe rocked her gently, as she often had in her early years, when Daphne's child sometimes went from happy little girl to a sobbing fury in the blink of an eye, as if she wept for all she had lost at birth. All Chloe could do back then was hold her until Verity calmed and slept, or Lady Virginia managed to divert the little girl from her woes with a joke or a funny story about her own misspent youth. This time there was no Virginia to make light of such woe and Chloe felt terribly alone and as bereft as Verity.

'Where shall we go, Mama?' the desperate question stuttered from Verity's shaky lips as she battled dry sobs and looked tragic, as if all Chloe had been worrying about for the last weeks was crushing her, too.

'Oh, my love,' Chloe responded with tears backed up in her own throat as she realised she should have had this conversation with her daughter as soon as she came home. 'I don't know if we can stay here, but Lady

Virginia left me a full year's salary in return for a trifling charge she laid on me. I have enough saved to live comfortably on for a year or two after that, if I should choose not to look for a new post yet, and Lady Virginia left you an annuity, so you will never starve. Please don't run away with the notion you're an heiress, though, will you?'

'Then I shall not. I love her even more though, now I know I shall be able to look after you one day, Mama, when you are too old to do it yourself.'

Chloe went from the edge of tears to fighting laughter. 'We probably have a few years before I'm too bowed with age to work, darling,' she said with a straight face.

'You're laughing at me, aren't you?' Verity accused.

'I'm sorry, love, but I'm not even eight and twenty yet. That might sound as if I could shake hands with Methuselah on equal terms to you, but I feel remarkably well preserved when my daughter is not making me out to be an ancient crone.'

'That's what age does to a person, Lady Virginia told me,' Verity informed her with a solemn shake of her head, as if she saw through her mother's ruse.

'Lady Virginia was at least fifty years older than me, Verity love, and that was only what she admitted to. Her age varied every time someone was rude enough to try to find it out. I'm unlikely to follow Lady Virginia into the grave for a great many years yet and you must stop fretting about me.'

'But what if you die in childbed, Mama? I can tell Lord Farenze wants to marry you and ladies die giving birth, particularly when they're old.'

'Why would Lord Farenze want to marry me?' Chloe

asked; shocked that her brain picked that rather than thinking how to reassure Verity ladies gave birth safely time after time at much more than seven and twenty.

'Oh, Eve and I realised ages ago,' her daughter said, as if it was so obvious she was amazed anyone could miss it.

'I hope you kept that conclusion quiet then, as you couldn't be more wrong.'

'Bran and Miss Culdrose agree with us.'

'And whatever would the rest of the household make of such a silly idea?' Chloe asked faintly, dread at facing even the smallest scullery maid eating at her lest they were already speculating about it.

'They think Mrs Winterley will put a stop to it, but Eve says her father takes no notice of what his stepmother says and even less of what she thinks.'

Chloe sighed and decided she could put off telling Verity the story of her own birth no longer, if only to scotch any false hopes of becoming Eve's stepsister, but her niece's eyes were red and tired after her crying bout and the sad tale of Daphne's love affair must wait for another day.

'Lord Farenze is a viscount; I am his housekeeper and lords do not marry servants. Forget such wild flights of fancy and get into bed, love. Your Miss Thibett would be the first to say you need a decent night's sleep before you're ready to face world trade and the laden caravans of gold, jewels, silk and spices that will be winding their way through far-off, exotic lands even as we speak.'

Her imagination caught by the idea of those processions of camels laden down with fine cloth and exquisite treasures, Verity allowed Chloe to walk her to her room and help her undress, then get into bed. Verity asked for a story and how to resist when she usually insisted on reading herself to sleep and this might be the last time Verity let her be her mother? Chloe dreaded telling her the tale of her birth and felt like crying herself by the time they wandered a little way along that ancient road in their imaginations and Verity's eyes got heavier and heavier until she slept at last.

Chloe let her voice trail away, then gazed at her precious child as if she had to fill her mind with Verity as she was now. Tomorrow Verity might hate her for a pretence begun when nobody else cared enough about Daphne's child to save her from death or a lonely life at the mercy of the parish.

Shaking her head to keep back the idea things were better as they were, Chloe went to her own room earlier than usual to struggle with the knot her life seemed tangled into all of a sudden. Someone had lit a fire for her and she knew exactly who had ordered it. Luke's thoughtfulness at a time when he had hundreds of other things to think about made tears sting as she gazed into the glowing flames and wondered how he'd ever managed to fool anyone he was an unfeeling recluse.

She loved Luke Winterley and finally admitted to herself she had loved him far too long. The fact of it, fresh and vital in her heart as she knew it would be to her dying day, made her content and full of hope for all of a minute. Yet if she emerged from whatever fate her family had told the world she had met to wed my Lord Farenze, Verity would be exposed as the reason

Lady Chloe was supposed to have died with her sister in the first place.

Her brothers would walk through fire rather than publically admit they'd let one sister give birth with only her twin to help her and a rapidly sobering midwife, then forced Chloe out to starve with her dead sister's child after even that ordeal didn't kill the poor little mite and they had to rid themselves of her by other means.

Chloe sat watching the fire with tears sliding down her cheeks as she bid farewell to a dream she hadn't let herself know she had. She had Verity and a secure future many a woman left with a child to bring up alone would envy her. Verity's future was secure as well and she ought to be dancing on air. Instead she must fight the heavy weight of grief and an urge to sob her heart out on the threadbare rug she had decreed good enough for her bedchamber, so at least nobody could accuse her of gilding her own nest.

Luke could condemn her thrift and look at her scratch bedchamber with offended distaste, but she had lived among the cast-offs of a bygone age most of her life and was used to making do. Carraway Court had been neglected and down at heel for as long as she could remember and the older servants would shake their heads and say how different it was in her grandfather's day, before their mother wed her lord and he took all the rents, then left the Court to go to rack and ruin.

Even then they whispered of gambling and extravagant mistresses and how even an earl couldn't bring such low company to his late wife's home with her daughters in residence. Chloe wondered bitterly why her father and brothers cared so much about the family name when they blighted it so enthusiastically.

A sentence from Virginia's letter slotted into her mind as if her mentor had whispered in her ear and a possible plan formed. Lady Tiverley was an amiable feather-head, but she was the daughter of a far richer and more respectable earl than Chloe's father had ever been and moved in the highest social circles. If such a lady whispered the truth in a few well-placed ears, could Daphne and her romantically mysterious child become the heroines of such a sad tale? It was a faint hope and her heart beat like a marching drum at the idea she and Luke could love openly after all.

Then she remembered Daphne lying in that rough bed, dying and feverishly demanding that Chloe promised her never to love a man so recklessly. She wasn't Daphne, or a vulnerable seventeen-year-old girl with no protector now, though. Anyone who wanted to take advantage of her would have to get past Luke Winterley first, even if he was the one wanting to take it. She smiled at the thought of him holding aloof from Farenze Lodge for so long, because she had said *No* and they each had a daughter who would be damaged if she didn't. He could deny it as often as he pleased, but her love was a noble gentleman from the top of his midnight locks to the tip of his lordly boots and how could she not love him? It was admitting it she had trouble with.

First she must talk to Verity and insist Luke told his own daughter the truth about them as well. Lying in bed, torn between wild hopes and abject terror, the weight of four people's hopes and dreams seemed to press her into the mattress. Even as the wonder of 'perhaps' made her heart lift with joy and her toes and a good many other places tingle with anticipation, Chloe couldn't bring herself to believe her impossible fairytale might actually come true.

Fumbling Virginia's letter from the pocket of her neatly discarded gown, she jumped back into bed and relit her candle. She had talked Verity to sleep; now she let Virginia do the same for her. Chloe was very glad in the morning that her candle had sat firmly in a night stick, since it had gutted without her even being aware she had gone to sleep with it alight and slept peacefully the whole night long.

Chapter Fifteen

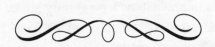

'I need to speak with you privately, Mrs Wheaton. Meet me in the Winter Garden in half an hour if you please,' Luke demanded when he tracked down his housekeeper to the linen room, where she seemed to be having an urgent consultation with the head housemaid about torn sheets, of all things.

From the flash of temper in her magnificent eyes at his order he felt lucky he hadn't come across her alone and she had to keep to her role in front of the maids. He smiled like a besotted idiot as he ran down the back-stairs, as if it was what a viscount did, and went out to the stables to speak to Josiah Birtkin about travel arrangements and how this place could be kept safe and cautious whilst he was away. The thought of being parted from Chloe, Verity and Eve while he carried out Virginia's quest added a bite of nerves to his elation as he finished his conversation and went to seek a far more crucial one.

It could be another clear morning, if only the mist would clear. Instead it hung about this sheltered valley and he wondered if he should have asked Chloe to meet him outside on a day when frost seemed to hang in the very air, waiting to crystallise their breath. The wintery statue at the heart of the place was still staring into the distance, but Luke resisted the urge to confide his thoughts to his unresponsive stone ears. Some things were so private they should only be said to the person concerned.

'There you are,' Chloe's pleasantly husky voice observed from so close it made him start and her frown turned to a satisfied smile.

'As you say,' he drawled as annoyingly as he could manage and from the flags of colour burning across her cheeks he'd succeeded a bit too well in rousing her temper this time.

'How dare you order me to meet you out here in the middle of my duties like this? What do you imagine the household will make of such a hole-and-corner encounter, Lord Farenze?'

'That I wish to speak to you in private and can hardly do so inside with so many eager ears tuned to our every move, I expect,' he replied with a shrug part of him knew was wrong when he was master and she was playing the upper servant.

'Why would you need to be private with me?' she demanded haughtily and Luke took a deep breath of frosty air and prepared to tell her.

'So I may ask you to marry me again, of course,' he managed to say casually, as if it was what viscounts always did of a foggy morning, when they employed housekeepers as magnificent as this one.

'Just like that?' she demanded and he wondered if

he'd miscalculated by stirring her into enough fury to be her true self instead of Mrs Wheaton.

'No, not just like that,' he said with a stern frown of his own. 'After a decade of denial and deception—' he heard her draw breath to annihilate him with negatives '—I'm done with pretending it doesn't matter that we wasted ten years because I was too stupid to see past your disguise and my wife's shoddy little love affairs to the woman you truly are, Chloe Thessaly.'

'You can't call me that here,' she argued with a shocked look about in case old Winter at the centre of the garden might pass her identity on.

'Nobody is in earshot and there are eight-foot-high hedges all about us, but are you ashamed of me then, my lady?'

'Never that, my lord,' she shot back so urgently he had to hide a satisfied grin.

'Then when do you intend telling the world who you truly are?'

'When the time seems right,' she muttered crossly and shifted under his steady gaze. 'Oh, I don't know,' she admitted with a heavy sigh. 'Soon,' she added as he continued to watch her as annoyingly as he could manage when all he really wanted to do was kiss her speechless and a lot more it was as well not to go into right now.

'When Verity is of age, or has run off with the boot boy perhaps? Or when hell freezes over and I'm so old and grey even you don't want me any longer?'

'I shall always want you,' she said unwarily and he couldn't help his broad grin at the declaration he most wanted to hear on her lips.

'Marry me, then,' he managed to say before he could launch himself at her like a lovestruck maniac.

'You could do so much better,' she said, avoiding his eyes as she watched the stony statue as if he fascinated her and Luke found he could even be jealous of inanimate objects now.

'I could ask nobody better suited to be my wife,' he assured her as he cupped large hands about her face, so she had to look up and let him see the doubts and questions in her amazing violet-blue gaze, as well as the heat and longing that made his heartbeat thunder with exhilaration and desire. 'I never met a woman I honoured so much or wanted so badly, Chloe,' he told her shakily and hoped he had managed to put all he was feeling into his own gaze, for once. 'You've made me into me again,' he said and grimaced as all the words he couldn't put together clogged up in his head. 'I don't have the right words. I've been trying not to admit it for a decade, but I love you and I won't stop doing it, even if you walk away.'

'I can't marry you, Luke.'

Chloe let herself gaze up into his fascinatingly hot grey eyes and saw pain and anger there before he decided *No* wasn't enough this time. It felt as if the frantic beat of her heart might choke her as she gazed up into all she'd ever wanted and had to say it anyway. Love *was* there in the flare of gold about his irises, the hidden depths of green at the heart of his gaze that looked back at her.

Luke, Lord Farenze, was finally showing her the tender places in his heart, the hopes and dreams in his complex mind and she was hurting him all over again.

Tears swam in her eyes as she thought of the young man he'd been—scarred so badly when his dreams were trampled in the dust by his shrew of a wife. He needed her to love him back, and love him back she truly did, but it didn't mean she could let him marry her and make Verity into a bastard again.

'Why not?' he breathed, so close she wondered how she could still be so cold.

'I have a daughter,' she said sadly.

The blighted hopes and dreams young Chloe once wept over so bitterly while missing stubborn, noble, infuriating Lord Farenze in her bed seemed as nothing, now she had to renounce everything mature Chloe wanted to give her lover.

'Oh, Luke, don't frown at me and shake your head. I know you're a good man and I'm a coward, but I can't let Verity grow up with Lady Daphne Thessaly's shame blighting her life. You need a pristine wife with an innocent heart, not me.'

'Why would I want a tame little tabby kitten when I can have a lioness who'd fight for our cubs with her last breath?' he said with a refusal to be fobbed off that made temptation tug so powerfully she had to look away.

'I am fighting for one of them now.'

'No, you're denying we could fight the world for her together. I won't accept this as your final answer, Chloe Thessaly,' he said with a determination that made her knees wobble and her breath come short. She loved him so much she felt herself weakening and turned to watch the foggy garden to stop herself admitting she would only ever be half-alive without him.

'Virginia's quest for me is to find out who Verity's father was. I will do my best to do so, but after that I'll wed you, whoever he turns out to be,' he told her.

It sounded as much a threat as a promise, until he ran an impatient hand through his sable pelt of hair and let out a heartfelt sigh. 'Lord above, but you're a proud and stubborn wench, Lady Chloe Thessaly,' he informed her with exasperation.

Chloe sighed at the angry intimacy of them here in this foggy garden and longed for a forever after to spend with him. She spared a thought for Virgil, begging Virginia to wed him rather than be his scandalous lover as she would have offered to be. They must have realised after two previous marriages bore no fruit there was a strong chance she was barren, but even that didn't seem as huge a barrier to love and marriage as Verity's future happiness was to her.

'I'll wed you or nobody,' Luke told her so stubbornly she almost believed him and her unhappiness seemed about to double. 'Although heaven only knows why I'd saddle myself with such a steely female for life,' he grumbled.

'How charming. You look very much like a grumpy mastiff denied a juicy bone right now, my Lord Farenze.'

'What a sad pair we are then; you look like a queen about to have her head cut off,' he replied, eyebrows raised and a challenge to deny it in his sharp look.

'Nobody else would want us if they knew what a sorry pair we are,' she agreed.

'They'd better not want you, but if we're not to be united in marital disharmony, I suppose I'd best be off about Virginia's business,' he told her with a look that said it was her fault. They could be married inside the week and have a wedding night before he went, if not a honeymoon on the way.

'Wait for a better day,' she urged, all the imaginings of a woman terrified that her lover might never come back taking shape in her mind.

'If I wait out one more night under the same roof as you, Lady Chloe, I shall either run mad or break down your door from sheer frustration. I need to be gone, but first you have to tell me everything you can remember about your sister's visit to Scotland all those years ago.'

'I don't know much, she never told me.'

'Tell me what you do know, then, for it is sure to be more than I do.'

'Daphne went off to our father's Scottish estate to stay there with his sister while her husband was in Ireland, supposedly to be instructed how to go on in polite company, then make a début of some kind in Edinburgh society. My father was deep in debt by that time and had secretly agreed to marry her off to a pox-ridden but very wealthy old duke as soon as they could fool the world she chose such a fate of her own free will.

'Papa was furious when his plan went awry and the old man wanted his money back and Daphne was sent home in disgrace. We were sent away so she could have Verity at a remote and tumbledown property on Bodmin Moor that my father had won in a card game and couldn't sell, but Daphne still refused to tell me who her lover was. She said it was best I didn't know, then I wouldn't be embarrassed when I was presented and had to meet his relatives.'

'He must come from a gently bred family at the very

least then; she could have met one of the neighbours during her time on your father's estate, I suppose, properly out or no,' he said with a preoccupied frown.

Chloe thought fascination with his quest was already overtaking his frustration that she'd refused to marry him, but she put that grief aside for later and did her best to help him with what was probably an impossible task.

'Daphne was desperate to escape marriage to that dreadful old reprobate, but she had always dreamt of a gallant hero who would come and rescue her from the lonely lives we lived at Carraway Court. I wouldn›t be surprised if she took any lover happy to have a sixteen-year-old girl in his bed in a desperate attempt to get herself with child and escape marriage to such a man.'

'She was no older than my Eve when your father tried to sell his own child to the highest bidder, then? What sort of a father would consign his own child to a life of such misery and frustration?'

'The Thessaly sort,' Chloe said sadly, regretting the gaps in hers and Daphne's lives and contrasting them with my Lord Farenze's fierce love for his only child. 'He was no sort of father at all and only wed my mother because she was heiress to the Carraway fortune. I don't suppose he was faithful to her, or even particularly kind. Such a hard-hearted man can do a fearsome amount of damage to his children, so Daphne and I ought to have been grateful he favoured our brothers and despised us as mere girls, I suppose.'

'He was your father and ought to have been proud of his spirited and beautiful daughters. But why did he send her to Scotland with his sister and not you?'

'Because I was openly rebellious and Daphne always chose the course of least resistance, then did as she wanted to as soon as his back was turned. He thought she was meek and tractable and would do as he told her, in so far as he thought of either of us as beings and not his chattels to be disposed of as he chose.'

'Miserable old fool.'

Somehow his round condemnation of her late father made her smile, even if it wobbled and flattened at the thought of all that cold idiocy had cost the Thessaly twins.

'He was, but you can see why Daphne longed so desperately for a lover when she had so little affection from anyone other than me in her life, can you not?'

It came out more as a plea than a demand he understood her twin and she was grateful for the warmth of his hands as he folded her cold ones in his and watched her with a mix of admiration and exasperation in his intent gaze.

'And what of Lady Chloe Thessaly? Was she supposed to stand alone and become the prop for her weaker sister whenever a lover let her down? You must have felt so alone, my love, so forsaken, when your sister and companion was bundled away like that.'

'I always knew that one day we would be parted. Daphne needed to be loved and supported and I had to hope she would meet a man strong enough to do both, until Papa came up with his plan to wed her to a monster. Every day we were apart I was scared she'd do something dreadful to evade what he had in mind for her.'

There, she had almost admitted it for the first time in her life. She had been terrified her sister would find the prospect of that marriage so impossible to endure she would choose death over it.

'It was almost a relief to me when she returned to Carraway Court unwed and with child by a lover she refused to identify even to me,' she added, because he might as well know all her secrets now the worst one was out in the open.

'Oh, my love,' he said, everything she longed for and couldn't have in his dear eyes as he watched her without condemnation. 'What a heavy burden your wretched family made you carry when you were too young to bear even half of it.'

'I grew up very quickly,' she said with a would-be careless shrug, but he drew her closer instead of letting her stand further off and clasped their hands between them as if he never intended letting her go for very long.

'No wonder you thought me such a paltry creature when I made you that dishonourable proposition ten years ago,' he almost managed to joke, despite the pain of that driven declaration spiky between them even now.

'I didn't, Luke, I thought you were the only man I might ever love enough to accept it. Then I thought of Verity and had to say no for all of us.'

'Aye, and you were right to do so, but if only I'd let myself delve deeper then, looked a little harder at Mrs Chloe Wheaton and all the witchy secrets you didn't know and I thought you did.'

'I wouldn't have told you anything back then.'

'Probably not, but it would be good to remember that I tried.'

'I think you did,' she almost whispered and somehow it sounded so loud on the freezing air she looked about and wondered how they must look to a casual observer, this potent lord and his encroaching housekeeper.

'Whereas I think I was a fool until very recently. Now stop distracting me with might have been and let me get this confounded quest over and done with, before I decide to consign it to the devil and stay here and lay siege to you until you finally agree to wed me after all, my Chloe.'

'None of it will go away,' she warned.

'Maybe not, but life and hope must win out over history and gossip. I have to believe it and so ought you, my darling. Coming to terms with our future will keep you out of mischief while I am away.'

'As if I need any sort of occupation with your house to spring clean and put back in order for you,' she said brusquely, but suddenly all the barely hidden energy of nature in January felt as alive in her as it was in the bulbs pushing through the cold earth even here, in the frozen realm of Winter.

'I'll return to you,' he promised, all that life and promise in his dear eyes as he held their clasped hands up to show her they were pledged on a level even she couldn't deny,

'To us?' she offered as a sort of compromise, since they agreed Eve should stay here while he was away and Verity would become a weekly boarder for now and it felt as if a family was forming between them whether she wanted it to or not. 'Will that do?'

'For now, and that brings me back to my quest—what sort of lover would your sister have favoured?'

'A young Adonis, such as my Lord Mantaigne might have been ten years ago, if he was less cynical, which

I doubt,' she said after thinking clearly about that lover for the first time since she realised her twin was with child by him.

'He was never so and had better keep away from this Thessaly twin if he wants to keep a whole skin,' Luke said crossly and she smiled.

'I prefer dark and brooding Border raiders.'

'Stop trying to hold me here with half-promises, woman. I'm off to find this idol of your sister's with his feet of clay. After I confront him and beat him to a pulp, I shall be able to come back and wed you at long last.'

'As if that will solve anything. I said no and I've got work to do,' she told him huffily and pulled out of his arms to walk away with the sound of his surprised laughter echoing in her ears.

'Insufferable, stubborn, impossible man,' she muttered as she marched inside, then darted into the flower room when she thought she heard someone coming downstairs.

Chloe splashed frigid water from a jug waiting to warm up enough to be used to refresh the few vases of flowers available at this time of year and gasped in a deep breath. The impossibility of it all threatened to suck the elation and hope out of her, but this time it wouldn't go. That had been her last no and they both knew it. He was a risk she had to take when he got back from Scotland, whatever the result of his quest might be. She was going to take that risk on love Daphne warned her against with her dying breath. Risk or not, she was going to have to jump right into it and trust him not to let them both drown.

She felt a little less convinced he'd manage it when she came down the elegant front stairs of Farenze Lodge on a fine spring morning six weeks later, ready to begin the grand clear out of hatchments, black veiling and all the other trappings of mourning Virginia had ordered must take place as soon as possible after her death. Chloe knew she should be as happy as she ever could be here without her beloved employer and mentor, but somehow knowing she was a coward took the joy out of the spring sunshine and dulled the sight of a flurry of primroses and violets brightening the edge of the still-leafless woods.

She still hadn't found the courage to tell Verity who she really was. She felt weighed down by her own folly as she helped the maids take down the dark veiling from gilt mirrors and statues and open the blinds in all the rooms kept half-dark until today. Holland covers were removed from the furniture in Virginia's splendid boudoir and the last bequests were matched to the list Mr Poulson left, ready to be sent to new owners with a note or a personal visit from Eve, her father or the housekeeper to hand over a memento of a much-loved lady.

Life was going relentlessly on all round her and Chloe felt the past threaten her happiness like a pall. She looked the same soberly correct housekeeper she'd been for so long, but felt nowhere near as serene and composed as she appeared while she awaited Luke's return and the end of his quest to find Verity's father.

Luckily, none of the neighbours knew Luke enclosed long letters to her with the sealed packet he sent to his daughter every week. Eve always handed them over with a lack of expression that said more than Chloe wanted anyone to know about her relationship with the girl's father. Yet with Eve's middle-aged governess here now to keep her pupil busy and all of them respectably chaperoned, Chloe knew Luke was making her own continuing presence here as unremarkable as possible and could only love him all the more for it.

'He's courting you,' Bran had pointed out when the latest letter came and Chloe hastily hid it in her pocket to read as soon as she could make an excuse to be alone.

When she did, she sat pouring over every word and could almost imagine he was here, telling her who he'd met and what he thought of the part of Scotland where Daphne stayed at first, then some sharp observations about her paternal aunt, Lady Hamming, that the lady would certainly not enjoy if she read them.

'His lordship is keeping me informed of some business he undertook for me whilst he is in Scotland,' she had retorted as briskly as she could when Bran made that accusation, knowing her blush was giving her away so badly they both wondered why she was bothering.

'His lordship is a good man, but not so good he'd write at such length to someone he was doing a favour, Mrs Wheaton,' the shrewd little woman told her.

'He can't court me, I'm a servant,' Chloe said numbly.

'Are you now?'

'Of course I am.'

'The nobility and gentry might see what they expect to when they look through any of us as doesn't slop their bathwater or knock over the silver, but you won't fool the rest of us that easy, my dear.'

'For all that, I'm still a housekeeper.'

'And a very good one you are, too, but it's not what you're born to.'

'As if most ladies of birth and expectations are not

brought up to keep house, when they're not too busy bearing heirs. Even if I was born a lady, why would I want to become a brood mare for some chilly lord?'

'Because he's a man in every sense of the word and would be whether he was born a lord or a labourer, perhaps? Don't you go judging Lord Farenze by any other noble devils you've come across, Mrs Chloe. He suffered enough grief from a woman who wouldn't see he's got a good heart under that abrupt manner of his. Why don't you ask yourself if he'd grumble and glare at those as wants to poke about in his life to pass the time if he hadn't a wild, romantic yearning inside him to protect? He needs you, my girl, so are you going to make him happy or kick him aside like that heartless young madam he married when he was too young to know any better did, as if he was nothing?'

'You'd trust me with the happiness of such a good man? I'm not sure I would. I come from bad blood, Bran, best for him if he has no more to do with me.'

'Your girl's bad then, is she?'

'No, she's as sweet as a nut all the way through, which makes her almost a miracle considering the nest of vipers I hail from,' Chloe replied with a shrug.

'Speaking for myself, I don't judge a book by what's next to it and you should try looking in the mirror sometimes.'

'I do. How else can I be sure I look neat and tidy every morning?'

'Look closer and you'll see a stranger looking back— bad blood indeed.'

'I'm not worthy of him, Bran,' Chloe whispered as if to say it aloud admitted Lord Farenze really was courting his great-aunt's companion housekeeper.

'You won't be if you cower behind that cap and your blacks for ever and won't see what could be if you was to let it. He deserves better.'

'That's exactly what I'm telling you.'

'No, you've come up with a cartload of reasons why not, when he's set his heart on you. He deserves a woman who'll say yes to him and damn the devil.'

'I have a daughter to consider,' she argued stubbornly.

'And he doesn't? Don't you trust him to be a good father to your Verity?'

'Of course I do,' Chloe admitted, then sighed with relief when Eve came to find out why it was taking them so long to count napkins and write down an order for more and saved her from even more uncomfortable questions.

Looking at herself from where Bran stood, Chloe wondered why anyone would believe she'd been the bold, bad Thessaly twin, who defied anyone who stood in the way of what she or Daphne wanted or needed now. When her father decided to sell off his more tractable daughter, she recalled how cleverly he'd whisked Daphne away so Chloe had no idea where she was and found she wanted to lash out at him as fiercely now as she had then. How that fiery young Chloe would stare at the subdued woman she'd become. She had kept herself and Verity safe by refusing to live fully and love Luke for years and it was time to let that pent-up fury go and learn to live without it.

Lady Chloe Thessaly learnt young that love was a snare. It left Daphne dead and her with a child to bring up. Little wonder if she refused to trust her feral longings for my Lord Farenze a decade ago. He'd been gruff and hurt then and must have resented wanting her until he glowered at her more often than he smiled. The battered and cynical aristocrat he pretended to be back then was so unlike the ardently romantic young lover she'd once dreamed of that it was little wonder she'd been horrified to discover he roused passions in her she'd thought stone dead.

Chapter Sixteen

As a delicate and vulnerable baby Verity had needed Chloe to concentrate all her energy on her, but did she truly need it now? She considered how a mother could cope with her child growing up. Mrs Winterley had treated Luke like a cuckoo in her nest his entire childhood because she wanted her own child to inherit, but now that James regarded his own mother as sceptically as his brother did, how must it feel to be rejected by the very being you adored? Chloe felt a moment of motherly sympathy with the woman before she disliked her all over again for doing her best to make the half-brothers hate each other. Little wonder it took years for Luke to recover his faith in human nature with such a stepmother. Then his self-centred fool of a wife did her best to convince him he was cold and unlovable and compounded the damage before running away.

She recalled how warm-hearted and passionate he could be and blushed. Telling herself to keep her obsession with the master of the house a secret, Chloe set her maids the tasks of washing and cleaning the paraphernalia of mourning, then storing it in the darkest attic they had. When they were all busy, she took a half-hour of peace and quiet for herself and sneaked into the library to shut the door on the world.

No need for the entire household and Brandy Brown to know she always kept one or other of Luke's letters in her pocket to re-read when she wanted to feel he was close by; or that sometimes she just wanted to set out for the north to find him and to the devil with appearances and duty. She sat back against the cushioned comfort of the little *chaise* in front of the unlit fire where they had sat one memorable January afternoon and let herself hear his deep voice in her head while she read the words he seemed more able to put on paper than bring on to his tongue to woo her with when they were together. Wasn't that just like him? Yet would she love him half as much if he was glib and careless and ready to pour forth his every emotion?

Here on the West Coast of this fair land the gorse is in blithe flower outside my window, and the sight and heady, astringent scent of it reminded me so sharply of my prickly Lady Chloe that I had to set pen to paper in order to dream of you as I write and wish we could be together again, but this time in every way that word knows how.

Typical of him to begin with an insult, then turn it into a charm, she decided as she fingered the paper where his pen had scratched, then been mended and refilled with ink, bringing the scene to life so vividly it was almost as if she had been sitting nearby, shak-

ing her head at his impatient curses, while all that had
to be done before he could continue.

> *As dreaming of you is all I seem able to do at*
> *the moment, I might as well sit here and suffer*
> *the frustrations of the damned, while I imag-*
> *ine you with your knitted brows and a quick*
> *shake of that clever, unwise head of yours as*
> *you wonder if I have finally run mad from*
> *missing you in my life and especially in my*
> *bed.*

She stopped as she read that once again and stared
unseeingly at the wonderful portrait of Virgil and Virginia over the mantelpiece. As always, it showed two
lovers so lost in love they couldn't spare their very expensive artist friend time to look anywhere but into each
other's eyes. When her heart stopped racing at the very
idea of Luke here with her, saying things like that and
holding her as if he couldn't bear to let her go, she focused on the painted likeness of those other lovers and
frowned.

Was taking all your lover had to offer part of the true
generosity of love? How would she know, never having
been one in any sense until now? Even if it took a daring
leap of faith and imagination, the risk could be well worth
taking though. Sinking a little deeper into the cushions of
the *chaise* she'd shared with him the day Virginia's will
was read, she took up Luke's letter again and let herself
imagine him writing it with such un-Luke-like candour
it made a tender smile lift her lips at the very thought of
him putting so much on paper for her.

This is such a beautiful land, full of contradictions and surprises, so really it's a lot like you. I'm sure you'll like it when I get you here for a visit with no lost lovers to unmask at the end of it and, I sincerely hope, no forced politeness to a relative of yours I couldn't warm to if lost in an icy waste alone with her. I would rather snuggle up to an icicle than your once so famously beautiful paternal aunt, my Chloe.

Lady Hamming is still outwardly attractive, but not even her close family dare touch her, presumably fearing her chilliness is catching. I'm surprised she hasn't given poor Hamming frostbite or turned him into an ice statue after so many years of marriage, but he seems to consider her a marvellous curiosity it's best not to try to understand rather than his comfortably familiar companion through life.

Chloe smiled fleetingly at his vivid picture of an aunt she had no desire to know after she had conspired to sell Daphne to a depraved old lecher. Luke had laid her aunt's character open to her without any need for them to meet and she knew he was protecting her again. Chloe frowned and wondered why she wasn't offended by the notion—especially after swearing never to let another man shape her life the day she left Carraway Court for the last time.

'Is it part of love; learning to let someone make your burdens lighter?' she mused out loud. 'I really wish you two would pay attention and answer a few of my questions,' she told the painted lovers across the hearth crossly. 'What can I be expected to know about true love, after being brought up a Thessaly?'

As if they had answered, which was clearly impossible, the portrait of the first 'princely' Earl of Crowdale and his devious countess in an exquisitely painted book of hours, before her father sold it, seemed to sparkle before her mind's eye. Little doubt those two rogues adored one another, she decided, recalling them turned towards each other and holding hands as if that was the bare minimum of contact they could endure. The Thessaly family made a good start on loving immoderately and against the odds. *What a shame so few of their line carried on the tradition,* she felt she was being told now and wondered if Virgil and Virginia would scold her wariness if they truly could see her now.

'Good point,' she conceded, 'although I never actually *knew* them.'

'You knew me.' Virginia's voice, even richer and more full of suppressed laughter and devilry than Chloe remembered, seemed to echo in her mind and add weight to lying, loving Lady Crowdale and her pirate lover. 'I'm one-half of us two, my dear Chloe, and a love like ours doesn't fade and die when facing a challenge,' the imaginary Virginia added.

'Death is quite a challenge,' Chloe replied out loud, very glad she had shut the door behind her when she came in here to read and dream of her love.

'Only if it stops you living in the first place,' Lady Virginia's voice seemed to add before she withdrew from their non-conversation and was only a painted image again: fabulous Lady Virginia, Comtesse, Marquise and now Lady Farenze, sitting for her third marriage portrait and unaware of anyone but the man she'd married for love.

Luke's letter continued, and how could she miss a voice in her head when his loving words were right here in front of her?

The only way Lady Hamming reminds me of you is in how opposite you are to her in every way. It's been like trying to chip away at granite to get anything about your sister out of her or hers, but at last Hamming let fall something about the 'sad business' as he called it last night, while we dipped too deep into a bottle of aged malt whisky he'd managed to hide from his wife and her equally frosty butler; it cost me the devil of a head this morning, but at least this visit north of the Border hasn't proved a wild goose chase after all.

I'm sure Hamming could have been a decent man with more will-power and less frost in his life, but he was busy on his Irish estates that spring, so her ladyship was unchecked by any softer impulses her lord may have. He knows something was done in his absence, but it will probably cost me a few more sore heads to get the whole tale out of him.

I really don't know how you manage to think yourself unimportant to me when I'm risking my poor Sassenach constitution to find the name and fate of your sister's mystery lover. Apart from that, and being parted from you and Eve

*when I least want to be, I must admit that I have
an easy enough role in all this.*

*Poor Peters seems to be faring less well in London, since he had to treat with some of the worst
rogues the place can hold and visit its lowest hells
to find the true depth of your elder brother's decline. It truly is a decline, Chloe, in every sense
of the word. The wider world appears to think
your younger brother more led into evil than devoted to it, but the current earl would make Francis Dashwood and his silly Hell Fire Club blush.*

*Nobody in Crowdale's inner circle would be
surprised to hear how deplorably he and your
father treated you and Lady Daphne and little
Verity, but Peters tells me a very wealthy City
merchant is rumoured to be about to permit
Crowdale to marry his only child, a seventeen-
year-old, naïve schoolgirl available to pawn for
a title at just the wrong moment. Any whisper
of his heartless conduct towards his little sisters
and niece until that alliance is sealed will blight
the whole plan.*

Chloe gasped with pity for the very idea of that unfortunate girl being left at the mercy of such a man. Her
brother certainly wouldn't balk at wedding an innocent
for her father's money when his father had done the
same thing to her mother. She resolved to do whatever
she could to stop the marriage, but not even her disgust
at such a scheme could dim the glow of happiness she
felt at being loved by such a fine man as Luke Winterley. Most men who lusted after an upper servant would

have schemed to get her dismissed, or forced her to become his mistress ten years ago, but even now Luke had gone away and let her be when she begged him to, while he waited for her to believe the unbelievable.

For years he'd avoided this house when he clearly loved it, in order to make sure an upper servant of his great-aunt could raise her child in peace. Bran was quite right; he was an exceptional gentleman. She recalled how brusque and bad-tempered he'd been about it with a smile. The promise of such a rare love was so breathtaking she could hardly bring herself to believe it was within her reach. To reassure herself it was, if she dared accept the wonder, she re-read the ending of his letter.

You must take every care of yourself whilst I'm not there, love. I have sent Josiah to stay at Miss Thibett's school, with that lady's full knowledge and permission, so your girl can be kept safe whilst I gather the whole tale of your sister's adventures. Then Peters can give it verbatim to that ambitious alderman and even he won't be able to dismiss it as a warm story thought up by one of Crowdale's detractors. Peters seems to have some surprising connections of his own, so one or two vigorous and wary rogues will be joining the staff at Farenze Lodge soon to outfox anyone intent on harming you to keep me quiet, if it should come out I have been asking questions about Daphne and Chloe Thessaly's disappearance.

Please say and do nothing reckless in the meantime, since yours and Eve's welfare are crucial to me and your brothers are clearly desperate for the girl's dowry and will do anything to make sure this sad tale and their appalling treatment of their very young sisters never comes out, or at least not until the marriage is safely over and cannot be revoked.

Believe me a blind fool if you like, but I bitterly repent a decade of refusing to look into my own heart and find you there tonight, love. I'd rather live without a limb than endure another ten years without you, so even if you can't return my feelings, please don't run away again and disappear as you did from your father's house all those years ago. I'll run mad fretting about your safety and happiness if you remove me so completely from your life. I shall stop now, before I sink myself for ever in your eyes by begging pathetically for anything you feel able to offer me. You must give that freely and I must turn into a patient man.

I think of you with every other thought and for a curmudgeonly old bear like me to say that you must know I mean it,
I am, now and always, your Luke Winterley, whether you want me to be or not.

Chloe caught herself staring into thin air and smiling broadly at a mental picture of him as he signed his name at the end of her letter. When she read his words again it all seemed so simple. She could echo her love back at him across the miles between them without a second thought.

'Oh ,I want you all right, Luke Winterley,' she told

the place where he'd signed his name as if it might bring him back all the sooner, 'And I wouldn't love you half so well if you were more charming and less bearlike,' she whispered softly. Then went to make sure her maids were setting about the spring cleaning whilst the master of the house was away, to stop herself from sitting and dreaming the whole day away.

Several days later Luke urged his weary horse onwards and fought his frustration that this was as fast as he could get to Farenze Lodge. He'd had the best horses money could buy under him all the way, but he still wasn't getting there fast enough. It was asking too much of this poor beast and he was weary to the bone, but fear drove him on relentlessly and he'd bid his head groom goodbye when the man had almost fallen from his saddle some time yesterday.

Nearly there, the words seemed to echo in his head with every step, but he still felt as if the devil was on his tail, his rank breath hot on the back of Luke's neck and the chaos of hell at his back. He'd racked his brains all the way south to work out when Chloe's wicked aunt began to watch him with active malice. He hoped he'd outrun the messenger she must have sent south as soon as she realised he was in Scotland to track down a pair of star-crossed young lovers, not to buy one of her husband's precious racehorses, or marry the last unwed Hamming daughter left on her hands.

In the end he'd realised Hamming must have told her about Luke's interest in Lady Daphne Thessaly's tragically early death and he cursed the woman's ability to prise information from her amiable but shallow lord. It wasn't hard to see where Chloe got her brains, but thank heaven she and her sister got their warmth and sweetness from their mother as well as their distant Thessaly ancestress.

His love could say what she liked about bad blood, but everything about her screamed her difference from her father, brother and icy aunt. If Lady Hamming was ever presented with a tiny baby to cast into the world alone or protect with her last breath, she would place it on that frosty church step, then walk away without a second thought.

There, at last, the Lodge was in sight and he asked his tired horse for one last effort as the urgency that brought him south as fast as he could get here needled him. At first glance all seemed serene and hope stirred that he was in time. As he rode into the stable yard and nobody came out to welcome him or take his weary horse, it was clear he was wrong and Lady Hamming was as coldly efficient in getting messages to her disreputable nephews as she was at everything else.

'Take him,' he barked at the stable boy who ran breathlessly into the yard and stood with his mouth open as if he'd forgotten who Luke was. 'Put him in a box and rub him down, then let him rest.'

Weariness forgotten, Luke jumped from the saddle and dashed towards the house, wondering what the hell had happened. He went through the back door and into the kitchen to save all the fuss of rousing Oakham and explaining why he had no luggage and looked more bearlike than ever.

'Ah, here's his lordship at last. Now we can relax and worry about you and your injuries while he sorts everything out, sir,' he heard Chloe say calmly as if she was welcoming a late guest to a party and he felt his temper snap.

'What the devil is going on?' he rapped out as he surveyed the crowd cluttering the kitchen with what he felt was excusable irritation.

'Mr Revereux has been shot,' Eve informed him calmly.

The man's name punched through the haze of weariness dragging at him and he blinked to bring the Adonis wilting on the scrubbed kitchen table into sharp focus.

'Has he now? I've been searching the length and breadth of Britain for the man and find him lying on my kitchen table? Good day to you, Revereux, do make yourself at home, won't you? Perhaps you'd enjoy a few covers and the odd side dish when you're done and the rest of my house and gardens are of course available for your enjoyment when you're not reclining on the kitchen table.'

'I think Papa is tired and hungry. He certainly looks as if he hasn't slept for days,' Eve explained his lack of hospitality with a furious sideways look for him and a sage nod for everyone else. Luke felt as if even her presence might not prevent him swearing long and fluently if someone didn't explain what was going on very soon.

'Of course he is. I dare say he's found out something crucial and travelled here far too fast to inform us of it, so do go and sit by the fire and rest for a moment, my lord.' Chloe finally spared the time to turn from her patient and soothe him, as if he were a dangerous wild dog she was trying to see the best in before he bit someone.

'Yes, I have,' he thundered, quite unappeased. 'I found out he was it,' he said with an accusing gesture at the pale and interesting-looking blond god trying to fight Verity Wheaton off without hurting her. She refused to be diverted with a hardy determination that reminded Luke strongly of her aunt.

'Then you are Verity's father, sir?' The question seemed to tumble out of Chloe's mouth before she could silence it and first she stared at the stranger, then had the gall to glare at *him,* as if he should learn to guard his tongue. Luke felt another check on his temper snap.

'I am,' the pale and interesting hero gently pushed his daughter's hands aside before he sat up to confront Luke with that knowledge, and what a fairer side of his nature told him was excusable pride in his daughter, as well as a challenge in the clear blue eyes Verity had inherited from him.

'My papa is dead,' Verity insisted with a frown nearly as fierce as the one Luke felt pleating his own brows on her face. At that moment he felt a deeper kinship with the bewildered, belligerent girl than ever, even as another man claimed her as his own.

'So some would have you believe,' the man muttered darkly and shot Chloe a look of angry dislike that made Luke's ire boil over like the saucepans he could smell doing the same in the background.

'If you weren't being physicked for that injury and lying on my kitchen table already, I'd knock you down for that,' he bellowed at the prone figure of his latest unwanted guest. 'Lady Chloe gave up everything to keep Verity safe and happy and you lie there and accuse her of usurping your role and scheming to keep the child to herself? You'll meet me for that insult as soon as you've recovered from whatever wound some worthy soul has inflicted on you to teach you some manners before I could do it for him, sirrah.'

'No, he won't,' Chloe said flatly, glaring at him for defending her integrity and he turned a blazing challenge on her instead.

'Why the devil not? He's the idiot who ruined your sister's life.'

'My father and brother did that. He saved her from a marriage that would have been hell on earth and I can't bring myself to think what they might have done to make me miserable if I'd stayed home to be bartered off to some rich roué as well. If Captain Revereux loved my sister even for a week or two, it was more than either of us had from any other human being after our mother died and I'm thankful for it.'

'Thankful to lose your twin sister? To endure what you have done? To be left alone with her in that shack in the hills Peters reports they consigned you to like a pair of unwanted puppies while she waited for her child to be born? Why forgive the sins of everyone in your life who wishes you harm and never mine, when I want only the best for you, woman? Well, I give in, I'll finally accept you don't want what I do and leave you to your happy family reunion while I take myself somewhere I can endure being regarded as a devil in human form more easily,' he said with a hitch in his voice he didn't care to hear at all.

Chapter Seventeen

Turning to stamp out again and ride as far as a fresh horse could carry him this late in the day, Luke stumbled over the doorstep, then righted himself like a drunkard. Just as well he did, considering Chloe rushed into the yard to confront him with her cap sadly awry and her auburn locks tumbling from under it. She would have tripped over him if he had tumbled on to the cobbles.

'Don't you dare say that, then walk away from me, you lubberly great coward,' she spat at him. 'How dare you come home, looking like something the dog didn't want, then snap and rage at the man who saved my daughter from the very men you were supposed to be protecting her from?'

'I suppose he has some excuse for being here.'

'Yes, and I have the good manners to thank him for it, whoever he might be. You challenged him for no good reason that I can see.'

'If you can't see why I would, then I'll leave you to your touching family reunion. The man is clearly everyone's hero but mine and you have no need of me.'

'You're jealous, aren't you?' she asked and gave him

a smug smile that made him squirm, but at least temper made him face her challenge with one of his own.

'Of course I'm not, the man's obviously an idiot.'

'How can even you say so, let alone believe it? My brother hatched a wild plan to abduct Verity, to keep me quiet about his past sins until his wedding was over and the poor girl bedded so it could not be annulled. Captain Revereux foiled it, then rode here with Verity up behind him and a bullet lodged in his arm, until Josiah recovered consciousness after being knocked out and he and Mr Peters rode to the rescue a little too late to be a great deal of use.'

'Then he is clearly your hero and I have nothing to do or say here.'

'And you're going to turn and walk away in a fit of pique? Go out of my life for another ten years...' Words failed her for a moment. 'How could you, you ridiculous, thick-headed, bad-tempered great *idiot*? You wrote me all those wonderful letters; full of love and hope, and let me dream of you loving me back. Now you're going to throw it all away because you're tired and you've lost your temper? Oh, go away then, you stupid great oaf. How could I ever think I loved you? I must be an even bigger fool than you are.'

He stood reeling when she turned on her heel with a huff of impatience and prepared to storm off and leave him there gaping after her like a stranded codfish.

'No, you don't,' he barked as he snapped out of his shocked stupor and grabbed her by the waist to physically stop her walking away from him. 'You're not going anywhere until you've explained yourself,' he told her gruffly.

'I'm not saying anything,' she informed him and tossed her head so the awful cap finally fell off and the sight of her glorious copper-gold locks down her back like hot silk nearly mazed him into slackening his grip and letting her go.

'Good,' he said huskily and snatched a hungry, explicit kiss square on her mouth at the instant she opened it to hurl some new insult at him.

She resisted angrily and a rational, gentlemanly part of him stood aside and tutted as the rest of him deepened the kiss. His grip on her softened, but he had to persuade her to need him back before he dared raise his head and admit she was right and he was a damned fool to even dream of walking away from her and this.

His inner gentleman was about to win the battle and let her go if this wasn't what she wanted desperately as well when she wriggled insistently against him. His heart in his boots, he waited for her to wrench out of his arms, then rage at him and demand he never came within a hundred miles of her ever again. Instead she flung her arms about his neck and held on to him as if she never intended to let him go. Fierce joy sang in his heart even as the appalling weariness of his forced ride threatened to wash over him and send him into a very unmanly faint.

'I missed you so much,' she informed him tearfully as she stood on tiptoes, meeting his tired eyes with a blaze of passion in her own. 'I love you, Luke Winterley, and don't you dare walk away,' she threatened fiercely. 'If you do, I'll walk in the opposite direction and *you'll* have to chase *me*, because I am a Thessaly and I do have some pride,' she told him; all they could be together in her mesmerising gaze.

'Oh, my Chloe, whatever would I do without you?' He breathed and hardly dared blink unless he was imagining the feel and fact of her against him and the wondrous promise she'd just made, in public, in front of rather a lot of witnesses as half his staff were standing in the kitchen doorway grinning like idiots.

'I feel the same about you, you great unshaven, smelly brute of a man,' she murmured, then kissed him as if he was her perfect pattern of a gentleman.

'It might be best if you came back in, Lord Farenze, ma'am,' one of the men Peters had sent to protect Verity interrupted them from the back of the crowd. 'Yon Captain Rever—whoever you said he was—has fainted and the cook's beating the kitchen maid with a soup ladle.'

'Oh the romance of it all,' Luke whispered against Chloe's lips as he forced himself to stop kissing the love of his life and met her laughing eyes instead. 'Life seems to await us in all its rich variety, my darling. Don't forget me whilst you deal with it in your usual inimitable fashion.'

'As if I could, my scruffy, disreputable lord,' she whispered, 'now let me go before I kick you in the shins as I should have done the instant you laid disrespectful hands on me, you great barbarian.'

'Virago,' he replied shakily.

Scandalously hand-locked, they went back into the once spotless and beautifully ordered kitchen and Chloe snapped a series of concise orders. Within minutes the hysterical kitchen maid had been sent to lie down in a darkened attic, Cook was sipping tea in her chair by the fire and looking sheepish while the footmen hauled quantities of water onto the hot plates to hasten the bath Luke knew he needed rather badly.

Eve somehow stopped Verity plucking the feathers out of the head housemaid's best feather duster to burn to revive the patient. Revereux woke from his faint of his own accord and was now insisting on getting down from his undignified perch as if he would never do anything so unmanly.

'Don't be an idiot, man,' Luke urged him roughly as Revereux tried to stand tall and accept the challenge Luke had thrown out in his flash of overwrought temper after finding Verity safe and sound and his mad dash south more or less unnecessary. 'Lady Chloe explained about your rescue of Miss Verity and told me in no uncertain terms that we are all deeply in your debt and I owe you an apology.'

'I was protecting my own,' the man stubbornly insisted, as if he could think of nothing he would like more than a good fight with his uncouth host.

'Shame you weren't about when the child needed you most then, isn't it?' Luke rebuked him grimly and met the man's pained blue eyes, so like Verity's there really was no questioning his claim to be the girl's father.

'Aye,' he replied with a deep sigh and looked easily as weary as Luke felt.

'I am here, you know?' Verity intervened even as Chloe sent Luke a warning glare to inform him he was making things worse for the poor man.

'Something I trust Lord Farenze and his daughter are about to remedy,' Chloe said and Verity looked as if she was about to argue. 'This is not the time for anything other than making sure poor Mr Revereux is made comfortable as he can be with a bullet wound in his shoulder—explanations can come later.'

'I don't know about that, but would you mind finding out how my poor horse does, Miss Verity?' the gentleman asked faintly. The girl still hesitated and Luke's admiration for her courage increased.

'Very well, but please don't think I'm too young or stupid to know what's going on,' she said sternly and managed her exit a great deal more gracefully than the master of the house had done.

As soon as Verity was out of earshot Luke watched Chloe ruthlessly uncover her patient's wound, despite his protests this was too public a space for a gentleman to remove so much of his clothing.

'Pray stop being such a baby,' she ordered the strapping sea captain, who bit his lip, then fainted again while she examined the wound for stray fragments of cloth and lead, then cheerfully pronounced the ball had passed along the fleshy part of the gentleman's upper arm and avoided any major veins or arteries.

She frowned in concentration while doing her best to remove every shred of fine linen threads from his wound then clean it with a solution of what smelt to Luke like rosemary and brandy, before binding it up with a pad soaked in herbs and honey and bandaging it in place.

'It's as well we're still only in March,' he observed as Chloe sat in one of the kitchen chairs with a relieved sigh and accepted a cup of Cook's best tea. 'The poor man would be mobbed with bees and wasps if he set foot outside later in the year.'

'It will stop infection, although Captain Revereux must have the constitution of an ox to manage to ride here from Bath with a wound like that draining him of energy all the way,' she said.

'True, although it would be as well if we wait to get the whole tale out of him before we declare him a hero. He doesn't strike me as being the type to dwell on his good deeds and he is a little late in rescuing his daughter from the wolves,' Luke said, glad he hadn't been called upon to test his limited knowledge of herbs and doctoring in his current state of travel-stained weariness.

'And Mrs Wheaton is quite right, Papa, you really do need a bath,' his own daughter told him with a fastidious wrinkling of her nose at the smell of sweat, road mud and horse so strong on him it almost drowned out the astringent herbs.

'I'm a trial and embarrassment to my womenfolk at the best of times,' he said with an unrepentant smile and went away to remedy it with an energy he'd have thought impossible, before Lady Chloe Thessaly admitted she loved him.

'Why did Lord Farenze call you Lady Chloe when you were arguing, Mama?' Verity asked even as she accepted Chloe's help to don a fresh gown and sat still for her to comb out her tangled mane of wheat-blonde hair.

'Because it's my real name, my love.'

'Then you are the daughter of an earl or marquis or duke?' Verity said as she held Chloe's gaze in the mirror.

'An earl,' Chloe admitted with a sigh.

'The men who tried to make me go with them, then

attacked Mr Revereux, said the Earl would have their hides if they let us escape. What an odd coincidence.'

'I'm afraid not, love,' Chloe admitted, wishing Verity was less intelligent for once.

'He is the same one, then? My own grandfather paid those men to kidnap me and attack anyone who got in their way? What kind of man would do such a thing to his own flesh and blood?'

'The earl who wanted to capture you is your uncle and not my father and I don't really want you to know what kind of man he is now.'

'I want to know why he thinks I would want to live with him when I'd rather be your next scullery maid. He had poor Mr Revereux shot because he stopped those bad men carrying me off.'

Chloe was unsure how much Verity had heard or understood of the arguments in the kitchen, so she took a deep breath and told Verity how she and Daphne grew up together on a rundown estate in Devon. How their father and brothers ignored them until they decided Daphne would net them a fortune as a beautiful and biddable young lady they could sell to the highest bidder. She couldn't describe Daphne's visit to Lady Hamming in Edinburgh because she didn't know about it herself, but she also admitted that her father, the Earl of Crowdale, thought their aunt should introduce his prettiest and most docile twin daughter to Edinburgh society before she married the old man he agreed to sell her to.

'Rumours that my father was in debt were probably flying about London and a London Season is very expensive. My aunt has always doted on her brother and nephews, so they knew she would do as they asked her to at no cost to them.'

'It's a sad story and I feel sorry for Aunt Daphne, but what has she got to do with that man who says he is my father?' Verity asked.

'Well, instead of marrying her to an elderly duke, your grandfather and uncles brought my sister back to Carraway Court in disgrace. They ordered me to pack enough for both of us, because we were going to live in the most remote place they could find since she refused to marry that rich old man. So I packed all I could in the time they gave me and was glad to quit the Court with my father and brothers stamping about there as if every breath we took was costing them dear.

'Our things were bundled into a farm dray and we were taken to meet the stage coach, then thrown off it at the turning leading up to a farmhouse high on Bodmin Moor, where no tenant would stay because it's so isolated you can only walk there or ride a single pony across the moor. It was miles from our nearest neighbours. The roof leaked in places and the wind howled across the moor as if the hounds of hell had been let loose to roam the earth. We were often cold and hungry as summer turned to autumn, then winter, and the local people would leave scraps of firewood and any vegetables they could spare us where our narrow track left the road. They had the kindness our own kin lacked and we might have died of cold and hunger if not for them.'

'Why did they turn on you because Aunt Daphne didn't want to marry some horrid old man, Mama?'

'Because she was with child,' Chloe admitted reluctantly.

'How old were you both then?'

'Seventeen at the turn of the year.'

'Then you must have been the one who was pregnant, Mama, since you had me when you were seventeen.'

'I'm sorry, my love, but your true mother was my twin sister, Lady Daphne Thessaly.'

'Then I'm a bastard,' Verity whispered blankly, the full nuances of that word seeming to hit her like a blow.

'A love child,' Chloe corrected her gently.

'And you lied; you pretended I was your child.'

'I admit there never was a Mr Wheaton, love. I had to make him up, so we could both be respectable and I could keep you with me while I worked to feed and clothe us both. I couldn't let my father take you away after your mother died and there was nobody else to look after you but me.'

'Where was he going to take me, then?' The question was without inflection and Chloe hated to go on with her story when Verity was already so shocked by it.

'Your mother was buried at a tiny church on the Moor where the vicar was a good Christian. I was so glad when my family sent for us so you would be fed and warm. I didn't ask what they intended to do until we were back at Carraway Court and I overheard an argument about which church to leave you at on the way to London.'

'Poor little baby,' Verity said as if talking about someone else.

Chloe longed to take her in her arms, but Verity looked as if the last person she wanted close to her now was the one who had lied to her and everybody else about who they both were for so long.

'I stole every coin I could lay hands on that night and

took what was left of your grandmother's jewellery. I'm sorry, Verity, but I sold it when I got to London and used the money to support us until I managed to get work. I'm a liar and a thief and you must hate me for pretending to be your mother.'

'You could have left me somewhere safe.'

'Abandon my twin sister's beloved child to an orphan asylum? No, I couldn't. I loved my sister dearly, but I already loved you more.'

'If not for me you would have a family of your own by now. Grandfather was too stupid to see how beautiful you are, but some fine gentleman would have married you long ago, if you didn't have me.'

'Nonsense, I was quite content to be the carroty-headed quiz of the family, my love, and I have loved being your mama, even if I am really only your aunt.'

'No, you're truly beautiful, Mama. Oh botheration, I know you're not my mother now, but I can't call you Aunt Chloe after all these years.'

'Then don't, but you do have a father after all, Verity. Until today all I knew about him was he was young and handsome and Daphne loved him, but from all appearances he is quite the hero and seems very ready to own you as his daughter.'

'Mr Revereux?'

'So it seems and the rest of their story is his to tell, since I don't know it and your mother kept him a secret even from me, for some reason best known to herself.'

'Would Grandfather and my uncles have kept me if they knew he was a gentleman?'

The comforting lie trembled on Chloe's lips for a moment, but she bit it back and shook her head. 'I suspect they did know and forced them apart. My father was a cold man and my eldest brother isn't much better. '

'Then I've had a better life than you did, Mama,' Verity astonished Chloe by saying practically. 'Lady Virginia loved us and I had you. I much prefer being me to living the kind of life you two had to at my age.'

'It wasn't so bad, our mother's aunts descended on us every summer to make sure we didn't grow into a pair of savages.'

'So you two ran wild, yet I endure algebra, logic and geography?'

'Such are the injustices of life.'

'You and Lord Farenze could have married years ago if you weren't Mrs Wheaton for my sake. That's an injustice and a shame if you ask me.'

'Since his lordship doesn't go into society and I can't see my father paying for me to come out even if he did, it's highly unlikely we would have met in my true guise, darling.'

'He has met you, though, and I think he loves you, Mama.'

'And I love him back, Verity,' Chloe admitted quite calmly now it was out in the open.

At times, she reflected, she could wish her precocious niece was a little less perceptive about the adults around her. It was probably because Verity had spent so much time with Virginia that she saw through social pretence. In a few years' time the beaux of the *ton* would need to watch out when Miss Verity Revereux-Thessaly was launched into their rarefied world.

'You two are going to get married like Lady Virginia

and *her* Viscount Farenze did, are you not?' she asked bluntly now.

'Lady Virginia was fabulously beautiful in her youth.'

'And so are you. Eve and I think this Lord Farenze loves you easily as much as the last one loved Lady Virginia,' Verity persisted stubbornly.

'I have had to work for my living, Verity. He really shouldn't wed a housekeeper.'

'He can do as he likes and I think you can, too, if you want to badly enough.'

'And I think you need your dinner sent up and a good night's sleep after all your adventures today, young lady,' Chloe said as Verity's eyelids began to droop. 'Why not climb into bed and I'll see if I can persuade Cook to send up a tray for you just this once.'

'I'm not ill.'

'Maybe not, but you've had a busy day, even by your standards. It won't hurt if you play the young lady and lie abed until noon if you choose to tomorrow either.'

'But I *am* a young lady, if all you have told me is true and my father intends to own me as his daughter.'

'Indeed, Captain Revereux seems the very model of a heroic gentleman,' Chloe said and managed to hide a nasty little stab of jealousy. Heroic and handsome Captain Revereux would soon win his daughter's admiration and love and where would that leave Lady Chloe Thessaly?

'I still like Lord Farenze best, though. He will never let anyone hurt me if he's my stepfather,' Verity argued sleepily and Chloe was glad the under-housemaid knocked at the door with the tray Cook had sent without waiting for an order.

She let her niece finish her soup and a syllabub, then sit up fighting sleep, as she had to let it all go down before she could curl into her warmed bed with a guard set before the fire and a weary sigh of relief.

'I'll stay with her, you're needed elsewhere tonight,' Brandy said, as she swept into the room with a bland smile while Chloe wondered if she should stay in case Verity had nightmares after such a day.

'Give me time to make certain all's well and Miss Thibett has been told Verity's safe and I'll be back to sit with her myself,' Chloe whispered and Bran shook her head and shooed her away like a farmer's wife chasing hens from her kitchen.

Chapter Eighteen

'Managing female,' Chloe muttered as she stood outside Verity's room, glaring at the blank and highly polished closed door.

'It takes one to know one,' Luke grumbled as he rose from his seat just along the corridor, then tugged her further away so they wouldn't disturb Verity.

'You think I'm overbearing, then?' she asked absently. It was wonderful to feel all that warmth and strength and maleness so close again.

'Of course I do, love. It's been your job for the past decade or more to be a managing female. You wouldn't be much good as a housekeeper if you weren't a little overbearing at times, now would you?'

He understood her and still wanted to spend his life with her. It was odd and unaccountable, but it felt dazzling to know that stubborn, clever, complicated Luke Winterley was indeed the wild lover of young Chloe's dreams, as well as his slightly gruff, everyday self to make it all real and possible.

'You don't mind that I'll never be able to turn myself into a meek and biddable little wife if you marry me, then?'

'I'd be deeply disappointed if you did, my fiery, short-tempered love. Does that mean you're thinking of saying yes to me at long last?'

'I refuse to discuss it when you're weary half to death and should probably be in bed instead of prowling about the place like a restless wolf. You clearly rode south so fast you nigh killed yourself and the poor horses you rode along the way.'

'My bed here never holds much attraction without you in it, Chloe, but I can't tell you how often I have wished for a faster way to get to you these last few days.'

'Or how many times I wished you were here,' she told him with promises of all they would be heady between them. 'How is the patient?' she asked absently, doing her best to tear her fascinated gaze from his smoky dark one in the dim light at the top of the stairs to the nursery wing they hadn't got round to descending yet.

'Revereux refuses to sleep. Unless we convince him Verity's quite safe until he can guard her like a mastiff with a bone again, he'll be running a high fever by morning.'

'Exasperating man,' Chloe said, fear that the Captain would insist on claiming his daughter still haunting her like a bad dream.

'As you have accused me of being one of those so often, I hope you don't expect me to condemn him for it. You do know Virginia's elder sister wed a Revereux though, don't you, my love?' Luke asked gently.

'I thought his name sounded familiar. Then I'm surprised he hasn't visited whilst I've been here, although

I'm very glad he didn't. It would be hard to deny my daughter is related to him now I've seen the strong resemblance between them. Do you really think Virginia knew who she might be and didn't tell me, Luke?'

'I doubt it. Can you see my darling great-aunt resisting such a wonderful chance to interfere in so many lives if she did?'

'Not really—it does seem an odd coincidence, though.'

'They do happen and Virginia and her eldest sister never did get on. Lady Revereux was rigidly respectable and even I have to admit Virginia was outrageous in her youth. Virgil was no saint either and I doubt the stiff-necked old stickler approved of their marriage. The current earl is a downright prig, so we'll have to wait and see if this fellow takes after him or has a bit of humanity in him to leaven all the Revereux starch he's probably inherited. Until we know how Revereux found Verity we won't know if Virginia knew or not, though, so we'd better keep the man alive for now.'

'Don't even joke about it, Luke,' Chloe replied with a shudder at the thought of Verity losing her father as soon as he'd found her.

'It was in poor taste, but what do you expect from a barbarian? It'll be your job to civilise me.'

'Maybe I like you as you are,' she said with a witchy smile.

'Hell cat,' he responded with a hot glitter of masculine interest in his eyes she'd thought he was too weary to feel after his epic journey south.

'Wolf,' she countered huskily, all the temptations of loving him fully running like a hot tide through her heart and mind.

'Mr Revereux refuses to take the potion the doctor left for him,' Culdrose interrupted them from the bottom of the next flight of stairs and Chloe stared down at the ladies' maid blankly for a moment.

It was a timely reminder there were other things to do than find Luke Winterley's faults fascinating and his wonderful qualities even more unique than she'd realised.

'It's quite like old times for Culdrose, I suppose,' she informed the patient crossly when she entered his bedchamber with Luke sauntering in her wake and openly enjoying the view.

'Why so, ma'am?' the patient asked with an impatient frown.

'Our late employer was every inch as stubborn as you are proving to be.'

'Sensible woman,' he muttered glumly.

'There are those who would argue, but did you never meet the lady yourself, sir, related to her as Lord Farenze believes you to be?' Chloe couldn't help asking.

'Only as a boy and I've been at sea since I was thirteen with very little leave spent in this country. I recall her telling me then that she might like me better if I didn't have such a high opinion of myself. She said if Bonaparte was to be defeated by vain boys I would be an admiral before I was thirty.'

'That sounds very like her, I should try not take it too much to heart, sir.'

'It's very difficult to remain a spoilt brat as a midshipman in the senior service, your ladyship,' he admitted with a rueful smile that tempted Chloe to like him more than she wanted to.

'Then why not take your medicine and prove it, Mr Revereux?'

'Slyly done, Lady Chloe, but if those rogues could get so close to abducting Verity in Bath, how can I risk fogging my wits when she's in the middle of an isolated country estate miles away from authority?'

'Because I know how to protect my own, Revereux,' Luke stepped forward to tell him and there was enough challenge in his deep voice to tell the man he was on shaky ground. 'Our enemies are now too busy avoiding their creditors to bother scheming against us.'

'Foreclosed, have you?' Revereux asked as if he understood the true facts of the matter far better than Chloe did.

'This very morning a friend of mine delivered a detailed account of Crowdale's past sins to the City merchant who almost let him wed his only child.'

'Heaven knows, they're heavy enough,' the Captain said with a restless movement against his pillows, then a quickly suppressed gasp at the pain it caused him that made Chloe flinch in sympathy.

'Heavy enough to finish him in this country; he'll have to flee if he's to avoid being imprisoned for debt, as well as various sins we won't broadcast for the sake of Lady Chloe and your daughter. '

'Since we're being so protective of my sensibilities, why don't you take this draught, sir, before I succumb to hysterics after such a long and trying day?' Chloe asked, glaring at both men as she tried to understand their veiled references.

'You don't fight fair, do you, Lady Chloe?' the patient asked with a wry smile that made her see why Daphne fell so deep in love with him.

'How can I when there are so many unfair advantages on the other side, sir? Gentlemen have a monopoly on dashing about the country engaged on adventures you refuse to explain to us dim-witted females. If I can wait until tomorrow to find out the facts of my sister's tragic love story, you can sleep and recover from your injuries and show a little patience as well. Verity and I wait on the whims of annoying males who feel they have a right to dictate our lives without asking us.'

'I feel sure half that tirade was directed at me, Revereux. It would be diplomatic to restore your strength before she takes you on again though,' Luke cautioned.

'And you'll swear to me my daughter is safe?' he asked with such painful anxiety that Chloe softened a little and even smiled when he directed his question at her, instead of dominant, masculine Viscount Farenze.

'I kept her so when nobody else cared a tinker's curse what happened to her, Mr Revereux, I will do so for as long as she needs me to,' she promised.

'Very well, do your worst then,' he murmured grudgingly and finally allowed himself to feel wretched.

Chloe nodded at the waiting Culdrose, who managed to tip a healthy dose down the gentleman's throat when he opened his mouth to argue he'd do it himself.

'No better than a stubborn babe,' Culdrose muttered grimly.

'Nor much more use than one right now,' he admitted wearily.

'Then you'll sleep like one if you know what's good for you,' Culdrose told him severely and sat in the chair by the bed as if settling in for the night to make sure he did as he was bid.

'I think we can safely leave her to it,' Luke whispered as he urged Chloe out of the room. 'The poor fellow doesn't stand a chance of stirring from that bed until he's healthy as a horse once again.'

'Would she could keep him there,' Chloe murmured and met his steady gaze with a shrug. 'I know, he's Verity's father. What if he wants to take her away, Luke?'

'We're still at war, Chloe, and I doubt he could leave the sea right now even if he wanted to. Verity has a perfectly good family to love and care for her and, in his shoes, I wouldn't even try to prise the child away from a woman she has no intention of being parted from.'

'Thank you for being ready to take us both on then, but I can't pretend he doesn't exist, can I?'

'Hardly, but come downstairs and dine with me, my darling. If I manage to stay awake long enough, we can talk about where we shall live and love and, if we're lucky, raise the rest of our vast tribe of children yet to be born.'

'I haven't officially agreed to marry you yet.'

'Then you'd better do so, Lady Chloe Thessaly. I've waited long enough to be your lover and refuse to be gainsaid much longer.'

'You're too tired to make love to Venus herself, if she bothered to step down from Olympus for such a disagreeable bear as you are tonight,' she told him as he took her hand and tucked it into the crook of his elbow. 'But I'm saying yes anyway,' she added.

'Good, I've waited over a decade for one of those from you, Mrs Wheaton. I intend to hear you say it again and again as soon as I've got my ring on your finger.'

'Not before then?' she asked, all her scruples forgotten as she stared up at him with a scandalous invitation in her eyes.

'In three days if I can get a licence quickly enough, lover,' he said implacably.

'You're turning into a puritan,' she said sulkily, rather insulted he could resist her now their marriage was so close. 'Three *days*?' she asked incredulously as that part of his statement finally got past the heady promises of their marriage bed.

'Our courtship has been quite long enough, we can marry as soon as you've found a gown that isn't made up from black bombazine.'

'I have a very nice grey-stuff gown for best,' she told him solemnly, running through an inventory of all the gowns unsuitable for a housekeeper Lady Virginia had pressed on her over the years in her head and selecting the most unsuitable of all.

Luke did his best to hide his horror at the idea of meeting her at the altar dressed so and Chloe laughed, then met his tired eyes with a teasing smile.

'It's all right, love, the neighbours will be shocked when they see me walk up the aisle in the splendid white ball gown Virginia gave me for my last birthday. As they will already be reeling at the secrets we will have to reveal about my past, present and future by then, I suppose we might as well give them something else to wonder about.'

'True. How do you feel about being the focus of gossip for miles around, my lady?' he asked as Oakham opened the door of the Green Parlour the family used before dinner when not entertaining.

'Indifferent on my own account, but a little worried about how it will affect Verity and Eve,' she replied, then Eve and her governess greeted them with a flurry of questions about the Captain and Verity and even that concern was laid aside for another day.

It took Captain Revereux two days to evade his nurse and make his way downstairs without Culdrose knowing he'd gone. Luke found him ensconced in the family sitting room before dinner and began to dislike him all over again. Eve was busy finding cushions to make the chair by the fire where Luke usually sat more comfortable for the interloper and Chloe was ordering a feast fit for a king in honour of his recovery.

Trying hard to be fair, Luke could see why an impressionable young girl like Daphne Thessaly would fall so hard for the young Adonis Revereux must have been, but couldn't quite suppress a sting of jealousy when Chloe fussed over the man as if he were a fallen god. He felt much better when Revereux fidgeted uncomfortably at so much feminine attention, then wondered if he might even learn to like him one day when the man called a halt.

'I am very well now and have always healed quickly,' Revereux said, so they sat and wondered who would ask the rush of questions they all wanted answers to, but felt too polite to launch straight into as soon as the man was feeling well enough to come downstairs again.

'When does your ship sail, Revereux?' Luke asked, as genially as he could when he was trying not to wish it might be tomorrow.

'In three weeks' time,' the Captain said with a frown

and Luke felt a twinge of guilt at reminding a guest he would soon have to depart, but only a twinge. He was feeling very impatient to get on with his wedding. 'She's been in dry dock for a refit, then I am to get her back for sea trials in a fortnight and, all being as it should be, we will embark a week later.'

'And where will you be bound, Captain?' Chloe asked, looking relieved he would shortly be out of the country, but Luke knew they would have to resolve Verity's future before the man left.

'I'll be sailing under sealed orders, Lady Chloe, so I really don't know.'

'How exciting,' Eve said with stars in her eyes, as if she dreamt of sailing the seven seas in a state of constant adventure and upheaval.

'Not really,' Revereux argued with an indifference to the idea Luke must remember to thank him for later. 'Apart from the danger and upset of a storm and the rush and alarm of battle, life at sea is sadly tedious and the men dread serving on the Caribbean station because of the yellow fever and the like. I hope we're not bound there, Miss Winterley, for I can't like the place for all its warmth and natural beauty.'

'Is it so beautiful, then?'

'Aye, and rich and devilish hot at times and the sugar plantations are worked by unlucky slaves I don't blame in the least for feeling rebellious and running away whenever they get the chance.'

'Oh,' Eve said, looking a little downcast. 'I'm sure I should as well and I'm very glad Papa has no business interests there after all. Will you not tell us how you found out about Verity and tracked her down and rescued her from her wicked uncles though, Mr Revereux? It sounds a very dashing tale and quite fit for one of Mrs Radcliffe's novels.'

'I dare say it was nothing of the sort and anyway it is a story that can wait, love, if the Captain wants to tell his private affairs to such a curious miss at all, that is,' Luke intervened before the poor man felt obliged to recount his ill-fated love story between entrées.

'Indeed, and dining *en famille* is a treat that can easily be withdrawn from young ladies not yet out.' Chloe reinforced his warning with a stern eye on Verity and both girls rolled their eyes at the unreasonable nature of parents, then behaved like a pair of unlikely angels.

'Would you like to take a brandy or shall we join the ladies and be sociable over the teacups, Revereux?' Luke asked at the end of the meal and thought he saw the man pale at the idea of returning to Culdrose's stern rule before he had to.

'I'd best avoid brandy for the time being. I don't want to risk lurching about like a drunkard until I've got my land legs again.'

'Then I'll bring my glass to the drawing room, if you ladies don't object?'

'I think we might bear that much dissipation calmly enough,' Chloe said.

Luke grinned, knowing he'd never find her company tedious if they lived to be a hundred, when she gave him a look that warned him she knew he was up to something and was in two minds about putting a stop to it.

At last Oakham and his acolytes were dismissed and Miss Yorke, Eve's governess, excused herself to write to her elderly parents. It was very close to Verity's bed time, but Luke was glad Chloe didn't send her away. This tale needed to be told and arrangements about her contact with her father and where she would live made before the man went back to sea.

'I think the time has come to tell your story, Revereux. I hope you won't mind doing so in front of Eve and myself, since I'll soon be Verity's uncle by marriage?'

'Neatly put,' Revereux said with a challenging look in those sharp blue eyes of his that said he would be no pushover if his ideas didn't chime with theirs.

'Why, thank you,' Luke said with an ironic bow.

'I will try to emulate you,' Revereux said with a sigh, then watched the fire and seemed to be staring into a past full of mixed blessings. 'I took a bullet in my side at the Battle of the Nile. I was eventually given shore leave to recuperate with my maternal grandfather, a minister of the Scottish church, since even the Admiralty decided they didn't want me back until I had some flesh on my bones.'

'Your poor mother must have been beside herself with worry,' Chloe said.

'She has one son in the navy and two in the army and often says the one who gives her the most worry is my brother Henry, who stayed at home and followed in his grandfather's footsteps. A practical female, my darling mother,' he said with a rueful smile that said a lot about his affection for her.

'I hope we'll have the chance to meet her one day,' Luke put in, to remind them time was wasting and Cully would be down to bear her patient off to bed again very soon.

'So do I, but to return to my tale, I was feeling better and growing restless and bored, as young fools of eighteen often do when they don't have enough to do. Then, one day I met a young lady walking the hills on her own and sadly lost. Not that she minded being so, she told me, since as she didn't know where she was, she hoped nobody else would either. When I pointed out that I now knew, she had a fit of the giggles and admitted I was right. I fell in love with her on the spot.' Revereux smiled broadly at nothing at all and even Luke couldn't help but sympathise.

If only he was heart-whole and still innocent when he'd first laid eyes on Lady Daphne's sister, he'd have done exactly the same. Deep down he probably had, he realised now, then refused to admit it to either of them for a whole decade; which made him more of a fool than Revereux, so he could hardly blame him for diving head first into love with a very different Thessaly twin.

'After that she used to get lost whenever her aunt took her eyes off her long enough for her to get away from Hamming House and I haunted the hills and moors around my grandfather's manse like a lost soul, hoping she would and I could meet up with her. Apparently her aunt had a splendid marriage planned for her and the vast settlements on offer that would set her family back on the road to riches. Daphne told me most of her family could go hang, but she was worried about what would happen to you when we wed and frustrated their whole rotten scheme, Lady Chloe. Her only regret was that our marriage would part her from you.'

'You were married?' Chloe said incredulously.

'I loved her far too much to risk leaving her unwed

and with child once I was considered fit for service again and sent back to sea.'

'Then how did she end up in that state and alone anyway?' she demanded fiercely.

Luke thought her magnificent as she defended her sister ten years after her death. Looking away to distract himself from the heady thought of the day after tomorrow he'd been forced to compromise on for their wedding, Luke saw his daughter and Verity were listening to Revereux's tale of star-crossed lovers with round-eyed fascination. Perhaps he should send them to bed? No, the last thing he wanted was either of them thinking a runaway marriage sounded deeply romantic, so far better for them to stay and realise the pain and sorrow that impulsive wedding had caused Lady Daphne and her impulsive young lover, as well as Verity and Chloe.

'I didn't know she had done so until I cornered your younger brother one night when he had drunk nearly enough brandy to sink a man o' war and threatened to beat the story out of him if he didn't tell it of his own accord.' He paused and sent his daughter and Eve a dubious look and obviously reached the same conclusion Luke had done and decided they ought to hear the sad end of his grand love affair after all. 'I owed him that much for standing by while his brother and the thugs he'd hired beat me within a hair's breadth of my life, then had me carried south and put aboard the next ship leaving for the East Indies.

'Imagine how I felt when I finally came back to my full senses and found out I was halfway to Java with the captain and all the ship's company to convince I was who I said I was, not some poor pressed fool who'd been in the wrong place at the wrong time. They couldn't have turned about and taken me back to my wife even if they had wanted to and I was lucky to have ended up on a good ship. The ship's surgeon treated my new wounds as well as the ones I'd nearly recovered from until the attack and the captain didn't have me shut in the brig for insubordination, or dropped off at the first port as a lunatic. I raged and resisted, but had to accept my fate and serve out my time until the ship sailed for home three years later.'

'Oh, you poor man,' Chloe said sadly.

She looked torn between pity and reluctance to let him off all blame for her sister's sorry plight. Luke's heart went out to her, but she had to accept Verity now had a father who deserved some say in his child's future. He waited for Revereux to finish his story and trusted Chloe to reach the same conclusion.

'Never mind me, Daphne suffered a fate I wouldn't inflict on a dog,' Revereux said, clenching his fists as he had to fight his still-raw feelings for his lost love. 'You know more of that than I do, Lady Chloe. I was a thousand miles away by the time the poor darling bore my child in that apology for a house your father and brothers sent you both to endure, as if that whole greedy scheme was your fault and not theirs.'

'Why did they do so when you were married?' she mused now, puzzlement and pain so dark in her violet eyes that Luke took her hand to show her she wasn't alone with it this time.

'Probably because we were wed, not despite it,' Revereux said gently and waited for her to realise what he couldn't say in front of the girls.

Unwed Daphne would still be young, lovely and sale-able, if shop-soiled; wed she was none of those things and had frustrated them of the fortune the raddled old duke was willing to pay for a virginal wife. Daphne had been meant to die and her baby along with her.

'No! Oh, Luke,' Chloe gasped as that fact finally bit deep.

Chapter Nineteen

'What happened when I was born?' Verity demanded and there was a wobble of uncertainty in her voice that made Chloe drag Luke in her wake as she rushed to Verity's side to cup her chin in her other hand, then smooth her hair and force her to meet her eyes.

'It doesn't matter, my love, you survived and I loved you from the moment you dropped into my arms screaming at the top of your voice. You were so perfect and so very much your own person, how could I help but love you?'

'I love you too, Mama, but I killed my real mother, didn't I?'

'No, darling, never think that. Your grandfather and uncles did that by abandoning us with not enough to eat and no money to pay for firewood or a doctor when her time came, but she never complained as I did while she waited for you to be born and we scratched a living from the vegetable patch and even resorted to poaching now and again, as well as foraging on the moor for whatever we could catch. She loved you so much she would have endured far worse to see you safe and healthy. Daphne loved you before you were born and I took over when she had to leave you, love. I'm a far better person than I would be if I'd gone on my merry way without you.'

'And when Lady Chloe Thessaly decides to love someone, they stay loved—like it or not,' Luke added with a wry smile.

'Even after ten years of stony silence and gruff discouragement to do anything of the sort from certain viscounts I could mention,' Chloe sniped.

'Even then,' he confirmed.

'You're a lucky man, Farenze,' Captain Revereux told him wistfully.

'Luckier than I deserve.'

'That's what Aunt Virginia said the last time I saw her, Papa. She said you were a lot luckier in love than you would admit of your own accord. I told her I wished you would find a viscountess before I came out, to distract you from growling at any man who looked at me like a bear who hadn't had enough for dinner,' Eve said.

'Did she now? And did you?'

'We did, and at least now I know that Lady Chloe will stop you making a laughing-stock of me when I make my début.'

'Oh, the joys of fatherhood,' Revereux said with a set look that told Luke and Chloe he was feeling low and wistful about all he'd lost.

'Just you wait until this young lady makes her come out before you dare to be smug about my coming ordeal then, Revereux,' Luke warned him.

'I believe I should like to have a father as well, if you

don't mind me staying with Mama and Uncle Luke most of the time,' Verity said earnestly and Chloe looked as if she was about to cry as she watched them assess the sore spots in this new world of theirs and find a way forward, even if it did feel strange and new.

'I don't think I would mind that at all,' Revereux replied huskily.

'Well, that's settled then,' Eve pronounced and nobody argued.

'Can you bear to part with Verity when Revereux is ashore, love?' Luke asked Chloe when the girls and the invalid were escorted to bed by their mentors and the two of them sat by the fire in the library before parting reluctantly for the night.

'Somehow I shall make myself do so,' she replied, staring into the fire to revel in the love, excitement and security of being held in Luke's mighty arms and dreaming about sharing all she was with him so soon now it was almost in reach.

'Verity will always need you, Chloe,' his deep voice rumbled and she felt the resonance of it as her heartbeat raced at such heady proximity.

'Maybe by the time he is home again she will have a cousin to keep me from fretting myself to flinders about their big sister,' she added, smiling at the thought of a solemn little boy or girl with Luke's complicated grey eyes wondering at the world in her arms. 'It really is hard work trying to sort out all these relationships, isn't it?'

'All that matters is that we love them, but do you

think the world is quite ready for another violet-eyed temptress or some mule-headed boy in our image?'

'I do, if you agree to take equal blame, but what if I can't give you children, Luke?' she asked him with the thought of Virginia and Virgil's great love affair, without children to make it complete, heavy on her mind.

'Then we will have to trust James weds a bride with more sense than him, then gives him a tribe of brats. Don't look like that, love, it didn't matter to Virgil and Virginia that they couldn't have a family, as they made one anyway. Mantaigne lived here as a boy and James and I spent our summers with them by rote, since my stepmama couldn't refuse to let Virginia and Virgil have my brother when she wished so badly he was the heir. She wouldn't allow us to come here together though; we might have learnt to like each other and she hoped I'd cock up my toes so he could inherit, so that would never do.'

'She has a cold and calculating heart,' Chloe said and turned to stare up at the wonderful man who'd taken to hiding his vulnerability behind apparent coldness and self-control far too young.

'I was better off on the wrong side of her than James was on the right one,' he said with a bittersweet smile.

'Promise me you won't wed a harridan if anything happens to me,' she said as she had to suppress a shiver, despite the warmth and temptation of him at her back and the glowing blaze in the fireplace to fend off the chill of an early March evening.

'Promise *me* nothing will, then,' he replied with a full-blown shudder she had to find flattering as he pulled her closer and dared the devil to take her away from him.

'You know I can't do that, but I will promise to love you with everything I am and will be for the rest of my life, Luke,' she said, all the love and delight she had in him in her eyes and the hope he could believe he was finally loved as he'd always deserved to be in her heart.

He kissed her deeply and passionately to prove it was mutual and her inner rebel hoped she'd finally broken his silly, gallant notion of waiting another two more interminable nights to make love to her. Unlucky for her that his will-power was as formidable now as it had been for the last decade then; he put a little distance between them and rasped a few deep, shaky breaths as he imposed that dratted iron control of his once more.

'Spoilsport,' she muttered darkly.

'Serpent,' he retaliated.

'Charming,' she sniped back, but the euphoria of finding her viscount had a wild, tender passion for her under all that aloofness of his made her constantly feel about to dance on air. 'I do love you, Luke,' she told him, unable to help herself, despite the drag of wanting and curiosity he'd roused in her once again, and left gnawing at her innards like some bittersweet wild fire.

'A shame it took you ten years to work that out,' he said with his unique Luke smile that sparked her to argue, mainly because he liked arguing with her almost as much as he did making love with her and just now he wasn't allowing them that alternative.

'You're the slow-top, not me,' she accused him.

'I am indeed—how else could I have thought of Pamela when I looked at you and wanted you so much it hurt all this time?' he admitted with a sad shake of his dark head that made tears pool at the back of her eyes, despite her euphoria that they were almost man and wife. This endless waiting really was playing havoc with her emotions, she decided, frowning at the flash of jealousy that streaked through her before she told herself not to be ridiculous

'You have truly forgotten her now though, haven't you?' she asked and held her breath for the answer, full of hope, but doubting any man could put such a betrayal behind him and truly trust again.

'She was a young man's nightmare, Chloe. Hearing about the one Revereux lived through tonight, mine seems a far lesser one. I got my lovely Eve and he endured tragedy and disappointment, then missed the first ten years of his daughter's life into the bargain. I'm a very lucky man, my darling. In two days' time I'll be far luckier than I ever deserved to be.'

'Now there, my Lord Farenze, I beg to differ,' Chloe breathed as she moved so she was kneeling on the *chaise* and could look down into his wonderfully complex gaze. 'You, my lord, deserve to wed a wife who will adore you, want you and live with you in glorious disharmony for the rest of your days. That's just as well, since that's exactly what you're going to get when I finally get you up the aisle.'

'Before God, I truly am a lucky man then,' he said and, if there was suspicious hint of moisture in his beloved grey eyes, she couldn't bring herself to tease him about it when tears threatened to flood her own and this was definitely not a time for crying.

* * *

'Virginia worked a happy ending to your tale then, despite your best efforts to be miserable, Lucius, old friend,' Lord Mantaigne drawled, as if the last months were a play that had been put on by his late godmother to keep him amused and stop him missing her quite so badly.

'No need for you to be so smug about it, you could be her next victim for all we know,' Luke said equably.

'Or me,' James said gloomily.

'Well, it certainly won't be me,' Captain Revereux put in with a grin at the younger of Chloe's two brides-maids. Verity returned his smile with a confidence Chloe told herself she had to be pleased about.

'I wish Virginia could have been here to see us marry though, Luke,' Chloe whispered as they toasted each other again and all she tasted was his quick, hard kiss on her delighted mouth. 'She would have been so happy today.'

'I'm sure she would.'

'Virginia knew we couldn't stay master and house-keeper for long if she managed to trap us under the same roof for more than the day or so you had allowed us up until then,' Chloe said confidently, sure now that was what her late mistress and best friend had intended all along.

'I like being your husband even better than I did being your impatient master, my lady,' he murmured wickedly for her ear only.

'And being your wife promises to better being your impatient servant, my lord.'

Luke groaned and whispered something very incendiary indeed that brought a rosy blush to the new Viscountess Farenze's cheeks and set her plotting to escape the company of their innocent daughters, before all restraint between them was finally cindered into ashes at long last.

Chapter Twenty

'I love you, Luke. So very much,' Chloe said in a shaky voice, stirring at last as the fog of bliss brought on by becoming Luke's wife in every sense of the word dissipated enough to allow her sufficient spare breath to speak.

'Good, it took you long enough to realise my sterling worth and agreeable temper was exactly what you needed to make your life complete,' he joked, with an echo of her own wonder in his eyes.

'Pompous idiot,' she said with a wifely look he seemed to find fascinating.

'Wife,' he murmured huskily, fascinated by a curl of red-gold hair trailing across her bare shoulder. He tested that word again on is tongue. 'My wife,' he murmured and she opened heavy-lidded eyes a little wider to take him in, naked as Adam and insufferably complacent about life as he currently appeared, and she sighed with contentment.

'What is it?' she asked sleepily.

'*You* are my wife,' he informed her as he kissed the disordered tumble of her wildfire hair over that satin-smooth shoulder, then eyed her as if tempted to work his way downwards and catch her in the sensual web he'd woven round so effectively last night once more. 'Lady Chloe Winterley is *my* wife,' he added, gloating over the fact of her as she stretched her sleek and very bare body luxuriously against his own naked form. 'My lawfully wedded wife,' he added for good measure.

'I think we have already established that fact,' she murmured, still half-asleep, but very willing to wake up to a new and very alert husband in her bed.

'Not to my complete satisfaction we haven't,' he argued, even as the gallant impulse to leave his new-made wife to recover from his amorous attentions seemed to fly out of the window and she put all the provocation she'd stored up over a decade into kissing her one true love back. 'I *love* you,' he distracted himself by saying as soon as he could. 'I love *you*, my Lady Chloe.'

'You haven't leapt out of bed and downed a pipe of port or a cellar full of brandy while I was asleep, have you, Luke? You sound drunk, even if you don't taste it,' she observed with a self-satisfied smile he took very personally indeed.

'I'm only drunk on you, love. Merry as a grig on my first taste of housekeeper and *very* personal companion,' he informed her with a smile that truly freed the wolf in him for the first time in ten years and, oh, but that wolf was *hungry*.

'I like the sound of being employed so intimately by my Lord Farenze—do you think he'll make a hard-working female like me a good master?' she whispered and let her hand wander towards a very rampant piece of evidence he would be a very attentive one, if this newest

Lady Farenze ever acknowledged any man her master and they both knew that was very unlikely.

'I know Mrs Wheaton drove him nigh mad with need of her every time he laid eyes on the impertinent female. Shall we see if he can return the compliment?' he whispered in her ear as he taught her the erotic potential of that delicately made organ with his busy tongue. She surprised a groan of delight out of him when she retaliated by exploring his manhood with a delicately curious fingertip.

'Mrs Wheaton wanted you back, Luke; she wanted back you so badly that she used to pace her room at night for the pent-up frustration of wanting you in her bed and not being able to have you there. She cried herself to sleep with missing you more times than she wants to remember right now, poor lonely, lovesick female as she was. I longed for you with every fibre of my being, when I was so young I couldn't imagine how anyone could want a man so much and not have him and for a whole decade after that. On nights when you slept under Lady Virginia's roof for one night, or even a slightly less miserly two of them, I shook with need in my lonely bed and wept for all we could never have.'

'And I had to leave after a few nights because I couldn't sleep for longing for my great-aunt's housekeeper in *my* bed. I wanted you so much I ached with it every time I was within thirty miles of the Lodge and you, Chloe. I had to stay away. There was no other way for me *not* to have you. You had a child to bring up alone and you were my great-aunt's housekeeper and another man's widow. How could I stay when you would have ended up my mistress and I knew that was less than you ought to be?'

'If I'd known you wanted me back like that, I don't suppose I'd have been able to stay away,' she confessed with a blush beyond the rosy flush of need already spread across her cheeks and down to places where she hadn't known she could blush until last night. 'Even for Verity's sake, I couldn't have stayed away if I'd known you wanted me as much in return, Luke,' she said and abandoned teasing for a moment to stare into his eyes with her heart in her own. 'I love you, you great gruff, noble idiot,' she said with wet eyes and a shaky smile. 'I love you so much I won't be able to pretend I married you because you were obliged to right Lady Chloe in the eyes of the world. I can't counterfeit polite indifference and yawn my way through the odd evening when we happen to have no engagements if we spend a Season in London. If you don't want me to give away the fact I feel as if half of me is missing whenever you're not near; that I long for you so deeply that the world is less shining and wonderful when we're apart, then you'll just have to leave me behind. In Somerset or Northumberland I can be Lord Farenze's besotted wife, who thinks about you every moment of her day, but you and Eve will have to leave me there while you go to London if you want to be fashionably indifferent to me in public, Luke.'

She reared up and dragged the bedclothes with her, since it was still only March and not even love could keep them warm when the fire had gone out hours ago and the chill of an early spring morning pervaded this splendid old bedchamber. Chloe propped herself above him as he lay prone against the bank of down pillows covered in fine and snowy linen and forgot what she had been going to say next in her fascination with watching him, her husband of a day.

'So dark,' she whispered as she swept a fingertip along the stern arch of his brow. 'So determined…' she lingered over the hard firmness of his jaw. 'So tempting,' she gasped as his lips parted to nibble that fingertip and his grey eyes heated to silver and steel and a hard flush of need swept over his cheekbones.

'So yours,' he rasped with such love in that dear gaze of his that she moaned in sheer awe. 'So ready to let the wide world know I love my wife, will always love her and have loved her for far too long in silence to ever be quiet about it again. Now I have my ring on your finger and you in my bed for the rest of our natural lives, I shall never be able to pretend I'm not fathoms deep in love with you. We won't be walking in Virginia and Virgil's footsteps, my darling. We've got our own road to travel, but I want the world to know we're every bit as besotted with each other as they were and intend to be so for as long as we live. Polite society will just have to accustom itself to that fact or keep away, wherever we are.'

'It sounds wondrous,' she told him with a dreamy smile.

'It will be,' he promised as solemnly as he had the day before, when they stood in front of the altar and made their vows before God.

'Well, that's all right then,' Lady Farenze informed her enthralled lord, then blinked and eyed him a little doubtfully. 'Are you sure the servants won't come in until we ring the bell?' she asked, as all sorts of possibilities suddenly suggested themselves when he gently shifted her over his prone body and she wriggled delightedly at all the wildly sensual ideas he was putting into her head with such promise in his wolfish gaze.

'Come now, love, this is one of Mantaigne's friend's households we're staying in whilst he's up in London, getting ready to be fashionably bored for the Season. Please be serious, wife,' he scoffed.

'Rakes, the lot of you,' she condemned.

'Not rakes, my love, wolves. A rake is a care-for-nobody seducer of any woman who presents him with an intriguing enough challenge. We lone wolves mate for life, which makes us all the more dangerous to unwary ladies like you.'

'Ah, but I'm not unwary any more,' she said with all sorts of untried promises in her violet eyes. 'Can we really?' she added as he splayed her legs over his narrow hipbones and she felt the full force of his arousal against her over-heated feminine core once again.

'I don't know, can we?' he whispered with a plea in his dear eyes to say how very much he wanted to, and a promise behind it that they would not if she felt too new at being a wife to ride to paradise in his arms like this.

'Yes…' she breathed as she solved his dilemma in the best way she could think of. 'Ooh, yes,' she gasped raggedly as she rose eagerly, then sank down on to the rigid and impressive length of his manhood and felt the fire and sweetness of mutual possession roar through her once again. 'I knew I needed to wake up with you, my lord, but until today I didn't know *exactly* why,' she told him as she held his fire and thunder-shot grey eyes with hers, saw the same flash of burning colour on his lean cheeks as she felt on her own.

'Ah, but you see, I did,' he managed to say and thrust up into her wet silken depths at the same moment as she bore down.

Chloe felt her breath hitch even more, her heart thunder in her breast and her core tighten on him as they strove together towards ecstasy and this time she knew what was coming and yearned for it, even as she knew a lick of sadness that, with that lovely, trackless completion, their congress would end, for now. But it ended so gloriously; so passionately, as she bowed back and moaned in extremity and he bucked and shouted his ultimate fulfilment as he shot his seed so high up inside her that spasms of their loving still rocked them when she sank down on to his heaving torso, feeling even more boneless and full up with wonder than last time.

As she lay splayed across him where their last flex of bliss beached her, she spared a brief thought for the sad, bereft Chloe of ten years ago who longed so desperately for love she had even fantasised over her mistress's stony hearted great-nephew.

'As well for me that I *didn't* know,' she observed as she used the light of the strengthening spring sun to peer down into her lover's tender, love-shot gaze. 'I might have humiliated myself and crept into your bed, whether you wanted me there or not, if I'd known this lay in wait for me there.'

'As well for both of us you didn't, then, because I had to learn to love before it could be like that. It never was so with anyone else,' he promised with such earnest need for her to believe him in his eyes that she nodded to admit he was probably right.

'I hate the fact that there ever was anyone else, Luke.

I can't help but begrudge this to every other woman who ever faced you in bed of a morning and rode herself to heaven on your lordship's most potent weapon,' she said with a wicked glance at his even now half-alert member that seemed to have a life of its own. He looked half-disgusted and half-resigned about it as he managed a sheepish smile for his new and very demanding wife.

'It's been more of a curse than a blessing to me until now,' he confessed and how could she not love the sheer mannish appeal of him as he lay there all gruff and un-defended?

'Has it really?' she said with a dubious gaze that somehow had to linger in fascination on the difference of him, the intriguing drama and details of his sex.

'Yes, when I met and married Pamela need and fury drove me nearly as hard as it did her, we were noxious to-gether, Chloe. Even you would not like the man we made of me between us back then. When she left I was more relieved than angry; she took the tortured need to satisfy her, to somehow please her when the only thing that truly delighted her was to have me force her in some way, and that went against all I wanted to be as her husband. I had a mistress after she went; I admit that to you frankly and can't bring myself to be sorry for it. She showed me that a woman doesn't have to be begged or coerced to let me into her bed, proved I was physically desirable in ways Pamela never tired of telling me I wasn't.'

'I swear I could tear the vicious little cat to shreds for hurting you so deeply, or at least I could if she was still alive.'

'I doubt it; you don't have enough malice in you to go about avenging yourself on my past lovers.'

'If any of them ever tried to hurt you, your Eve or my Verity, you might find yourself mistaken in that very flattering opinion of my character, Lord Farenze.'

'Maybe so, but luckily I'm not fool enough to look at another woman while I have a wife ready and willing to satisfy me quite royally in bed, and perhaps even out of it?' he suggested with a hint of ever more wicked possibilities in his deliberately melodramatic leer.

'Perhaps,' she echoed, her wild Thessaly imagination feeding her reasons to look forward to exploring them very urgently some time soon.

'What an idiot I was not to snap you up ten years ago,' he murmured as he kissed her tenderly and settled her head against his shoulder, so he could try not to dwell on those tempting scenarios while she was still a very new bride.

'What idiots we both were,' she said dreamily as she lay back against his powerful torso and simply enjoyed the warmth and reality of him after so many long, long nights fooling herself she could live without him.

'Hmm, and now we have a whole decade of loving to catch up on spread before us like a Lord Mayor's Banquet,' he murmured and it was a fit promise for the first part of Lady Virginia Winterley's expected year of wonders.

'Well, we won't have time for lying in bed when we get to Caraway Court, it sounds as if there's far too much to do for that,' Chloe said, wondering if they should have aped his last bride trip and risked the Lakes in springtime, instead of her childhood home that he'd bought for her, despite its ramshackle state.

No, she didn't want any part of her marriage to echo

Luke's first one and shivered at the very thought. He mistook it for her being cold and cuddled the bedclothes even more securely round them, then held her close until she dismissed the idea as nonsense. She and Luke loved each other wildly and completely and his first wife had only ever loved herself. It was a truth Virginia had pointed out when Chloe was still pretending not to care one way or the other about the current Lord Farenze. Now something restless and uncertain in her settled as she realised she might be his second viscountess, but she was also his first love.

'Think of the fun you'll have getting the place back to how it was in your however many times grandparents' time; it's a housekeeper's dream come true,' he teased her.

'Or her wildest nightmare,' she replied as she contemplated the mammoth task of restoring her childhood home to anything like its former glory, after so many years of shocking neglect. 'I hope you didn't pay much for it. After what my brothers did to Daphne they don't deserve a penny piece from either of us.'

'Little enough, and it was worth it for their promise to take themselves off to the Continent with the proceeds and never come back. Crowdale House and the London properties will have to be sold to pay off their creditors, but this seemed a good way of getting them out of our lives with as little embarrassment to you and Revereux as could be managed.'

'The Scottish estates will go as well, then,' Chloe said with a suspicion that was poetic justice.

'Revereux said he might bid for those.'

'I hope not, my sister would rather see him happy

than living in the past. She must have loved him very deeply to keep him a secret even from me. Verity is Daphne's best memorial and Adam Revereux should be content with her.'

'Aye, we husbands must all learn to be realists,' he teased and Chloe decided she liked his diversionary tactics and snuggled back into his arms to dream of the future as the spring sun shone in and a symphony of birdsong sounded in the ancient gardens below their window.

'Do you really not mind if I'm like Virginia and can't give you a child, Luke?' she asked, as the sounds of a new season and all the life and hope that came with it reminded her this was a time for new births as well as new beginnings.

'I already have one and so do you. Any more will be a bonus. James can spawn a procession of young Winterleys in his image and I'm not sure if I pity the world or James most for that repellent notion.'

'Wouldn't that make you dislike him all the more?'

'No, and I don't dislike him. In a way I pity him for having to carry the weight of his mother's frustrated hopes and dreams all these years.'

'You're a good man, Luke.'

'No, I'm a lucky man, Chloe, and the fact I've finally realised it is Virginia's finest legacy to me. Or should I count my wife as one of those as well?'

'Willed to you as her last bequest? I'm not sure I like the sound of that.'

'Not the fact of you, but the idea of you, perhaps? I think I learnt to hope the day I met your eyes across a cold expanse of January air and you couldn't bring yourself to look away and pretend I wasn't there for once. I was so sad and empty coming back to Farenze Lodge with Virginia dead and it seemed such a waste to know you so little and want you so badly. Oh, I haven't the right words to say it, but that day I knew we would be different. That there was a chance for us, a future that might be opening up in front of us and it looked more wonderful than I dared to dream I deserved.'

'I like your words, Luke. They're so much better than your grim northern silences,' she teased him a little, because it was tempting to give in to the tears stinging her eyes at the thought of him so lonely and grieving that day and this wasn't a time for sorrow. 'I love you, immoderately and passionately, and since ten years of enduring Lord Farenze's gruff rebuffs couldn't stop me doing it, I'm clearly going to suffer the affliction for life. I love you, Luke; today and tomorrow and every day after it that we spend on this good earth together.'

'I'm so glad you love me back and echo every word in my stony and tongue-tied Winterley heart, even if I'm currently hungry as a hunter and in severe need of my breakfast.'

'Oh, dear, that really is sadly unpoetic of you, my lord.'

'I know, my lady, but I'm a mundane man and, as such, could be a sad burden to you for many years to come.'

'I'll still take you, my love; I'm a workaday woman and quite hungry myself.'

'It's been a busy sort of a day and night, getting ourselves wedded and bedded at long last. I'll go and fetch us some breakfast,' he said and jumped out of bed as if about to tear off downstairs stark naked, then get back to her before the bed was cold.

'Luke, put some clothes on, you'll terrify the maids,' she exclaimed, trying to pretend the sight of his magnificent body, gilded by brilliant spring sunshine as the sun crept up the sky, hadn't put all thought of food out of her head.

'Very well, my lady, but don't you go anywhere while I'm gone, will you?' he said with a grin that made her knees knock too much to even think about getting out of bed quite yet.

'As if I would, but I do love you,' she told him with a besotted smile and how could she ever have thought his grey eyes were cold as he stared back at her, as if those words put every other thought out of his head but her.

'I love you too, Chloe, so very much,' he murmured and because he was a practical man he rang the bell instead of astonishing the servants, before leaping back into bed and rejoining his wife. 'Far too much to go anywhere for even that long today,' he murmured and kissed her so passionately and recklessly that they shocked them anyway.

* * * * *

THE MARQUIS'S
AWAKENING

Chapter One

Tom Banburgh, Marquis of Mantaigne, thought the polite world was about to be bitterly disappointed. If the wolfish glint in Luke Winterley's eye was anything to go by, he wouldn't be letting the former Lady Chloe Thessaly out of his bed long enough for her to go to town for a very long time, so the *ton* wouldn't be able to pass judgement on the new Viscountess Farenze until her new husband could spare her—some time in the next decade, if they were lucky.

'Can't this wait until after your wedding journey?' he asked with a sinking feeling in the pit of his stomach as Lady Chloe took a sealed missive from the neat reticule she was carrying. He should have been suspicious of that, since Luke was waiting to whisk her off on their bride trip and she hardly stood in need of whatever ladies carried in them when she had a husband all too eager to provide for her every need, and a few she probably didn't even know she had right now.

Feeling a fool for not remembering his godmother's

infamous will, even on this joyous day Virginia had done so much to bring about, he realised he'd stepped into the book room with the happy couple as naively as a débutante at her first grown-up party. As if they would have anything else to say to him before they left for Devon on their honeymoon but *here you are; you're next*.

'Here you are; you're next, I'm afraid, Tom,' Chloe said with a rueful smile to admit he wouldn't be pleased to take it and how could a few bits of expensive paper feel so heavy? 'Luke says we won't be back from Devon for weeks, and you must begin whatever you have to do for Lady Virginia before then if you're to get it done in the allotted three months.'

'Dash it all, though, it's the beginning of the Season,' Tom managed to utter after a heavy pause as he fought off a craven urge to throw the letter back at his best friend's new wife and refuse. 'Ah, well, suppose I might as well get it over with,' he said as lightly as he could while turning the letter over again, as if he might conjure it into someone else's hand if he put off reading it long enough.

'Look what my quarter of a year brought me,' Luke told him with a besotted smile Tom did his best to find nauseating.

'And can you see *me* neatly paired off at the end of whatever wild goose chase Virginia insists I carry out for her?' he demanded past a nasty little suspicion that was exactly what his wily godmother intended to happen, if Luke's adventures were anything to go by.

'One day you'll have to consider the succession,' Luke said half-seriously.

'I have and decided there's nothing very wonderful about the Banburghs, so who cares if there are no more of us?' Tom replied with a cynical smile that felt a lot better than the dread of being the next one on his godmother's list.

He ordered himself not to squirm under the sceptical mother's glance Chloe had perfected on her young niece. She and Luke would no doubt raise repellent quantities of brats in their joint images and be blissfully happy together for the rest of their lives, but he had no wish to follow in their footsteps and had managed without a family all his life.

'True,' Luke agreed with an impatient glance at the door. 'Why not leave him to read it in peace now, love? A very small part of me would like to stay and watch Mantaigne perform like a dancing bear in his turn, but the rest can't wait for us to begin our honeymoon.'

'I doubt your *best friend* relishes the task in front of him though, Luke,' she told her new husband sternly, then seemed to find it impossible to see anything but him once she'd turned her fascinated gaze his way.

'Have you any clue to what my quest could be, Lady Chloe?' Tom asked to remind the lovers he was still here, before it was he who needed to leave the book room in a hurry instead of them.

'Oh, that quest. No, I only hand out the letters,' Chloe said with a shrug that admitted she was so deep in love with Luke they were very poor company.

She flicked a glance at Tom's name and titles inscribed on his last message from his godmother and he was in danger of being ambushed by grief all over again. It was such a stark absence, having to acknowledge Virginia's wit, warmth and energy had left this world for the next. She and Virgil had lit up his life, and he felt the loneliness of losing both hit him anew.

'I had such plans, very seductive and beautiful ones they were as well,' he grumbled to hide his true feelings on such a joyful day.

'Rakehell.' Luke dismissed that objection with the wolfish good humour of a man about to have his own wildest fantasies come true. 'And where would be the fun in my great-aunt being predictable in death as she never was in life?'

'Fun for you, I suppose, Romeo, now your task is safely over.'

'True, watching you squirm is a pleasant side effect of standing at my own Lady Farenze's side while I watch three more idiots run about in their turn. If Virginia can see us from her place in heaven, I bet she's enjoying the view even more than I am right now.'

'Knowing her, it won't be some simple task easily got through and back to town before anyone misses me either.'

'Oh, I suspect those seductively beautiful plans of yours will, but we have to leave, and you need to discover whatever it is Virginia wants you to do in private,' the new Lady Farenze intervened.

'The fun's just starting—do we really have to go when it's getting interesting?' her lord said with the easy humour of a man whose task had come to a deeply satisfying conclusion.

'*We* do, Luke Winterley,' Chloe said with a severe look that only made him laugh.

Tom hadn't seen his friend and honorary brother this carefree since he was a dashing and hopeful youth, always game for a lark. The marriage his father arranged when Luke was barely twenty certainly knocked the youthful high spirits out of him far too young and he'd turned into a virtual hermit when the silly chit left him. After that Luke had locked himself away in his northern stronghold to raise their baby daughter and Tom blessed Virginia for managing to chip Luke out of frozen isolation, but he didn't want to be next the next victim on her list all the same.

'Well, we'll leave you to it then, Mantaigne. Try not to miss us too much, won't you?' Luke said with a mocking grin at Tom and a hot look at his lady that made her blush, then stride ahead of him, clearly in nearly as much of a hurry to begin married life as he was.

The door shut after them with a soft snick and Tom was left with the last letter he'd ever receive from his godmother, wishing she was here to tell him what maggot had got into her head this time herself. He'd spent the best years of his boyhood in this house and sometimes wondered if he had imagined his stark early childhood as the true lord of an ancient castle and vast estates, but master of nothing.

'Bonaparte's Imperial Guard could be marching about on the cliffs tonight and we wouldn't be any the wiser.'

Polly Trethayne shook her head, then remembered

her companion couldn't see her in the heavy darkness. 'I really think we would,' she whispered, wishing her friend and ally had stayed inside. 'If it *is* smugglers, we really need to be quiet.'

'Better for us *not* to know when they're out and about, if you ask me,' Lady Wakebourne grumbled a little more softly.

'I didn't and we can't simply sit back and let them use Castle Cove to land cargo whenever they fancy. The riding officers are sure to find out and report it, and the last thing we want is for the Marquis of Mantaigne to take an interest in Dayspring Castle for once in his life. He'll turn us out to tramp the roads again without a second thought and leave the poor old place to go to rack and ruin.'

'Even if he wants Dayspring to tumble down as the locals say, I'm sure he'd rather we stay than leave it empty for any passing rogue who wants a hiding place.'

'One or two may already be doing that and we are the rogues as far as the rest of the world is concerned. No, long may he stop away,' Polly argued.

Meeting Lady Wakebourne and finding this place abandoned on his lordship's orders was a small miracle and Polly had prayed every night for the last six and a half years for the man to stop away. Even the memory of how it felt to wander the world with a babe in her arms and two small boys at her heels for six long and terrifying months made her shudder.

'I doubt if anything would wrench him away from the delights of a London Season at this time of year, so I don't suppose we rogues need worry,' Lady Wakebourne whispered with an unlikely trace of regret.

Polly shook her head at the idea her practical and forthright friend secretly dreamed of playing loo and gossiping with the tabbies and dowagers of the *ton*, whilst the glitter and scandal of soirées and balls played out round them. Deciding she must be a freak to think the whole extravagant business sounded appalling, she wondered fleetingly how she'd have fared in that world if she had been obliged to make her come out in polite society. The idea was so far removed from her real life it made her want to laugh, but she bit it back and reminded herself this was serious.

'Surely you heard that?' she whispered urgently, listening to the night with the uneasy feeling it was listening back. 'I'd swear that was a window opening or closing on the landward side of the house.'

'The wind, perhaps?'

'There is no wind; nothing ought to be out here but foxes or owls.'

'Some poor creature could have got in and not been able to get back out, then,' Lady Wakebourne murmured.

'I refuse to believe bats and birds can unbar shutters or open windows,' Polly said as lightly as she could when this black darkness made her want to shout a challenge at whoever was out there.

'Tomorrow we'll go in and see for ourselves, but if you take another step in that direction now I'll scream at the top of my voice.'

'They will be long gone by then,' Polly argued, although she knew Lady Wakebourne was right and she couldn't afford to encounter an unknown foe in the un-used parts of the castle.

Her three brothers had to grow up and be independent before she was free to have adventures, but it was so hard to fight her wild Trethayne urges to act now and think later. At least memory of her father's reckless-ness reminded her to leash her own though; she was all that stood between her brothers and life on the parish, if they were lucky, and she had no plans to leave any of them in the dire situation Papa's death had left her in as a very naive and unprepared seventeen-year-old.

'At least we'll find out if these felons of yours exist outside the pages of a Gothic novel. If they do we'll have to get them to believe there really are ghosts at Day-spring Castle and leave us in peace with them.'

'Perhaps I should cut my hair and borrow a fine coat, then ride up the drive and announce myself as the Mar-quis of Mantaigne come back to claim his own,' Polly suggested as the most absurd way of scaring anyone out of the old place she could think of.

'And perhaps you should stop reading those ridic-ulous Gothic novels the vicar's sister passes on to us when she knows them by heart.'

'Aye, they're about as likely to come true as the idea Lord Mantaigne will ever come here without being kid-napped and dragged up the drive bound and gagged first. So ghosts it will have to be then,' Polly agreed, reluctantly admitting there was nothing to be done to-night, and followed her fellow adventuress back to the castle keep and the closest thing she had to a home nowadays.

* * *

'I should have sent the butler and housekeeper from Tayne on ahead of us, Peters. At least they might have found a few rooms at Dayspring undamaged after all these years of neglect and managed to make them habitable for us by now.'

Tom halted his matched team of Welsh greys at the gatehouse and wished himself a hundred miles away. Dayspring Castle was puffed up as his most splendid country seat in the peerages and guides to the county, but he felt a clutch of sick dread in his belly at the mere sight of it ahead, wrapped round the clifftop like a beast of prey from his worst nightmares.

'They would have given notice,' his companion argued. 'It would need an army of servants to get such a place in any sort of order after lying empty so long.'

'True, but wouldn't that army need to be directed by my man of business?' Tom retaliated against a not-very-well-disguised rebuke for neglecting the wretched place until it became the ruin he'd once sworn to make it.

'I like a challenge, my lord,' Peters said, and wasn't he a mystery of a lawyer now Tom came to think about it?

Nothing about this business was simple, though, and he supposed he'd have to admit the man had been useful to Luke in the part of the quest Virginia set him. According to James Winterley, who had a way of knowing things you didn't expect him to, Peters had helped a variety of aristocratic clients sort out the skeletons in their rosewood cupboards, including the Seaborne clan, whose shrewdness Tom would back against a corps of wily diplomats. So Tom had no choice but to trust this man to watch his back, even if the fellow saw too much of what lay below the surface of life for comfort.

'You're only here for three months, and heaven knows why Virginia thought I needed you by my side the entire time. Perhaps she expected you to force me up the drive at pistol-point if I lose my nerve.'

'The late Lady Farenze merely instructed me to meet you in Dorchester and accompany you here. I couldn't say what your godmother had in mind, my lord,' Peters said primly, but there was a world of disapproval in his gaze.

Perhaps the man was a Jacobin? Tom decided he didn't care if he was hell-bent on revolution, so long as they got on with this wretched business and left as soon as they found out what was wrong. 'I believe I mentioned my dislike of being "my lorded" at every turn when we first met,' he replied with a preoccupied frown at the neatly kept castle gatehouse.

'I'm supposed to be your temporary secretary here, not your equal, my lord.'

Tom found himself doubting that and how unlike him to look deeper into another man's life than he wanted him to. Lord Mantaigne had spent most of his adult life skimming over the surface of life like a pond-skater, and Tom shook his head at the picture of himself not caring about anything very much. He'd loved his godmother and Virgil, but they were both dead now, and at least he'd managed to keep the rest of the world at arm's length, except a voice whispered he'd let in Luke and his daughter and James. Now Lady Chloe and her spirited niece seemed to have chipped their way into a corner of what he'd thought was his cold heart, and how could he have been so careless as to let himself care about so many people without noticing?

He glared at a certain window high up in the ancient keep and stark memories rose up to whisper he was right not to come back until he had to. Virginia's last letter had told him one of her legion of friends had written to tell her something was amiss at Dayspring and he must go and find out what was so wrong with the place, but all he could see wrong with it right now was that it was still standing. Only for the woman who had taken in the feral little beast who had once existed in that keep and loved him anyway would he revisit the place despite all his resolutions not to.

'Whoever you intend to be, you'll have a poor time of it here,' he warned Peters as he slowed his greys to a walk.

'I expect I'll survive; I'm not faint-hearted.'

'Just as well. My last guardian only kept a few servants here once he took control of the estate for me, and I paid them off when I came of age,' Tom warned.

Peters shrugged as if he wanted to get on with his mission and leave, before he violated some lawyerly code and told a client exactly what he thought of his criminal neglect of such an historic property.

'I expect there will be a couple of rooms we can make habitable for the few days I intend to spend here,' Tom added glumly.

'Indeed, although the castle looks very well preserved to me, despite your orders it should not be.'

'And it's evidently a lot less empty than it ought to be,' Tom mused with a frown as he watched a plume of smoke waft lazily from a chimney in the oldest part of the castle.

The place had an air of being down at heel, but it wasn't the echoing ruin it ought to be after being left empty so long. There were deep ruts in the road leading down to Castle Cove that made him wonder even more who had stopped it falling into the sea. Virginia was right to make him come here to find out what was going on, and he pictured her impatiently telling him she'd told him so from her place in heaven. He had to suppress a grin at the idea of her regarding him with still very fine dark eyes and a puckish grin that told the world Lady Virginia Farenze was still ready to jump into any adventure going with both feet.

He missed her with an ache that made him feel numb at times and furious at others. Lord Mantaigne was a care-for-nobody, but he'd cared more for Virginia than he'd let himself know until he lost her. Still, one of his childhood resolutions was safe; he would never marry and risk leaving a son of his alone in a hostile world. The Winterley family might have trampled his boyhood vow never to care about anyone in the dust, but that one wasn't in any danger. He hadn't met a female he couldn't live without in all his years as one of the finest catches on the marriage mart, so he was hardly likely to find her in a dusty backwater like Dayspring Castle.

'Some traffic clearly passes this way,' Peters remarked with a nod at the uneven road in case Tom was too stupid or careless to notice.

Ordering Dayspring's ruin on what must seem a rich man's whim was one thing, but being judged stupid set Tom's teeth on edge. Was he vain about his intellect as well as finicky about personal cleanliness and a neat appearance? Probably, he decided ruefully. The last Marquis of Mantaigne already seemed to be learning more about himself than he really wanted to know, and his three months of servitude had barely begun.

'Heavy traffic as well,' he murmured, frowning at the spruce gatehouse and well-maintained gates and wondering if there was a link between those carts and whoever kept it so neatly.

'Perhaps we should follow in their hoof prints towards the stables? At least that way is well used, and the castle gates look sternly locked against all comers.'

'Since there are clearly more people here than there ought to be, I'll start as I mean to go on.' Tom replied.

'Maybe, but I don't have any skill with the yard of tin so I'm afraid I can't announce you in style.'

'I knew I should have brought my head groom with me and left you to follow on one of the carts, Peters. Hand it over and hold the ribbons while we see what this idle fool can do with it instead.'

'I never said you were a fool, my lord.'

'Only a wastrel?' Tom drawled as insufferably as he could manage, because being here prickled like a dozen wasp stings and why should he suffer alone?

'I don't suppose my opinion of anyone I work with during this year Lady Farenze decreed in her will matters to you.'

'I'm sure you underestimate yourself, Peters.'

'Do I, my lord? I wonder,' the man said with his usual grave reserve.

Tom wondered why Virginia had thought he needed someone to watch his back in what should be a straightforward ruin by now. Perhaps she was right, though, he decided with a shrug when he considered his non-ruin and the rutted lane down to the sea, but he still played down to Peters's poor opinion of him by raising an arrogant eyebrow and imperiously holding out a gloved hand for the yard of tin.

The greys accepted the change of driver with a calmness that surprised their owner as he produced an earsplitting blast and, when there was still no sign of life, gave the series of emphatic demands for attention he'd learnt from Virgil's coachman as a boy. He was about to give in and drive in the wake of those carts when the door slammed open and an ageing bruiser stamped into view.

'Noise fit to wake the dead,' he complained bitterly. 'Yon castle's closed up. You won't find a welcome up there even if I was to let you in,' he said, squinting up at them against the afternoon sun.

'I don't expect one here, so kindly open up before I decide it was a mistake not to have the place razed to the ground.'

'*You're* the Marquis of Mantaigne?'

'So I'm told.'

'Himself is said to be a prancing town dandy who never sets foot outdoors in daylight and lives in the Prince of Wales's pocket, when he ain't too busy cavorting about London and Brighton with other men's wives and drinking like a fish, of course. You sure you want to be him?'

'Who else would admit it after such a glowing summary of my life, but, pray, who am I trying to convince I'm the fool you speak of so highly?'

'Partridge, my lord, and lord I suppose you must be, since you're right and nobody else would admit to being you in this part of the world.'

'What a nest of revolutionary fervour this must be. Now, if you'll open the gates I'd like to enter my own castle, if you please?' Tom said in the smooth but deadly tone he'd learnt from Virgil, when some idiot was fool enough to cross him.

'You'll do better to go in the back way, if go in you must. It's a tumbledown old place at the best of times, m'lord, and there's nobody to open the front door. These here gates ain't been opened in years.'

Tom eyed carefully oiled hinges and cobbles kept clear of grass both sides of the recently painted wrought-iron gates. 'I might look like a flat, Partridge, but I do have the occasional rational thought in my head,' he said with a nod at those well-kept gates the man claimed were so useless.

'A man has his pride and I'm no idler.'

'How laudable—now stop trying to bam me and open the gates.'

Partridge met Tom's eyes with a challenge that changed to grudging respect when he looked back without flinching. At last the man shrugged and went inside for the huge key to turn in the sturdy lock and Tom wasn't surprised to see the gates open as easily as if they'd been used this morning. He thanked Partridge with an ironic smile and, as the man clanged the gates behind the curricle, wondered who the old fox was doing his best to warn that an intruder was on his way even he couldn't repel.

'I'm still surprised such an old building isn't falling down after so many years of neglect,' Peters remarked as Tom drove his team up the ancient avenue and tried to look as if he hadn't a care in the world.

'Some misguided idiot must have disobeyed all my orders,' Tom said bitterly.

Memories of being dragged up here bruised and bleeding and begging to be let go before his guardian got hold of him haunted him, but he was master here now and thrust the memory of that ragged and terrified urchin to the back of his mind where he belonged.

'Anyway, if I intended to let the place fall down without having to give orders for it to be demolished, I seem to have been frustrated,' he managed to remark a little more calmly.

'And I wonder how you feel about that.'

'So do I,' Tom mused wryly.

He accepted there was no welcome to be had at the massive front door and drove to the stable yard, feeling he'd made his point, if only to Peters and the gate-keeper. He saw two sides of the square that formed the stable blocks and the imposing entrance and clock tower were closed up and empty, paint peeling and a cast-iron gutter, broken during some tempest, left to rust where it fell. The remaining block was neat and well kept, though, and two curious horses were peering out of their stables as if glad of company.

'More frustration for you,' Peters murmured.

'Never mind that, who the devil is living here? I ordered it empty as a pauper's pocket and they can't be any kin of mine because I don't have any.'

'How did you plan to look after your team when we got here then, let alone the carts and men following behind?'

'The boot is full of tack, oats and horse blankets, so it's your own comfort I'd be worrying myself about if I were you.'

'I will, once we have these lads safely stowed in the nice comfortable stable someone's left ready for them,' Peters said with a suspicious glance about the yard that told Tom they had the same idea about such empty but prepared stables and what they might be used for this close to the coast.

'Keep that pistol handy while we see to the horses,' he cautioned.

Chapter Two

It didn't take long to remove the harness and lead the now-placid team into four waiting stalls and rub them down. Once they were cool enough, Tom and Peters hefted the ready-filled water buckets so the horses could drink after their leisurely journey, then they left them to pull happily at the hay-net someone had left ready. Tom was enjoying the sights and sounds of contented horses when the shaft of mellow afternoon sunlight from the half-open door was blocked by a new arrival. Pretending to be cool as the proverbial cucumber, he cursed himself for leaving his coat and pistol out of reach and turned to face the newcomer with a challenge that rapidly turned to incredulity.

'Ye gods!' he exclaimed, stunned by the appearance of a shining goddess with no shame at all, at Dayspring of all places.

'Minerva or Hera?' he heard Peters murmur in the same bewildered tone and felt a glimmer of impatience that the man was ogling the woman he urgently wanted himself. He could hardly wait to wrap those endless feminine legs about his own flanks and be transported to the heights of Olympus as soon as he could get those scandalous breeches off her.

'You should at least get Greece and Rome sorted out in your head before you make such foolish comparisons in future,' the vision said crossly, proving she had acute hearing, as well as a classical education and the finest feminine legs Tom had ever seen, in or out of his bedchamber, and he badly wanted this pair naked in one as soon as he could charm, persuade or just plain beg her to let him make love to her.

'I'll be happy in either so long as you're with me, Athene,' Tom recovered himself enough to offer with a courtly bow she should find flattering.

'And I have no time for such nonsense and nor do you, Mr Whoever-You-Might-Be. You're going to be far too busy reharnessing those fine horses of yours to that pretty little carriage and driving them back the way you came to indulge in such ridiculous fancies.'

'Why would I do that?'

'Because I demand you remove them from our stables immediately.'

'*Our* stables?' Tom's mind latched on to the possessive word among so many he could argue with and he wondered why it seemed so important she had no intimate other to pair herself with instead of him.

'Ours, mine, whatever you prefer. I'd certainly prefer you to go quickly and stop staring at my legs.'

'If you don't want them leered at, you should resume your petticoats. We males can't resist eyeing such fine feminine charms when they're so temptingly displayed without them.'

'A true gentleman wouldn't look,' she informed him, looking haughtily down a nose Hera or Minerva would have been justly proud of.

'Oh, but he would, wouldn't he, Peters? Peters is a proper gentleman, Athene, although I am only a nobleman myself,' Tom said, not at all sure he liked being looked at as if he was a caterpillar on a cabbage leaf.

'So you say,' she said sceptically.

Tom had often wished the world could see beyond the wealth and prestige he'd been born to and now he wanted an unlikely goddess to be impressed by them? Folly, he told himself, and goddesses didn't wear an odd mix of outdated clothes that looked as if they'd belonged to a few of his ancestors before they found a new glory on her.

'So I know,' he managed coolly enough.

'Prove it then.'

He laughed at the notion he needed to and at Dayspring of all places. Should he thank her for distracting him from the ordeal he'd thought this homecoming would be without her? 'Do you expect me to produce a letter of introduction from the patronesses of Almack's, or an invitation to Carlton House? Perhaps the record of my birth in the local parish church might do the trick—what would you advise, Peters?'

'Any one might be a fraud,' she argued before Peters could open his mouth.

'And I'm not prepared to prove myself on my own

property, madam,' Tom said, deciding it was time to bring the game to an end.

'Everyone in the neighbourhood knows the Marquis of Mantaigne never sets foot beyond the clubs of St James's or the ballrooms of Mayfair during this season of the year and has sworn not to come here as long as he lives. You need to think your story out better if you plan to masquerade as that idle fool.'

'You think me more useful and less vain than Lord Mantaigne? Hasn't anyone told you appearances are deceptive?'

'Not as badly as yours would have to be,' she said as if it was a *coup de grâce*.

Stray curls of russet-brown hair had worked free from the impressive plait hanging down her back to dance about her brow and distract Tom from a subject that kept slipping away from him as he wondered why she was so irresistibly female when her dress and manner were anything but.

'Blue,' he mused out loud as he met the smoky mystery of her eyes under long dark lashes. Her unusually marked eyebrows made her frown seem exaggerated and her smile a delicious flight of mischief, or at least he thought it might be, if she ever smiled at him, which currently seemed unlikely. Just as well really, he supposed hazily; if she ever gave up frowning he might walk straight into the promises and secrets in her unique eyes and fall under her witchy spell for ever.

'No, they might be grey,' he muttered as he tried to disentangle smoke and mystery from reality. 'Or perhaps even a little bit green.'

He saw shock in the bluey-grey marvel of her eyes, with those intriguing rays of green in their fascinating depths when she widened them, as if suddenly realising they were staring at each other. She shot Peters a questioning look, as if Tom might be a lunatic and the lawyer his unlucky keeper.

'I am the sixth Marquis of Mantaigne and have been so for most of my life,' Tom informed her testily, 'but who the devil are you?'

'None of your business,' she snapped back.

'How ironic that I've come back after all these years and nobody seems to believe I have the right to, don't you think, Peters?' Tom mused to play for time whilst he gathered his senses.

'Much about life is ironic, my lord,' Peters said unhelpfully.

'Aye,' Tom drawled with an emphatic look at his reluctant hostess that should make her blush and run to fetch whoever tried to lend her countenance.

Not that she had any idea of her own looks, he decided with a frown. She must be close to six feet tall to meet his eyes so easily, especially when looking down her haughty Roman nose as if he was the source of an unpleasant smell she hadn't been able to track down until now. Most of her inches were made up of leg and he almost wished he carried a quizzing glass so he could infuriate her all the more. Not that she didn't have a superb body to match those long and slender feminine legs of hers; dressed in form-fitting breeches, flowing shirt and a tight spencer jacket as she was, he'd be a fool *not* to notice she had a fine collection of feminine curves to go with them.

The wonder was she could roam round Dayspring in such a guise without a pack of wolves hunting her as such beasts usually did any unprotected female. She must be able to go about unmolested, though, since she hadn't stopped doing it, and that made him take her more seriously than he wanted to. If ever he'd met a feminine disaster waiting to happen it was this argumentative young goddess and he hadn't time or energy to cope with the challenge she presented just now.

'You don't look like any of the portraits of past Lord Mantaignes scattered about the castle,' she informed him with the sort of infuriated glare he hadn't been subjected to since he last annoyed Virginia.

'I doubt if one of my father survived my former guardian's rule here, but I'm told I take after him,' Tom said, wondering why it mattered.

'Don't you know?'

'I don't remember either of my parents.'

'That's as may be, but none of the pictures look like you,' she said accusingly.

He sighed in his best impression of a bored society beau and hoped she found it as superior and annoying as he meant her to. She took a long look at his dusty but perfectly fitted boots, then her gaze flicked dismissively over the coat Weston would no longer be quite so proud to admit was his handiwork lying nearby, but he saw the odd giveaway sign she wasn't as confident of his nonentity as she wanted him to believe. Her breathing came a little short and there was a hint of desperation in those fine eyes, as if the truth was too much to cope with and she wanted to fend it off as long as possible.

'I dare say you know the State Rooms better than I do. My guardian never let me explore that part of the house when I lived here,' he admitted, trying to shrug off the feeling he'd revealed too much.

'The villagers do say Lord Mantaigne's guardian was a cruel man,' she conceded, thinking about rearranging her prejudices, but not yet ready to turn them on their head.

'How tactful of them,' he said with a bitter smile.

Why the devil had he let Virginia bullock him into coming here? Tom wanted to be out of this intimate stable in the fresh air. With hints of fish and brine, seaweed and wide oceans on the breeze from the sea, at least that was something his guardian had never been able to take from him. How could he have forgotten that and all the other things he loved about this place, despite the neglect and cruelty he'd endured? He'd never wanted to set eyes on this place, but the scent of the sea settled a strange sort of longing in him for home that he hadn't even known he had until he got here.

He used to risk his life creeping down the hoary old stones of the North Tower as soon as his bare feet were big enough to cling to the bumps and cracks in the rock. Grably was too much of a coward to kill the 'spawn of the devil', he had called Tom when no outsiders were listening, but he wouldn't have shed a tear if Tom had fallen to his death and saved him the stain of murder on his mean and twisted soul.

'I suppose you could be him,' a very different

keeper of Dayspring Castle admitted begrudgingly and wrenched his thoughts back to the present. 'You're the right age, but Maggie said his little lordship looked an angel fallen out of Heaven and you don't look angelic to me.'

'You know my one-time nurse then?' he said, sounding far too eager. That reminder of the one constant in his life after his father had died, until his guardian sent her away, caught him unawares.

'I knew Lord Mantaigne's childhood nurse before she died,' she said, eyeing him as if unsure his word could be trusted or not.

Not, Tom concluded, at least not if she was aware of her own allure as she stood in the shadowed gloom of the stables and stared at him as if she could read his sooty soul. Not, if she was possibly the most un-likely virgin lady he had ever met, with her mannish garments, unmanly figure and a mass of unruly hair barely held by the tail she'd plaited it into some time during the last week.

An unforgivably urgent desire to see the heavy weight of it about her naked shoulders like rumpled silk taunted his body and his senses. Half hiding and half enhancing a figure he knew would be as perfect in real human flesh as any classical statue of a two-thousand-year-old goddess carved in ancient Greece, he could picture it rippling over the fine skin he suspected was creamy and satin smooth where the sun hadn't reached her not-quite-redhead's skin and tinted it pale gold.

Considering nothing about her seemed quite sure how to be, she was a very definite snare for a man who liked his ladies bold and confident of their own charms. Her hair wasn't quite red, brown or blonde and he'd already had that silly discussion with himself about her eyes. He could feel Peters's cool gaze on him as he realised what the unwary goddess wouldn't let herself see—that she was in the presence of a lone wolf and could be very unsafe indeed. If not for where they were and what he'd been sent here to do, she would be in more danger than Peters realised, but Tom couldn't afford distractions until he got to the bottom of a very odd barrel of fish.

'*Knew* her?' he asked after he'd racked his brains to recall what they were talking about before he got distracted again.

'She died five years ago,' his mystery snapped.

'I have no resident agent here,' he said stiffly. 'Nor have I kept in contact with anyone in the villages.'

'Something they know all too well,' she condemned, and he suddenly felt impatient of his would-be judge and jury.

'Something they can now complain about directly to me, if I ever manage to leave these stables and meet any of them,' he said wearily.

'Is he really the Marquis of Mantaigne?' she asked Peters, as if unable to trust his word, and Tom bit back an impatient curse.

'Ask yourself if he could be anyone else, ma'am, and I suspect you'll have your answer. I'm his employee, so you can't trust me to tell the truth. Lord Mantaigne could terminate my employment if I was to argue against him.'

'As if I would dare,' Tom allowed himself to drawl

and felt he'd almost won back the detachment he prided himself on.

'He looks useless enough to be a marquis, or he might if he was wearing that dandified coat,' she allowed with a nod of contempt at a once-exquisite example of Weston's fine work.

'Do you think there might be a compliment hiding somewhere in that sentence if I look hard enough for it, Peters?' Tom asked as if they needed a translator.

'I wouldn't bet your rent rolls on it, my lord.'

'Paulina! Oh, Polly! Wherever are you hiding yourself this time?' a brisk soprano voice called before being drowned out by what sounded like a pack of large and hungry dogs barking as if they were eager to sink their teeth into any passing stranger—be he a marquis or a commoner.

Tom's guardian used to hunt him down with his pack when he thought he'd had his freedom for too long. Remembered fear made him cast a swift glance in the direction of the hunt kennels his guardian had built far enough away for their howls not to keep him awake at nights. Luckily his companions were too busy to see it and he clamped adult self-control on childhood fears and reminded himself he'd learnt to like and trust dogs since then.

'I know you're in the stables because these misbegotten hounds insist you are, so who does the curricle belong to?' that brisk voice added from much nearer at hand.

'Which question would you prefer me to answer first, Lady W.?' the goddess shouted over the hubbub.

Paulina-whoever-she-was sounded as calmly unruffled as any woman could with such a commotion going on in her stable yard, but shouldn't that be his stable yard? And why did he feel a need to claim the property he'd been tempted to destroy all his adult life?'

'How many times have I told you not to call me by that repellent nickname?' the newcomer demanded.

'So many I wonder you still bother,' Paulina replied as Tom peered over her shoulders and managed to meet the lady's shrewd blue eyes. 'He claims he's the Marquis of Mantaigne and this is Lady Wakebourne,' Paulina said as if not quite sure how to introduce a possible impostor.

'Lady Wakebourne,' he said, searching his memory for clues to how the lady fitted into the complex patchwork of the *ton*.

He dredged up the tale of a certain Sir Greville Wakebourne, who had bankrupted a great many people before putting a bullet in his brain several years ago. This lady, who had evidently been a true beauty in her youth, was probably his widow, but it was impossible to tell if she mourned the swindler or not. She didn't look as if she dwelt on him or anything else in the past, so vivid and vital was her presence in the here and now.

'Lord Mantaigne,' she greeted him with such superb assurance he was in mid-bow before his brain reminded him he was the host here and not the other way about, but he carried on anyway.

'Weren't you one of my godmother's coven of regular correspondents, my lady?' he asked and felt Polly-Paulina's gaze fix accusingly on him, as if he'd been trying to deceive her about his identity instead of trying to convince her he really was rightfully lord and master here.

'Please accept my condolences on her death and desist from using such terms in future,' Lady Wakebourne told him with a firmness that told him she was every bit as stubborn as the goddess.

'Is he really the Marquis of Mantaigne?' Polly-Paulina asked, sounding so disgruntled she must be taking him seriously.

'Of course he is—why would anyone else admit to being a notorious rake and dandy?' Lady Wakebourne replied before he could say a word, stern disapproval of his chosen way of life plain on her striking countenance.

'They would if it meant getting his possessions along with his reputation,' Paulina-whoever-she-was muttered.

Outraged barking had waned to a few vague snuffles and the odd whine as the owners of those formidable canine voices sniffed about the curricle for concealed villains. Now two huge paws hit the bottom half of the door and a shaggy head joined Lady Wakebourne's attempts at blocking out daylight. The creature appeared comical until its panting revealed a set of strong white teeth the hounds of hell could be justly proud of.

'Get down, sir,' Lady Wakebourne ordered the enormous animal irritably. 'If you must take in any stray lucky enough to cross your path, Polly, I wish you would train them not to dog my footsteps as if I actually like them.'

'But you do,' Polly said, seeing through Lady Wakebourne's frown as easily as the large hound seemed to, given he was now watching her with dogged adoration.

An impatient bark from lower down said the hell-hound was blocking the view, so he sank back to sit next to a busy-looking terrier with a thousand battle scars and a cynical look in the one eye he had left. He met Tom's gaze in a man-to-man sizing up that was almost human, and if a dog could snigger this one did in a crooked aside. An elderly greyhound with an aloof look that said *I don't get involved, so don't blame me* and a lolloping puppy with some spaniel and a great deal of amiable idiot completed the canine quartet. Even Tom couldn't bring himself to blame them for the sins of the pack of half-starved beasts his guardian had once used to terrorise the neighbourhood and his small charge.

'Not in the house, I don't,' Lady Wakebourne asserted, as if it was her house to be pernickety over if she chose.

Tom frowned as he searched his mind for a reason why the widow of a disgraced baronet was living in his house without his knowledge. 'I expect several carts and their teams before dark, my lady. Can anyone help us make more of the stabling usable?' he asked the simplest of the questions that came into his mind.

It felt strange to be so ignorant of his household, especially when there wasn't supposed to be one. Two coachmen, several stalwart grooms and three footmen were on their way with supplies to make camping in a ruin bearable and they would need somewhere to bed down as well. It would be too dark to do much more than sleep by the time they arrived, but he'd often sought the warmth of the horses at night as a boy and one more night in the stables wouldn't hurt him.

'No, but the northern range is better than the west. It takes less battering from the winds that come in from the sea,' Polly-Paulina said with a sly glance at Tom's riding breeches, shining top-boots, snowy white shirt and grey-silk waistcoat. He wasn't dressed for heavy labour, but she seemed happy about the idea of him doing some anyway.

He had no old clothes here and wouldn't don them now if he had, so he hoped there was a copper of hot water over the fire betrayed by its smoking chimney. Tom met the girl's hostile gaze, determined not to prove as useless as she clearly thought him.

'We'll need pitchforks and a wheelbarrow, buckets and a couple of decent brooms. You will have to re-mind me where the well is,' he prompted as she stayed stubbornly silent.

'The boys can come in from the gardens this late in the day to help, Paulina. They are probably disgrace-fully dirty by now anyway,' Lady Wakebourne said with a caution in her voice to remind her fellow interloper some tact was needed when dealing with the owner of a house you were living in without his knowledge or permission.

For a long moment Paulina the Amazon glared at Tom, as if quite ready to lay aside any pretence of civil-ity and risk expulsion. He raised one eyebrow to ques-tion her right to be furious with him, but she seemed unimpressed.

'Very well,' she finally agreed without taking her eyes off him, as if he might steal the silver if she did so.

He couldn't help the mocking smile that kicked up his mouth, because it was his silver, or it would be if it hadn't been taken away years ago.

'Lunar, go and fetch Toby,' she told the huge beast, as if he would understand. 'Go on, boy, go fetch him in,' she added when the bigger-than-a-wolf dog put his head on one side and eyed Tom and Peters as if not sure it was safe to leave them here.

'Maybe he'd feel better if we went with him?' Tom suggested lightly.

'The boys would run away from such a dandy,' Paulina-Polly muttered darkly, shooting him a look that said she wouldn't blame them.

'Perhaps it would be better if you went yourself then,' he said blandly.

The hound sat on his mighty haunches and eyed first him, then his younger mistress, as if awaiting his cue to protect her to the last breath in his amiable body.

'Or you could make it a clear to your mixed pack of hell-hounds we're not going to rip each other to pieces when their backs are turned?' he added.

'I would have to be certain myself,' he thought he heard her mutter under her breath, but then she seemed to make a huge effort to be civil and held out her hand as a sign to their canine audience that peace reigned.

Tom took it, wondering at the state a lady could get her hand in and not care. A glance at her short nails and tanned skin, nicked and scarred here and there from her labours, did nothing to warn him how it would feel in his broad, well-manicured palm. *Ah, here she is, at last*, an inner voice he ordered not to be so foolish whispered. He felt emotions he didn't want to examine stir and threaten something impossible at the feel of work-hardened calluses on her slender fingers and finely made palm.

She shouldn't have to work at anything more strenuous than pleasing herself and me, his inner idiot whispered in his ear. A shock of something hot and significant he'd never felt before shot through him like a fiery itch. It was too much of an effort to shake her slender hand then let it go as if she was just a new acquaintance.

'I'm honoured to meet you, Miss Paulina,' he said as lightly as if they had met in a Mayfair ballroom or, heaven forbid, Almack's Club. He'd long ago resolved never to venture there again for fear of the tenacious matchmaking mamas and their formidably willing daughters.

'Trethayne,' Lady Wakebourne said abruptly. 'Her name is Miss Trethayne and since she has no elder sister that is all you are required to know.'

Tom felt the girl's hand tug insistently in his, realised he was still holding it like a mooncalf and relaxed his grip with unflattering haste. No wonder she was glaring at him now, and the vast hound was growling under his breath, rather than running off to fetch Toby from the garden as he was bid, whoever Toby might be.

'Three tired teams and their drivers will be arriving here in the next couple of hours, so I suggest we put aside questions of what a Trethayne and you,

Lady Wakebourne, are doing here under my less-than-comfortable roof and get on with preparing the stables to lodge them as best we can.'

'Something you should have thought about when you set out,' Miss Trethayne informed him, and Tom bit back an urge to defend his right to visit his own house if he wanted to, or even if he didn't.

'And if you expect me to put off examining your presence here, perhaps you should lay aside your hostility,' he suggested coldly.

Part of him wanted to trade words with her until the sun went down, for the sheer pleasure of gazing at her scandalously displayed form and extraordinary face, but the rest knew better. She had fascinating eyes and then there was that strong nose that should make her a character, not a beauty, but didn't. Her mouth was too wide to fit an accredited beauty as well, but it was as full of unstudied allure as the rest of her. There, hadn't he just ordered himself *not* to catalogue her graces? Fully recognising his desire to kiss her deeply and urgently would be folly; best not think of such fiery needs when dressed in tight buckskin breeches—for all they concealed of his errant masculine urges he might as well stand here buck naked.

'You'd best get on with cleansing the Augean Stables before it's pitch dark and you can't see what you're doing, then,' she said with a shrug, opening the stable doors with a glance of contempt at his once-spotless linen and expensive tailoring.

He was glad to see it contained none of the cynicism in Lady Wakebourne's gaze as she silently challenged him to keep any lustful thoughts he might harbour about Miss Polly Trethayne strictly to himself. Bracing himself to meet the assorted hounds at closer quarters with suitably manly composure, Tom stepped out in Miss Trethayne's wake and blinked in the late-afternoon sunshine. The four dogs sat to attention at a stern word from Lady Wakebourne, looking more comical than threatening as they watched her as if they knew they'd violated the laws of hospitality by being uncivil to guests.

'Lunar, Zounds, Ariel and Cherubim, otherwise known as Cherry,' the lady introduced them. 'Lunar, give a paw,' she commanded the great hound, who was clearly reserving the option to bite Tom if he misbehaved.

The terrier, Zounds, let out a gruff bark; Ariel looked regally indifferent, and Cherry rolled onto her back and waved all four feet in the air in a frantic plea for attention.

'Hussy,' Lady Wakebourne said with a sad shake of her head that didn't deceive anyone, and the half-grown spaniel-cross waved her paws to tell her mistress she still wanted her belly scratched, hussy or no.

Chapter Three

❧❧❧

Polly watched the castle's official reception committee behave in character and sighed. It was too much to hope the man would be scared of Lunar's mighty build and need to protect them to his last breath. She had sensed fear in the tall figure at her side and tried to convince herself it made him less of a man, but then he'd sauntered out of the stables in her wake as if he hadn't a care in the world and confounded her again. How could she not admire a man who confronted his fears with such style, even if she didn't want to like anything about him?

Cherry decided a pantomime of what she wanted wasn't doing the trick and yipped a command in his lordship's direction, so he bent to give the pup a full belly rub she enjoyed so much she let out a little moan of delight and threatened to surge to her feet and jump at him in an excess of joy.

'No!' Lady Wakebourne ordered firmly, so Cherry simply demanded more fuss, and Polly felt the rich echoes of his laugh prickle like a warning along her spine.

'Misbegotten hound,' Lady Wakebourne said, and Cherry wagged her tail as if it was a huge compliment.

'Go get the boys,' Polly ordered Lunar and Zounds, and they bounded off, or at least Lunar bounded. Zounds skittered after him as fast as his uneven gait would allow, and Ariel weighed his options and decided he would like a run, so he streaked after them like the wind. Cherry saw she was being left behind, gave Lord Mantaigne an apologetic lick and dashed off as well.

'The pump?' his lordship asked Polly with one of those exceptionally irritating eyebrows of his quirked in an imperious question.

'There is no pump, only a bucket on a rope,' she said to him with a nod at the most deeply shadowed corner of the yard.

This was no time to soften towards him and join in the mighty clean it would take before the empty stable block was at all usable. Polly fetched the giant key to the tack room on the other side of the quadrangle, daring him to complain at the decay he'd caused in the first place. They'd fought his wilful neglect since the first day they happened on the castle, so he could see for himself how hard that struggle was for an hour of his soft life.

He didn't look soft as he turned the key in the ancient lock without apparent effort. It was beyond her strength to move it without both hands and much cursing and swearing, and Polly told herself it was wrong to ogle his magnificently displayed physique as blatantly as he had done hers and sighed under her breath. His coming here would change everything, and all the wishing him away in the world wouldn't alter the fact he was home at last. An untamed part of her was intrigued and even a little bit triumphant about the fact he'd been well worth waiting for.

Well, he didn't know about the Polly she kept well hidden, and she certainly wasn't going to tell him. Nor was he going to lord it over them; not after neglecting this wonderful old place so shamefully a battalion of thieves could have hidden here without any risk of being challenged. She recalled her father telling her nobody could make her feel small and insignificant unless she let them and bit back a smile as she wondered what her adventurous parent would make of his tall and all-too-significant daughter now.

Not a great deal, a sneaky voice whispered in her ear, but she hid her self-doubts behind the mask of confidence Papa had taught her to use to outface her enemies. Except she couldn't afford to be headlong and reckless and arrogant as he'd been the first to admit a true Trethayne was by nature and intent. He had lost every penny they ever had, and a good few they didn't; then he died during an insane midnight race across the moors to try to recoup his losses with a mad bet on his favourite horse.

Claire, her stepmother, had died when her smallest brother was born, so seven years on from Stephen Trethayne's reckless and untimely death Polly and her little brothers lived on whatever they could grow or make at Dayspring Castle, which went to show what happened when Trethaynes refused to rein in their wilder impulses. At times she had longed for a life of passion and adventure instead of hard work and loneliness, but Polly only had to recall how it felt to be seventeen with three little boys to raise on nothing and the urgency faded.

Yet a dart of something deep and dangerous had shot through her at first sight of this handsome golden-haired Adonis, staring back at her as if she was water in a desert. It still sang somewhere deep down inside her as if he'd branded her with warm lightning. She shivered at what might be, if she wasn't four and twenty and father, mother and every other relative they had never had to three little brothers, and if Lord Mantaigne wasn't one of the richest and most powerful aristocrats in the land.

She shook her head at the ridiculous idea of him wanting her as other than a passing fancy she was not willing to be. Trying to distract herself, she wondered how many horses and servants were on their way with the luxuries he would demand as his right. She could imagine him a great lord or prince in medieval times on a grand progress about the land with a huge entourage of brightly arrayed courtiers and an army of servants to answer his every need along the way. If Dayspring Castle was once capable of housing such a household, it certainly wasn't now. She scaled down his retinue to a couple of carriages and a few carts laden with boxes of superbly cut clothes to deck him out in style.

He would need a valet to keep such splendour bandbox fresh and wasn't it lucky the thought of him mincing down Bond Street carrying such an item after a visit to the milliner made her want to laugh? Whatever she thought of him, and she wasn't sure she wanted to know what that was; even she couldn't accuse him of being effete.

She would like to, of course, but she couldn't delude herself so badly. Not with his powerful breadth of shoulder and heavily muscled arms on show when he stood there in his shirtsleeves ready to begin his Herculean task. He had narrow flanks and long and sleekly muscled legs, finishing in those damned boots of his that made him look more like a tidied-up pirate than the mincing marquis her imagination had painted him.

His hair might have started out the day in neatly ranked waves or even the artful disorder some of the dandies affected, but now his golden locks were in such disarray he must be as impatient of a hat on such a fine spring day as she was herself. Which didn't mean they had anything in common. The fine cut of his immaculate waistcoat; the stark whiteness of his linen shirt and beautifully tied neckcloth all argued the Marquis of Mantaigne was used to the finest money could buy. Miss Paulina Trethayne had long ago resigned herself to life shorn of all her kind took for granted and sniffed, as if doubtful he could lift a pitchfork, let alone wield one.

'You'll get very dirty,' she warned, as if he couldn't see the dust and smell the unused staleness of the air inside long-neglected stables for himself.

'I'll wash,' he said indifferently, letting her implied insult pass as he surveyed the dust of ages in front of him. 'We'll need those buckets and something to scrub with as well as more hay and straw, if it can all be got at short notice.'

'Enough of both are in the barn and there's more in the rickyard,' she said, and he raised his annoying eyebrows again, as if surprised they were so organised. He might not be so pleased when he realised animals and crops came ahead of people in their household and there would not be enough to feed him in style.

'Good, we'd best get on with it then, if you'll tell us where a couple of decent brooms and buckets are, then leave us to our labours, Miss Trethayne?' he said, as if he swept and washed down stables every day dressed in Bond Street's finest and with that fallen-angel smile never wavering for a second.

Mr Peters eyed the blanket of stale dust and detritus overlaying everything and looked as if he had better places to be. Moved by his mournful look at his neatly made coat as he took it off, as if he was bidding goodbye to his sober raiment and tidy appearance for ever, Polly went to make sure fires were lit under the vast coppers in the laundry to provide baths for the lord as well as his man. If there was only water for one, doubtless the marquis would take it all and let his fastidious aide sleep in his dirt, so there was no point trying to make him even more eager to leave by skimping on such necessities after their hard labour.

Tom and Peters were almost unrecognisable as the lord of this ancient pile and his supposed secretary by the time all four cartloads of luggage and provisions rolled down the rutted drive. It was dusk and on the edge of true darkness by then and the grooms and stable lads seemed delighted to be at journey's end, even if it didn't promise more than a roof over their heads against the coming night. Their calls to each other and exclamations at the state of the roads and their new lodgings made the yard livelier than it must have been for decades. Tom shook his head as if he was Lunar trying to dislodge a persistent fly and dust and old cobwebs threatened their handiwork with a new sprinkling of ancient history.

'Hercules had the River Styx handy to divert through the Augean Stables,' Peters remarked gloomily as he swept up the dislodged dust and followed his broom outside into the fading daylight, before Tom could make more work.

'And the nice warm Aegean to bathe in when he was done,' Tom said with a grin at his once-pristine companion. 'You look as if you've been pulled through a hedge backwards, rolled in the dust and trampled by a herd of wild horses.'

'I feel filthy,' Peters said disgustedly, and Tom laughed.

'Ah, but you must admit the place is full of surprises,' he said.

'Aye, it's confounded us so far,' the man said as if that wasn't a good thing, but hard work had settled some of the tension of the past few days, and Tom didn't intend to fall into a gloom again.

'At least there's not much chance of being bored for the next few weeks.'

'Boredom can be a good thing, given the alternative,' Peters said with a sigh, but Tom turned to greet his head groom and managed to ignore him.

'There's good news and bad, Dacre,' he informed the man cheerfully once Dacre reported a smooth journey and they had compared notes on the roads and the state of the horses after the easy run they'd had today.

'I can see the bad part of it, milord, so what's to be happy about?'

'Mr Peters and I have swept and scrubbed the unused stables as best we can, so we can house the horses in reasonable comfort and safety. If your lads go and fetch bedding and feed from the barns over yonder, I dare say the nags will be as happy as we can make them, even if I don't hold much hope for the rest of us. I trust you didn't push the teams so hard we can't water them when you find a few more buckets?'

'Not I, but it's as well we brought plenty with us, my lord,' Dacre said with a disapproving look at their handiwork.

Tom's head groom always disdained anything he hadn't ordered himself on principle, but, since Amazonian Miss Trethayne had sent her three young brothers and other assorted urchins to 'help', Tom knew they had achieved a lot. Luckily the lads had soon grown bored with sweeping up choking clouds of ancient dust and cleaning windows and melted away to find more amusing things to do.

'Never mind, Dacre. Barnabas will be here with the riding horses any moment, he can help you restore order in the morning,' Tom said.

'I'll try to be grateful for small mercies then, my lord.'

'For now the horses need your attention and I hope

you find all their gear on the wagons in the dark. A few moth-eaten brushes and a curry-comb with every other tooth missing won't do the job after their journey.'

'Very true, my lord. Now you leave the beasts to me while you go and turn yourself back into a gentleman.'

'Of course. Why else would I pay you so handsomely? Even when you think it's your duty to set me down like a scrubby schoolboy with every other word.'

'Somebody has to do it, my lord,' Dacre replied dourly. 'Her ladyship trusted me with the job when you was a lad, and I'm not done hoping you'll toe the line one day quite yet.'

'Do let me know when you consider me mature enough to run my own life, won't you?' Tom said cheerfully.

Knowing he could relax and leave his horses and men in good hands now, he wondered if he and Peters would have to make do with a very quick dip in the still not-very-warm April sea he could hear whispering against the foreshore of the cove below the castle. There was no chance of him getting a wink of sleep if he tried to bed down in all this dirt, even if it was in a stable, so the sea it would have to be and what else had he expected of the wreck he'd made of his former home?

'Polly said we were to bring lanterns to light you and Mr Peters inside,' little Joshua Trethayne's childish voice piped up as the glow of them softened the fast falling darkness in the stable yard. 'But you're to be careful because the whole place will go up like a tinder box if you let one fall, or so Lady W. says. Oh, and you're not to be late for supper if you have to scrape the dirt off to be in time.'

'Bagpipe,' Master Henry Trethayne condemned his little brother in his halfway between child-and-man voice. 'Lady Wakebourne said we're to say there's enough hot water for two baths in the coppers, but you'll have to take them in the laundry house, because there's nobody to carry water up and down stairs for you.'

'And there's the biggest pie we ever saw ready for dinner and we're starved,' the boy Tom thought was called Joe said from behind the three brothers.

'We'd best hurry, Peters,' Tom told his filthy companion, wondering if he had that much dust and dirt on his once-immaculate person as well. 'Do you know if there's any soap to spare, boys? Or must I search the wagons before we come in?'

'I sincerely hope not, my lord,' Peters said as if he'd experienced quite enough misplaced optimism for one day, 'you would get dust and dirt on everything.'

'Aye, there's soap all right,' one of the skinny urchins Tom thought more at home on a London street than rural Dorset said gloomily, 'more of it than a body should have to put up with in a whole lifetime, if you asks me.'

'That's because you're a mudlark,' Henry Trethayne said cheerfully.

'Then at least I ain't a pretty little gentleman.'

'D'you still think I'm pretty now?' Henry asked as he lunged for his friend and wrestled him to the ground.

'Please ignore them, my lord,' his elder brother said loftily, but Tom's night vision was good enough to see him eyeing the pair with the wistfulness of an adult looking back on the pleasures of his youth. 'They know no better, I'm afraid.'

'Clearly,' he said as solemnly as he could. 'Now, about that soap and water? Could you point us in the direction of it so we're rid of our dirt before the ladies see us? We'll get a fine scolding if we venture inside looking like this.'

'Hmm? Oh, yes, Josh will take you, won't you, Josh?' the boy said absently, weighing up how best to intervene as a third boy launched himself into the fray and maturity felt less important than evening the odds.

'Come on then, Mr Lord,' the youngest Trethayne ordered cheerfully.

'You don't want to join in?' Tom couldn't help asking as they walked towards the castle with the noises of battle fading behind them.

'I'm the smallest and weakest. It would be foolish *and* painful to do so,' the boy informed him as if he was the grown up.

'True,' Peters said with a heartfelt sigh.

'Younger son?' Tom couldn't help asking.

'Something like that,' his companion replied in his usual guarded tone when Tom tried to learn more about this enigma of a man than the enigma really wanted him to know.

Tom forgot his companions and everything else when Dayspring Castle loomed ever closer out of the half-dark. Its air of down-at-heel raffishness was hidden by the coming night and the feeling of malevolent power he recalled all too well from his childhood was in command once more. Then it had seemed to have a real, beating heart tucked away somewhere, hellbent on showing him he was as nothing compared to the grand history of Dayspring and its warrior lords.

His breath shortened and his heartbeat began to race, as if he was on the edge of the same panic he'd felt every time he was dragged back here from an attempt to run away as a boy. Back then he'd usually betrayed his terror by being physically sick or, on one terrible occasion, losing control of all his bodily functions as his guardian and that terrifying pack of dogs bayed at him from the castle steps and he felt the snap of savage jaws held just far enough off not to actually bite, but close enough to be a boy's worst nightmare come horribly true. Thank Heaven Peters knew nothing of that awful moment of weakness as he remarked what a fine place it was and how he might envy its owner, if it wasn't close to ruin.

'It's not a ruin,' Joshua Trethayne said as if he loved it. 'The North Tower is dangerous and Poll says we're not to go there, even if someone could *die* if we don't. Jago says it's haunted, so I don't want to go up there anyway and Toby can say I'm a coward as often as he likes, but I really don't want to know who the ghost is.'

'Quite right,' Tom said dourly. 'He's not worth meeting.'

'I would consider meeting any ghost a memorable experience, even if their very existence is beyond the realms of logic to me,' Peters argued.

Tom was tempted to growl something disagreeable and stump off towards the laundry house he remembered as a warm, if damp, hiding place when he escaped his prison in the North Tower to roam about the countryside. Frightened of the smugglers and other unpredictable creatures of the night, he would come back here to sleep in the outbuildings and feed on scraps of food carelessly left out by the laundresses and grooms. With adult perception Tom realised that was done deliberately and felt a lot better about being back here all of a sudden. At least some of the people who once lived and worked here had cared enough about the ragged little marquis to leave him the means to stay free and safe for a little longer.

'I was kept in that tower for several years by my wicked guardian, Master Trethayne. So, no, there are no ghosts up there I can assure you. I'd have been glad of their company, feral boy as I was back then.'

'That's what Poll said Jago was when Lady W. found him: a feral boy,' Josh Trethayne said, and Tom could have kicked himself for saying too much about his past in front of this acute young gentleman, although there had to be rumours still flying about the area of shocking goings on up at the castle before Tom was taken away to be brought up by a very different guardian to the one he'd begun his career as an orphan with.

'I dare say he and I would have got on well if we had met when I was young, then,' Tom made himself say cheerfully as he tried to dismiss the past. 'Right now I'm sharp set and filthy. Do you think your sister and Lady Wakebourne will mind if I eat in my dirt?' he asked to divert the lad from what he'd revealed about his early life, lest he have nightmares of that long-lost boy shut up in the tower alone.

'Yes, her ladyship says she has her standards, however low she's fallen in life, and cleanliness costs only a bar of soap and some hot water, which is just as well since she can't afford much more. We told her we'd be happy to save on the soap part to help out, but Poll insists it's a price worth paying.'

'Bad luck,' Tom said sympathetically, recalling earnest arguments with Virginia on the same subject he'd been secretly relieved not to win when he looked back with a shudder on being filthy and on the brink of starvation at Dayspring Castle, before his life took an unexpected turn for the better with her arrival in it.

Polly stood up from stoking the fire in the communal room they'd made from the great parlour of long-ago lords of Dayspring Castle. It had been little more than a huge lumber room until they came, but now the oak-panelled walls and mix of ancient furniture gathered from other neglected chambers shone with beeswax.

Richly coloured cushions made even awkward old oak chairs comfortable enough to sit and doze in on a winter evening. The fact they were made from the good bits of brocade or velvet curtains too old or damaged to repair probably wouldn't go down well with the owner of this faded splendour, but she really didn't care. No doubt Lord Mantaigne would condemn them for making a home here and turn them out tomorrow anyway, but today they had more right to be here than he did. Given the neglect he'd inflicted on his splendid birthright, if there was any justice he'd have no rights here at all.

'Ah, there you are,' the man observed from the doorway and she turned to make some sarcastic comment on his acute powers of observation.

'Heavens,' she said lamely instead and felt her mouth fall open at the sight of a very different Lord Mantaigne to the man polite society fawned on like fools.

'I believe "Lawks" was how your cook put it,' he said, and drat the man, but his grin was pure charm, and suddenly she understood all that fawning after all.

'Prue's not *my* cook, she's a friend,' she argued, but there was no bite in her tone as she gazed at perhaps the dirtiest nobleman she'd ever laid eyes on.

He shrugged, and a clump of grey dust-covered cobweb fell from of his once-burnished curls and drifted softly to the threadbare but spotlessly clean Turkey carpet. 'Whoever she is, she is a wonderful cook if the delicious smells coming from her kitchen are anything to go by.'

'She is, and they are,' Polly agreed lamely.

'She has invited me to eat with you all, once I've dislodged the dust of ages from my person and can sit down to it like a civilised human being.'

'That sounds like her,' she said, still trying to enmesh her image of the wicked and sophisticated aristocrat she'd hated for so long with this rueful, sweaty and filthy man who seemed very ready to admit the joke was on him.

'I offered to marry her, but she says she's already spoken for,' he added, and she refused to like him— yes, that was it, she simply refused to be charmed. He wasn't going to subvert Paulina Trethayne with his easy, intimate smiles, or the glitter of mischief in those intensely blue eyes that invited her to laugh with him and bid goodbye to the wary distrust she wanted to keep between them like a shield.

'It will take you until midnight to get yourself clean enough for that,' she blurted out, and he laughed as if at a brilliant witticism. She felt it as if he'd reached inside her and jarred her whole being with that one rumble of masculine enjoyment. 'And I refuse to wait here like a waxwork while you preen and primp and peacock yourself back into a state of suitable splendour and the rest of us go hungry, so you'd best hurry up.'

'You thought me splendid before I acquired all this dirt then, Miss Trethayne?' he asked with an ironic bow that lost some of its effect when a twig from some ancient bird's nest fell on the carpet at his dusty feet and he had to stoop down even further to pick it up.

It would be silly to find it admirable in him to consider whoever had to keep this place clean. Of course she didn't think he was anything of the kind and reinforced her disapproval with a glower that might be a little overdone. The sight of it certainly seemed to cheer the contrary man for some reason, and he clicked his heels in a mock-military salute, then stood as upright as a soldier on parade.

'I can quite see why your brothers are terrified of your wrath, Miss Trethayne. You must set very high standards of cleanliness and good behaviour.'

'They are *not* terrified of me,' she told him with the feeling of having been caught kicking puppies, making her meet those blue, blue eyes of his with shock and reproach in her own before she remembered he was a master of manipulating those about him and glared full at him, since he was so determined to get her attention.

'No? And they seem such well-behaved and sensible lads,' he lied with a straight face.

Dote on them though she might, she had no illusions about any of her lively and headstrong brothers and nobody had ever accused them of being less than a handful, even when they were on their best behaviour.

'You know very well they're nothing of the sort,' she said dourly.

How had he tricked her into saying any such thing within such a short time of his arrival? She would have sworn to any other outsider that her brothers were the best boys she had ever come across if they even tried to tell her the Trethayne brothers were a touch wild and ought to be confined to the care of a strict schoolmaster until they learned some manners. Now she was admitting they were a trio of noisy and argumentative urchins to her worst enemy and he was her worst enemy, wasn't he?

'I like them,' he claimed, and that was just plain unfair of him.

'So do I,' she replied repressively and stared pointedly at the spider about to drop off his elbow onto Lady Wakebourne's favourite chair. 'If you don't go away and take your livestock with you, there won't be any dinner left for you to devour when you get back from restoring yourself to your usual state of dandified magnificence in an hour or two,' she told him nastily, but this man brought out the worst in her and that was that.

'Scared of spiders, Miss Trethayne?'

'No, only marquises, my lord.'

'Very sensible, you really wouldn't want one of us in your hair,' he said as lightly as if she hadn't just shot a dart past his armour, but somehow she knew she had and felt a twinge of shame twist in her belly that she refused to consider more closely until he'd gone. She wasn't scared of him so much as her own reactions to him and neither of them needed to know that just now.

'Go away,' she said dourly, and the wretch did with one last, thoughtful look back at her that said he wondered exactly why she wanted him gone so badly. 'Why were you looking for me?' she called after him, feeling as if he'd taken some of the air and all the excitement out of the room with him and contrarily wanting it back.

I bet lots of women can't help themselves whenever he's around, a bleak, repressive inner voice whispered, but she ignored it as best she could.

'Because Lady Wakebourne thought you would know where my valise has gone. If you will excuse me, poor Peters is very likely shivering himself into an early grave out in the laundry room right now, since he refuses to enter the castle in a state of nature after his much-needed ablutions. I, of course, have no such gentlemanly scruples and will be perfectly happy to run about the place stark naked as soon as I've washed the dust and dirt of the last century or so away and feel restored to my rude self again.'

'Sam Barker took it up to the South Tower. That's where all the men sleep,' she said in a strangled voice she hardly recognised as her own.

'I must remember to thank him for such a kindness,

but I don't think he'd want me searching the place from top to toe and getting dust everywhere right now, do you?'

'I'll find him and ask him to bring it out to you,' she said in a loud voice she told herself wasn't in the least bit squeaky with panic as the idea of this particular man appearing in the hall of his ancestors and naked as the day he was born sent a shudder through her that had nothing at all to do with her being cold.

'My thanks, Miss Trethayne,' he said as smoothly as if they'd been discussing the weather, then he sauntered away to join poor Mr Peters in the laundry as if he would never dream of wondering how it would feel if they happened to be naked at the same time.

Chapter Four

Polly was glad to be alone as the very idea made her clamp her legs together against a hot rush of wanton excitement at her feminine core that felt sinful and delicious in equal measure. 'Oh, heavens,' she husked on a long, expelled breath that felt as if it had come on a very long journey all the way from her boots.

The most appalling images of a naked, sweat-streaked and vital Lord Mantaigne were cavorting about in her head like seductively potent demons now. He was disgusting, she told herself, and in more ways than one. He was certainly physically filthy, and she ought not to find that the least bit appealing in the man. There had even been a streak of ancient grey dust right across the front of his disgracefully open shirt and, come to think of it, that garment had clung to him as if it loved him as well. She could recall exactly how the dust darkened across the bare torso visible under that once-pristine linen and the powdery stuff had clung to the sweat on his tanned and glistening skin like a fond lover.

If she had dared let even a hint of her fascination with his work-mussed person show, he would have played on it as shamelessly as an actor in a melodrama, but even willpower couldn't control the physical response of her body to his now he'd gone and her wicked imagination had taken over. Of course it was folly to wonder how it would feel to be his equal in sophistication and passion and flirt right back at him, to risk the shame and scandal of being a fallen woman for the absolute pleasure of being such a devastatingly masculine yet civilised and urbane man's lover. He was an accomplished breaker of women's hearts and it was good that she was nothing like the females such finicky men of the world chose as their paramours.

She brushed a hesitant, wondering hand tentatively over her breeches and up to her slender waist with the feeling she was leaving stardust in its wake, then she gasped as she realised where her too-vivid imagination was taking her again. So horribly conscious of her own body that she suddenly felt as if it had a life and demands independent of the rest of her, she slammed a door on the image of lordly Lord Mantaigne luxuriating in the makeshift bathing room they'd made in one of the laundries. It would be steamy, the air warm from the fire Dotty would have lit for the comfort of the weary labourers as they got rid of all their dirt, because Dotty had a soft heart under her gruff manner and she openly admitted making men comfortable had been the mission of her youth.

Thank goodness the self-appointed castle laundress was middle-aged and didn't continue with her life's work in quite the same way nowadays. The image of his lordship in his tub with a very willing and gleeful female seemed utterly disgusting somehow, as the one of him in it with the likes of her that hesitated on the edge of her thoughts never could be, even though her everyday self wished it was.

'Oh, no, the valise!' she yelped and ran out of the room to find Sam Barker before there was the slightest risk of the marquis carrying out his implied threat to parade about the castle naked if someone didn't produce his clothes in time. 'Useless dandy,' she grumbled as soon as she'd run Sam to earth in the kitchen and met his amused gaze as he reassured her the master of the house had already been safely reunited with his clothes and there was nothing for her to panic about.

'That's what he thinks,' she mumbled to herself as she went back upstairs to put out a few of their precious store of wax candles in honour of their unwanted guest.

'So, what do you think?' Tom asked his supposed secretary-cum-agent-cum-lawyer half an hour later.

'Nobody would think you even knew what a broom looked like now, let alone how to use one,' Peters told him distractedly as he did his best to shave by the light of a flickering candle.

'That's not what I meant,' Tom told him grumpily, wondering why the world thought him such a peacock. 'I was asking your ideas about the self-appointed keepers of my castle.'

'From what I've seen so far, they seem a very mixed bag.'

'True, but I'm ready to defer to your superior knowledge of the criminal classes. Do you think any are active law-breakers?'

Peters seemed to consider that question more seriously as he wiped the last of his whiskers from the blade of his razor and was himself again, whoever that might be. 'I doubt it,' he said, as if the fact surprised him as well.

'So do I,' Tom said with a preoccupied frown as he used the square of mirror his confederate had vacated to brush his hair back into gleaming order. 'I suspect Lady Wakebourne would have them marched out of here faster than the cat could lick her ear if she had the slightest suspicion any had gone back to their old ways.'

'It's not just that. They respect her and Miss Trethayne. Even that battered old rogue in the gatehouse seemed more concerned about them than his own doubtful claim to employment and a roof over his head.'

'So why are two ladies living in what should be an abandoned barrack with a pack of reformed rogues and criminals?' Tom mused as he decided he was ready to face the world outside the castle laundry once again.

'Some don't seem the type to have ever been out-and-out rogues, so maybe they were all victims of an unlucky fate.'

'Maybe, but what sort of circumstances would set two ladies so far apart from their kind? They must have been dire to leave them squatting in such a bleak old barn of a place, scratching a living from whatever they have managed to find here to sustain some sort of life on.'

'Dire ones indeed,' Peters said starkly, confirming Tom's own conclusions.

He frowned at his now-immaculate reflection and came to terms with the idea he couldn't simply come here, take a look round and walk away again as he had half-hoped when he was given Virginia's letter ordering him to come here, find out what was amiss, then make up his mind if he wanted to demolish the castle or accept the duties and responsibilities that went with being born the heir of Dayspring Castle.

'Dire indeed if I meant to bring in a full staff and live here, since they would then have to leave the place.'

'And you don't?'

'Of course not, man. Would I have avoided it like the plague all these years if I had the slightest desire to settle in and play lord of all I survey here?'

'I really couldn't say, my lord,' the supposedly quiet and unassuming Mr Peters said, as if he had his own opinion about Tom's feelings for the place but was keeping it to himself.

'Good,' Tom drawled, squaring his shoulders at the suspicion the man might be right.

'Is Lord Mantaigne's bedchamber ready yet?' Lady Wakebourne asked Polly from the doorway of the great parlour.

'It would take an army to make that echoing barrack room ready for him,' Polly snapped back and felt the new tension in the air now the rightful owner was back in his castle. 'They can both sleep in the South Tower with the rest of the men,' she added, knowing all the same that nothing here was ever going to be the same again. 'We can't get them into the staterooms fast enough for my taste, but lodging the man in a musty and bat-ridden chamber in the empty part of the house won't endear us to him in any way.'

'And we don't want him to feel more uncomfortable than he has to here.'

'No, indeed,' Polly agreed with a weary sigh.

'Nor should we allow him the chance to form any wrong ideas about a lady residing under his roof, my dear. You must resume your petticoats in the daytime as well as at nights now, Paulina, whether you like them or not.'

'I don't. They're confoundedly restricting and make it well-nigh impossible to for me to do any work,' Polly complained, knowing her ladyship was right.

Casting a last glance round the comfortable room at the odd family they had made out of a pack of rootless strangers used of an evening, she wondered how many would stay in their own quarters tonight to avoid the puzzle of how the sweepings of the King's Highway dined with a marquis. Biting back a wistful sigh for yesterday, when they had no idea the impossible was about to happen, she nodded her agreement and bit her lip against a furious protest against the darker whims of fate.

'Never mind, my dear, it won't be for long. The boy must loathe the place, given the terrible things the locals whisper about what he endured here as a boy, and this is the first time he's been near Dayspring in twenty years. He probably won't be back for another twenty, once he's done whatever it is he came here to do.'

'And whatever that might be, he certainly didn't expect to find us here,' Polly answered glumly. 'I can't imagine why you wrote to his godmother about whatever is going on here. You must have done that months ago, since the old lady has been dead three months,' she said sharply, as all those nights when she had lain awake worrying about whoever was making incursions into the castle at night reminded her Lady Wakebourne was a devious woman.

'He is the only person who can tell them to go, my dear. I wasn't going to risk you losing your temper one day and confronting them, then maybe leaving those boys of yours even more alone in the world than they are already.'

'Oh, then I suppose I can see your point,' Polly conceded reluctantly, knowing she had a tendency to act first and think later, although of course a measured risk was perfectly acceptable and she had weighed that one up already and decided she needed more information before taking it.

'And I am very fond of you, my dear. I want you to be safe and happy as much as any of us.'

'Thank you, I am very fond of you to,' Polly admitted.

'Then there is no harm done between us?' The lady actually sounded anxious about that and Polly had to nod and admit it.

'No, but I now know you are a splendid actress and will be very wary of you in future.'

'I don't think I'll take to the stage to repair my fortunes even so. Now run along upstairs and put some petticoats on, my dear, if only for my sake.'

'Very well, but I still hate them.'

Going back across the courtyard to the women's quarters, she climbed the stairs to her lofty room and washed hastily. Trying not to give herself time to think too much, she bundled herself into the patched and fraying quilted petticoat, wide overskirt and unfashionably long bodice she wore when she absolutely had to. It felt ancient and impractical, and she hated the corsets she had to wear to make the bodice fit and the curb the heavy skirt put on her long stride so she must mince along or hold them so high they were indecent and defeated the purpose of wearing them in the first place. Without the hoops and panniers the gown was designed for, it hung limply about her long legs, but it was the only gown she'd found that wasn't so short on her it was more revealing than her breeches, so what couldn't be cured must be endured.

Until she had come here and discovered the liberty of breeches and boots she must have spent her waking life enduring the wretched things, she supposed with a sigh. As she lifted her skirts to descend the stairs without tumbling down them, she wondered how she'd borne it for so long. She minced impatiently into the housekeeper's kitchen they used instead of the vast castle kitchens and tried hard not to knock anything over now she felt several feet wider than usual.

'Oh, for goodness' sake, girl, you'd look a fright even without the sad state of your hair,' Lady Wakebourne exclaimed as she turned from stirring a saucepan for Prue with a look of despair at Polly's unfashionable array.

'What's wrong with me now?' Polly replied defensively.

'It looks as if you last ran a comb through it about six months ago.'

Polly raised a hand to feel if she was right and realised the hasty plait she'd twisted it into first thing this morning had gone sadly awry and she might as well be wearing a bird's nest on her head. She felt herself blush at the spectacle she must have made when Lord Mantaigne first laid eyes on her. She wasn't surprised he'd let his gaze linger on her long legs and what curves she had to her name so impudently now. No, she was, she had to be. His preoccupation with her long limbs proved to her that any reasonably formed female body would do for him to bed a woman, she reminded herself militantly.

'I'm not primping and preening for any man, let alone him,' she said, even as the idea of sharing a meal with that finicky, arrogant aristocrat looking as if she had been left out in a tempest for a day made something deep inside her cringe.

'Don't worry, I think we would know that, even if you did the rest of us the courtesy of taking a brush and comb to that wild mess now and again.'

'I'm not going all the way back to my room to try and turn myself into a sweet and docile lady for the marquis's benefit.'

'Not much risk of you ever being one of those, Miss Polly.' The girl stooping over the fire to turn the spit for her sister Prue straightened up as far as she could to eye Polly critically. 'If you wouldn't mind watching this for me, your ladyship, I could take Miss Polly along

to my room and tame that tangle into something closer
to how it ought to look.'

'Of course, Jane dear. Far be it from me to stand
in the way of such a noble undertaking,' Lady Wakebourne said cheerfully and took over the task with an
ease her former friends might find a little distasteful if
they could see her. Since they had turned their backs
when she found out her husband had gambled away
his fortune, Lady Wakebourne's dowry and a whole
lot more before he shot himself, Polly was very glad to
have missed out on knowing them.

'You have such beautiful hair, Miss Polly,' Jane said
when she finally persuaded Polly to sit still on a three-
legged stool in her bedchamber on the other side of their
makeshift kitchen from the men's sleeping quarters,
where the heat of the fires at least warded off the chill
from the southwest winds and ancient walls left too long
without enough fires powerful enough to warm them.

'It gets in a mess as soon as I've finish tying it back
every morning.'

'That's because it needs thinning here and there and
if you'll let me take a few inches off the ends, I'm sure
you won't find it so hard to manage,' Jane said shyly as
she undid the heavy mass, then brushed and combed it
into a crackling and vital cloak about Polly shoulders.

Even her hair seemed imbued with some of her impatience with being primped until suitable for the lord
of Dayspring to set his noble eyes on so he wouldn't be
put off his dinner. Polly wondered how long Jane had
wanted to be a lady's maid and it was a hope unlikely

to ever come true, given society's prejudices, so if playing one for a night made her feel better, Polly found she could keep still after all.

'Do what you like with it then,' she said with a restless shrug.

'Only if you promise to sit quiet,' Jane chided, then produced a pair of sharp scissors and began snipping at Polly's hair as if shaping it was a work of art. 'Sit there while I fetch a branch of candles. I can't see well enough to do this properly,' Jane said just as Polly was beginning to hope she'd finished.

So Polly had time to sit and wonder why she was doing this. Surely she didn't want that popinjay to admire her as he might have if their eyes met across a crowded ballroom? She squirmed at the idea of being sized up as the other party in a wild and fleeting affair by a society rake and told herself it was because her seat was too low and rather hard, not because the very thought of Lord Mantaigne made her feel as if a crucial part of her insides might be melting. She despised unprincipled dandies and who could doubt he was one of those when he wore that ridiculously elegant get up as if he was about to take a stroll across Mayfair instead of camp out in a dusty and crumbling castle?

If she'd first seen him sauntering down Bond Street in that exquisitely cut coat, tightly fitting pantaloons and gleaming Hessians she would have shot him a scornful look, then forgotten him as a man of straw. If he'd raised his perfect top hat from his gleaming golden curls and bowed as if he knew her, she would have given him the cold stare of a lady dealing with an overfamiliar gentleman and moved on with a dismissive nod. How she wished she had seen him like that, in his natural orbit and revealed for what he was under the cool light of a London Season.

Except she had only ever heard about such beings in Lady Wakebourne's tales of former glory. Miss Paulina Trethayne had no youthful rites of passage to look back on; she had never stood on the verge of womanhood, waiting nervously to meet a hopeful youth who might marry her and make her and her children secure for the rest of her life, or might gamble and whore his way through every penny of his fortune and her dowry. She never would now and, since she was already a woman who knew the best way to feel secure in life was to rely on herself; that was just as well. If she came across the Marquis of Mantaigne outside the castle walls it would be as his unequal in every way and she refused to regret it.

So why *did* a part of her she didn't like to admit existed long to dance with him at grand society balls and drift about the dance floor of Almack's Club during a dazzlingly intimate evening of gossip and dancing? The flighty Paulina Trethayne she might have been, if things had been very different, stopped twiddling her thumbs in boredom with the mundane life she had been forced to live beyond the playgrounds of the *haut ton* and livened up at the idea of dancing with such a man, intimately or not.

Polly wondered how much of the wilful and contrary young girl she had once been was left in her soul, breathlessly green and curious as ever. It felt as if she was on the edge of something life changing and potentially wonderful and nothing could be further from the truth. She looked sideways into the square of mirror Jane and her sister had rescued from somewhere and saw a beanpole dressed in a jumble of hand-me-down clothes with a rough cloth draped over her shoulders to collect stray hairs. What was worse, the lanky creature was staring back from that pane of silvered glass all soft-eyed and dreamy with a silly smile on her face.

Idiot, she condemned her inner fool. *You know exactly what happens to such romantic dreamers.* With impatient revulsion she turned her head sharply away and was about to get up and ruin Jane's day when the girl came bustling back into the room as rapidly as her twisted limbs allowed.

'Sit down and have a bit of patience for once in your life, Miss Polly,' she ordered, and Polly folded her long legs back on to her perch and meekly did as she was bid. Just because dreams stopped being rosy when reality broke in, it didn't mean Jane's secret ambition deserved to be pushed aside as if it didn't matter.

'There's so much to do,' she protested half-heartedly, but Jane frowned with the air of an expert interrupted in a vital task. 'And that mincing fop wouldn't care if I sat down to dinner wearing a sack.'

'But you should,' Jane reproved her gently, and Polly felt ashamed for not caring she had straight limbs and an acceptable, if lanky, female form when Jane must long for such luxury every time her legs refused to obey her.

'It's been years since I needed to,' Polly admitted softly and they were both silent for a while, Jane busy with her self-appointed task and Polly wondering how her life might have been, if Papa hadn't been so feckless and the boys so very young and dependent on her when he died.

'There, I've finished,' her companion said at last. Polly sighed with relief and got ready to get up and go about her interrupted evening without another thought for her reflection in that unforgiving mirror. 'No, you don't. You have to at least take a look at yourself now I've done all I can at short notice,' Jane protested.

'I'm still me,' she argued, snatching a glance in the mirror to pacify Jane. 'It looks a little wild for my tastes,' she said, eyeing her newly barbered and carefully arranged hair dubiously.

'Not wild; cut and dressed to frame your face properly. You have beautiful hair, Miss Polly. It's a crime to bundle it up as best you can and hack bits off it when you get impatient with the weight of it like you do. Come to me whenever it gets in your way and I'll soon have it looking lovely again.'

'You can't make a silk purse out of a sow's ear, Jane, but since you enjoy cutting hair you might as well practise on me as anyone else.'

'You're a fine-looking lady, Miss Polly, and it's high time you realised it,' Jane said with a militant nod. 'His lordship won't be able to take his eyes off you tonight.'

'Flatterer. You know perfectly well I'm a quiz at my last prayers and I don't care a jot what that lordly fribble thinks of me,' Polly said as she left the room and walked straight into a wall.

Blinking at the odd fact it was a warm and very well-dressed wall that smelt of Lady Wakebourne's best herbal soap and clean linen, she groaned very quietly as she replayed her own words in her head.

'Forgive me,' Lord Mantaigne said with meticulous politeness as he set her at arm's length and stood back. 'I seem to have got sadly lost in my own castle.'

'I'm sorry too, Lord Mantaigne,' she said stiffly as she pulled back from the impact he had on her senses as if he'd stung her. 'I didn't see you out here.'

'Little wonder, you'd have a job to see a shooting star in all this gloom,' he grumbled rather dourly.

'What did you expect after so many years of doing your best to let this poor old place fall down, a diorama put on in your honour?'

'Even I am not that unreasonable or deluded. No, I expected a great deal worse than this and should thank you all rather than complaining about shortcomings I caused in the first place,' he admitted. She refused to find the sight of him running a distracted hand through his now wildly curling golden locks endearing. 'I expected we would have to camp out in an outhouse or sleep in one of the barns. Hence all those wagons and so many provisions for the horses until we could buy more.'

'I'm relieved to know the space was not entirely taken up by your clothes,' she said before good manners could catch up with her tongue.

'What a very high opinion of me you do have, Miss Trethayne,' he said so smoothly she wondered if anything touched the real man under the gloss and glamour. She must have imagined her scathing opinion of him had hurt, for there was nothing in his eyes but mockery of them both for standing here trading insults whilst their dinner was waiting and they were sharp set.

'This is a fine and noble heritage, my lord, and I don't approve of your wilful destruction of it,' she said dourly. There seemed little point trying to be sweet and polite when he was about to put her family out of the only home they had.

'Some things are better left to rot,' she thought she heard him mutter.

'People harm other people. Buildings merely endure our faults and caprices, as this one testifies all too well, but they have no feelings about us.'

'Thus speaks the voice of experience?' he asked with too much perception for the empty-headed Bond Street Beau she so badly wanted him to be.

'Of course, none of us would be here if we had anywhere else to go,' she replied with a shrug meant to deflect more questions.

'And I suspect you think I have no right to ask,' he said with a look in his deceptive blue eyes that promised he would find out anyway.

'Since you're sure to turn us all out now you have turned up, you have no right to know anything about us.'

'And if I don't?'

'You will, once you are properly settled here you won't be able to help it. What could Lord Mantaigne have in common with a ragtag band of beggars?'

'I'm surprised you haven't listened to the tales of my childhood that must be raked up when someone wonders why I don't cherish it as my forefathers did.'

'For some strange reason I admit I can't fathom, your people are loyal to you. We were told you disliked your guardian and he went mad, but they don't give out details to newcomers, and you must know we'd still be those if we'd been here decades.'

Polly caught a flash of emotion in his watchful gaze, then it was gone as if he didn't allow himself such luxuries. He was touched his people felt something for him; she could have sworn it in the brief moment he left himself unguarded. It shouldn't matter to her if he felt endless sonnets of overblown emotions or none at all, but if she wasn't careful she could find this contrary and deeply irritating man fascinating and that would lead her to places Polly Trethayne could not afford to go.

'Such loyalty is beyond me,' he admitted with a rueful shrug.

'Indeed?' she made herself say as if it was a puzzle she didn't care to enquire any further into. 'It must have been as long a day for you and Mr Peters as for the rest of us, my lord. Perhaps we should agree to eat and sleep before we resume arguing how your arrival will change Dayspring Castle in the morning.'

'We might as well, but tonight I can say thank-you for saving my house from dereliction and my staff from an uncomfortable night in an abandoned wreck and a cold supper, Miss Trethayne. I'm sure you would say that was all I deserve, but you must admit Peters and my servants are not to blame for my misdeeds.'

'They are welcome to share what little we have and I didn't do it on my own,' she said, but could tell from

the twitch of a smile at the corner of his mouth that
he'd noticed her side-step his share of their hospitality.

'Then let's agree there will be time enough for a report on all you and your friends have managed to save
from my neglect another day,' he allowed, but there was
a steely purpose under the limpid blue of his eyes now
that ought not to surprise her. He'd already proved a
very different marquis from the one she'd despised for
the past six and a half years, so it was little wonder he
kept surprising her.

Managing a half-hearted smile of greeting for her
friends and Mr Peters when they finally reached the
Great Parlour together, Polly did her best to fade into
the background when Lady Wakebourne greeted his
lordship like the Prodigal Son. Even those who ought to
know better seemed dazzled by the presence and glamour of a real live lord in their midst. She tried to tell
herself he was really a wolf in very handsome camouflage, but even to her the fact of him outdid the image.

If only she could have held on to her first impression
of him as a man of fashion; spoilt, idle and self-obsessed
as the Regent himself was reputed to be. Hating him
would be so much simpler if that cliché was nearer the
truth than this complicated rogue. She slanted a glance
at him being polite to his guests as if they were the no-
blest gathering in Europe and frowned at him for not
being high enough in the instep to put her off feeling
this unwanted connection between them.

And she couldn't fool herself into thinking he was a
soft and dandified gentleman who loafed about Mayfair

raking, gambling and doing whatever else idle young lords did to relieve their boredom any longer either. She was in a very good position to affirm there wasn't a spare ounce of fat on Lord Mantaigne's lean but powerful frame and he didn't get like that by going to bed with the dawn and rising too late to see more than a glimpse of daylight. This afternoon his grey-silk waistcoat had clung so lovingly to his muscular torso and narrow waist she suspected many otherwise respectable women would be eager to examine the fit and quality of it for themselves if he gave them the chance.

Luckily she had already given herself a stern lecture on the differences between such women and Polly Trethayne and she trampled down any lingering spell her first sight of him had cast and told herself she would now be immune. There had been a sharp moment of *Ah, here he is* before she felt the heat of those bluest of blue eyes linger on her long limbs and remind her she had given up all hope of respectable marriage the day her father died and left nothing but a mountain of debt behind him.

She had dared all she had in her to keep the boys with her, but that was dare enough for one lifetime. She couldn't consider the dishonourable intentions of a rake, or dream of might have been if things were different. The boys were not yet grown and she wasn't free to meet any rash promises those hot blue eyes of his had made her, even if she wanted to and of course she didn't want anything of the sort.

Yet still his magnificent physical presence was still emphasised by the long-tailed dark coat of a fashionable gentleman dining with friends, and she was still a sentient female with the use of her eyes. How could she *not* look at him and be reluctantly impressed, despite all her resolutions not to be? Clearly no Cumberland corset was necessary to give him a nipped-in waist and even the idea of his tailor having added buckram to pad out those muscular shoulders was laughable. She wondered what the fine ladies and gentlemen of the *ton* would make of the Marquis of Mantaigne sweeping his own stables, then spreading straw for his horses and waiting until they were fed and tended before taking himself off for a much-needed bath in the castle laundry.

The gentlemen might laugh up their sleeves while they secretly envied him his fitness and cheerful good humour as he got very dirty indeed, but the ladies would be too busy with less straightforward thoughts and impulses to listen to jokes at his expense. Polly knew that because she'd experienced a terrible urge to watch him at his labours this afternoon and had almost peeped through a knot hole in a shutter at the back of the building in an effort to do so. Somehow she found the strength to turn away, but considering he'd found her in his sweat-and-dust-covered glory afterwards anyway she might just as well have indulged herself to the full.

Now she squirmed in her seat as she waited for the men to sit once the women were in their accustomed places at the table, despite the marquis being a lord and most of them of far lower rank than any ladies he was accustomed to dining with. The heat that ran through her at her shameful thoughts of him sweaty and dishevelled and naked before jumping into his bath told her she found this particular lord far too desirable for her own good. She was suddenly very glad their precious beeswax candles were placed sparsely and flickered now and again in the draught from an ancient window. At least nobody would know she was blushing at such a scandalous idea in this mellow and uncertain light.

Chapter Five

For a while it was quiet in the room while they ate hungrily after a hard day of toil and travel. The silence was testament to Prue's fine cooking, Polly told herself as she slanted a look at Lord Mantaigne every now and again to make sure he was duly impressed. If he kept Prue on to cook for him, she and Jane would be safe. A plan to point out the skills and talents of her fellow interlopers took shape in her head as she tried to distract herself from his all-too-vivid presence next to her as everyone else had insisted, as if she was chatelaine and he the lord. He might employ them as a skeleton staff or caretakers if she convinced him how loyal and hardworking they were, despite the odd quirk that led to them being rootless in the first place.

'Were you and Mr Peters on the road for long today, Lord Mantaigne?' Lady Wakebourne asked politely.

'Peters joined me at Dorchester, but the rest of us took the journey from Derbyshire slowly to pace my team and let the wagons catch up every day.'

'They look fine beasts and your team are highsteppers, aren't they? I don't suppose they enjoyed being held back like a string of donkeys,' Tobias declared, and Polly glared at her eldest brother for breaking his absorbed silence. How typical that the only thing to divert him from his dinner was the team of perfectly matched greys now happily settled in their stables.

'The dray horses were bred for strength and not speed and can't match the pace of my greys, so we made slow progress by the standards of a true whip, but it was an easy enough journey at this time of year,' Lord Mantaigne said with a ready smile, and Polly had to stifle an urge to tell her brothers to be quiet and eat their dinner so it might be over with sooner.

They had little chance to converse with gentlemen, isolated as they were from local society by their poverty and dubious status as unofficial residents of Dayspring Castle. One day she must face the puzzle of finding suitably gentlemanly occupations for three quick and energetic boys who no longer enjoyed the privileges they'd been born to. For now she supposed it would do them good to see how easily a true gentleman conducted himself in company, but she hoped they didn't learn any of the idle, rakish and expensive ways this one could afford to indulge in along the way.

She loved her little brothers fiercely and would never be without them, but it was hard to be father, mother and everyone else to them. The burden felt especially heavy now they must make a new life out of nothing again. Dayspring had given them a life of peace and usefulness after their lives became a wasteland. If they hadn't stumbled on Lady Wakebourne in as sad a case as they were and this place so temptingly empty and forsaken, they would not have had it, though, and Polly sighed at the idea of taking to the roads again, in search of some other place to live until someone claimed it back. She fought a deep-down weariness at this constant struggle to keep her family happy, healthy and hopeful and told herself to count the blessing of a roof over their head and good food in their bellies for one more night.

'Your sighs could rival the gusts even the shutters can't keep out tonight, Miss Trethayne,' Lord Mantaigne remarked.

'It's been a long day, my lord. I suppose I must be weary of it,' she replied, refusing to squirm at the disapproving look Lady Wakebourne shot her to say she should remember her manners and make polite conversation.

'I suppose you must be,' he said blandly. 'I could be a little tired of it myself if I let the idea take root.'

'Aye, your lads from the wagons was worn to a thread. We took their share of stew and what bread we could spare to the stables so they didn't have to wash and shave until morning,' Dotty Hunslow said cheerfully.

Polly smiled a 'thank you' for that attempt to lighten the tension she'd caused with her edgy feeling they were walking on eggshells. By not being able to put her fear out her head that they were about to be homeless, she'd probably made it more likely they would be ejected than not.

'My thanks for making Dacre and my stable lads comfortable, ma'am,' Lord Mantaigne said as politely as if Dotty was a patroness of Almack's Club. Polly had to admire his manners, even if they highlighted her poor ones. 'I warned them not to expect much at the end of their journey, but you have made a liar out of me.'

'Even though you hate the place?' Sam Barker, the one-legged sailor who arrived here without a penny in the pocket of his ragged breeches, said from his seat with its back to the window where the worst of the draughts came in.

'Even so,' Mantaigne replied with a straight look. Sam met it with a challenge, then a nod, as if admitting this lord had backbone, despite his sins.

'And who can blame you for that, my boy? Now, we're at dinner, not the local assizes, Sam Barker. Let us talk of matters conducive to good digestion rather than past sins,' Lady Wakebourne said gently, and Polly was almost ashamed of her own determination not to see good in the man. It would be dangerous to like the spoilt aristocrat at her side and that was that.

'This is far too delicious a meal to mar with mine at any rate,' Lord Mantaigne agreed, 'but where has the artist who produced this fine meal hidden herself away?'

'She's not an artist, she's Prue,' Polly's littlest brother, Josh, informed him with a nod to where the sisters were sitting, flushed with pleasure at such praise.

'Then thank you, Mrs Prue. If the Prince of Wales gets word of your culinary skills, you'll be gracing his kitchens at Carlton House as fast as he can carry you off.'

'Oh, I wouldn't like that,' Prue said shyly, and Jane nodded wisely by her side.

'I'll be grateful if you continue here then. Tomorrow I'll find you a couple of assistants, though, as my arrival has doubled the number of people you cook for and more will have to be found if the old place is to be put in any sort of order.'

Lord Mantaigne offered such help so lightly Polly frowned, certain he meant his offer to have a limit. It sounded like a 'for now', until he decided what to do with this unwanted part of his splendid inheritance. Even if he ordered repairs to stop the castle from falling down, he would order it closed up again afterwards.

'What about the rest of us?' she blurted out and instantly regretted it.

Her sharp query arose from a stab of intense envy. He had so much while they could live on a small portion of it—if only he'd stay away. The others were shocked she had raised such a topic at the dinner table, gasped at her temerity, or sat in their seats, fearing they'd be turned out now she'd asked what no one else dared.

'Well, really, Polly!' Lady Wakebourne exclaimed.

'Coo, Miss Poll, you ain't half got a big mouth,' Jago said admiringly.

'A good question, but perhaps not an aid to good digestion,' Mr Peters said wryly.

'Do you ride, Miss Trethayne?' Lord Mantaigne asked coolly when the murmurs of agreement or dissent had died down.

'Of course I do,' she said scornfully, before she remembered she always did so astride and had no ladylike habit, or even an old-fashioned and not particularly ladylike one such as this shabby and decades-out-of-date evening gown.

'Then meet me in the stable yard after breakfast tomorrow and show me what you've been doing here. Once I know that, I shall be in a better position to decide what comes next.'

'You can't ride about the place dressed as a young man now his lordship is here, child,' Lady Wakebourne put in with genuine distress in her voice. 'You won't have a reputation left to whistle down the wind if you gallop about the countryside alone with such a gentleman looking like some heathen amazon.'

'Nonsense, ma'am, we shall take Peters with us. He's more of a proper gentleman than I shall ever be, so nobody will dare to think ill of us in his sober presence. My consequence is much improved since he entered my employ; I preen myself on the appearance of virtue without the effort of reform.'

'I am, of course, suitably grateful for your good opinion,' Mr Peters said in his usual quietly ironic fashion.

Polly wondered at the steel under his words. Who was Mr Peters to dare challenge a man of rank and power, even if he did it so subtly it took sharp ears to notice it?

'You need not fear for Miss Trethayne's reputation in such company, Lady Wakebourne,' Lord Mantaigne finished with an air of settling the question.

'Since I don't ride, I must be content with your word as a gentleman you will chaperon Miss Trethayne as effectively as I would, Mr Peters?'

Polly was touched by Lady Wakebourne's concern for a reputation already in shreds, given her unusual mode of dress and the life she had lived these past few years.

'Of course, my lady, it will be my pleasure,' the enigmatic secretary agreed with the deference he refused his powerful employer.

'Should I be feeling sadly cast down by your lack of faith in my gentlemanly instincts?' the marquis mused with a smile in his eyes Polly mustn't find disarming.

'Probably,' she replied and lowered her gaze to her plate in the hope Prue's cooking would put tomorrow to the back of her mind.

'You are about as easily cast down as a distant planet, young man,' Lady Wakebourne muttered into her soup.

'How well you seem to know me, ma'am—were you a long-standing friend of my godmother?'

'Oh, no, she belonged to a more sophisticated set than I aspired to. My maiden aunt was one of her bosom bows, but she's been dead for fifteen years or more now and I doubt you remember her.'

'Virginia had a variety of terrifying friends who would interrogate me about my morals and intentions in life and the shameful state of my neck and hands when I was a grubby schoolboy. I dare say your relative was a sweet little lady with a doting fondness for small boys and would not dream of such an inquisition?'

'I never found her heart of gold if she possessed one, which I doubt.'

'Oh, dear, who was your particular tartar in petticoats, then?'

'Miss Euphemia Badlerstone,' Lady Wakebourne said with a shudder Lord Mantaigne echoed, and Polly felt it set off a twinge of heat and dangerous fellow feeling stir deep within her once more.

'I remember her only too well: a lady of great perception, little patience and a devastatingly frank tongue.'

'I would think less of you if you pretended she was sweet, gentle or charitable,' Lady Wakebourne said indulgently.

Polly only just bit back a groan at the thought her friend was about to adopt another lone boy. This one was certainly not in any need of her fierce protection and frustrated maternal love. Lord Mantaigne was clearly able to take care of himself, and Polly couldn't imagine how any woman would see his all-too-evident strength and boldness and feel in the least bit motherly, because she certainly didn't.

Something told her he was even more complex than she'd first thought under his shell of indifference, so she tried to let his genial small talk wash over her as she ate her dinner. Then she went through the plans she had for tomorrow in her head in order to put them off for a day that might never come now he was here. This was the true business of her life: ensuring there was enough to eat and a safe place for her family to sleep. Things she grew up taking for granted were a vague memory for Toby and Harry and a myth to Josh and she was all that stood between them and destitution. She would keep standing there, though, and this feral attraction to a marquis could not be allowed to get in the way.

Heaven forbid her boys ever looked like Jago, Joe and Benjie did when Lady Wakebourne lifted them down from the cart she had driven back from London. None of them could blame their new friend for snatching three little exhausted climbing boys from their master one night as he lay drunk in the gutter on their earnings, but for a long time they lived in dread of someone connecting Lady Wakebourne's last desperate appearance in polite society with their disappearance. She had gone to see if anything was left from the disaster her husband had wrought to add to what they could grow or make from a mouldering castle and its neglected gardens.

It was a reminder Polly must still fight to make sure her boys were never dependent on cold charity. Thank heavens all but Josh were too big for such a trade now, but it took months for the sores on Jago, Joe and Ben's poor burnt and soot-encrusted feet to heal, longer for their shocked eyes to spark with mischief and to this day Jago had nightmares about being trapped in dark and ever narrowing chimneys. He was still only twelve years old, and Polly caught herself glaring at Lord Mantaigne for having so many chimneys in need of small climbing boys to clean them.

She had no right to judge him, she reminded herself. How would she have been by now if she had lived the life of a lady of quality? Ladies were not supposed to question the grand order of things and even the thought of such a little life made her yawn. Lady Wakebourne misread it as weariness and rose to her feet as if she had been waiting for someone else to wilt so she could too. Gathering her female troops about her, she was gracious as the men sprang to their feet.

'I think we might as well retire, ladies,' she remarked. 'There is a great deal to do in the morning and no point wasting candles if we're only going to nod over our needlework.'

'Until the morning then, Lady Wakebourne; Miss Trethayne; ladies,' Lord Mantaigne said with a bow that made no differences between them.

'Boys, you might consider yourselves quite grown up and able to sit up half the night plaguing your elders, but I do not. Bedtime, my lads,' Lady Wakebourne ordered.

'Will he let us stay, Poll?' Toby asked her quietly as soon as his younger brothers were asleep.

'I doubt it,' she had to admit because he was too old to be fobbed off with a shrug or a diversionary tactic.

'We'll come about somehow, though, Sis, don't you worry,' he said with a grave look that ought to be beyond a boy born to comfort and privilege, even if there was little of either in his life now.

Toby was the only one of her half-brothers old enough to fully remember how it felt to wander the world with nowhere to go and an ever-dwindling supply of money to do it on. Polly had tried so hard to make their new life an adventure; to encourage him to look forward to every day as full of hope and possibility instead of fear. She had felt enough of that for both of them and memory of it made her heart thump.

'We shall be together, that's all that matters,' she replied with an attempt at light-heartedness he met with a brave smile.

'I'm a man this time, Poll,' he told her sleepily.

'You are, love, but men still need sleep, and you've had a long day, so let tomorrow take care of itself.'

'You will discuss anything important with me, won't you?' he asked, and yet again she had to face the reality her brothers were growing up without much more prospects in life than Jago, Benjie and Joe.

'Of course, and we're the bold and bad Trethayne family, don't forget.'

'Aye, of course we are,' he mumbled with a sleepy sigh and slept as suddenly and completely as a boy must after a day of action and excitement.

'Oh, love, may you dream of better things,' she whispered softly, dousing the candle before tiptoeing out by memory.

'Are they asleep?' Lady Wakebourne murmured when Polly shut the door as softly as ancient oak and a heavy latch allowed.

'Yes, it would take an army marching about the courtyard to wake them now.'

'Then come to my chamber and talk while we take some of that claret Barker found in the inner cellar. I dare say you'll get no sleep without it, despite what I said when we left the great room tonight.'

Polly and Lady Wakebourne crossed the courtyard to the women's quarters together. No doubt Lord Mantaigne would find it amusing such barriers existed in such a ramshackle household, but it was a matter of pride to confound those who called them vagabonds and misfits—not that many villagers dared say so after they met Lady Wakebourne. Polly bore the lantern to light them to the stout door of the inner courtyard and a suite of rooms that once belonged to the castle steward.

'Hold still, girl,' her companion demanded, using both hands to try to raise the latch holding the ancient studded oak door firmly shut. 'What's the point of being half a foot taller than you should be if you can't act the footman once in a while?'

'None at all I dare say,' Polly replied placidly, wondering why the lady's blunt comments didn't set her teeth on edge as any slight criticism by Lord Mantaigne did. 'Would you like me to try?'

'No, keep that light steady and I'll do well enough.'

'May *I* open it for you then, my lady?' the marquis's deep, amused voice asked out of the gloom.

Polly wondered why instinct hadn't made her nerves jump the moment they stepped out of the tower door into the darkness, since he was obviously strolling about the inner court, making what he could of his domain in the pitch dark.

'Of course you can, Mantaigne, it's your door.'

'I apologise for its intransigence,' he replied as if he'd escorted them home from the play and conducted them to their door as a proper gentleman should. He shifted the heavy iron latch the other side of the wrought handle with one hand and gently pushed open the door.

'Well done, my boy,' Lady Wakebourne said as if he had just achieved some hugely difficult quest and took advantage of the lamp left burning low in the little hallway to sail upstairs before Polly could follow her.

'I suspect we're being left to settle our differences and stop making her uncomfortable, Miss Trethayne,' he said as she frowned after her so-called friend.

Differences could be good. Particularly if they kept you from having silly daydreams of what might be for her and this potent and infuriating lord if life had only been different. She would still be nigh six foot tall and he would be as armoured against her in a Mayfair ball-room as he was in the starlit darkness of a Dorset night. Any other reasonably young and not unattractive lady might tempt him to test her virtue once they were alone with the sea whispering on the shore and spring seeming to soften the very air around them, but Polly Trethayne was in no danger.

'I don't think we'll ever be bosom bows, my lord. We have neither interests nor acquaintances in common,' she said as distantly as she could when her foolish inner self wanted to rail about his immunity to her as every move he made seemed of unique interest to her.

'We should give each other the benefit of the doubt until we know better, but if you'd like to confide your dearest secrets in me I'll try not to broadcast them,' he said so blandly she felt her palm itch to slap the smile off his face.

'I would sooner tell them to a town crier,' she muttered darkly.

It simply wasn't acceptable to find his answering chuckle disarming. They had moved away from the circle of light cast by the lamp he'd hung on a hook by the old door to light her way back. Now it felt too intimate in the shadowy courtyard for her peace of mind.

'Yet we must rub along over the next few weeks if I'm to do what I set out to here. If you and your friends remain here, we must reach some sort of truce and make it obvious Lady Wakebourne is your very strict chaperon. There is no other way we can live under the same roof without scandal, and I'm not the one gossip will reflect on most. This isn't a fair world, Miss Trethayne, and we have to pretend we respect each other if we're to stay at Dayspring with any appearance of respectability,' he said soberly, and drat him for being right.

'I suppose so,' she admitted reluctantly, and that won her another soft masculine laugh that made her shiver with warmth and feel the natural order of things had been upended.

'And I'm really not such a bad fellow if you ignore my shortcomings,' he said as if he was coaxing a wary dog to like him.

Ridiculously offended he showed none of the caution he would have used toward any other lady of her age and single status, she squirmed at the prickly discomfort of being close to him. He was so oblivious to her as woman he'd hardly noticed she was one since that first heady moment when he seemed to see it very clearly indeed, but how stupid to feel piqued by his indifference now.

'I'm sure your friends hang on your every word and deed, Lord Mantaigne, so you hardly need me to join in. I am squatting in your grand castle with my friends and family and your coming must change that, so you can hardly expect me to welcome you with open arms. You'll turn us back into beggars and vagabonds sooner or later, however nicely you try to wrap it up in ifs and maybes.'

'You're not like any vagrants I ever came across,' he muttered, as if his inability to slot them into convenient places troubled him.

'I suspect they're not like them either, if you can see past rags and desperation to the person underneath. I've had all the sneers and slights most beggars get thrown at them over the years, my lord, but words only sting for a while and blows are much harder to shrug off.'

'Someone hit you?' he asked indignantly as if it was an affront he would dash off on his charger to avenge in blood.

'Of course, and attempted worse when I said them nay. I was a beggar woman with a babe in her arms and two children clutching at her skirts. Why else do you think I stopped wearing them in the end, my lord?'

'For ease and to fit the hard labour you undertake, I suppose,' he admitted with a shrug she could feel rather than see. 'Maybe you're right and I am only a man of fashion and not a deep thinker,' he added.

'If you truly believe that, you really are a fool,' she said impatiently.

'You are a very forthright female, Miss Trethayne.'

'And you're a cunning opponent, Lord Mantaigne. You deflect difficult questions so ably I don't suppose your foes recall asking them in the first place.'

'Yet you have an uncomfortable knack of clinging to them whatever hares I put up to divert you, but I really didn't set out to be your enemy.'

'Since you own this place and I've been living in it without your permission for nearly seven years, that makes us enemies whatever you set out to be.'

'First I'd have to care about Dayspring and I'll never do that. If you and your friends living here means I need never come back, you can all stay until doomsday as far as I'm concerned.'

'For a man who doesn't care you're almost passionate about your birthplace, my lord,' she pointed out slyly.

Polly saw him flinch now her eyes were accustomed to the faint starlight even in this dark corner of the courtyard. The idea she might have caused him pain gave her no satisfaction at all and sparked a little echo of his hurt in her own gut. It was worrying to feel such connection to a man far outside her reach and experience. She retreated into the darkest pool of shadows lest he could read her too easily back.

Tom caught the faint movement even as he tried to defend himself against her curiosity. No, that was harsh; he couldn't accuse her of so simple a human failing. This odd mix of a woman now trying to hide her thoughts in darkness as she wouldn't let him had lived her life shorn of the pretences, as well as the comforts, of her kind. No wonder she was impatient of the strategies he used to fend off anyone who wanted to know the Tom under his wealth, fashionable clothes and titles.

He felt a nigh overwhelming urge to let her find him and couldn't recall feeling such connection with a stranger since the day Virginia had marched into his life and changed it for ever. His mouth quirked in a reluctant smile as he recalled how little he'd liked his godmother for breaching his defiant hatred of the world that could treat him as this one had so far. Virginia took no notice of his barricades either; she marched straight over them with one impatient shake of her still-handsome head and informed him he was to live with her from now on and everything would be different, beginning with a haircut and a bath. Even that threat didn't stop something

hard and brittle at the heart of him from cracking open
to let a new Tom step out.

The man who grew out of that boy sighed for the
awkward and mistrustful urchin he'd been and almost
wished himself other than who he was now. Once he
was gone Polly Trethayne could do what she wanted
with Dayspring and he mustn't wish he could be at her
side, wanting it too.

Chapter Six

'What the devil was that?' Tom demanded as the echo of a distant thud carried through the still night.

'Damned if I know,' she whispered, sounding more gruffly impatient than he was. 'Someone has been getting into the closed-up wings of the house at night and we don't know what they want or how they get in.'

'Smugglers?' he suggested grimly, knowing there was a risk the local rogues were emboldened by his hatred of the place to use it for their own ends.

'You must know better than that, my lord. You spent your earliest years here, even if you now live as far away from the sea as a body can get.'

'Aye, too much starlight,' he agreed as he listened for any other signs they were not alone out here in the night and felt the prickle of her so closeness shiver against his skin in the intimate dark.

Confound it, but even listening for what shouldn't be in the night wasn't enough to divert him from this ridiculous consciousness of her so close and feminine and even more goddess-like than ever in her shabby and ill-fitting gown and old-fashioned petticoats.

'News will have got about that you're here by now as well,' she warned, and he supposed she was right, given the network of gossip and intrigue that operated so effectively in any areas where the free-traders ran their illicit cargoes.

'Maybe that's what spurred them into action,' he wondered out loud.

'Then what brought them here last week or the one before?'

'When did it begin, then?'

'I felt there was something wrong before the turn of the year, but I wasn't sure until a couple of weeks ago. Now I need to know how they get in and out and why they seem to be looking for something, rather than hiding it or fetching it away as you would expect the free-traders to do. Everyone knows the castle is all but empty and anything left behind is so heavy or useless it has no value, or it would have been taken away for safe keeping when the castle was closed up. Either they are curious youths hell-bent on some sort of secret carouse, or your second guardian did not clear out the newer parts of the castle as well as he did the older one where we live. I can vouch for the fact he did a very good job indeed on our quarters.'

'Virgil Winterley was an efficient man. When he and my godmother decided to do something they always did it to the best of their ability—they took me on when anyone else would have blenched and run away at first sight of the sullen brat I was then.'

'I find that difficult to believe, my lord.'

'That I was sullen or a brat?

'You are almost too much in control of your temper and I can't visualise you as the furious and defiant urchin even my littlest brother can turn into at times.'

'Oh, visualise it and multiply it by a dozen, Miss Trethayne,' Tom told her softly, his thoughts in the past with the resentful, terrified boy he had been for the three years of his early life between five and eight when his first guardian controlled his young life with sadistic thoroughness. 'I'm astonished Virgil didn't bundle me up, drive halfway across the country and leave me on the madhouse doorstep for my old guardian to take back, however few wits he had left.'

'So old Maggie was wrong about you being so angelic, then?'

'You should have listened a little harder. She might have said I *looked* like an angel as a child, not that I ever behaved like one. From what little I recall before Philip Grably turned her off, my old nurse was far too honest to tell anyone her former charge was aught but a spoilt and hasty-tempered urchin.'

'She did say you'd have turned out as proud as a turkey cock if that devil hadn't tried to break your spirit, but she truly loved you, my lord. She was still mourning her inability to defy the man and stay with you last time we spoke.'

'I don't remember anything much of my life before my father died. It feels as if someone built a wall between before and after.'

'You were very young, so little wonder that you can't recall much.'

'For all I know I could be my father's bastard smuggled into the nurseries one night when his wife wasn't looking, as my guardian told me I was on one memorable occasion.'

'I think that unlikely.'

'Aye, but a great deal about my life seems unlikely now I'm back here.'

'Us included?'

'You especially. You're the most unexpected surprise of all.'

'And not a very welcome one either, I suspect.'

'Oh, no, you have rarely been more wrong. It's not every day a man meets a goddess in breeches, and I wouldn't have missed the experience for all my castles and unearned wealth put together.'

Tom felt her start at his clumsy reminder he was a vigorous and lusty man under all his fine plumage and she was a magnificent and very desirable female under her rag-bag of a wardrobe. He'd been doing so well until that moment as well and he cursed his normally glib tongue for failing him with a woman who felt a lot more important than any of the impeccably bred young ladies trailed under his nose by their hopeful mamas had ever been to him, try how they might to catch themselves a marquis. He felt as if every word they said had a significance that was almost terrifying as they whispered of the past out here in the now and listened for intruders into an empty and echoing mansion nobody wanted to live in. If he'd read about himself and his odd mix of feelings in a book he wouldn't have believed a word of it, but here he was, senses more alert than he ever recalled them and every male cell in his body awake and alert towards the very female puzzle at his side.

'We weren't talking about me, my lord. I would like your help tracking down whoever is here under cover of darkness, but if you're going to be facetious I'll find out alone.'

'That you won't,' he muttered as he cast his mind back to that first soft and distant thud as another fainter one carried across the yard on the clear night air.

'Smugglers trying to remove a cargo before I can look closely at the place or employ a proper staff?' he suggested as her tension told him there was no point pretending he hadn't heard.

'There have been lights on the upper floors now and again as well,' she admitted reluctantly, as if she suspected local rumour would reach him sooner or later and he would wonder why she hadn't told him about them.

'Seen by those out in the night who should not be, I suppose?' he asked laconically, remembering his own nodding acquaintance with the night-hawks from his childhood. 'The local poachers didn't betray me to my guardian although he'd have winked at their sins if they did; so why would I hand them over to the local magistrates now?'

'Because you're no longer a child and hold our fates in your hand?' she said bitterly, and once again he felt the pull of connection between them as he saw how hard her life must have been these past few years and cared that she had suffered so much for the boys she obviously loved more than her own comfort.

The Marquis of Mantaigne famously cared for nobody and here he was teetering on the edge of worrying about a pack of strangers and one in particular. It wouldn't do. He must find out what was going on here as Virginia asked and leave without a backward look. He might leave an echoing, half-empty barrack behind him, but it would be a well-run one if Peters had a say in the matter.

'I'm just a man like any other, Miss Trethayne,' he defended himself against her scorn and wondered why.

'And you're making too much noise,' she muttered distractedly.

Her preoccupation with whoever was invading his castle in the dark clearly overcame any faint interest she might have had in him until someone trumped it. He felt piqued that she could so easily dismiss this wild curiosity to know more. He'd been so sure it was mutual, but perhaps he flattered himself. Maybe she was immune; his warmth and scent and the sound of his voice didn't do anything spectacular to her senses, now her sight was blunted by darkness, as hers did for him.

He wanted to employ every sense he had to learn all about her, but could he really feel such strong attraction to a woman who only wanted him to keep quiet or go away? Unless he chanced a rebuff and violated the laws of hospitality by kissing a guest under his roof to find out, he'd never know. Now the idea was in his head it was the devil of a job to ignore the temptation to do just that and risk an Arctic reception to find out if she was as indifferent to him as she wanted to be. No, only a rogue would do that and he wasn't quite one of those yet, so he exerted his brain and came up with an answer that almost made him groan out loud.

'Surely you don't intend to go and see for yourself?' he asked incredulously and could have sworn he saw her bite her lip and silently curse that lucky guess. He hadn't thought even she was that wild and reckless until that giveaway silence told him he'd hit a nail on the head.

'Not if you won't be quiet I don't,' she managed with a snap that wouldn't carry on the night air.

'And do what?' he gritted as softly as he could between his teeth, shaken by the thought of her confronting some villain in the dark.

'Find out,' she muttered impatiently, as if it was so obvious she couldn't imagine why he had to ask.

'Not on your own you don't,' he was surprised into arguing as she took things into her own hands and stole away as silently as if part of the shadows herself.

He grabbed her hand and felt her start and get ready to demand he unhand her, as if she was royalty and he was committing treason by touching without permission. He smiled grimly into the darkness as he felt the firmness of her long, slender hand in his, the work-worn toughness of her skin and the realness of a woman who made her own way in the direst of circumstances. It felt right there, as if it belonged, and that would never do. A sharp bolt of awareness shot through him as it had at first contact with this warm, all too live woman against his skin back in the stable yard. Drat it, but he wanted her as he couldn't recall wanting a woman so urgently since he was a desperate and callow youth and there wasn't a hope of having her and being able to look himself in the face next day when he shaved.

You're playing with fire, Mantaigne, he warned himself sternly, but he kept hold of her hand through her resistance, then silent acceptance he wouldn't let her flit off into the night and tackle who knew what invaders on her own. Recalling all those illicit adventures he'd risked in the darkness of this very place when he crept down from his tower and evaded capture for a day or two, he felt as if a cold place in his heart had warmed as he set out with her.

You're not alone at Dayspring this time then, Mantaigne? Virginia's voice seemed to whisper out of the night as he crept along the darkest part of the courtyard and through the elaborate arch that gave access to the newer parts of the castle.

No, it seems the nights here are full of things that ought not to be, he replied in his head as he might if his beloved godmama were witnessing this unlikely adventure.

Good point, he almost heard her say, and his sense that Virginia was here vanished as he felt Polly Trethayne's hand tense in his and the very alive woman at his side took up all his attention once more.

He sensed her impatience with him even as he felt her draw an arrow on his skin. Biting down on a gasp when it felt as sensuous as half-a-dozen nights in his current mistress's bed, he reminded himself it was only her way of directing him in the dark. Anyway, it wasn't right to lust after a lady he had only met today and who lived under his roof. It wouldn't be right to lust after her if she'd been his best friend since childhood, he reminded himself with a wry quirk of his lips, but knowing it didn't seem to stop him. Allowing himself be led for once, he peered through the shadows at the firmly closed side door he knew led into the grand wing.

Glad she couldn't follow any stealthy intruders inside, he soon found out he'd misjudged her. He muffled a curse as she tried once again to wriggle her hand out of the grip he was having the devil of a job to make firm but not painful. Somehow he managed it and heard a soft grunt of frustration before she surprised him by dipping down to delve in a nigh invisible nook in the carved archway with her other hand to extract a key. All sorts of question about the keys to Dayspring Castle that were supposed to be lying in Peters's trunk in the ancient castle armoury flitted through his mind. Best not to ask how she got this one, he supposed, as she bit off an annoyed hiss at his continued grip on her left hand and fitted the key in the lock with her right.

Tom did his best to put aside the thought of the fine pair of Manton's best duelling pistols sitting uselessly in his own trunk. He supposed there was a faint hope Miss Trethayne might have a pistol concealed in the pocket of her ridiculously ancient gown, but he was probably giving the bird-witted female too much credit for common sense. She really needed to carry one if she intended to delve every mystery Dayspring held, but something told him she was as unarmed as he was.

Now she was silently turning the key in the modern lock his lawyers had probably ordered fitted when he abandoned this place to its ghosts. It must have been oiled, and he revised his opinion of her foresight up a notch as his anger at her for being even more reckless than he'd thought her went up several more. He was tempted to shout a challenge and hope it sent her quarry scurrying down whatever rat-hole they'd come from. He would do it if he sensed a threat the rat would turn and bite, then track the vermin another day, when she was busy interfering in someone else's life. No, this was her life, more than it ever would be his, and now they were in here it behoved him to pay attention. The ifs and maybes of feeling some sort of connection with this wretched female that neither of them wanted might go away if he ignored them hard enough, except the low hum of excitement in his body as her hand tightened in warning on his told him that was very unlikely.

She nudged him to help her close the door as silently as she had opened it, then tried to push the key into his hand to let him know she wanted it locked again so she could flit off alone into the profound darkness in this part of the castle he hated most. He silently refused to take it. Hearing her huff an annoyed sigh, then turn it herself, he frustrated her as she tried to brush him aside again. She couldn't afford to demand out loud he let her go so she could run her head into any reckless adventure that came her way uninhibited by his presence.

His senses reached past the exploration his baser instincts were urging him to make of this warm and reckless female, and he told himself any distraction must be welcome. He was almost rigid with need in this heavy darkness as parts of his imagination he couldn't seem to control any more demanded an intimacy they should never have. If she felt even a tithe of the same affliction, she would never admit it. For all her outrageous attire, air of confidence and what he judged to be mature years for a single lady, there was a curious innocence about her. She had done all she could to keep the wary barrier of strangers between them.

Now they were here, he suddenly didn't want that barrier there any more. It made him feel lost in this sense-stealing darkness. He had spent most of his life avoiding this place and now he was wilfully courting the worst parts of his nightmares with the most unlikely siren he'd ever encountered at his side. Any moment now she might find out what a coward he was at heart and somehow it mattered far more than it should what this penniless and vagrant female thought.

No, that was quite enough worrying about Miss Trethayne's all-too-obvious contempt for the Marquis of Mantaigne; they were here now and might as well find out what they could. Apart from her, he scented only dust and disuse, and the droppings of generations of bats and mice on the air. For a moment he wished he'd brought his best spaniel with him to track the intruders, but a housebreaker would hear Rupert coming long before the eager animal could corner him. Tom tried not to miss Rupert's eager good humour and liking for his master anyway, telling himself he hadn't set out to endear himself to anyone who loved Dayspring Castle so could hardly be surprised Miss Trethayne only held his hand now because he refused to let her go.

He swallowed a curse as his knee connected sharply

with the carved newel post and he held his breath as
even that soft thud echoed in the empty hall. As it died
away he only just stopped himself whispering an excuse, then tried to put his memories of the layout between them and the silent blackness inside this echoing
barn. Shutters kept even the faint starlight out and it felt
as if the house was listening. Fanciful nonsense, but
anything could be lurking in those shadows and Tom's
heart thumped, then raced; remembered fear snapping
at his heels as they crept up the steps. It felt for a moment as if his guardian might leap out of the night to
shout out half-mad accusations and taunts, then try to
beat him senseless again. Tom licked suddenly dry lips
and forced his old fears aside. He was more than big
enough now to knock the weedy little tyrant down these
stairs and into Hades, if he wasn't there already.

Lord Mantaigne boxed and fenced with the best; rode
the finest horses as hard as if the devil was on his heels
when the mood took him and famously drove to an inch.
He was a Corinthian and, if he cared enough to lead
anyone, he could lead his chosen pack wherever he decreed they should go. Reminding himself of his usual
light-hearted indifference to the world, he still felt the
warmth of Polly Trethayne's hand in his as they stole
up the marble stairway together and was grateful not
to be alone here this time all over again. Over the smell
of long years of neglect he caught traces of soap and
woman and fresh air, as if she had brought the scent of
the spring itself here with her.

With his other hand he trailed an exploring finger
through twenty years of dust and found finely tooled

mahogany under his fingertips. It felt smooth and oddly warm under his hand, as if the old place was wistfully welcoming him home despite all he'd had done to it since he came of age.

On the top step they paused to gauge the silence. Tom felt her brace as if ready to rush into whatever trouble might be waiting, but he tried to convey the fact he was listening intently and they needed to gauge the dangers ahead before they dashed towards them. There; he heard a faint creak of distant movement on the other side of the state rooms from where they stood. He frowned into the darkness, knowing from bitter experience it was impossible to creep down the oak-boarded enfilade undetected.

'The back stairs are made of stone,' he murmured, as close to her ear as he could get so nobody could over-hear.

He felt her nod, the whisper of a fine curl against his skin, and could picture her as vividly as if she was lit by half-a-dozen flambeaux. Despite the old clothes and her impatience with all things feminine she would look magnificent in her outmoded gown, but he was the Marquis of Mantaigne and she was a beggar-maid. He would have to fight his blazing attraction to a reluctant goddess and get on with whatever he had to do here, then leave.

Knowing his way by the uncomfortable memory of all the times he'd crept in and out of the servants' hidden passageways about the house, he pulled her away from a board that always creaked and wasn't sure if he was glad or disappointed when the door to the servants' stair swung silently on its hinges.

'We'll have to go down to come back up,' he warned her, so close to temptation he could easily breach the fractions of an inch between them and kiss her, if he wasn't such a noble man and didn't know he'd get his face slapped if he did.

'Hurry up, then, we'll die of old age before we get there at this rate.'

Fighting the seductive feel of her breath so near to his own ear, he could sense her lush mouth close enough to set about a sensory exploration. He'd not dreamed how much he'd like his lover to embark on such an intimacy until tonight and ordered himself to forget it again. He went down the steps in front of her, to stop her dashing into any trouble she found at the bottom of them and leaving him behind.

They were at the foot of them now and in the dark and echoing passage, built broad enough to get a horse and cart through to the vast kitchens and storerooms a great household once needed. Miss Trethayne gave a small sound of impatience and softly muttered, 'Shame on you', as their steps were softened by years of dust and detritus. His feet seemed to slide out from under him as he turned to listen to her in the darkness and whatever he'd slipped on shifted and tumbled him in a heap with Miss Polly Trethayne dragged on top of him by their linked hands.

'Oof!' he barked involuntarily and managed to shift her weight slightly as he got his breath back, hoping she wasn't aware how delightful he found the feel of her curves against his winded body.

Not even the listening silence all around them could divert him from the delicious feel of nigh six feet of Miss Polly Trethayne lying prone on his torso. For a long moment it seemed as if she felt it too; a breath-stealing anticipation; an odd belief she was uniquely right in his arms. He heard an unsteady sigh, felt her heartbeat thud against his own ribcage. He reached for her, cupped her head with reverent hands and drew her down until their lips met in a breath-stealing, open-mouthed kiss that made his world shift and left him desperate for more when she raised her head and made a soft sound halfway between a mew of protest and a regretful moan for more, then she was wriggling frantically to get up and he must act the gentleman again, somehow.

Her mouth had been so wondering and curious, then eager on his in those few moment that he felt a new world open up, then be snatched away. 'Be still for a moment,' he murmured, certain he'd embarrass them both by acting on this foolish urge to keep her here if she kept thrashing like a captured mermaid in his arms.

'No, let me go,' she demanded breathlessly, and he hastily opened his arms as soon as he caught a note of fear in her whispered voice, shame rising in a mortified flush he was glad neither of them could see in this musty gloom.

'Precious little point in us going on now, I suppose,' he observed as carelessly as he could while counting his bruises as he tried to calm his errant body.

'Thanks to your clumsiness,' she informed him crossly.

'Indeed, I'm sorry my foot slipped in the dark. You would have done better without me,' he admitted grumpily, wishing she seemed as deeply affected by that hasty kiss in the dark as he had been, and frustration thrummed through him like a fierce gale.

'Nobody else knows this place as you do,' she said as if she had to give the devil his due, even when she didn't want to.

'A misspent youth,' he replied as lightly as he could. In truth, he used to creep down in the dead of night to sneak food, hoping his guardian's lackeys were too drunk to drag him upstairs for a beating.

'I heard you were just a boy when you left, so you hardly had time to indulge in one here,' she argued softly.

He really didn't want to talk about this when he already felt so vulnerable to her, as if he'd had a layer of skin peeled off him and had let her too close after that unwary kiss to fend off her questions as he'd like to.

'I was eight,' he admitted flatly.

'Poor little boy,' she murmured.

'Not as poor as Lady Wakebourne's waifs or even your own brothers would be without their fierce protectors. Do they know how lucky they are?'

'When we march them to their lessons every day and they have to do without the ponies they want to pay for them? What do you think?' she whispered.

It seemed education came before riding for boys lucky enough to live under this roof nowadays and yet he didn't hear a hint of self-pity in her tone. Tom felt something heavy threaten to move in his chest and re-make him. Simply being here had threatened to un-dam a torrent of feelings he'd kept to himself since leaving twenty years ago and now this.

Appalled by the idea this woman might come to mean far too much if he let her, he did his best to wall that wild notion up behind my lord's facade of careless man about town, for her benefit as much as his. She was the oddest sort of lady he'd ever come across, but didn't deserve to be shackled to a fool like him if they were discovered lurking in the dark. He scrambled to his feet, brushing down his once-fashionable attire and wrinkling his nose at the feel and smell of dust and dirt under his touch once again.

'Dashed midden,' he muttered grumpily, then tensed as stealthy footsteps sounded on the stairs from the other side of the building. Grabbing Polly's hand out of sheer instinct and a worrying urge to protect her at any cost, he dragged her behind one of the great pil-lars that held the weight of the cantilevered stairs above and whispered to her to keep quiet. He felt her fury at his presumption and squeezed her hand in what he hoped felt like an apology as well as a plea to do as he asked for once. His pulse raced at the contact of her skin against his once more, even as he wondered at himself for not feeling on edge with apprehension instead of frustrated desire.

'I tell thee I heard a noise down here,' a strongly ac-cented voice echoed down to them. Tom wondered how many felons were infesting a place no self-respecting burglar would walk half-a-dozen steps out of his way to break into.

'It's only rats,' a more-educated voice informed him, and Tom shivered at a register in it he couldn't quite place and didn't like one little bit, then felt her fingers tighten about his as if she was trying to reassure him and that pulse of wanting turned into something far more dangerous.

'They're the biggest rats I ever did hear then, Guv'nor,' the first man muttered as if not sure why he bothered arguing.

'This whole place is an infernal rat-hole; what else would it be?'

'One of them band of gypsies as lives here. I'm sure they heard us last time we was here, but still you keep coming back. They'll inform on us if you ain't careful.'

'Not they—if they do they'll be out of here faster than the cat can lick her ear. No magistrate will listen to a pack of vagrants.'

'You're lucky they're only squatting here, then. I'd sooner be on the streets than live here myself, what with all them ghosts and witches they whispers about in the taproom of the Raven late at night.'

'They're nothing but a pack of smugglers, you superstitious fool, of course they tell tall stories to keep strangers away from the coast on dark nights so they can carry out their trade undisturbed,' the other man said contemptuously.

Tom hesitated between a need to challenge him and a deeper one to keep Polly as far from this dark business as he could get her. From the tension in her fingers it felt as if she might be able to read his mind and that was a danger he really didn't want to think about, so he worried about his castle instead. Reminding himself he didn't care what happened to the place didn't ring quite true now he was actually here. Perhaps he cared more than he wanted to, but if it wasn't for this idiot he wouldn't have had to come here and find out Dayspring meant something after all.

'Tall tales or no, I can't abide the place.'

'Fool,' the leader said with contempt that set Tom's teeth on edge.

'I ain't the one spending every night you think the gentleman ain't at work searching this old ruin for a pot of fairy gold, though, am I?'

'It's real, I tell you. The old fool raved about his treasury, insisted I get him in here so he could die with his riches around him.'

'Shame he stuck his spoon in the wall before you did then, weren't it?'

Tom stiffened as their whispered conversation sank in and he decided they were fools to discuss their mission where they could be overheard. His one-time guardian was put in a lunatic asylum once Virgil challenged his fitness to be anyone's mentor. The man had ruled Dayspring for three years, though, and could have done what he liked here for all the trustees cared. Tom listed his larger assets in his head, but there was nothing important missing, so what had Grably convinced the more educated idiot was hidden in a house stripped of valuables when Virgil closed it?

'Mind your tongue,' the man said, and suddenly Tom

knew why he'd shivered at the sound of his voice. Snapping orders like that, he sounded so like Tom's guardian they must be related in some way.

'Can you see aught?' his reluctant companion asked, as if he sensed them in the shadows or thought some ghost the locals had scared him with was waiting to haunt him if he came closer.

'No, there's naught to see. You're nervous as a spinster.'

Tom felt Miss Trethayne's hand tighten involuntarily, as if it was a personal insult. He supposed she was unlikely to marry, penniless and responsible for her three brothers as she was. She might be at her last prayers by the time the last one flew the nest, but any woman less like the proverbial spinster he found hard to imagine. He was touched by her plight and wished he could see a way to offer her a respectable way out of it.

If he tried to settle a competence on her, she might find a suitor besotted enough to take on her three brothers, of course, but she wouldn't accept it and they were not related so he couldn't even suggest it. Paying a man like Peters to wed her stuck in his craw, even if he agreed to do it. Then there was this fierce desire he'd been struggling with since he set eyes on her in those outrageous, disreputable breeches of hers. Tom reminded himself his biggest ally in his fight to keep his hands off her was the lady herself, then remembered to listen to these housebreakers instead of worrying about things he couldn't change just in time to catch their next bad-tempered exchange.

'We've tramped up and down too often to see if anyone else has been down here,' the second housebreaker was saying resentfully.

'If I'd known we'd need to check this filth for foot-prints, I'd have flown across it like a bat. It was rats, I tell you, now get up here and help me search the state rooms before one of that ragtag band really comes to see what we're up to.'

'I don't like the look in the old bruiser's eye and he ain't past milling either of us down, if you ask me.'

'Fortunately I'm not that foolish.'

Chapter Seven

The housebreakers' voices faded as they went back up the stair arguing. Tom felt Miss Trethayne tense as if getting ready to creep after them and wondered if the wretched female had some sort of death wish.

'Let them go,' he murmured as urgently as he dared.

'Coward,' she accused in a bitter little whisper, and he was surprised how sharply the accusation stung.

'If you were a man, you'd meet me for that,' he replied gruffly.

'Then go after them before they can get away,' she said, quite unimpressed by his offended dignity, and this time he had to muffle a startled laugh.

'And do what?' he demanded laconically.

'Find out what they are doing here.'

'Oh, why didn't I think of that? Let's just go and ask the nice housebreakers why they're searching an empty house in the middle of the night and how they got in to do it in the first place then, shall we?'

'I admit they won't want to tell us, but I'm sure you can awe them into it.'

'And what will you do while I'm busy?'

'I could hold your sword if only you'd thought to bring one,' she mumbled crossly, as if seeing the foolishness of her scheme, but still refusing to admit it.

'How remiss of me,' he murmured as he stifled the fantasy of impressing her by confronting two villains with bare fists and the few wits she'd left him.

'Yes, it was,' she agreed and surely that wasn't a huff of suppressed laughter?

'Next time we embark on one of your nocturnal adventures, I'll make sure I'm armed to the teeth,' he said solemnly, and her hand relaxed in his as they fumbled their way back the way they'd come. 'First we'll plan it a little better,' he added when they were by the side door again, and she fumbled for the key.

'I want to know how they get in and out.'

'Patience, Miss Trethayne, we need to know who our enemies are before we let them know we've smoked them out at the time that suits us best.'

'Why not catch them first and ask questions after?'

'At least I know now that the legendary impulsiveness of the Trethaynes hasn't been exaggerated,' he murmured, determined not to admit he was unwilling to let her risk injury and worse at the hands of an unknown foe. Nothing was more likely to send her smashing recklessly back into the house to confront danger than knowing she was being kept out of it for her own good.

'They made me angry,' she admitted with a shrug once they were on the other side of the door, and he slid the key back in his pocket before she could appropriate it again. 'We may be beggars, but we don't scavenge in the dark, stealing whatever we can lay our hands on. They come and go as they please while we stay out of the way of the magistrate as if we're in the wrong. What right do they have to look down on us when we work every hour God sends not to be a charge on the parish?'

'If I tell the authorities you have my permission to live at Dayspring, nobody will be able to tramp about the place willy-nilly in future.'

'And you think men like that will take notice? The law is run by and for the rich, Lord Mantaigne. It takes a dim view of those who're too poor to pay it to look the other way.'

'There are plenty of good magistrates,' Tom argued lamely.

'Luckily for us, Mr Strand is an indolent one. He'd turn a blind eye to anyone not robbing or murdering in front of his nose rather than leave his fireside on a night like this one.'

'Which must have been a good thing for you at times,' Tom pointed out absently, frowning at the notion any criminal who wanted to run tame about the area had a virtual *carte blanche* to do so if the local magistrate was as lazy as she claimed.

'True, and luckily he's terrified of Lady Wakebourne. A royal scold from her has saved us from eviction more than once.'

'I will let him know Dayspring is my business and who does or doesn't live here has nothing to do with him.'

'A nicely ambiguous reply—have you ever thought of taking up your seat in the House of Lords?'

'How do you know I haven't?'

He heard her snort of disbelief at the very idea and tried not to let her opinion of him as an idle and useless fool hurt. It was true he disliked politicians in general and avoided allying himself to the Whigs, Tories or Radicals, but he had a conscience and often voted on it. He even spoke out about causes close to his heart on occasions, for all the good it ever seemed to do. Since he had met Miss Polly Trethayne's incredible eyes earlier today, with that flash of contempt in them to make him wonder about himself more than was quite comfortable, he'd been wondering if it was time to stop taking life quite so lightly and properly espouse a few of those causes.

Since they exchanged that hasty kiss in the darkness her low opinion of him stung even more, and he fought off an urge to plead for her understanding and a better opinion of him. Her contempt was a useful shield between them, her scathing opinion of his morals and motives might keep him from falling on her like the ravening beasts he'd hated the very mention of when she spoke of the casual violence she'd met on the roads before she got to Dayspring and a sort of sanctuary. He sighed and wished her warmth at his shoulder and her scent on the air wasn't quite so intimate and endearing and that he wasn't quite so drawn to the prickly female. Begging sometimes seemed a fine idea if it would win her over and get her back in his arms for a lot longer than she had been tonight.

'What on earth have you two been doing in the dark all this time?' Lady Wakebourne demanded the instant they approached the still-burning lamp he had hung by the old steward's lodgings. She had obviously grown tired of waiting for Miss Trethayne to come in and was keeping watch for her ewe lamb to make sure she was safe from the big, bad wolf.

'Suddenly I know exactly how your Mr Strand feels,' he murmured and heard that delightful huff of feminine laughter again and felt the warmth of it to his toes.

'Terrifying, isn't she?' she whispered back, then stepped forward to greet her mentor with a serene smile. 'You did mean us to settle some differences and make everyone else less uncomfortable, didn't you, Lady W.? We had a lot of differences to sift through and it took some time, but I think we have finally agreed on a truce of sorts, have we not, Lord Mantaigne?'

'Indeed,' he said as solemnly as he could with the thoughts of what they had actually been about crowding into his mind. 'Miss Trethayne has agreed to take me and Peters on a tour of the closest parts of the estate, starting tomorrow,' he added.

It might test that truce to the limit, but she couldn't run round trying to find out more about tonight's unwanted visitors on her own if she was with them. With any luck it would take days to familiarise himself with his estates and in the meantime he and Peters could find out what the devil was going on here and do something about it while she was busy.

'You think you're so clever, don't you, my lord?' she spat so softly he was sure Lady Wakebourne had no idea how far from a truce they were.

'No, being clever is far too much effort. It must be

low cunning,' he muttered before bowing to her with such exquisite grace and wishing her a good night, so she had to curtsey back and return it with such over-done sweetness he knew she secretly wished him anything but a good night.

Polly had no choice but to follow her ladyship into the little entrance hall, but she went past the wretch without letting even a thread of her gown touch him. In the kindly shadows cast by the single candle he was as immaculate and exotic as he'd been at dinner. She told herself it was a timely reminder how far apart they truly were. Awareness of his subtly powerful body sent prickles of unease shivering across her skin like wildfire and yet he looked calm and unaffected as if she had never fallen on top of him and felt the brilliant jag of attraction shock between them.

She took the lamp and held it lower to hide the flush that was making her cheeks glow and told herself it was as well if her ladyship didn't look too closely at his lordship's once-immaculate clothes. She'd kissed the man, for goodness' sake, sunk down and seized his mouth in a hasty snatched kiss that still sent shivers of awareness and want through her like a fever she couldn't seem to break.

'For heaven's sake, girl, I can hardly see a foot in front of me,' Lady Wakebourne chided so Polly had to raise their lantern to light the way after all.

Lord Mantaigne gave a warm and almost sleepy-sounding chuckle that made her think even more darkly sinful thoughts of rumpled bedsheets and sleepless nights of far too much intimacy. What had the wretched man done to her? She heard her own lips let out a muffled moan of denial as the thought of waking up beside him crept into her secret thoughts and settled in. No, he was an impostor—a rich and idle aristocrat, but not quite the harmless and noble gentleman he pretended to be. Nothing about his gaze—smoky with shadows as well as hungry and mysterious in this soft light— seemed either safe or gallant.

He knew he was a handsome and powerful man in his prime and she was painfully aware she was an awkward and gawky female, aware of him in every inch of her lanky body. All the time her head was trying to block him from her senses, she'd felt the power he could hold over her wilder senses, if she let him, and ordered herself to be very wary indeed.

He could walk right over a woman's most tender hopes and dreams and make them his before either of them realised it, then he'd walk away. Whatever else he was capable of, a deep-down sense of fairness told her he wouldn't inflict pain on another human being in pursuit of his own pleasure. She wondered about all the women who'd loved him, then watched him go without a backward look. The shudder that racked her at the very idea of being one of them was a powerful antidote. She imagined the desolation he'd leave in his wake when he left her and recoiled as if he'd brandished a lethal weapon instead of that rueful smile.

She raised her chin and met his eyes with as much indifference as she could summon. He stepped back and nodded as if to admit she couldn't take a lover of any sort and certainly not one like him. His bow said she might be right and he gently closed the door before either of them quite took in the fact he was gone.

'The boy has far too much charm for his own good,' her ladyship murmured and ignored Polly's sceptical snort with the queenly indifference of a true lady.

'If you say so,' Polly replied in as neutral a tone as she could after such a day and gave a weary sigh as she lit her ladyship back upstairs and whispered a soft goodnight before running up the next flight of steps to her own room.

She slept well only because she was exhausted by a day of toil and tension, but woke with a feeling of unease and the half memory of unquiet dreams. She scrambled into her work clothes, sparing a cursory glance as she brushed, then plaited, her hair. Once she was as ready to face the day as she would ever be she looked round her cosy room in the eaves, just in case this was the last time it was her home and not an old attic most would think old-fashioned and inconvenient. If they had to leave here, she would miss it more than her childhood home, but there was so much about Dayspring she had learnt to love and its owner obviously hated. This wasn't a significant part of the castle, but there was a wonderful view of orchards and parkland and a glimpse of the sea even from this side of the castle.

Going downstairs, Polly could almost sense the people she knew falling into places none of them had taken any notice of for years. A gap was yawning between those who had lived here as equals until yesterday. Soon she would have to don petticoats and whatever jumble of skirts they could put together out of the attics as a matter of course. She tried to picture herself looking clumsy and overgrown in the narrow skirts and high waist of the current mode and had to smile wryly at the very idea. Put ostrich feathers on any bonnet of hers and she'd make a sight to frighten small children and skittish horses.

Not that she could afford fashion, she reminded herself, and batted away the thought of Lord Mantaigne stunned speechless as she swept into the room dressed in a gown designed to make the best of her queenly height instead of the shabby and ill-fitting monstrosity of last night. Nonsense, of course. The most dazzling beauties of fashionable society must fawn on him like bees round honey and Miss Trethayne of nowhere at all still had too much pride to join in even if she could.

'Good morning, Miss Trethayne.' Mr Peters rose politely from the breakfast table to greet her, then looked significantly at her brothers until they stood as well.

'Good morning, sir, and a very fine morning it is too, but who are these polite young gentlemen? I can't say I recognise them.'

'It's us, Poll,' Henry told her wearily, as if wondering about her eyesight.

'May we sit down now, Sis? I'm hungry as a horse,' Toby asked.

'Of course you are, love, please carry on before you fade away in front of me,' she said, exchanging a rueful glance with Mr Peters that probably looked intimate to Lord Mantaigne when he strolled into the room.

'Good morning,' he said coolly, and she had to have imagined a flash of anger in his lazy gaze before it went unreadable again.

'It's going to be a lovely day,' she offered because she didn't want the boys to pick up on her worries about the future, or her jumbled feelings towards the marquis.

'Indeed, but the sea is still cold,' he said, helping himself from the pot of porridge set by the fire to keep warm.

'Don't say you've been for a swim, Mantaigne?' Mr Peters asked, seeming as startled as Polly that his employer would indulge in such bracing activity.

'I believe it's allowed if you have skill enough not to drown,' he said as if there was nothing unusual about a fashionable beau battling the full force of nature on such a bracing morning. Although the sun shone there was a lively breeze and taking on the waves must have been hard going.

'Don't even think about it,' his secretary said with a shudder, 'I can only imagine the fuss if you drown when I'm supposed to guard your back.'

'A task that should never have been set to you, my friend,' Lord Mantaigne drawled, but there was steel under all that careless élan.

Polly had spent years picturing the Marquis of Mantaigne as a spineless fool, ready to whistle his magnificent heritage down the wind on a whim. Under the expensive clothes and effortless elegance was a dangerous man, and last night proved how seductively the real Marquis of Mantaigne called to a wildness in Miss Paulina Trethayne she'd thought long gone. It would be as well if she avoided him as often as she could when this morning's ride about the estate was over.

'Prinny would take your land and fortune and give your title to one of his cronies,' Mr Peters mused. 'I'd have to tell the Winterleys how you met your end, though, so I'd really rather you didn't perish at sea during my time here.'

'Should your brothers need a schoolmaster I can recommend Peters as perfect for the role, when he's not too busy lecturing a fool of eight and twenty who's been going his own way far too long to listen.'

'About eight and twenty years of his life, by my reckoning,' Mr Peters murmured into his porridge, and Polly chuckled, then squirmed self-consciously under Lord Mantaigne's impassive scrutiny. She only just resisted the urge to put out her tongue and set the worst sort of example to her brothers.

'Thank you, but the vicar teaches Tobias, Henry and Jago. Josh and the younger boys have lessons with some of us here and I suspect Mr Peters has far too much to do already to join in with that thankless task,' she said to fill the silence.

'D'you think Mr Barker will tell us how he lost his leg today, Poll? He told Toby and I'll soon be as old as he is.'

'You're five years younger than your eldest brother, Joshua Trethayne, and some things have to wait until I say so,' Polly intervened before Toby and Henry could. 'And don't argue,' she added firmly.

'Why not? You're only a girl,' Josh muttered darkly.

'No, she's not, you ungrateful little toad,' Toby told him.

'No, for Miss Trethayne is your sister and for some odd reason she seems to like you,' Mr Peters said solemnly, and Josh grinned delightedly at the implication it took a doting gaze to see past his worst traits. Polly wondered why she couldn't be attracted to the man instead of his employer.

Oh, no, that was it, wasn't it? She was conscious of Lord Mantaigne on too many levels. Why did she have to feel a warm shiver of *perhaps* run over her skin at the very idea of being alone with a nobleman's secretary instead of the nobleman himself? Because she was a Trethayne, she supposed fatalistically, and they never did anything by halves. Falling headlong for the most unattainable man she'd ever come across would be a disaster bigger than any that had befallen her so far. There must be no more midnight adventures with him then and, after today, no daytime ones either.

'Still here, boys?' Lady Wakebourne asked from the doorway. 'Jago and Joe and Ben have already got their boots on.'

'And I expect Mr Partridge is waiting,' Polly prompted.

Some of the squatters had found work in the village of Little Spring, but Partridge had insisted on walking there and back with the boys ever since lights were first seen in the cove below Dayspring. Toby and Henry bolted the last of their breakfast and ran off to join their friends at a nod from Polly, and Josh dashed after them. Wishing she could do the same, she made herself eat in a suitably ladylike manner despite the sinking feeling in the pit of her stomach. Better to walk in Lady Wakebourne's shoes this morning, but the lady was so determined not to trade on her title that Polly was careful not to impinge on her self-imposed tasks.

'Shall we meet in the stable yard in half an hour for our tour of the estate, Miss Trethayne?' Lord Mantaigne asked.

'I'm ready now,' she said, because it seemed better to get it over with.

'Which of the spoilt beasts in your stable would you like saddled, then?'

'I always ride the black cob, but he won't let a stranger near him.'

'He must be a hard ride, and I dare say he's headstrong as the devil,' he remarked, trying not to call Beelzebub an unsuitable ride for a lady.

'He refuses to plough and I couldn't endure the thought of him being abused as a carriage horse.'

'Not to a coaching company or the mails, but I know a man who would treat him well and give you a good price. Can he be handled by anyone else?'

'Once he trusts you he's more amenable, but I found him wandering on the heath and he'd been beaten, so I could never let him go to someone who would try to break his spirit,' she said carefully, wondering if she could refuse a reasonable offer for her favourite when she would soon be homeless.

'I wouldn't suggest he might find a home with my friend if I doubted his ability to tell a rogue from a spirited beast with his worst masculine traits intact.'

'There's a lady present, Mantaigne,' Mr Peters protested, and Polly set him a little lower in her estimation and his master a little higher.

'Miss Trethayne doesn't want to discuss the latest fashions or how many fools crowded into Prinny's last squeeze at Carlton House, Peters.'

'I might,' Polly heard herself say as if someone else had taken over her tongue.

'I beg your pardon, ma'am. Then I must rack my brains for the details as best I can at this hour of the day.'

'You must know I have no knowledge of either subject,' she said gruffly. 'I would look ridiculous in London fashions and feel like a fish out of water at Carlton House, but a cat can still look at a king.'

'I know what you mean,' Mr Peters said with a wry look that won back some of Polly's respect and seemed to sink him in his employer's. 'I often wonder if Prinny wouldn't be happier if he'd been born on a fairground instead of in a royal bed.'

'It must make a fine spectacle, but I would hate to take part.'

'It's hot as Hades and noisier than a parliament of crows. I'd certainly give a good deal not to sit through another of Prinny's never-ending banquets,' the marquis said with what looked like genuine revulsion for all that show and waste Polly had read about in the discarded newspapers that sometimes came her way at third- or fourth-hand from the local squire.

'If your entrée to such places was withdrawn, I dare say you would feel the snub all the same,' Mr Peters said quietly.

'I expect you're right, but if we're all finished we might as well adjourn to the stable yard before the morning has gone, if you agree, Miss Trethayne? I hope you will ride one of my horses today. Although he will be nowhere near as fast or fiery as your own mount, you would be doing us a favour. A full stallion will never tolerate the presence of our hacks without a lot of fire and brimstone.'

He was right of course; Polly had been hoping Beelzebub's antics at the proximity of other males, even if they were geldings, would put a premature end to the tour. She resigned herself to hours in the disturbing man's company as both gentlemen stood back for her to lead the way, then carefully didn't look at anything less than six feet off the ground lest they be accused of ogling.

Dotty Hunslow was sitting on the granary steps, smoking a short pipe and exchanging flirtatious glances with a wizened little man who looked like a former jockey. He jumped to his feet and did his best to look as if he'd been busy all morning, and a warning glint sharpened Dotty's knowing gaze.

Unease prickled down Polly's spine as all the risks of having too much contact with a lord like this one ran through her mind screaming. No, he wouldn't give her a second glance if she was properly dressed and that was just as well. He could ruin her and her brothers' slender prospects in life if she wasn't very careful, and the throaty murmur of her inner wanton whispered it would be a very pleasurable descent, before sensible Paulina dismissed the idea as completely impossible.

No, she would have to find time to search the attics for skirts long enough to hide her legs from him and his fellow rakes so he would turn his hot blue eyes elsewhere.

'Please saddle the grey for Miss Trethayne, Dacre,' his lordship ordered as if it was an everyday occurrence for a lady to ride astride.

'He's feeling his oats,' the little man argued.

'Miss Trethayne usually rides the black cob, so Cloud will seem like a docile pony in comparison.'

'Cloud it is then, ma'am,' the small groom said with a nod of limited approval.

'Thank you,' she said, trying not to feel self-conscious in front of the stable lads while she waited for the animal to be saddled. 'Oh, you're a handsome lad and a true gentleman, aren't you, sirrah? I warrant you'd hunt all day if you had to,' she greeted the powerful-looking animal as he arched his neck at her like a circus horse and waited to be admired.

He was as big a rogue as his master from the look of him and her opinion of Lord Mantaigne rose as he laughed at the grey's antics and told him not to be such a commoner. He sobered as he cupped his hands to take her booted foot and boost her into the saddle.

'I don't hunt,' he said, eyes flicking in the direction of the tumbledown kennels Polly knew lay on the far side of the yard so as not to disturb anyone in the castle with the restless baying of the hounds.

'You don't enjoy the exercise then, my lord?' she asked a little breathlessly, trying not to be impressed as he boosted her into the saddle as easily as if she was a foot shorter and as slender as a fashion plate.

'Perhaps I pity the quarry,' he said lightly.

She was still wondering about that remark as they set off. She'd heard whispers that a miserable child-hood had led to his hatred of Dayspring, but all that had mattered then was that he stayed away. Eyeing the powerful figure of the now very real Marquis of Man-taigne, Polly tried to see past it and wonder about the man under the careless elegance.

He was relaxed in the saddle of his fine horse as if he hadn't a care in the world, but she sensed wari-ness in him, an unwillingness to feel the appeal of this fine place on such a beautiful spring morning. Would a bright but abused boy learn to guard his thoughts and emotions from his persecutor? Yes, she decided, and any woman tempted to love him would have to fight her way past the shield wall he still kept them behind. She pitied her, whoever she turned out to be. To throw your bonnet that far over the windmill would mean being prepared to risk everything without any guarantee he would even want her once she'd done it.

Tom expected the parkland to be overgrown and small forests to blur the beautiful landscaped gardens his grandfather had paid Lancelot 'Capability' Brown to design for him. Instead the park was close-cropped by sheep and a herd of cows grazed the meadow by the lake that dreamed under the spring sun as he remem-bered it doing on days when he'd escaped his prison to wander his own land like a poacher in constant fear of discovery.

Not even that sense of such freedom being short and

forbidden spoiled the joy of a spring morning in this wide landscape then, but that was quite enough of the past. Today the trees looked as if they'd been kept tidy by foresters. He ought to ask Miss Trethayne how that could be when he didn't have any, but he let himself feel all the promise of spring about them instead and saved the argument for later.

'Where are we going?' Peters asked and saved him the trouble.

'To the Home Farm, through Cable Woods, then down into Days Magna,' Miss Trethayne said concisely.

'A neat slice across the closest parts of the estate,' Tom conceded and saw from the tightening of her lush mouth how his pompous reply annoyed her.

Since he couldn't make her his mistress, and she was nothing like any marchioness he'd ever come across, he told himself it was good to see the look of impatient contempt back in her fine eyes. He must do his best to keep it there for the next couple of weeks and then he could return to London or Derbyshire, leaving them both more or less unscathed.

'Who has the Home Farm?' Peters asked, and it was a reasonable enough question, so why did Tom feel jealous, as if he was the one who should be having easy conversations with Miss Trethayne and not Peters?

Perverse idiot, he condemned himself and urged his horse a little ahead, so he could leave them to talk while he watched this once-familiar landscape for changes. Yet he took in very little of it for listening to their conversation and keeping enough attention on the road in front of them to make sure he didn't fall in the dust and make himself even more of a fool than he already felt as he fought the need to have all her attention focused on him and him alone.

'The Allcotts have held it for generations,' he heard her answer Peters question obliquely and wondered why she was uneasy about it.

'And do I have a forester?' he turned in the saddle to ask.

'Several, my lord,' she said, and there was that sense she wasn't telling him the whole story again to pique his interest and let him convince himself his interest was nothing personal.

'Don't expect me to believe they come from the same family who felled trees here from the dark ages on, then. I well remember my guardian railing that he couldn't keep a male worker on the estate thanks to the press gangs and fishing boats and quarries robbing him of manpower.'

'I suppose those alternatives were more attractive,' she said so carefully he knew her thoughts were busy with all the rumours she'd probably discounted about him and Grably and how bad it had been at Dayspring once upon a time.

'Yet they came of their own free will once I ordered the place kept empty? Perhaps they fell my timber for nothing out of the goodness of their hearts,' he said blandly, and her gaze slid away from the challenge, as if she didn't want him to read secrets in them.

'Maybe they wanted to keep faith with the Banburghs?' she suggested.

'My father died, and I turned my back on them. I

can't see the locals feeling aught but contempt for the Banburghs,' he admitted harshly, conscious of Peters's shrewd gaze as well as her discomfort with the subject.

'Maybe they felt guilty?'

'I hope not; the fifth marquis is dead and I don't care.'

'No, of course you don't,' Peters said, and Tom sensed the two of them exchanging rueful glances behind his back and fought temper and something a little less straightforward—surely it couldn't be jealousy?

To be jealous he'd have to want Miss Trethayne as irrationally as Luke and Chloe Winterley had wanted each other during their decade of estrangement. So that meant he simply could not be jealous. He didn't want to ruin or marry her, so he must be immune to her smoky laugh and everything that made her unlike the pursuing pack of would-be marchionesses he dodged so carefully at *ton* functions.

'No, I don't,' he echoed as coolly as he could. 'So let's stop dawdling like a trio of dowagers and get on with our day,' he added to put an end to the conversation.

Chapter Eight

When they got to Home Farm he could see nothing wrong. Allcott was at the local market buying and selling cattle, but the neat-as-a-pin house and yard spoke of a diligent master. Yet Mrs Allcott didn't meet his eyes when he complimented her on her hen yard and the neat gardens and the thriving orchards surrounding the ancient stone house.

'Tell your husband I'm well content with his tenancy,' he tried to reassure her.

'Thank you, my lord, he'll be glad to hear it,' she said, her mouth in a tight line, as if it might say something it shouldn't if she let herself relax.

'Are you going to tell me why I might think Allcott an unsuitable tenant if I had actually managed to meet him, Miss Trethayne?' he asked when they were in open country again.

'He's a fine farmer and a good man,' she said defensively.

'And?'

'He was pressed into the navy as a lad and spent ten years at sea. They let him go after Trafalgar.'

'And the navy don't give up experienced seaman in times of war unless they can find no further use for them.'

'No, Allcott was blinded as well as lamed in the battle,' she replied as if she expected him to rescind the tenancy of Home Farm on the spot.

'Then he's an even more remarkable farmer than I thought,' he said tightly, angry that she thought him such a shallow fool.

'He knows more about soil and seed and weather with four senses than most men do with five,' she said as if she needed to defend the man anyway.

Squashing another of those nasty little worms of jealousy, he nodded at the outskirts of Cable Wood ahead of them. 'Is there anything I should know before I meet these woodsmen I've heard so little about?'

She couldn't mean anything to him, or he to her, he reminded himself, so it didn't matter that she thought him a hard-hearted monster. He only had to imagine the reception she'd get if he introduced her to the *ton* to shudder on her behalf. The fops and gossips would make her life a misery and the wolves would ogle her magnificent legs, raise their quizzing glasses to examine her lush breasts and tiny waist with leering attention, then pounce on her as soon as his back was turned.

He'd probably have to kill one or two to punish such disrespect, then flee to the Continent even though Bonaparte controlled most of it. No doubt she would follow, cursing his black soul while she lectured her brothers about the places they were seeing on their less-than-grand tour. No, the very idea of Miss Trethayne making the best of things at his side like that really wasn't as seductive as it seemed and he had plenty to keep him occupied here for the next three months without fantasising over a woman who would like to pretend he didn't exist.

'What are you doing your best not to tell me this time, Miss Trethayne?' he insisted wearily as she hesitated over answering his question honestly or leaving him to find out for himself.

'One or two of them are a touch impaired,' she said tightly.

'Can they do their job?'

'Of course, you only have to look around you to know that.'

'Then why expect me to turn off men who keep the rides neat and my woods just so?'

'Because they could get no work elsewhere.'

'Until today not even my worst enemies have accused me of following the crowd, yet you seem to have done so before we even met, Miss Trethayne.'

'You turned your back on a heritage most men would give their right arm to possess in a fit of pique. What did you expect the folk who depend on the castle and estate to think of you after that?'

A fit of pique? Oh, damnation take the dratted woman. Had she no idea what beatings and hardship the ragged little lord of all this had once endured? The old mess of rage and hurt pride and that feeling of being cut off from the good things in life threatened to spill out of him. If he let her, she'd wrench details out of him he hadn't even confided to Virginia. No, if his beloved godmother couldn't coax the details of his old life from him, he wasn't dredging them up for the amusement of a vagabond Amazon queen determined to think the very worst of him.

'How very tedious of me,' he drawled as indifferently as he could manage.

'Oh, why pretend? You watch every change here like a lover looking for changes in a beloved he hasn't seen for too long, yet you expect us all to believe you hate the place and don't care a tinker's curse what happens to it? No, my lord, I don't believe you and why should you stay untouched by life? You behave as if you are a summer butterfly; too gorgeous and empty to understand life isn't only made up of sunny days and nectar.'

Tom felt Peters try to meld into the quiet wood like a green man. Part of him admired the trick, but the rest was busy fighting a ludicrous idea this woman had the right to rage at him. Tall and magnificent in her man's saddle, she met his angry gaze as if it cost her nothing and if only life was different he might have agreed.

'I don't think I should care to start life as a caterpillar, or make a quick meal for a hungry bird or frog,' he managed with a careless smile and a shrug that made his horse sidle, as if it sensed the turmoil Tom was trying so hard to ignore.

'Perhaps you're right, my Lord Mantaigne should be eaten by something nobler than a slimy little creature with a harsh voice.'

'Aye, he ought, Miss Trethayne, but if it makes you feel any more charitable towards me, I'll admit I have missed the Mantaigne lands, if not the castle that goes with it.'

'I beg your pardon, my lord. I forgot our unequal stations and trespassed on your privacy,' she said as if he'd intended a subtle rebuke by reminding her he was a marquis and she was only here because he hadn't been for decades.

'I think I preferred you in a rage,' he said, her unexpected humility shocking the truth out of him.

'I don't suppose you'll have to wait long for that. I've never been very good at minding my tongue,' she admitted with an almost-smile even as her sharp eyes picked out the deep marks of a heavily laden cart on one of the cross-rides, and she veered off to examine them more closely.

'I don't think Miss Trethayne is concerned that your phantom woodsmen have been shirking their duties, do you?' Peters muttered as if Tom might not have noticed.

'No,' Tom agreed, frowning as an image of similar ones leading to the cove at Dayspring reminded him this could be a dangerous coast for more reasons than unexpected currents and powerful spring tides.

He wished he'd listened harder when the subject of evading hefty government duties on so many things arose. This was his place, his heritage, and it was time he took some responsibility for it. He wondered about quizzing Polly Trethayne about the so-called free-traders, but something about her closed expression told him she would evade his questions. He decided Partridge would be his best source of information. Even if the old rogue wasn't involved with the gangs who ran this stretch of coast, he wouldn't be able to help himself finding out as much as he could about them.

The woodsmen were working on a tangled mess of dead trees and brambles he supposed he should be ashamed of. Most had strong backs and put the arms they had left to good use. Did Miss Trethayne really think he'd dismiss them for having served their country, then been discarded when the enemy fought back? From the sharp and defensively hunched shoulders that came his way once they realised who he was, she wasn't alone in that view of him. Tom silently cursed his careless reputation and picked out the leader of the now-quiet foresters.

'Good day,' he said in a voice he knew would carry round the clearing.

'Good day, milord,' replied the giant who had been hefting a huge axe until he laid it down so carefully Tom knew he'd been tempted to swing it in his direction.

'Aye,' he said with a grin that acknowledged what a tempting target he made for an angry man, 'it certainly seems to be.'

'It's spring and the sun's shining.'

'It is now,' Tom said with a nod to the carefully cleared brambles and other brush waiting for the bonfire nearby. 'You have let light in on years of neglect, so I must thank you for doing a fine job here.'

'Must you, milord? That ain't the way I heard it.'

'I understand you doubt my intentions to the Dayspring estate, but I'm not used to having my words questioned when they're hardly out of my mouth,' Tom said evenly, holding the giant's remaining eye steadily and feeling as if the man would like to challenge him, but didn't quite dare.

He raised his voice so the other men could hear him clearly in the now-silent clearing. 'You have obviously worked hard and, if you continue to do so, I won't import my own woodsmen when they had far rather stay at home and do the job they know. Consider yourselves employed, gentlemen, and let me know honestly how many weeks' pay you have done without. I am home and things will be different at Dayspring from now on.'

'That's what I'm afraid of,' the leader said bravely, and Tom nodded at the reference to his boyhood determination to let the castle and estate go to rack and ruin.

'I'm man enough now to realise a pile of stones and its lands have no part in the cruelties of men. I shall take a proper interest in the Dayspring estates from now on, even when I have to be elsewhere.'

'Until yon castle falls into the sea?' the man said with a gesture in the direction of the distant towers visible over the top of the tallest trees in the woods that protected Spring Magna from the harshest of winds from the sea.

'Did you never say hasty things in your youth?' Tom replied. 'I'm not sure what I'll do about the castle yet, but I want the estate put in order and kept that way.'

'About time,' his disrespectful head forester informed him sternly, but luckily Tom preferred plain speaking to toadying.

'Aye, the Banburghs learn slowly, but do it well in the

end,' he admitted and thought he heard the odd murmur of approval. The man in front of him and Miss Trethayne seemed unconvinced, but Tom resisted an urge to demand what else they needed to hear, because he probably didn't want to know.

'Are you going to bring in a bailiff and outsiders to work the estate, my lord?' this doubter asked.

'I won't bring in my own woodsmen if that's what you mean. Why would I uproot men who want to stay at home and bring them here when they're not needed?'

'Because they've got all their arms and legs and everything else we left behind after we took the King's shilling.'

'I see work well done and, as long as you're content, I'm happy to have you carry on. Some of you might prefer work more suited to your skills and experience, but that's for a time when I've leisure to examine the fine details of how this estate should work in future.'

'With some fancy new man you'll bring in to run the Castle estate, my lord?'

'Perhaps, but for now if you have a problem you will have to come to me.'

'Where would I do that, then, milord?' the man asked warily.

'I'll be at the castle for a while yet and intend to find a suitable manager before I leave. An estate this size can't run well without someone at the helm.'

'We have a captain,' he said with a nod at Miss Trethayne that made her blush as no flowery compliment from a Bond Street Beau could.

'I said a *suitable* manager,' Tom said clumsily. She

would hear his words as lack of confidence in her rather than a statement that it was too dangerous for her to ride about alone. 'I'm very grateful to Miss Trethayne, but it's not a burden I can leave on her shoulders for ever. You can come to me if a new man wants to make changes you don't agree with and I'll always give you a fair hearing.'

'Sounds like paradise,' one of the men joked sceptically, but sly smiles and the odd laugh greeted his sally all the same.

Tom thought his battle largely won, but the leader wasn't convinced. Apart from the eye-patch over his damaged eye, it wasn't until he moved that the halt in his gait made it a wonder he'd managed to keep both legs. Tom decided he wouldn't want to be a naval surgeon who tried to take this man's leg off if he wanted to keep it as the big sailor-cum-woodsman sneaked a glance at Miss Trethayne, and what a fool he was not to have seen it straight away. Of course, the man was in love with her.

Now he was home the big woodsman could either take up the role of head forester or chance his luck with the smugglers, while as for Miss Trethayne…

Yes, and what *would* Miss Trethayne do with herself if she left Dayspring? Even if she didn't have her brothers to care for, Tom couldn't see her as a lady's companion or governess. He supposed she might catch a widower or a cit if he contrived a Season for her in one of the minor watering places, where her looks and goddess-like presence would eclipse her years, height and lack of fortune. Or he could shame Lord

Trethayne into meeting his obligations. He doubted Miss Trethayne would take a penny-piece from the selfish old dog now, though, and he hated the idea of her having to lower her pride if she decided it was too expensive a luxury for a woman with three little brothers to provide for.

So what the devil *was* he going to do? He could marry her, but picturing her towering over every other female in a set of court feathers when she was presented at a Court Drawing Room as the new Marchioness of Mantaigne made him shudder. Yet how else could he rescue the stubborn female from the impossible situation she was in simply because he'd come home and she had nowhere else to go?

Polly tried to pretend she wasn't there while Lord Mantaigne made the acquaintance of his woodsmen. She had no connection to the family who'd owned this land since the first Banburgh claimed it and built a stronghold. The truth was she was jealous of the current marquis's ownership and his right to neglect it, then turn up and take it back while she, who loved it, would have to leave. The injustice of it might have made a Jacobin of her, if it hadn't been for the memory of her French stepmother starting at shadows and paling whenever she recalled the Terror.

The rightful owner of Dayspring Castle had come into his own. That phrase had a ring to it she would have laughed over only yesterday, but today there was nothing funny about it. She could almost picture her father giving one of his careless shrugs and telling her blithely that nothing stayed the same for ever. He was probably right and she might not have been able to hold the castle and estate together for much longer. The late-night incursions into the castle had been troubling her for weeks, and she thought of last night with a shiver of mixed emotions that shot through her and sent poor Cloud dancing as he sensed her turmoil through the bit she forced herself to relax her grip on so she could at least conceal it from the fine animal she was riding and his equally fine master.

Now the wretch was climbing into his saddle with an easy word to his new employees and turning his chestnut gelding towards the ride where she and Mr Peters sat silently waiting. Lord Mantaigne had a knack for getting what he wanted, and she let herself wonder for all of a minute what he might want of her. A swift and trouble-free departure after she had explained how things stood here, she suspected. She slanted him a stern look as he followed in her wake, because she knew the way and he'd let himself forget it, and tried to behave like a rational woman.

'Do you think they'll stay?' he asked once they were out of earshot.

'Most have families to support. They don't have much alternative,' she told him as evenly as she could.

'It's thanks to you they're usefully employed though, is it not?'

'I'm sure someone would have suggested they could usefully tame your woodlands and perhaps sell the wood to make it worth their while sooner or later if I had not.'

'And a wild wood makes a fine hiding place for vag-abonds and villains the local magistrates could well do without,' he said, and Polly wondered if he was re-membering smugglers liked wild places and hidden tracks to hide the pony trains that carried goods away from the coast.

'And those who like to avoid *them* might resent the loss of cover,' Mr Peters said shrewdly.

'I doubt that would be seen as a bad thing in Days Magna,' she replied absently, wondering if he was right.

'Are you telling me the free-traders are unwelcome round here, Miss Trethayne?' his employer asked as if she was trying to muddy the waters.

She recalled how sharply his gaze had focused on a careless footprint left on one of the less-obvious tracks and how he'd frowned at the deeper-than-they-ought-to-be ruts on the road down to the sea. The man did his best to hide a rapier-sharp mind under that air of lazy indifference, but she was beginning to see through it to the real man underneath. She wondered if he knew how many of his talents and intelligence were wasted being the idle man of fashion he pretended he was.

He wouldn't think it a waste, she answered herself cynically. Gambling and carousing and defying the devil was a game to him, along with seducing other men's wives and charming anyone who wasn't yet con-vinced the Marquis of Mantaigne deserved all the trea-sures and comforts he'd been born to.

She only just managed to bite back a tirade on the subject of gentlemen who thought they had a right to anything they laid greedy eyes on and decided to want. No, that was just being lazy. Wrong to add him to the leering beast who had thought a penniless female like her was fair game, she knew he wouldn't dream of forcing himself on a woman without anyone having to say so. Yes, there was a hot glitter in his blue, blue eyes when they rested on her too long, but she felt a new excitement stir deep inside whenever that happened so she couldn't deny it was a mutual wanting. It left her wondering how she would feel if they satisfied it, but that was never going to happen.

'They are part of everyday life here, but sometimes it isn't comfortable to know they pass too close,' she replied to his question about the smugglers and hoped he thought her silence had been because she was considering her answer, not the chance of being anyone's lover, but more especially his. 'The villagers know they must either accept the fact the Trade runs through the area like a seam or leave it. Evading the duty on goods that puts them out of reach of all but the very rich is often seen as their God-given right as free-born Englishmen,' she managed to say coolly.

'So I've heard,' Peters said grimly, and she hoped he wasn't thinking of taking on the deeply rooted traditions of the whole area single-handed.

'Even if the customs officials manage to catch them, the magistrates round here wouldn't prosecute hard, and no jury would convict them if they did,' she warned them, then squirmed under Mr Peters's cool gaze and wished she'd held her tongue.

'It's not the Trade itself that vexes me, or even the

ruthless nature of the smuggling business for anyone who gets too close, but Bonaparte's use of his damned guinea boats to subvert our currency,' Lord Mantaigne argued.

'I doubt that's the only reason he winks at the smuggling trade,' Polly said and felt the tug of conflicting loyalties most people must, if they stopped to consider it as other than a local way of life that had been going on since anyone could remember. 'I wouldn't have wanted to live in the days when the Hawkhurst Gang and their like terrorised everyone for miles around, but I can't roundly condemn a trade that puts a few luxuries in the hands of folk who labour for a pittance while their masters enjoy every indulgence they can think up, however foolish it might seem to the rest of us.'

'You sound like a revolutionary, Miss Trethayne,' his lordship drawled.

'Do I, my lord? How very shocking of me,' she replied lightly.

'I know there is much that is unequal and unfair in this country and no wonder working folk look at what others have and want it for themselves, but consider how it would be if the French Emperor invaded us as he has so many others. For all their talk of liberty and equality they treat their conquered nations like vassals and plunder them of treasures and, worse, I should hate to be a young and attractive female under such a regime. Those who hail Bonaparte as a liberator and a lawmaker should take a closer look at Spain and see how it feels to live under his heel.'

Polly allowed herself a shudder and blessed the fact

she wasn't on her usual mount. Beelzebub would have bolted at the feel of her involuntary flash of terror as she thought of the fate so many women had met at the hands of victorious invading troops in this horrifying, never-ending war.

'I would not wish to be an enemy nobleman in such a world either,' she pointed out.

'No, I think I'd better arrange to expire on the barricades if the worst should ever come to pass. I don't relish the role of a craven captive, or trying to ransom myself at any cost while my tenants and workers look on with contempt.'

'For heaven's sake, will you stop joking about the things you care about the most, man?' his usually meek secretary snapped, clearly as close to the end of his tether with the foppish aristocrat Lord Mantaigne pretended to be as Polly was.

'It is deeply exasperating,' she agreed.

'My apologies, the last thing I ever set out to do was prove tedious. To relieve you both of the trouble of bearing with me any longer I will leave you and flit off on a selfish errand of my own. Why don't you take my conscience here into Spring Magna instead of my unworthy self and introduce him to anyone who is interested for me, Miss Trethayne? I'm sure you can assure them everything they least wanted to hear about me is true and they must hope I shall depart as unexpectedly as I came amongst them,' Lord Mantaigne said as coldly as if he truly wished the estate was desolate, his castle in ruins and himself a hundred miles away.

'Well, that put us properly in our place,' Mr Peters observed calmly as he watched the marquis ride away.

Polly couldn't help but admire his horsemanship as his powerful, supple figure adjusted to the pace of his galloping steed as if by second nature. He confused and angered her by turns, yet felt an odd tug of sympathy for him haunt her as she exchanged a rueful glance with Mr Peters and considered how they'd been ordered to spend their afternoon without him.

'It will put the local rumour mill in a fine spin if we go on together without him, Mr Peters. You could always ride on alone and introduce yourself to the folk of the Spring villages. They will be pleased with any sign the marquis is taking an interest in them and are sure to make you very welcome. I might as well return to the castle and help with the spring planting since I seem to be redundant here.'

'That was not well done. Lord Mantaigne is a man of more impulsive character than he wants us to know at times, but I cannot let you ride alone. I may not be a native of this place, but I do have eyes in my head and can see that large groups of men have been marching about this land all too recently for my comfort. You must not take risks with your personal safety, and only think how Lady Wakebourne and your brothers will feel if anything untoward happens whilst you're out alone.'

'I have been out alone, as you call it, for years.'

'Then it's a very good thing we arrived when we did,' the man argued, and Polly only just suppressed an unladylike grunt of disagreement.

'I could learn to dislike you nearly as much as I

should your employer if you insist on being right all the time, Mr Peters,' she said half-seriously.

'I fear it is a sad failing in my half of our species, Miss Trethayne,' he replied with a mournful shake of his head that disarmed her and made her feel a fishwife for taking her fury with the marquis out on this man all at the same time.

'And of mine to argue. You really are wrong this time as well, though, because for us squatters it isn't a good thing at all. With your coming, we must leave the castle and it is never a good thing to be rendered homeless twice.'

'However maddening his lordship might be, he won't turn you out to wander the roads with your family and friends like the lost tribe of the Israelites. I can see signs of an unknown number of people determined to invade your sanctuary, though, and well before we turned up. It could be a very good thing the owner of Dayspring Castle arrived before they could succeed, despite your mixed views on the matter.'

Polly noted how neatly the man had his own plans for the afternoon running as they retraced their route from the castle even as she had half her mind on arguing with him. She went along with him, though, because she was safer in his company and it gave her time to think. Soon she would catch herself thinking it a good thing they were here as well, if she wasn't careful.

If their lives were different, how would it feel to arrive at Dayspring as a guest of Lord Mantaigne with her stepmother and Papa? For all of a minute she indulged in an air dream of herself superbly dressed and elegantly coiffured, stepping down from the carriage to meet the warm blue gaze of an admiring Marquis of Mantaigne. In such circumstances it might be quite all right to feel the same rush of heat and wonder as when they actually did meet; in a stable, among the faded and patched up rags of Dayspring's glory days. Instead of being dressed in silks and finest muslins she'd looked more like a scruffy youth—sweaty and weary and windswept after another busy day trying to keep the wolf from the door.

The differences of how they really were fitted neatly into that one scene. He was rich and powerful and unforgivably handsome; she was poor, powerless and awkward as a heron in a hen yard. *That's how my life really is*, she told herself sternly, trying to focus on what her real and adoptive family were going to do now Lord Mantaigne was back in his castle after all these years. Or he would be if he hadn't just galloped away from it in a temper, and suddenly the unease she'd been feeling for the past few weeks left her worrying about his safety instead of her own or her family's.

He would make an irresistible target for a villain lurking in still-untamed parts of the woods, or he might stumble on one of the secluded coves the landsmen used to hide their illicit cargo until they could be carried inland under cover of darkness. Marquis or no, he might never be seen again if he was unlucky enough to come upon them taking goods inland by one of the hidden lanes that scored the remotest parts of this countryside. Sometimes a Revenue Cutter lurking offshore would spur men into taking unprecedented actions, like moving a cargo by day, or setting an armed guard over their most precious hiding places.

Even if he was simply set upon by a rogue on the lookout for an easy mark, he would yield a fine haul. His clothes and boots alone would bring in several months' wages for a labouring man, even at a fraction of their true value, then there was that fine gold fob-watch she'd seen him consult earlier today and his signet ring as well as the plain gold pin in his spotless muslin neckcloth.

Before she got to the end of a list of things about my Lord Mantaigne that could be profitably marketed by an attacker they were in sight of the castle and she had to put aside her horrifying inner picture of him lying naked and unconscious by some distant roadside. Maybe he would be held for ransom, and how on earth would they raise the enormous sum any sensible villain would demand for his safe return?

No! She must stop this nonsense; he was nothing to her, and it was up to Mr Peters to look out for his employer and answer the marquis's friends if he went missing, if he had any of course.

Once she was home again, Polly did her best to go about the normal business of her day as if she hadn't a care in the world, or a marquis who ought not to be allowed out without a suitable chaperon on her mind. By the time he rode into the stable yard as darkness was all but on them, looking as if he hadn't a care in the world, she had a thumping headache and decided to have an early night as Lady Wakebourne suggested with an anxious frown at Polly's tense and pallid face.

With any luck she wouldn't dream at all and could forget about an annoying aristocrat without a care for anyone in his handsome head as easily as he had about her and Mr Peters this afternoon.

Chapter Nine

That day set the pattern for the Marquis of Mantaigne's return to his primary country seat. Whenever it didn't pour with rain he spent his days exploring the estate and its villages, with or without his secretary at his side. If he stayed home he was polite and surprisingly easy with the interlopers at his once-grand mansion and they did their best not to ask what he intended to do about them as days grew into weeks. Polly felt like the outsider as her friends and family came to look on him as a genial and civilised gentleman. So why was she the only one who felt as if she was constantly waiting for the second shoe to fall?

Her life had narrowed to the park and gardens, and she supposed glumly that it would prepare her for a time when they must leave and patch together some sort of life elsewhere. One day she came home from working in the fields around Dayspring to find a beautiful riding habit draped across her bed. For a moment she enjoyed the sheer pleasure of seeing the richly dyed forest-green fabric lying there in the dappled sunlight slanting through the ancient leaded windows. There were depths and shifts in the folds that told her it was the work of a master weaver and she knew that colour would suit her to perfection, if she had any intention of wearing it.

Knowing she was being stubborn and ungrateful, she still felt her temper rise to dangerous heights at Lord Mantaigne's presumption. If the man didn't like her as she was he could tell her so; this was an attempt to force her into the role of a meek and properly dressed female without him having to point out her clothes were unladylike and shocking even to a rake like him.

She refused to fit into a neat little niche where spinster ladies with no prospects must live. She couldn't cram herself into such narrow confines even if she wanted to, she concluded, with a severe nod at the beautiful garment lying there like a false promise. How did he expect Miss Paulina Trethayne to force herself into the cramping styles of a proper lady when she hadn't a penny to her name she hadn't earned through working his land when his back was turned? Surely he didn't think local society would blink at such an unlikely spectacle and make space for her?

The very idea of the derision that would greet her if she tried to cramp her long limbs and unladylike lope into the mincing gait and quiet littleness of a spinster's day-to-day life made her cringe. He was setting her up to be a mockery, and she felt the sting of it, even as she slammed the door of her bedchamber and ran back down the stairs to find the wretched man and berate him for taking this latest chip out of her self-confidence.

He didn't need her to accompany him about the estate while he was visiting folk who only a few weeks ago had turned to her for help and advice. They had little choice but to ask her for what little help she could give them after years of neglect by their lord, but now they'd forgotten how long he'd left them leaderless and bewildered and she might not even exist for all the need they had of her now. She hoped they never came to regret relying on a man who might easily forget them for another decade.

Fighting her hurt at being forgotten in the dazzling presence of the latest Marquis of Mantaigne, Polly felt weariness pinch after her latest day of hard physical labour. She was driving herself and the men who worked the smallholding they'd made in the castle's vast kitchen garden too hard, but fear of being left with nothing again goaded her on. This was their last chance of a good harvest and it ought to be the best one they'd ever had. If they could make enough money from their crops this year, maybe they could sell the surplus and set up a small farm elsewhere. It wouldn't be Dayspring, of course—nothing could equal the noble old stronghold by the sea she had come to love so much—but they'd work hard to make it a different home.

As she strode across the inner bailey and looked for my Lord of Mantaigne instead of avoiding him, Polly wondered why nobody else worried about the future. The marquis was with a stranger when she tracked him down to the little parlour he had appropriated as a study-cum-estate office and the surprised-looking visitor, trying so hard not to look at her legs, made her more uncomfortable than if he had leered like an uncouth lout. She hung back impatiently while Lord Mantaigne escorted the man outside and bade him a cheery farewell without ever managing to say who he was and why he was here in the first place.

Anyone would think the lord was the land steward he had still not appointed, despite his fine promises, and not a noble fashion plate, Polly told herself scornfully. Yet even she had to admit he looked like a hero from Ancient Greece in the mellow evening light, the long shadows from the setting sun lending his features such stern definition even she couldn't accuse him of being a soft dandy. She saw him laugh at something the man said and once more felt the pull of attraction even as a frown pleated her brows and she shook her head impatiently.

At this distance he looked like a gilded lord out of a legend—a modern King Arthur about to unite his ravaged kingdom with daring deeds and the circle of charm such beings cast on their friends as well as their subjects. Except he was real. And here. Every female impulse in her felt the siren call of such a compelling and deeply masculine man, even when he didn't know he was making it.

She drew a picture for herself of the woman he would happily pull close to kiss and caress in the fading May twilight as their visitor rode away. She would stand no higher than his heart. His true mate would be an intensely feminine beauty with hair of a paler gold than his own, eyes as compellingly blue, but softer and a great deal more demure. There would be a special grace to her slender limbs that not even her detractors could deny and, as one of those detractors, Polly was quite sure she would try very hard to do so.

His ideal woman's voice would be soft and low, and Polly was horribly certain she would sing like an angel. She added a low-cut, narrow gown of gossamer and fairy-dust and knew the wretched female would have sensual curves and a lovely line to her slender limbs to hold him to her for life. Already she hated the smug creature and waved a hand in front of her eyes as if she could erase the differences between such a paragon and herself just by wishing.

She glanced down at the mud and dust-stained work boots she'd once seen as a necessity of life and now regarded as a mark of how little she had in common with the ladies she should have grown up with. Then came her ridiculously overgrown legs, encased in ancient breeches she had found in an attic, discarded by their original owner decades ago in the belief they were too shabby and threadbare to wear even for rough jobs about the castle and the poor probably weren't poor enough to want them.

When she was growing up she often felt a freak, her overlong limbs tangling in her skirts and tripping her up at the most awkward moments. Now she knew she was a female others would mark out as extraordinary for all the wrong reasons and why on earth should it matter to her if the marquis watched her every move or kept his distance as sternly as she'd told herself she wanted him to ever since that first day and night at Dayspring?

She remembered the titters of some other girls when she fell on her nose in church one Sunday not long after her sixteenth birthday. She had crushed the brim of the new bonnet she had longed for so passionately. The pretty delicacy of it hadn't suited her, as one of them unkindly pointed out when humiliated tears streamed down Polly's sore face and bloody nose. Her stepmother had loyally informed them such cattish remarks were neither pretty nor delicate and said more about them than they did about her daughter. Even so Polly had seen the worry in Claire's dark eyes when she hugged as much of her strapping stepchild as she could still reach and whispered one day she would grow into herself and be magnificent, but those commonplace little girls would just be little and commonplace for the rest of their lives.

Loss twisted in her gut as painfully as the day Claire had died when Josh was born. Something in Polly's father seemed to die with her and grief for both of them fought its way past the anger Papa's ruin and reckless death brought with it and she let herself see how deeply he'd loved Claire and how impossible he had found life without her at last. It didn't make the things he'd done to forget his terrible grief right, but suddenly they were more understandable.

The possibility of loving so passionately might trip her up as well, but maybe she had inherited too much sense from the first wife Papa had wed with his head for such a headlong risk of everything she was for love. *Idiotic woman*, she chided herself, *haven't you just con-*

gratulated yourself on being a prosaic female and now you're longing to be the exact opposite?

'He has me in such a spin that I don't know what I do want any more,' she said out loud this time and heard the soft murmur of her own voice sound round the little room with horror.

What if someone was close by when she gave away so much she wanted to keep to herself? Sneaking a look to see if she really had given herself away, she saw nobody and heard only the cool silence of a place with history in every shadow. Fanciful nonsense, of course, Polly decided with a wry smile for her sudden outbreak of lunacy. She touched one of the cool old pieces of glass in the leaded window that overlooked the yard where the marquis and his visitor were still talking earnestly. If she closed her eyes and pretended hard enough, the image she saw through that glass might be him. In another dimension she might reach through and touch the man's very soul instead of the far-off untouchable reality.

There now, at last the marquis had said his farewells and the stranger was riding away. No time like the present, she told herself, and braced her shoulders for the argument she'd been promising herself as she did her best to recall why she was so angry with him in the first place.

'Miss Trethayne, you must have found the habit your friends have worked on so diligently from the stern expression on your face,' he said genially, as if he'd been expecting the flare of temper in her eyes and was finding it a little too amusing.

'If they made it, how come the material is so fine?' she demanded, telling herself she felt so frustrated and suspicious because arguing with him was like trying to wrestle with a shadow; the moment you thought you had a grip on it, it faded and all you were left with was a mocking smile and frustration.

'I remembered seeing a trunk full of such lengths of cloth hidden away in a room tucked away under the eaves that you and your friends must have missed,' he said, a tension in his eyes she might have welcomed a few moments ago to remind her how distant they really were from one another. Now it made her uneasy, tugged at some connection between them she really didn't want to know about.

'Then it's rightfully yours,' she said and shot him a baleful look.

'Ah, but it's not my colour,' he quipped.

'Don't shrug me off and don't treat me like a charity case.'

'I would never be so rash or so rude, even if you were anything of the kind and you're not,' he said sternly, as if he thought the rest of the world spent too much time tiptoeing about her temper.

'You have no idea what it's like to have nothing,' she replied defensively.

'Do I not? If you'd seen the ragged boy who used to risk his life climbing out of the highest tower window up there and down the outside of his own castle in search of scraps to fill his hungry belly, you might change your mind about my ignorance.'

'But you didn't really have nothing,' she argued

weakly, pity for such a desperate boy causing a lump of sadness in her throat she knew he would hate.

'And neither do you. You have a family who adore you; friends who would walk barefoot to reach you if you were in trouble and the whole neighbourhood sings your praises at me until I'm almost sick of the sound of your name on their tongues.'

'None of them need me now you are here.'

'Just as well, since you've been hiding behind a set of harrows or pulling weeds out of turnips or whatever else you've been finding to do with yourself all the hours God sends these past few weeks in order to avoid me.'

'I wasn't hiding.'

'Were you not? If nobody else could have done any of those tasks, then I bow to your superior knowledge and must consider you sociable after all.'

'You know very well there was nothing uniquely skilled about any of the jobs I've done lately.'

'Perhaps you ought to let someone else do them then. I've offered anyone who wants work all the employment they could dream of in my sadly neglected pleasure gardens, woods and the acreage the castle once kept under its own management. Kingwood wants to retire and tells me he's only been farming the land you and your friends couldn't cope with because he felt he owed it to my father. You have no idea how humble I'm becoming under the goad of such words, Miss Trethayne. Everyone here thinks my father a much better man than I'll ever be, although I can't remember much to back that opinion up. In fairness, he could hardly be a worse master than I have been, so the competition is not fierce.'

'They want to admire you,' Polly heard herself say softly and wondered how he'd turned her from raging virago into his sympathetic champion in so short a time. 'Some would even love you, if you let them.'

'Love is the most unreliable of human emotions, Miss Trethayne. I do my best to avoid feeling it or asking for it from others.'

'Then I must feel sorry for you, my lord,' Polly said with a corrosive feeling of disappointment and pity nagging at her as she turned to walk away.

'Don't. I'm perfectly content with friendship and mutual respect.'

'I hope it keeps you warm in winter then,' she murmured and would have gone back to her eyrie to take a second look at the riding habit that now sounded like a gift of love, except he held her back with the lightest of touches on her arm.

'So do I,' he said far more seriously than usual. 'I also hope you'll accept Lady Wakebourne's scheme for your joint futures when she proposes it, Miss Trethayne. The lady has no family and those wild young rascals of hers to bring up on her own somehow. I don't think you'd want her to struggle on alone, even if the idea of me freezing to death on an Arctic ice-floe would probably cost you no qualms.'

'You're so wrong about that,' she told him, meeting his eyes for a long moment. 'It would cost me a great many.'

'But you have a tender heart, Miss Trethayne. I dare say you would make a push to rescue your worst enemy from such a chilly ending,' he said, and there was something in his gaze she dared not read, something that spoke of more than lust or mere liking for her and that simply couldn't be a possibility between them.

'Perhaps I would,' she agreed with a faint smile.

'And you will listen?'

'I would always give such a good friend a fair hearing and try my best to be reasonable about whatever it is she has to say.'

'If that's what it takes to render you open to reason, I must wish I was your friend then.'

'So must I, my lord,' she said rather sadly.

'Could we not try it?' he offered, and for a moment the chance of such an unlikely relationship tempted her to take the admiration in his gaze and warmth of his hand in hers to seal a bond between them.

'I don't think a marquis could be friends with a beggar,' she said and hated herself for being less democratic than he was as she made herself turn away.

'I don't think that so-called beggar can be friends with herself until she accepts we are each of us more than a rank or a piece of ignorant name-calling,' he said quietly as she went to walk away.

She hesitated, wishing so hard she dared accept his olive branch and see him in the same rosy light as the rest of the unofficial residents of Dayspring Castle did.

'I expect you're right,' she said tritely and made herself leave, before she swore undying devotion to him, or even blurted out some disaster of an emotion he would dislike even more.

Thinking back to his idea that she would be happy to hear he'd met such an awful end, she fought down a denial it almost hurt her not to voice. Of course she didn't want anything to happen to the arrogant lord of Dayspring Castle. The very idea of him enduring such hardship when she wasn't there to try to make it less hurt her. Tears blurred her vision before she blinked them back as she strode off to her room to find clean clothes to put on after the bath she so badly needed.

Half an hour later Polly sat back in her tub of hot water in the women's bath-house with a contented sigh, then reached for the soap Lord Mantaigne had insisted on sending for as a luxury he refused to live without. He wasn't the man she'd thought him at first sight of all that perfect tailoring and gilded splendour, but he wasn't the man he thought either. She'd done her best to pretend he was just a London dandy, but he was so much more. If he ever stopped keeping the rest of the world at arm's length, he would be an extraordinary and unforgettable man. It was the waste of such magnificent potential that made her want to cry, though, not a more personal sort of desolation that she wasn't the woman to unlock it.

Washing off the sweat and dirt of her labours, she did her best not to think of making love with the wretched man like this, with her limbs all smooth and warm and naked and her feminine curves undisguised by mannish clothes and rough labour. What would he make of her if he could see her naked? The very idea shot a hot quiver of anticipation through her like an arrow of molten gold, but that was a silly idea, wasn't it?

Gold was far too soft even for Cupid's arrows and

she didn't care to even consider being pierced by one of those. A knot of pure heat still clutched in her belly, though, and on down to whisper all sorts of impossible echoes of him and her at her deepest and most secret core. She considered what he might look like similarly naked and as curious about her as she was about him and blushed in places she didn't know she could blush. Would he want her if he saw her like this? Would his manhood betray the fact a vigorous and healthy male would always want a reasonably well-formed female, if the chance arose to be closeted with her hot and naked in a steamy room with a fire lit in the corner to make it cosy and intimate? Probably, but a cynical voice whispered in her head that it didn't mean she would be in any way special to him and he would be the sun and moon to her if she wasn't very careful.

She ran a speculative hand down the long sweep of her wet thigh and shuddered with feminine curiosity, longing for his hands to shadow hers there and admitting for once how very much she wanted him as her lover. Even the thought made her breasts grow heavier and tighter, and she cupped them to push them up and wonder. How would it feel to have my Lord of Mantaigne seize one hot, tight nipple in his knowing mouth and suckle, even as his long fingers played with the other so it didn't feel left out in the cold?

Polly gasped at where her wicked imagination was taking her, hastily snatched her hands away and reached for the rosemary-and-soapwort infusion Lady Wakebourne made up especially to clean the mud from her hair. She cleansed every lock until it squeaked, then poured the jugs of water over her head, adding the one of icy cold, drawn from the well lest any of the others proved too hot, for the last rinse of both her hair and her unruly body. There, that ought to chill the ardour out of her; shock her into seeing how impossible such a coupling was for both of them.

He would probably leave her with child and she would leave him with regrets and a duty to care for her and her by-blow for the rest of their lives. No, no and no. She would never do that to a man like him, one who would have to find a suitable marchioness one day. Pretend how he liked to be a care-for-nobody, he would suffer the guilt of the damned about any lady whose life he'd ruined in the eyes of the world, once the heady passion was spent and he woke up to find himself the other half of such an unlikely pairing with her.

Her tender smile wobbled at the thought of him arguing he hadn't a soul for her to concern herself with, as he surely would if he was here and knew what sinful wonders she was thinking about. He knew so little about himself it shocked her. It was as if the neglected and abused boy he'd once been had taken the hard things his obnoxious guardian threw at him and secretly owned up to them, as if every word was true. She was sure that was too simple a way to explain it, but she ached for the boy he had been and the man he really was.

Was the *ton* really so wilfully blind they only saw the gilded nobleman he offered up for them to wonder at? She supposed it was a brilliant act; his pose of shallow and vain aristocrat, more concerned about the knot in his cravat than the state of the world or the well-being of his fellow man. Perhaps he showed up less as the man he really was there than he did here, set as he would normally be amongst the brilliant but shallow pleasures of the *haut ton* and pretending to be as indifferent as the next care-for-nobody to the affairs of ordinary humanity.

He'd offered work to those who wanted it here though. That smile played about her mouth again and it was as well there was no mirror in the women's bathhouse to show her how gentle it went at the thought of him pretending to be indifferent, even as he gave the local men a chance to wean themselves away from the smuggling trade or the sea, if they chose to take it.

If he really thought they would lose the chance of a night's work as tub-men and gain luxuries a working man couldn't dream of otherwise, he was probably doomed to disappointment. At least he was giving them a chance to earn an honest living, though, and it would be good to see the Banburgh estates worked as they should be once more, or at least it would be for everyone but the gangs who had used the neglected woods and byways as the ideal conduit from coast to warehouse.

There, she had got through roughly towelling the water from her heavy hanks of hair and drying her over-receptive body without longing for the impossible again, here with her, loving her as she secretly longed to be loved exclusively by him. Was that it? Was she afraid of falling in love with the marquis? Worse even than that disaster—was she already halfway there?

Well, if she was it was about as much use to her as a lunatic longing for the moon, so she had chosen a man who would do her no harm—since it would never even occur to him to love her back. She was nearly six feet tall with four and twenty years of life in her dish; had three beloved obligations who would need her until she was old and grey *and* she habitually wore breeches in preference to petticoats, for goodness' sake. How could he consider her as a potential lover when she was about as ineligible even as his bedmate as a woman could be?

Seizing the delicately carved comb she had felt guilty about taking from one of the bedchambers in the closed-up and neglected part of the house, she began tugging at the tangles in her hair as if it was their fault she was undesirable. Not only was that ridiculous, but it hurt, so, taking a deep breath, she made herself begin at the ends and work towards her crown until every tangle was banished. As it began to dry the firelight picked out red and gold and russet lights in the curls it sprang into wherever Jane had cut the full weight of her heavy locks away.

It was stupid to be vain of a mane of hair she often thought couldn't make up its mind how to be, but the weight of it on her naked shoulders felt silky and rich and sensual. Telling herself it was as well to be realistic about her own attractions, she unwrapped the bath towel, another of Lord Mantaigne's luxuries she couldn't bring herself to argue against using, and felt as if even her skin was more sensitive than it had been before he came here. She felt as if only his sigh against the softness of her shoulders, or the whisper of a finger-tip on her arm, might set a blaze of something sensual and irresistible running over her like wildfire.

You are a deluded idiot, she chided herself as a hot shudder of wanting probably made it a good idea to plunge back into the rapidly cooling water and wash away the very idea. She'd been in here far too long already, though, and what if anyone suspected she had been preening and dreaming and longing for impossible things, instead of simply scrubbing herself clean and getting ready to face his lordship's indifference once more with a mental shrug and roll of exasperated eyes?

For once Polly took some trouble about dressing for the evening ahead because she did have a certain amount of pride after all. She grimaced at the latest ill-fitting gown with its wide skirts and unfashionably long bodice. She'd snatched it from the usual attic as the only other one left that would be long enough for her without the wide hoops designed to make it the first stare of fashion decades ago when a fine Banburgh lady ordered it from her mantua-maker.

She looked a quiz, she decided as she fumbled her bare feet into the old-fashioned high-heeled shoes that added another few inches to her already impressive height. At this rate she would be given a torch and told to stand instead of a light on the headland to keep ships away in a storm. Well, this was the truth: Miss Paulina Trethayne in all her unadorned plainness. She felt a twinge of regret for the jewellery she'd been forced to sell to pay some of her father's debts and feed the boys until she could beg, borrow or steal enough to keep them all from starving. Her mother's gold locket or single row of pearls would have diverted one glance from the stark lack of style in anything she was wearing.

The magnificent diamond ring Claire had managed to keep hidden somehow throughout her frantic flight from the Terror in France was hidden safely away behind a neatly re-mortared stone in Polly's bedchamber to be sold to help her boys one day. So far Polly had managed to tell herself *not yet*, but soon it would have to be *now*.

'Ah, there you are, my dear,' Lady Wakebourne said absently when she slipped into the dining parlour at the last moment before Prue would tell her she was too late and must make do with whatever she could forage in the kitchen.

'I was too dirty to sit down to dinner without a bath,' she told whoever might be interested.

'You shouldn't be slaving in the fields like a peasant girl,' Prue said sternly, and her sister nodded a solemn agreement.

Toby frowned at the last of his rabbit stew as if it suddenly tasted less savoury and shot her a worried look. 'We should help you instead of idling at the Vicarage all day,' he told her as if he'd suddenly grown up and become the man of the household.

'I'm not idle,' Henry objected, 'I work hard.'

'No, but you're a natural scholar, Hal, and love your dusty old books. I don't see much point aping the little gentleman much longer and pretending I have the least bent for learning, though, because I haven't.'

'I doubt any of us struggled to provide you with an education in order for you to throw it in our faces, my lad,' Lady Wakebourne chided with a glare at her own protégés that Jago returned with a shrug that said he wasn't going to complain about a lack of hard work after his years spent cleaning chimneys from dawn until dusk.

'I don't think any of us could describe you as little gentlemen without being accused of stretching the truth mightily,' Lord Mantaigne intervened before Toby could dash out and sign on as cabin boy on the nearest merchant ship and his littlest brother as powder-monkey to a man o'war.

'I promised your mother I would raise you as gentlemen, so you're not getting out of your lessons that easily, young man. And you promised her you would do as I said until you were one and twenty. By my reckoning, I have another six years of blissful obedience to my every whim to look forward to,' Polly said with a steady look for her eldest brother, then a wistful glance at her dinner.

She had worked up a mighty appetite at her labours and was very sharp set, but her brothers took precedence over everything else until she'd convinced them there was no point setting out to see the world before it had an idea they were coming.

'Let your sister eat in peace, Tobias,' his lordship said quietly, and Polly waited for a protest, but none came.

Toby held his new friend's eyes with a steady challenge for a long moment, then seemed to accept some unspoken reassurance Lord Mantaigne was giving him and grinned like the schoolboy he still was.

'Can I have some more, then?' he asked Prue, who pretended to be shocked by his huge appetite, as usual, then helped him to another plateful and muttered about growing boys who grew cheekier by the moment.

'You know very well I'm your favourite,' he replied with a grin, and Polly had to fight a smile, because he was quite right. Prue loved the way Toby enjoyed her food so openly and he also had the easy charm of generations of piratical Trethayne males to call on when he chose to use it.

'You take no notice of him, young Henry,' Prue said and piled another helping on Hal's plate unasked.

He grinned and ploughed his way through it with nearly as fine an appetite as his elder brother, but he was more comfortable in his own shoes and accepted he was loved as easily as one of the mixed pack of dogs lying fast asleep in front of the fire seemed to do. Little Josh had worn himself out chasing about the countryside on some mischief and had already been packed off to bed before he went to sleep in his dinner. Polly took time to wonder at how different her brothers were. Each had a special place in her heart and she would lay down her life for them if she had to, but did she love them enough to lay pride aside and let Lord Mantaigne offer them some golden future she could not?

The hint of it was in the air, the promise of a different life for them all in his vague reference to a plan he and Lady Wakebourne had been hatching between them. She wondered at herself for not wanting to snatch hold of it with both hands. How would the boys feel in ten years' time if they lived on a rich man's charity? And how did Mr Peters feel about his lot in life now? She shot him a wary glance as she did her best to recall Claire's teaching that real ladies took small bites and chewed their food to stop herself gulping Prue's stew down as fast as she could before running out of the room to escape all these uncomfortable problems.

The answer was that Mr Peters seemed content enough to play second fiddle to his employer, most of the time. She frowned at the notion he also seemed braced for some long-expected burden to fall on his shoulders and that odd idea didn't answer any of her questions. All Toby and Henry and Josh needed to do was make a path for themselves through life, though, and she hoped it would lead them to happiness and middling prosperity. They had an honourable name, but nobody would expect them to shoulder the heavy weight the head of a noble family had to bear.

She ate her fill and drank a little of the wine so long left to age or even spoil in my lord's cellars and thought about that weight. The Marquis of Mantaigne carried such expectation, so many demands on those broad shoulders of his, so how could she let her brothers become one more? The long put-off notion of trying to get the head of her family to help her again surfaced. The mellow claret turned bitter on her tongue at the thought of asking the arrogant old man who'd looked down on her father for anything, after he'd thrown her and the boys out of his house as if they'd polluted it and ordered her never to come back. She gulped her wine so carelessly it went the wrong way and she demonstrated all too clearly why she'd never be any man's conformable wife by spluttering and going red as a beetroot at the dining table.

'Try to breathe slowly and evenly and you'll soon be right as ninepence again,' Lady Wakebourne urged comfortably as Polly did her best not to cough at the same time as she mentally pushed the imaginary Marchioness of Mantaigne out of the room and slammed the door in her smug face.

'Tea, Miss Polly, that's what you need,' Prue said sagely and went off to make some before she could argue.

It would take a lot more than a cup of smuggled Pekoe to right the trouble that ailed her, Polly decided. She let Lady Wakebourne lead her from the room and sit her down in the slip of a room she'd christened her drawing room, as if she was still the prosperous squire's daughter of her youth, though, and enjoyed being soothed and mothered for once. Tomorrow was soon enough to face the very adult problem she had been fighting not to admit she had since the moment her eyes first met Lord Mantaigne's across one of the Dayspring stables.

Chapter Ten

'What are you planning to do about them then, Mantaigne?' Peters asked when he found Tom on the old outer walls watching the moon rise over the sea.

'Schools for some, trades for others. Boys need to be busy and will get into trouble if they're not occupied, whatever Lady Wakebourne thinks about turning her urchins into little gentlemen. The adults must decide what they want out of life for themselves, since I can't do everything. There will be posts here if they want them, but not the sort of freedom they have had until I came back.'

'For some that was only freedom to starve, but what of the ladies?'

'Ah, yes, the ladies. Now they really are a conundrum.'

'One beyond your ability to solve?'

'It will take some thought and a measure of cunning,' Tom replied with a frown at the calm waters below and the cloudless twilight sky above them. 'At least there's no need to worry about smugglers tonight—it's far too bright a moon for them to risk being out and about,' he said, as they were a lesser problem than the one Miss Paulina Trethayne and Lady Wakebourne's presence here had set him.

'I don't worry about them much on any night. There's little point doing so when half the coast is actively involved in the trade and the other half wink at it.'

'Aye, it would be a bit like trying to keep water in a sieve,' Tom admitted with a frown at the calm scene that was so at odds with the turmoil inside him.

'Which is why you don't ride to certain coves or visit outlying farms at the wrong time of day, I suppose?'

'I've never been one for tilting at windmills,' Tom said with the uneasy feeling he might be lying.

'And there's trouble enough close to home.'

It was more of a statement than a question, and Tom didn't know if he least wanted to think about who was managing to invade his castle right under his nose, or what to do about a female unlike any other he'd ever encountered.

'You are a clever lawyer, Peters, but Rich Seaborne tells me you're an even wilier investigator of knotty problems certain rich and powerful men would rather you did not untangle.'

'Does he, my lord? I wouldn't have thought Mr Seaborne so ready to wag his tongue about the shady affairs of such men to anyone who asked him.'

'Oh, don't worry yourself on that head; I had the devil's own job prising even that much information out of him. He only admitted to knowing you as anything other than a lawyer when I told him of my mission from my godmother and the fact she had engaged you to come here with me to guard my back and investigate my enemies. He said she wouldn't have asked you to do so on a whim, nor would you have agreed to come here if it was as easy a task as it appeared.'

'These incursions into a near-ruinous castle don't have the feel of anything truly sinister about them to me,' Peters said as if he was a connoisseur of the worst sort of criminal mind and this one wasn't up to his mettle.

'No, I suspect it's a mean little affair, much like the rest my one-time guardian had running in his lifetime. His nephew seems even less effectual, if also slightly less mad, than he turned out to be.'

'Yes, he does seem to have been a bully of the worst sort, but a coward with it, I suspect,' Peters said as if that was all the world needed to remember of Philip Grably, and Tom wondered if he was right.

'He was a twisted and devious coward and bully, though. All the tales I hear of my father when I ride about the estate and villages have made me realise he knew this place like the back of his hand. I can't help remembering how Grably used to rave he loved my mother better than any other man and how dared my father lay his filthy hands on such a perfect and fragile woman when he wasn't fit to black her boots? I suspect he might have murdered my father, for all the good that could do him when my mother was already dead. Perhaps he thought he was avenging her, or who knows what he thought when he pitched his supposed best friend down a two-hundred-foot drop onto the rocks below five years after she died?'

'That's a grim suspicion to live with, Mantaigne,' Peters said with sympathy Tom would have felt uncomfortable with only weeks ago.

'Aye, but it could explain how my father stumbled so close to the edge of a cliff-path he walked every morning and knew better than anyone.'

'It could, but if so it's a secret Grably took to his grave,' Peters agreed quietly.

'True,' Tom replied with a frown at a certain window in the old part of the castle where the women had their quarters. 'And the Trethaynes are alive and under my roof. Their welfare trumps old sins.'

'Indeed,' Peters agreed so blandly that Tom decided he didn't care if the man thought he was a besotted fool or not.

'Don't *you* think it strange even a junior branch of such an old and powerful family was left to beg, borrow or steal their daily bread?'

'Profligacy has brought many a rich man to ruin,' Peters said with such austerity Tom wondered if that was a reason a clever and devious man might become a lawyer and whatever else the man was when he wasn't busy.

'I know, but Lord Trethayne's fortune seems intact. I don't know how the man could leave those children to starve when he should feel a moral duty to look after his nephew's family, even if the idiot didn't leave them to his care until they were grown. That seems the logical step for the nephew of a lord to take when he began to breed so many boys with his second wife, don't you think?'

'The late Mr Trethayne doesn't sound like a sensible man.'

'No, but his second wife fled to this country after the revolution in France. She must have known first-hand how it felt to lose everything and would have pushed the idiot to make some provisions for her children, however feckless he was otherwise,' Tom confided the unease he'd felt about that destitution ever since he found the family here scraping a living on his land.

'I believe his ruin began after the lady died, but it happened nearly a decade ago and I can't recall any details. Nobody mentioned he had children when the tale of his rash dealings and sad end went the rounds, so I didn't think it remarkable Lord Trethayne disclaimed all responsibility at the time. Now I can see that you're right; it's odd and needs looking into, if only to find out why he didn't help them. I expect I will find out more in London at this time of year than I could at Trethayne's country seat, so I'd best arrange to be summoned there urgently before the week is out if you truly wish me to take this any further.'

'Aye, I do, and I'm sure the place is teeming with crimes and misdemeanours awaiting your attention by now,' Tom said with a mocking grin to offset Peters's knowing smile that he cared enough about the Trethaynes to go to so much trouble on their behalf.

'At least I'll be spared the tension in any room when you and Miss Trethayne are in it for the next few days. I half expect crockery or candlesticks to start flying round the room whenever you meet without one of Miss Trethayne's brothers or Lady Wakebourne there to make you guard your tongues and tempers,' Peters replied with a look that told Tom he also wondered if he was about to be punched in the nose.

'Well, don't, Miss Trethayne is too much of a lady to vent her temper on innocent bystanders. If I can remind Lord Trethayne of his duty to his family and the fact she and her brothers are his responsibility, at least they might be able to go home and excuse the rest of you such a state of civil war at the breakfast table.'

'She will never agree to go anywhere near the old vulture after he left her to tramp the roads with three little boys when her father died,' Peters cautioned as if warning him not to get his hopes up.

'The trick will be to present things to her in the right terms,' Tom said with a feeling finding those words wasn't going to be as easy as he made out, especially as his best words seemed to desert him in Miss Trethayne's company and all sorts of wrong-headed ideas took their place.

'I doubt a poet could come up with those,' Peters cautioned.

'I can't let her leave Dayspring with nothing in her pockets and an easy mark for any rogue who might threaten or exploit her and her band of fellow vagrants.'

'If I were you, Mantaigne, I'd look a little deeper into that particular charitable impulse before you lose something precious without ever realising you had it.'

Tom felt his way along that sentence and found knots in it. There was a deep sadness in Peters's expression he'd never thought he'd be allowed to see, and Tom fumbled to pretend he hadn't seen that glimpse of the man's private self Peters wouldn't relish sharing with the likes of him.

'Just as well you're not me then,' he said facetiously and saw Peters's frown at his refusal to be counselled.

He might have learned to love his childhood home again, had even let the sad old house and grounds and the folk on the estate into his life as far as he could, but he wasn't ready to give up everything he'd learnt about surviving in a hostile world. If he let himself care about everyone within his orbit he'd collapse. Too many people depended on him for him to risk burdening himself with a wife and a ready-made family and hadn't he decided on his way here he had true friends in Luke and his family? So he should be able to look forward to the end of Virginia's three months with the lightest of hearts.

Yet, despite her poverty and unconventional life, Polly Trethayne wasn't a female he could stow in a neat little corner of his life labelled 'mistress' and forget the rest of the time. She wouldn't fit, for one thing; for another he didn't want to leave her less than she was now and embittered by his betrayal into the bargain. He wanted her with a passion he couldn't recall being this fierce even as a spotty youth desperate to find out about sex and any female who'd let him have some with her. What he felt was a freakishly heated physical attraction that would burn out as soon as he got her out of his castle and as far away as he could put her. Even a few miles away would be good enough for now, though.

He felt the gap in his heart and mind at the idea of being a stranger to her and hers again. He licked his suddenly dry lips and tasted her on them, as if her lush mouth had only just parted from his instead of the gap of *impossible* that stretched between them. He was the one who walked away; he'd made that gap and would always have to make it.

Haunted by the idea he might look back on this time with the bitter regret Peters seemed to feel about some lost chance at love he regretted, he made himself remember where and what he was. With Peters probably noting the reminiscent smile Tom found himself giving at the thought of creeping through a dark and dusty mausoleum with Polly Trethayne's hand in his, it was high time he remembered the Marquis of Mantaigne cared for nobody again, especially not for a female he'd never be able to ignore as so many of his peers did their wives once they'd got their obligatory heir and spare. And when had he jumped from mistress into marriage, even in his head? Heavens, but he'd been right after all; the woman was a danger to herself and everyone else and the sooner she left the better.

'Anyway, we must make sure the felons plaguing my castle are run to earth,' he said. 'Neither of us can leave until we find out what the devil they're up to.'

'Until we catch them in the act again as you so nearly managed to that first night, or find out why they want to explore this dusty barrack of yours at any time of day, you would seem to be stuck here then, my lord,'

Peters said with a lack of respect Tom was beginning to admire. If the man ever did treat him with some, at least he'd know he'd earned it.

'Hell's teeth,' he exploded with frustrated rage.

'You have nigh on a month left on your slate, my lord,' Peters pointed out less than helpfully.

'And you know just what you can do with that happy reminder, don't you?' Tom asked sarcastically and decided he'd been tried enough for one day. 'I'm going for a walk,' he told the man with a glare that dared him to say it was nearly midnight and he needed to have a care until their night visitors were unmasked.

'I hope your groom can put up with your moods better than I can whilst I'm in London, my lord, since it seems to me you need a bodyguard more than you do a lawyer at the moment.'

'At least I'll be able to cheer myself up with the thought of you ploughing through piles of dry and dusty documents and listening to tedious old gossip while I'm here and you're in London though, Peters.'

'I could ask Miss Trethayne for the details, I suppose and persuade her to confide her sad tale to me. It would save us both a great deal of time and trouble.'

'Only if you don't like the way your head currently sits on your shoulders, Peters,' Tom told him grimly, an image of Peters and Polly Trethayne discussing her life so far as rain beat intimately on the mullioned windows and the outside world seemed far away punching into his gut like a fist.

'I do. Lovely, spirited and unique though I think she is, Miss Trethayne is not for me and nor am I for her.'

'Just as well,' Tom said, 'I'll see if I can find out if anyone on the estate knows where Grably went when they removed him from Daybreak while you're gone. Someone else might have heard him raving about his treasure and the most precious things at Daybreak he'd make sure I never got to lay my filthy little hands on.'

'You're sure that's what he said all those years ago?'

'He bellowed it loudly enough for half the village to hear him when Virgil demanded he returned everything he'd taken from me, but I'm in no humour to think of him right now. Get on with delving into the Trethayne family fortunes and tomorrow I'll go through that mountain of rolls and boxes in the Muniment Room myself.'

'It's a full moon tonight and your villains won't even need a lantern,' Peters warned him as if he knew there were a pack of wild ideas skittering about in Tom's head, but somehow the Trethaynes' well-being seemed far more important than a few dusty *objets d'art* and mementos of a mother he had no memory of.

'I'll watch my step,' Tom said as patiently as he could manage as he set off to reacquaint himself with Day-spring by moonlight.

At least the exercise might improve his temper and allow him a few hours of sleep uninterrupted by fantasies of a softly warm and satiated Polly Trethayne asleep at his side and tangled round him with sleepy-eyed ardour when they awoke together. Sometimes he couldn't get her out of his head long enough to relax into oblivion for a few hours, but even when he could, waking up alone felt stark and lonely. Thinking about his light-hearted affairs of the past, he shook his head and wondered why this woman threatened to be essential as breathing to him.

He strode on through the silvered landscape and vividly remembered how magical this place was to the small boy he'd been when night and the moonlight offered him escape from his guardian's thugs and mood swings and invited him to explore a new world. At night the place was alive in a very different way and Tom hoped the poachers and landers were staying home tonight in deference to the power of the nearly full moon.

Which thought brought him right back to where he started and the heady fantasy of returning to his own bed to find a sleepy-eyed goddess in it all warm and welcoming and murmuring unlikely promises. Drat the wretched woman, would she never give him a moment's respite? Thinking of such impossible and significant souls as Polly Trethayne, he realised now why Virgil had never seemed quite content when Virginia was out of sight and sighed at the idea both of them would be highly amused by the sight of him acting the fool over a woman like this.

Once he'd sworn never to dance at another being's bidding and here he was back at Dayspring on Virginia's orders and pining for a woman he couldn't have. At least he was trying to make peace with the past as Virginia must have intended when she sent him and Peters here to find out what had gone amiss at Dayspring. That ought to be enough even for his ever-interfering godmother, and at last Tom saw the joke was on him as he paused by the lake to moodily skim stones across its otherwise mirror-like stillness.

A moorhen shrieked a protest, then hastily fell silent as a hunting barn owl scoped the edge of the trees on silent wings and a vixen barked to her cubs to behave themselves and come away from somewhere close by. They were noises of the night he'd been so familiar with once upon a time he marvelled that he'd forgotten how good it felt to enjoy the freedom of his own land in the dark, when nobody else but smugglers and poachers and creatures of the night wanted it and a forlorn boy could feel free of all that made his days hideous. Even though he'd hated the castle back then because his guardian lived in it, he'd loved the land and still did. Another lesson learnt, he decided with a resigned sigh as he wondered if that was another reason for his godmother's demand he spend a season here and never mind all those childish oaths never to set foot in the place again.

'Damn it, Virginia, I'm here, aren't I? Shouldn't that be enough for you when I swore I'd never set foot in the place again until you went and died on me and left that confounded list of things to do behind you,' he murmured into the night air. He could have deceived himself into thinking he heard her argue less than the best was never good enough for her godson, thank you very much. 'God, I miss you so much,' he whispered to the now-still lake and the moonlit shadows and decided restlessly wandering the cliff-paths all night wouldn't do anyone much good and he couldn't avoid his bed for ever because there was no Polly Trethayne in it, waiting for him to come home and make love to her in the heady shadows of my lord's currently humble bedchamber.

Polly had been out of sorts for the rest of the evening. When the fire was burning low and conversation lulled to a sleepy murmur she looked up from a reverie about what lords and their secretaries talked about when nobody else was listening and caught Lady Wakebourne's eyes resting on her. For a while she tried to join in the relaxed chatter after the day's work until her thoughts took over and she lapsed into silence again.

If Mantaigne was here, no doubt he'd manage to annoy her in all sorts of subtle ways. And yet... And yet nothing; he was just a man and much like any other. Under his fine clothes and fastidious grooming he was still only another son of Adam. For a supposedly idle man he had a set of very powerful muscles on that lean body of his, though, and she had a feeling he was as impressive without a stitch on as he was with all that fine tailoring and spotless linen not doing a very good job of concealing his manly perfections from the eyes of the world.

He swam in the sea every morning whatever the weather, just for the sheer pleasure of pitting himself against the elements so far as she could tell. Then there were all those long hours spent in the saddle and it really wasn't quite right for her to long for an excuse to ride at his side and simply watch the play of his well-honed muscles over that long body of his as he moved as one with his horse. He might have helped her out in her quest to find fault with him, she decided crossly, but, just when she was ready to find him as idle and frivolous as he wanted her to, he would do something that showed how unlike the image he worked so hard to portray he was underneath those fine clothes.

She recalled him on that first day, dust and ancient cobwebs clinging to his sweat-sheened skin until she'd challenge his fashionable friends to even recognise him under the grime. Heat rushed through her at the memory of him so utterly male and yet so endearingly boyish in all his dirt. That hot bolt of what must be carnal desire unnerved her.

She'd spent years thinking herself a freak for *not* feeling the wanton urges some women seemed to be brought so low by. Now she was yearning like a schoolgirl for a man who very likely wished she didn't exist. Horrified to catch herself sitting among her friends, a dreamy smile on her face, she tried to make sense of the various strands of conversation and join in, but it was like trying to weave cloth out of cobwebs and the chatter faded into the background again as sorting out her feelings towards the lord of Dayspring Castle took centre stage once more.

The man was a walking conundrum, she concluded, frowning at the empty fireplace. If she understood him a little better, maybe she could put him out of her head and get on with her life. At first sight he'd looked almost too perfect, like a hero out of a myth rather than a real man. She supposed she'd been as taken in by his surface polish and glamour as everyone else after that first bolt of heady shock that here was the man she'd never let herself dream of, standing there watching her with whole worlds of promise in his blue eyes. Something told her that shield was part of a game he played with his fellow man even then and perhaps that accounted for her irritation with him as soon as she realised he wasn't put on this earth to make her feel unique and feminine and *found*.

Could such a self-contained man let anyone see him as he really was? She doubted it, but if he did she hoped she wasn't here to see it. There, she had admitted it, even if only in her thoughts. She wanted to be his special female, the one to unlock his guarded heart and make herself uniquely at home in his arms. Well, she could want as much as she liked, it would never happen. How could it when she was herself and he was Marquis of Mantaigne?

'Woolgathering again, my dear?' Lady Wakebourne asked softly.

Polly realised the others had said goodnight and gone to their own quarters without her even noticing. 'Apparently,' she admitted, finding her gaze hard to meet.

'High time you got some sleep if you're planning more relentless toil in the morning, my dear,' her ladyship told her, and Polly meekly got to her feet and took a last look round the now shadowy parlour.

How much longer would they be able to sit together so sociably at the end of a day's work like this? The question added another layer to her discomfort as she followed her ladyship down the grand stone stairway and outside into the twilight. So much was changing here and Polly knew her driven urge to work hard stemmed from a need to fight those changes and pretend all would be well again. That was obviously impossible; they lived in a different place and time now and she should accept it and plan her next move.

'Did Lord Mantaigne really find that lovely cloth for my new habit in an attic we managed not to discover somehow?' she asked as they made their way across the courtyard and she did her best to curb her long stride to her ladyship's shorter pace.

'Yes, he thinks the box must have been thrown in a dark corner when his grandmother died and the fabrics she planned to have her London dressmaker make up for her were forgotten. Lucky for us, since if they had been turned into clothes we'd have had to look at you dressed like a scarecrow for evermore.'

'I shall ignore that comment as best I can, but it must have taken a deal of work to make it up so beautifully.'

'We love you, my dear,' the lady said simply, and Polly battled tears.

'It's so long since anyone said so,' she admitted huskily, 'and I love you too.'

'Thank you. After Greville shot himself I thought I was too bitter and twisted up with fury and grief to love anyone again, but you and your brothers and the unlikely friends we've gathered along the way taught me otherwise. You have made a lot of difference to a good many lives, Polly. I hope you'll see how special you are one day and how very lucky those boys of yours are to have such a sister.'

'I only did what any sister would,' Polly protested uncomfortably.

'Most would have sent their brothers to a charitable

institution and done whatever they had to in order to make their own way in the world. Not many would put their half-brothers before their reputations and any prospect of a decent marriage. I would not have done what you did at seventeen; I was far too selfish and pleased with myself for such a sacrifice back then.'

'You would have done exactly as I did. The boys had done nothing to deserve what happened to us and I couldn't let Papa's folly cost them a future.'

'At the price of your own,' her friend pointed out gently.

Polly paused before she spoke, wondering why they'd never talked this freely in all the years they had known each other. 'I was too young to see that then and now my brothers' needs outweigh mine.'

'You are still human, child—you can't rule passions and emotions out of your life because your father seems to have indulged in far too many of them. If you ever need a listener, I'm an older and wiser woman than I was once,' Lady Wakebourne offered as if she thought Polly might stand in need of a confidante before too long.

'Finding a new home and some sort of future for Toby and Henry and Josh is more important than my little worries,' she said as if that was all that mattered in her life, as indeed it had to be.

'You're still too young to shoulder such responsibility. I really hope your father was properly ashamed of himself for leaving you in such dire straits.'

'He always thought we would come about.'

'When that last ill-considered venture took every penny he had?'

'It could have worked,' Polly defended her feckless father.

'And you should have had a life of your own, instead of being provider and protector to those heedless boys before you were out of the schoolroom.'

'They're not heedless, and I'm happy here—or I was until we were found out,' Polly argued. 'Anyway, I would never have taken in polite society.'

'Nonsense, you may be taller than the average, but the polite world would be well pleased by the sight of you if you'd ever had a Season in town.'

'There we must differ, so shall we forget building castles in Spain and go to bed, my lady?'

'Aye, although whether you'll sleep when you get there is a very different matter,' Lady Wakebourne said as if she knew a little bit too much about Polly's restless nights and disturbing dreams for comfort.

Chapter Eleven

'Someone was skulking about the castle again last night, my lord,' Partridge the gatekeeper informed Tom about a week after Peters left for London and Miss Trethayne resumed her petticoats.

The idea he measured out his days by her actions disturbed him more than any rogues ambling about the disused wings of the castle in the dark. Unluckily for him, she looked even more magnificent in skirts than she did in breeches. Lady Wakebourne was obviously intent on torturing him, since each garment produced out of that accurst trunk in the rafters suited her protégée better than the last.

First there was that dratted habit, draped so delightfully about her long limbs and feminine curves he could hardly concentrate on staying in his own saddle whenever she was wearing it, let alone any of the places he was supposed to be taking such an interest in. Then there was a dark-crimson monstrosity, made from finest silk velvet with such a sneakily modest bodice he was certain its wearer had no idea how immodest it truly was. The colour suited her and the fine stuff clung to every sleek and lovely line of her and when she moved he badly wanted to know how it felt between his touch and the warm woman underneath.

He only just suppressed a groan at the very thought of her hips swaying gracefully in front of him as she'd preceded him into the makeshift dining room last night. As if that wasn't bad enough, this morning she was wearing a deep-sapphire abomination of the very finest wool, made up into a morning gown, of all things, with a lawn fichu gathered almost to the neck that ought to be just what he'd been longing for last night, but was more of a disaster than the last instead. He was learning the magic of the hinted-at rather than the blatant whilst he tried to eat his breakfast now and he really hadn't wanted to know how well a fashionably high waistline showed off her firm, high breasts and magnificent length of leg.

Had he groaned out loud at the shattering memory of her sitting at the breakfast table, greeting him as if not quite sure he was the urbane gentlemen everyone around her seemed to think him? Wise woman, he told himself distractedly, as he met Partridge's speculative gaze with a rueful grin. He doubted much about his ridiculous preoccupation with Miss Trethayne's artfully designed new wardrobe had escaped the shrewd scrutiny of yet another man outside his natural orbit. There were so many of them at Dayspring he almost added himself to the list, but a terrible feeling of belonging was creeping up on him unwanted.

A good job this man knew how to keep secrets then;

Tom decided to ignore any minor crimes he'd committed in his hot youth and trust he hadn't brought them with him from London. Partridge was the main reason the odd assortment of people living in his castle had gone unmolested for so long, so Tom could trust him where they were concerned, even if he was less certain about the man's relationship to the free-traders and his supposed lord and master.

'You're quite certain this business has nothing to do with guinea boats or smuggling spies in and out of the country? I might wink at the Trade for the sake of my tenants and half the inhabitants of the south coast, but I won't look the other way if they run traitors or Boney's guineas in and out of Castle Cove.'

'They wouldn't do it now you're here anyhow. Folk round here are more loyal than you deserve and they'd never tell the landers you don't go in that part of the castle if you can help it.'

'I'd hoped nobody would notice.'

'I've lived a lot longer than you, my lord, and not much passes me by.'

'Which would make you a good gatekeeper.'

'So I'm told.'

'Ah, so there *is* a lady in the case. I thought so somehow.'

'Love gets to us all in the end, if we're lucky enough. The real trick is to recognise it when it hits you between the eyes, my lord,' the man said blandly.

'And to know it for the passing joy it is,' he muttered grumpily.

'But then it wouldn't be love in the first place, would it, my lord?'

'No, damnation take it, it wouldn't and it isn't. We were talking about intruders and thieves, Partridge, not fairy stories.'

'So we were, my lord. Then it's high time we found out who's getting into your castle and why they keep coming now you're here and busy at long last.'

'Perhaps we'd best find out what they're looking for, then,' Tom said, resigned to searching the part of the house he'd managed to avoid since his first day back.

'Stands to reason they wouldn't keep coming if there was enough of them to search properly in the first place.'

'So it won't take many of us to catch them.'

'You want this kept quiet, milord?'

'Yes, the place is all but empty and no sane felon would bother to break in.'

'Aye, most everything was taken away years ago. They certainly ain't busy picking apart state beds and all that fancy stuff you lords have built into your palaces. Folk round here are good at not seeing things, but they'd notice if the old place was being emptied bit by bit and the pickings trundled past their windows of a bright night when everyone's at home where they ought to be for once.'

'Or they'd have to get it past you,' Tom said thinking that the most difficult part of the whole unlikely business.

'True, so how many of your men can you trust, my lord?'

'All of them, but they're grooms and coachmen, not redbreasts or hedge creepers. I'd rather keep this to ourselves and plan a surprise my unexpected guests won't be able to refuse.'

A couple more weeks crept by with the skies overcast and dull and sometimes a heavy shower of rain before the sun came out for a few brief moments to show how spring ought to be, in a more settled country. Polly wondered if the local smugglers were the only ones happy at the sight of dull skies as the Preventatives stayed by their fires even when the moon hid in the clouds. She stared out of the rain-soaked window one morning after breakfast and wondered why she was still here, almost a season on from Lord Mantaigne's arrival at his castle and what should be her cue to leave.

The boys had gone to their lessons, and Polly didn't know what to do unless the rain let up enough for her to go outside. She didn't know what to do most of the time even when she was out nowadays anyway.

It was nearly June now and long past the usual time for spring cleaning, but Lord Mantaigne still wouldn't let her hire a small army to sweep away the dust and grime of decades from the newer parts of this vast place. She didn't know how he resisted the need to have the past purged from his castle, but somehow he still did and why it should matter to her was an even bigger mystery. Once he was free of the dust and shadows of the past, the marquis would be able to raise his family here. She could think of no better cure for the harsh memories of his childhood than a pack of well-loved and well-fed boys of his own to make him forget the deprived and resentful one he had once been himself.

Lady Wakebourne stubbornly refused to tell her what plans were being hatched for their futures, but part of her knew they needed to go. It was time for new beginnings, and she must be banished too, she decided, still with a huff of annoyance at them both for being so secretive. Apparently several of the middling houses in Castle Magna were being refurbished, and Polly wondered if the marquis had it in mind to put them in one of them. Close to the woods and with miles of coves and dunes to explore nearby, it would be ideal for the boys, but she really didn't want to live so close to the castle. She would have to smile and be grateful and pretend she didn't care when Lord Mantaigne wed a suitable lady and made her the mother of the children who would run wild at the castle instead of her brothers and their friends.

For weeks she'd been trying to come up with a plan to allow the boys to stay under Lady Wakebourne's benign wing while she somehow found a place for herself with no carelessly irresistible marquises close by to make her feel a stranger in her own skin. In her opinion the marquis should be kept in Mayfair for the good of the female population of Dorset. It was ridiculous to feel uniquely drawn to him, to know no other man would ever touch the hidden feminine depths of her as he had done. Well, it might be ludicrous and on the edge of dangerous as well, but that didn't mean she was going to stop feeling it because they no longer lived under the same roof.

She had hoped it was a silly infatuation she could get over as swiftly as it came, like a spring cold or a fever, but he'd been here nearly two months now and she longed for him more ridiculously with every day that passed. It was time she began to plan a life without him, more than time. If they shared a house much longer she'd let herself fall in love with the dratted man and that would be an even bigger disaster.

She was young and healthy as a horse; she knew more about running a large estate than a lady ought to and was capable of anything her sex allowed her to do. The fact that was such a pitifully small number of things could not stop her making plans. It hadn't taken her long to realise she wouldn't be a very good companion to the sort of nervous and fainting lady who usually needed one. Now Polly made up an ideal employer in her head and started her on a series of fanciful and raffish adventures that would keep them both well entertained without any need of tatting or reading sermons to snoring invalids. She was in the midst of planning her escape from the amorous attentions of her imaginary lady's discarded lovers when Lord Mantaigne came in and found her staring out of the rain-soaked window as if spellbound by the dismal view.

'Not even a Revenue Cutter would brave the Channel on such a day, so you can't be staring at one of those,' he remarked genially, but she refused to look at him.

'Even I am permitted the occasional daydream, Lord Mantaigne,' she told him as distantly as she could manage when his very presence in a room could make her heart race like Ariel after a rabbit.

'Really? I wonder you find the time,' he said with a long look that told her he'd noticed she went in the opposite direction to any he took of late.

'They don't take long,' she lied, 'and this rain give me an excuse to sit and twiddle my thumbs with a clear conscience.'

'How would we English manage without the weather as our favourite topic of conversation, I wonder?'

'Very ill, I should think. In better climates people must have to put so much more effort into the niceties of everyday life, don't you think?'

'On topics such as that one, I do my best not to think at all,' he said with an impatience that made her look him in the face out of sheer surprise he could dismiss the very small talk he'd been using to fend off the rest of them since he got here.

She blinked at the shock of seeing him anew. Every time he was out of her sight she dearly hoped her memory had exaggerated the impact of his looks and personality and every time he came back into it she knew what a vain hope it was.

I really want to kiss you, she heard a wild and reckless part of herself long to murmur to him like a siren, as if there could ever be anything more than tolerance between them. Thank heavens her sensible side had control of her tongue today. She could just imagine the horror with which he'd hear such a blatant invitation.

What if another Thomas Banburgh from this honourable idiot replied, *And I want to do more than just kiss you back, Paulina*—would she let him? Probably, so it was as well she hadn't put either of them to the test.

'Was there something you wanted, my lord?' she made herself ask with such distant politeness he ought to take it as a hint and leave her alone again.

Always, it felt like a whisper on the air as he met her gaze with more than she'd ever thought to see in the hot blue of his clear irises. Had he said it? Or was it wishful thinking? She heard a pair of masculine boots stamp outside the quiet room as silence stretched between them inside, and she cursed heartily under her breath. One kiss would not have made her into a wanton and it seemed a small comfort for all the years she would probably have to spend seeing my lord and his lady go by her new home, like a stray cat watching a king and queen.

'Partridge wants to know where my guardian went after he left here, although why he can't come in and ask you if you know himself is beyond me,' the marquis said loudly. 'Virgil told me it was best I didn't know and he didn't want to lest he be tempted to ride over and strangle him one dark night.'

'Virgil was your new guardian?'

'Yes, his wife was my godmother and they took me into their home and civilised me as best they could when they found out what a poor thing I'd become.'

Polly's heart ached for that small, vulnerable version of him. 'My godmother sent me a book of stern sermons for my confirmation and I never heard from her again. Why worry about your guardian now, though?'

'Not to wring the man's neck—he's already dead, so I couldn't if I wanted to,' he replied and raised his voice a little. 'For pity's sake, stop stamping about out there as if Miss Trethayne and I are discussing state secrets, man.'

'It was my idea, see?' Partridge told her when he finally sidled into the room as if she might bite.

'What was?'

'Folk here'll talk to you as they won't to his lordship or me,' the man said awkwardly, and Polly was intrigued by an unspoken dialogue between the master of the house and his self-appointed gatekeeper they thought she didn't know about.

'So you're taking all this trouble to find out where a lunatic spent the last few years of his life?' she asked, and her old friend shifted and look uneasy, but neither attempted to answer her question. 'Nobody ever mentions him anyway.'

'I'd like to forget he existed myself,' the marquis muttered, 'but we need to know something now and it's like trying to pin down a wraith.'

'Old Mrs Allcott might be able to remember where he was taken, if she's having one of her better days, or your lawyers would seem to be a safe bet to know where the man who did you and yours so much harm was put, don't you think? What a shame Mr Peters is absent at the very moment you need to find out so urgently.'

'Of course, her daughter-in-law said she was housekeeper here once and knew the place inside out,' the marquis said with an impatient frown, as if he now felt a fool for trailing that question so temptingly in front of her on a rainy day when she'd just admitted to being bored.

Then there was her niggling suspicion that Mr Peters had gone to London to find out anything he could about herself and Lady Wakebourne. She understood their past might affect Lord Mantaigne's future wife's tolerance of his dependents, but it felt intrusive and rude of them to delve about in the catastrophes that had overtaken them and led them to Dayspring when it was perfectly plain he didn't want to set foot in the place himself.

'What a shame you didn't think of her before you asked me, my lord,' she said blandly, a challenge in her eyes as she made herself meet his.

She felt a fool for not realising that, while the smugglers moved on as soon as they knew he was back at Dayspring, the feeling they were not always alone here hadn't gone with them. Adding that to her unease about the future and whatever he might stir up from her past, she was amazed at herself for being so wrapped up in trying not to want the man she'd almost forgotten how much depended on her being awake and alert for any threat that might hurt her brothers.

'Yes,' he agreed tersely, doing a very good job of concealing his thoughts from her so she felt more shut out of the real life of Dayspring than ever. 'I can't find the plans drawn up for improvements to the public rooms, which were due to be made just before my father died. Needless to say they never happened afterwards and I began to wonder if Grably took them away. I want the roof repaired this summer and it would save a lot of time if I had those drawings.'

'True, and Partridge is going to be your clerk of the works, is he? How very sensible. I'm sure everything will go on splendidly with or without those plans,' she said as if she almost believed them. 'I don't suppose the people left here when your former guardian was taken away would have let him take more than the shirt on his back. He may have burnt some of the estate papers before he went, of course.'

'True, so that settles it then,' Lord Mantaigne said with a heavy sigh.

'It does?' she said brightly, wondering what unlikely tale they'd invent next.

'Yes, I'll have Peters search the Muniment Room one last time when he gets back, but it seems likely the job must be done again.'

'No reason I can't look, is there, m'lord? I can read,' Partridge offered.

'I'm sure Peters would be delighted if you did.'

'Least I don't mind getting my hands dirty,' Partridge said and stumped out to begin a task none of them quite believed in.

Polly suspected they were looking for any secret ways in and out of the castle. The newer parts were built after a bloody civil war and a wary lord could well have ordered an escape route built to the sea in case it happened again.

'We've offended him now,' Lord Mantaigne said ruefully.

'I expect so, but you do it so well, don't you?'

'I do, don't I?'

'One more way of keeping us lesser mortals at a distance, I suspect.'

'Then it doesn't appear to be working since I came here.'

'You do yourself an injustice, milord, I feel I might as well be in the next county right now. Do you let anyone past that wall you keep round your heart?'

'Not very often,' he said with a shrug that said that was a good thing.

He also looked as if he had a hundred places he'd rather be, and Polly concluded he was only staying here because he wanted to distract her from the subject they had been discussing. He was doing quite a good job just by being here, but probably not the one he intended. She ought to be finding out what he and Partridge were really up to, but all she could think about was him. Silence stretched as he struggled not to tell her to mind her own business, and what right had a beggar like her to enquire into the state of a marquis's heart in the first place?

He wasn't going to admit he kept his essential self as shut up in that tower room as his guardian had the rest of him as a boy. Nor would he own up to the need that felt so strong she could almost touch it. And why would he when they were about as far apart as two people could be?

Yet only her presence had stopped him facing down those intruders that first night and, if she let him do as he wanted and keep her out of the way next time, he would take risks she couldn't seem to think of without a chance the bottom might drop out of her world if he got himself murdered, just because he was such a stubborn great idiot. He would certainly take on the rogues himself rather than trust anyone else to do it for him.

'Then you should,' she argued with his determination to always walk alone. 'You will never be truly alive if you don't.'

'Why, for Heaven's sake? I'm perfectly happy as I am.'

Polly found his ignorance of all he might be more touching than any conscious attempt to garner sympathy, but my Lord Mantaigne didn't need sympathy, did he? He didn't need anything he couldn't buy or charm out of those who only wanted to be charmed or bought, or so he obviously believed.

'I suppose you'll never know unless you try,' she said huskily.

'Don't even think about it,' he ground out as if denying what was there in the room with them and pushing them to explore a lot more than a mere friendship hurt him physically yet he couldn't stop doing it. 'Just don't.'

'All right then, I won't,' she whispered back, hoping Partridge really had gone to search through dusty piles of documents the lawyers hadn't thought worth taking away. It was as well to only lose one man's good opinion at a time, and she was very fond of the gatekeeper of Dayspring Castle.

'I've tried so hard not to touch you or kiss you again, you do know that, don't you?' Lord Mantaigne said with a feverish glint in his eyes that confirmed it and made her feel a lot better about the brazen course of action she was about to take.

'Be quiet, rattle-pate,' she chided him gently and took it.

Well, she would regret it for ever if she didn't, so she

kissed him, since he was being such a gallant marquis they might be in their dotage before he got round to it. Wanting him so badly made her ache in places she hadn't known a woman could ache for a man and she really had a lot of experience to make up in a hurry. Even so, this was playing with fire and it flashed and roared into a blaze even as he met her kiss for kiss. He tasted of rain and fresh air and himself and it was like all her birthdays as a child piling into a whirlpool of excitement and promise and hope all mixed together.

Then he took over the kiss and made it deeper; more sensual; unique. She had known, but not known. He was experienced and compelling and he knew how to make that fire slide under her skin and speak to the same force in him as they stood, mouth to mouth. Who needed words when there was such a use to put their tongues to? He slowed the pace, showed her how to enjoy the scenery on the way to a destination she'd never visited or expected to visit. It was subtle and somehow beautiful and how could he think himself isolated and unlovable when he had all this magic in him?

He gave a soft groan against her lips, and she felt the shake in his mighty body. Despite all that fine control of his, he needed her and that sucked her into another layer of wanting him altogether. He licked the swollen line of her lips with sensuous little darts of his tongue where they almost met, and she sighed with pleasure so he had a way to dart inside. This was so much more than a kiss now—more of a pagan dance he was showing her true, wild inner self as they explored and deepened and fed the heated delight that was taking over every inch of her body.

Even dancing wasn't close enough now. Mind and body united; touch and thought all wrapped up in needing this one man as she never would any other. His arousing, worshipping hands explored her narrow waist, down over the lithe curve of her hip and rested on the neat softness of her feminine buttocks, and she wriggled shamelessly until the urgent evidence of his need of her rose emphatically against her hot, wet core even through his gentlemanly breeches. Her soft, clinging and light-as-air skirts were a fragile barrier between them now. She appreciated them as she never dreamed she could when she put them on this morning.

It would take only one flip of the fine-spun stuff and the gossamer petticoats underneath to leave her open to such pleasure it made her breath catch at the very idea of it. One more fiery impulse and he'd be there, inside her—doing something about the delightful pain that was winding her so tight it hurt not to have him there. Instead of held back and still apart, they could have everything, right now. They could soar into sweet, hot darkness together; dizzying and brilliant as racing up to the moon. It was there; on their tongues, in their reaching, exploring hands, in their lips; as if they had to take all there was to take and love every second.

A surge of heat and pleasure sang though Polly. She wanted to meld with the pure essence of Thomas Banburgh and forget he was a lord and she was a pauper. She swayed into their kiss to deepen it even further, because she knew he wasn't going to let that happen and she desperately wanted him to spin beyond thought, beyond restraint with her. He was who he was and she was who she was and she felt him clamp fearsome self-control on the rigid need she could feel through his fine clothes and hers as well.

'Noble idiot,' she muttered reproachfully.

'If I was that, I'd never have got so close to losing control,' he said unsteadily, leaning his head against her bowed forehead as if he didn't want to break contact, but being kissable and not beddable was an agony she wouldn't share.

'You didn't, I did,' she said wearily and heard the jag in her voice as she said goodbye to so much they could have been and faced reality.

'I'd only harm you in the end and I'm not worth it.'

'Don't try to hide the truth behind your imaginary shortcomings. I am a nobody; less than that even as far as your kind are concerned. I was born a lady, but now I'm less than a beggar because I've fallen so far. Tell me I'm not a suitable mistress if you have to, but don't hide it behind polite lies.'

'How can I when it's not true? You're as good as any other woman I've ever met and I wouldn't offer you so little,' he told her with a fierce frown.

'Damned with faint praise,' she managed to say as his words sank in and she couldn't find even a trace of lover-like adoration in them.

'I lose any smooth words and easy compliments I ever had the use of when I'm with you. Maybe I left them at the castle gate the day I arrived and ogled at you like a looby,' he admitted with a flush of colour across his hard cheekbones that made her hope he had been a little bit besotted with her after all, even if it was only at first glance and seemed to have worn off.

'I'm not sure if I'm delighted or insulted by that lack.'

'Neither am I,' he said with a wry grin.

She felt a tug of temptation to smile back at him and pretend it didn't hurt, but it did. 'Don't expect me to interpret your lack of a glib answer, I obviously have no idea what makes you lords of creation tick along to your own tune,' she said as coolly as she could manage. She wanted to rage at him for rejecting what they could be to one another—and that was little enough, in all conscience—but she wasn't going to give him an excuse to sidle away from her as if he'd been right not to trust her with much of himself.

'And I really didn't draw back because I wanted to insult you, but more because I didn't, you know?'

'Yet somehow you managed to without trying.'

'Aye, well, clearly I'm a rogue of the worst kind.'

'Are you, my lord? I wonder.'

'Don't, but you do make me wish myself otherwise,' he said, so perhaps she'd made a small dent in his mighty defences.

His hand shook when he cupped the back of her head and drew her closer so gently she felt breakable. She looked up to meet his brilliant blue gaze defiantly and saw so many questions in it tears stung her eyes instead. No, she had her pride and made herself gaze back at him with desire bold and brazen and bare for him to see what she might have been with him, and what he could be with her, if he wasn't denying all that made them right together in defiance of all the wrongs the world would whisper.

'You're not the man you think you are,' she told him firmly.

'And you're not quite who you believe either, have you thought of that?'

'No, but Partridge might be back any moment and the rain is stopping, so it's clearly time for us to consider other things besides there not being a you and me for anyone to worry about, my lord.'

'I will, if you will,' he murmured and kissed her so gently it hurt.

'Go away,' she said unsteadily, the thought of a day spent dancing round each other as if nothing untoward had happened tearing at her like a battle wound.

'Will you be all right?'

'I'm always all right,' she said, 'it's what I do best.'

'There I have to argue, even with a lady,' he told her with the ghost of his wicked smile.

'Go and find your plans, my lord—even Partridge doesn't deserve to search through some endless piles of documents alone for much longer.'

She thought she heard him mutter something uncomplimentary about the family archives, but went back to her window until he stamped out of the room in a show of masculine bad temper, as if she was the one who had put a stop to what could have been a glorious lovemaking and not him.

The great blundering idiot would probably ride himself and his unfortunate horse to a stand-still in the rain now and all because he wouldn't admit he was subject to the same needs and emotions as the rest of humanity. Never mind what he felt or didn't feel for her, he was grieving deeply for his beloved godmother and wouldn't even admit it to himself.

Would a man who felt nothing for his own kind spend so much of his time finding out all he had omitted to do in the past two decades and do his best to put it right? Would he put himself out to find work for her mixed bag of fellow squatters if he was the care-for-nobody he did his best to pretend he was? No, and he wouldn't try to find a place for Lady Wakebourne and herself to go to when they left either.

Sure enough, there he was, racing his beautiful bay gelding through the park as if the devil was on their heels. So much of her wanted to be out there with him, full of life and strength and risk, that she turned away from the last glimpse of them tearing into the rain-soaked landscape she had come to love so much with tears blinding her to anything closer by until she blinked them away and reminded herself she wasn't the sort of female who sat indoors and cried for no reason on rainy days when the whole of nature seemed ready to weep with her.

Chapter Twelve

'Has it ever struck you that the intruders we thought were prowling round the Stuart wing of the castle could be choosing moonlit nights to avoid the free-traders, Lady W.?' Polly asked Lady Wakebourne over the luncheon Prue insisted they took in the 'Drawing Room' while the rest of the self-appointed staff had theirs in the kitchen.

For a while Polly had tried to insist nothing had changed with the marquis's homecoming, but the air of restraint and discomfort in the otherwise cosy kitchen had soon defeated her. Now she reluctantly bowed to the divisions that seemed to have grown up between gentry and working folk once more. It was tempting to blame his lordship, but fairness made her admit he'd done nothing to put those barriers up, he had given in to the fact they existed much as she had herself.

'I do my best not to think about the smugglers who infest this coast, or anyone else who might be wandering about in the night when I'm in bed. And don't call me Lady W. in that vulgar fashion.'

'If you really mean to adopt me as well as your mixed quantity of urchins so Lord Mantaigne can get us out of his castle, then you'll have to let me to call you something other than "your ladyship".'

'As if you ever did treat me with much respect,' Lady Wakebourne scoffed.

'Yet I still respect you and might even have admitted to loving you now and again, if you recall?'

'You know it's mutual,' Lady Wakebourne said. Polly felt her own smile wobble as it occurred to her it wasn't only Lord Mantaigne who had held back his feelings these past few years.

'I also know you stood with me when the rest of the world turned its back and without you I would have been so lonely I can't even bring myself to think about it. Besides that, who else can understand the things that concern me most? I love my brothers far more than they like me to admit now they're so grown up and manly, but they aren't interested in where their next pair of breeches is coming from or how to keep them well and happy on nothing a week.'

'You're far too young for that to be the beginning and end of your ambitions now, my dear, so at seventeen you were unforgivably youthful to be left to bring them up without a penny to bless yourself with. I would be a very hard-hearted female if I'd turned my back on you and those three little boys then.'

'And you're certainly not one of those, are you? Do you ever intend to tell Lord Mantaigne how your great-aunt somehow contrived to interfere in his young life, my lady? No, don't try pretending she had nothing to do with his timely rescue from his awful guardian because I know you as well as anyone can by now. Hearing how it was done might help him live here and not see that monster around every corner when the rest of us must leave.'

'And you take a humane interest in the man's welfare, I suppose? Do you really take me for such a fool, Paulina?'

'No, but you know as well as I do it's all I will ever share with him.'

Lady Wakebourne gave Polly a steady look as if she would like to argue, then sighed and shrugged her agreement that there was no future for a lady of no means at all and a rich and powerful marquis. 'Nevertheless, I am always here if you need to talk to someone about it. Carrying your burdens alone as you have had to all these years has made you both older than your years and at the same time as inexperienced as a débutante at her first ball. Promise me you'll come to me if you need a woman's advice or even a sympathetic ear?'

'If I ever come up against a problem Lord Mantaigne doesn't resolve before I have a chance to make my own decisions, I will,' Polly said bitterly and knew how much she had betrayed when she saw the look in her acute friend's dark eyes.

'How very ham-fisted of him,' the lady said with a glint of unholy satisfaction in her gaze that left Polly torn between agreeing and feeling even more hurt.

'We are better having as little to do with each other as possible when we must live under the same roof.'

'If you say so, my dear,' Lady Wakebourne said so equably Polly gave her a suspicious glare.

'Anyway we were not talking about me and the lord and master of this poor old place, we were discussing how your relative came to intervene in his childhood.'

'Well, no, we were not if we intend to be strictly accurate. You made an unsubstantiated observation and I didn't deny it.'

'That's splitting hairs.'

'No, I once made a promise and I don't easily go back on one of those.'

'But I was right, wasn't I?'

'If you make your own connections, I suppose it wouldn't break the letter of any agreement we might have made to keep quiet about Lord Mantaigne's early life for his own sake.'

'Cunning of you.'

'Yes, isn't it?'

'And you didn't recall this place was empty by an inspired chance either, I suppose?'

'No, and I made Virginia no promises on that front. She made sure the right backs were turned when I appealed to her for a chance for us to make some sort of a life for ourselves here since we had nothing. It wasn't as if his lordship wanted anything to do with the place and she agreed we were better than some villainous gang of rascals taking the place over.'

'Rather than the rascals who live here now?'

'Aye, we are something of a mixed bag, are we not?'

'At times I can't help feeling sorry for Lord Man-

taigne for having to endure our ramshackle company,'
Polly admitted ruefully.

'Don't waste your pity; he's enjoyed it, for the most
part, and it distracted him from brooding on things
he'd rather forget.'

'I suppose he does like the boys and seems to get on
remarkably well with Barker and Partridge and one or
two of the others. You could be right.'

'Of course I am; it's one of the privileges of middle
age. Another is noticing it isn't only the boys and those
two rogues he likes.'

'He does get on well with Jane and Prue and I'm
sure if Dotty was twenty years younger he'd like her
far too much.'

'If you say so, my dear.'

'She must have been lovely in her prime, don't you
think?'

'Not if I can help it, for goodness knows what she
got up to back then.'

'I hate to think.'

'Best if you don't, but you have so little grasp of your
own attractions it might be dangerous if your marquis
wasn't nearly as bad. I never came across two people more genuinely ignorant of their own qualities that
sometimes I feel as if I'm in the midst of one of Shake-
speare's comedies.'

'Except it's not very funny.'

'If I had charge of the ending, it would be,' Lady
Wakebourne said with the happy ending she would
write onto their sad little tale in the almost-smile she

gave Polly as their eyes met in an admission it was nigh impossible.

Polly looked away to try to tell them both it wasn't even worth speaking of and tried to recall what had got them on to this dangerous ground in the first place. 'You still haven't answered my original question,' she said as she retraced their steps and remembered her theory about those moonlight nights.

'Which was?'

'If those intruders you have always done your best to pretend you didn't believe in come here at the best times to avoid being spotted by the smugglers? I suppose that says either they are afraid of them or think they'd be recognised.'

'Either I suppose, if they exist at all outside your fancy, my dear.'

'Oh, they do, Lord Mantaigne and I heard them inside the closed-up wing the first night he was here, so at least now I know my ears do not deceive me.'

'And I know you two are reckless and headstrong as a pair of runaway horses.'

'Don't change the subject, although while we're on the subject of who knows what and when, did you really contrive to get word to Lady Virginia there was something wrong here before she died?'

'I'm sure she had her sources in the area. The late Lady Farenze had a wide circle of friends.'

'If she was half as all-knowing and infuriating as you, she could have run a spy ring for all anyone else would have known about it.'

'Lady Virginia was far more of everything than I

am, Paulina. Such a shame you never knew her, for you have much in common.'

'I think not,' Polly said stiffly, horrified at the image of a formidable lady looking down her aristocratic nose at her.

'If nothing else, you could have compared notes on Lord Mantaigne, since you both dote on him.'

'I certainly do not dote on that stiff-necked idiot of a man,' Polly ground out gruffly and wished her ladyship a brusque farewell until later so she could go and watch out for him to return from his afternoon of avoiding her in peace.

Later that afternoon Mr Peters rode back up the drive in time to meet his employer coming the other way. Polly wasn't watching for either of them by then, of course, but she happened to glance out of the a window overlooking the coast road and wondered how two gentlemen could be so wet and muddied and yet so vital she longed to be out there with them just to find out what they were talking about. Whatever it was that kept them out there longer than any sensible creature should be on such an inclement evening, it must be of absorbing interest, or so confidential they didn't wish to be overheard.

How might it feel if she happened to be the true lady of this ancient castle? Perhaps one of the previous ladies of Mantaigne had stood at this very window, watching for her lord to return from court or some foreign war and seen him at last on the horizon. She could have waited with breathless longing for it to be really him, this time, at last. Imagine how that lady would feel knowing he was safe and back with her again, joy surging through her at the sight of him, breathless with longing to lie in his arms all night again, desperate to be held close and told how deeply he had missed her every moment they were apart and she had held his fortress for him in his absence.

It seemed that dreaming of another time and different ways of being lords and ladies had let her think of herself as his lady as she never had in the here and now. The how she might have been as Lady Paulina of Mantaigne was queenly and proud instead of beggarly and defiant, her carriage fluid and assured as she swept down the stone stairway from the Great Parlour to greet her lord. She knew he adored her just as she was; that he knew she would defend his lands and his people and their children like a she-wolf protecting her cubs. A mighty lord needed an independent lady then, for how else could he know his lands and people were safe when he was not at home?

She shook her head and told herself not to be a fool. Not only was that then and this now, but here and now was real and there and then was not. Something about Peters's and his lordship's earnest conversation told her they believed some important problem had been solved by that mysterious trip to London, and it made her shiver to think that would be that. Now his lordship would leave and perhaps never come back. Even that phantom lady of his queening it over the neighbourhood seemed better than never setting eyes on the wretched man again, or only once in a long and weary decade when he might come back to see if his castle had fallen into the sea quite yet. Lady Wakebourne was right to accuse her of doting on the man and knowing it at least gave her the sense to distance herself from him.

If it was in any way mutual, he wouldn't have been able to turn his back on her and ride away from her this morning. She had offered herself to him so blatantly and he had all but blushed and said a polite 'no, thank you'. Shame rushed into her cheeks in a hot flood of colour, and she leant one on the cold window pane to cool it and saw with horror his lordship's rain-dark head raise as he caught sight of her. Gasping a denial she had been watching for his return like some faithful hound, she jumped away and refused to look back, but it was too late—the image of him soaked to the skin and his fine clothes plastered to his body as if they couldn't love him enough was stamped on her mind's eye.

Even from so far away she'd seen the intensity in his blue gaze as if not even that much rain would douse the heat in it. Drat the man, but he called to the wild instincts and hot blood in her. Her heart was pounding, her body roused and eager and her breath coming short through parted lips. She caught sight of herself in a watery old Venetian glass mirror almost too old to do its work any more and put suddenly cold hands to her hot cheeks. She looked wanton and, worse, enchanted; like a silly maiden in a fairy story put under a spell by the very sight of the handsome prince who had come to rescue someone else. Well, she wouldn't be the bereft spectator on his life. She was her own person and that was that. Easy enough to think it, but telling her body to let go of all those seductive images of her curled about him all loved and sated against that mighty, muscular body proved much more difficult.

'I wish a lady like that one would look at me as Miss Trethayne just did at you,' Peters joked down below in the stable yard as he and his latest employer led their tired horses through the stable doors Dacre had flung open as if he'd been waiting for his lordship to come home too.

'If I ever catch you watching her with that glint in your eyes again, I'll black at least one of them for you,' Tom told him brusquely and for once couldn't have cared less what his supposed secretary thought his feelings for Miss Polly Trethayne might be.

'No need, I have the sense to see when a woman has hardly noticed I live on the same planet, even if you are wilfully blind about your feelings for her.'

'A little less of both than I was when you left for London,' Tom said softly as the image of her, warm and dry and wistful as she gazed out of that window like a princess in her tower wishing she had a prince on the way, replayed through his mind.

'Less wilful, or less blind?'

'How plain do I have to be? I know she is like no other woman I ever met, that any man who could call her his would need to thank his maker on his knees for her every morning and work hard to deserve her for the rest of the day and into the night.'

'A delightful pastime, no doubt, but why does there

seem to be a "but" running under all that promising infatuation?'

'You have the devil of a sharp tongue, man; are you related to the Winterleys by any chance?'

'Not that I know of,' Peters said as soberly as any judge, but Tom was beginning to know him well enough to be certain he was laughing at both of them for some reason best known to himself. 'And the "but"?'

'But I'm hardly the sort of man who deserves the love of a good woman.'

'If we all had to wait to be worthy of that, the human race would have died out long ago.'

'Yet if what you say is true, Miss Trethayne will soon have the chance to meet a man who can offer her so much that I cannot.'

'A castle, perhaps? A comfortable lifestyle at the heart of the *ton*? Or do you think she might prefer a fortune not even laying out funds to support half the countryside can make a dent in?'

'Please don't think accusing her of being a gold-digger will make me furious enough to give away some phantom truth about my feelings for Miss Trethayne, Peters. I'm not some naive young fool up from the country.'

'It might be better if you were.'

'Better for whom?'

'For you of course, my lord,' the man said abruptly and made way for one of the grooms to take over caring for his tired horse as if he couldn't endure the company of such an idiot for very much longer.

'He's right, lad,' Dacre informed him.

'Not you as well,' Tom mumbled with a tight frown he hoped would put the man off one of his homilies.

'Me more than anyone, m'lord. Her ladyship trusted me to keep you from riding straight to the devil when you was younger than Master Josh and I ain't done yet.'

'Thank you,' Tom said as the fury died out of him at the sight of genuine concern in the old groom's eyes. 'You always were more patient with me than I deserved.'

'High time someone was,' Dacre said gruffly, as uneasy with speaking of his feelings as Tom had ever been, but doing it all the same.

How humbling to know his old friend had more courage than he did, but perhaps this was his day for being humble.

'Any woman worth her salt wants to make her own choice, boy, and that one's worth a lot more,' Dacre told him with a severe nod and went to fetch the warm mash he had ready for the unlucky gelding who had gone so hard for him all afternoon.

'Anything to say?' he challenged the weary animal as he finished grooming it and stopped to pet him. 'No? You must be the only one who hasn't today,' he murmured in the gelding's responsive ears and even his own weariness wasn't enough to blot out the feeling he'd done the most stupid day's work he'd ever done by walking away from all he could be as Miss Paulina Trethayne's grateful lover.

Polly refused to go across the courtyard to dinner that night and sat in her lofty room, staring into the fire that would never have been lit on a soaking May evening before the marquis came home. She sighed at the thought of how much had changed here since she saw him that first time, like some gilded god come down from Olympus to play stable hand for a day.

Feeling sad and forsaken and thoroughly out of sorts with herself and the rest of the world, she tried hard not to turn into a watering pot when Toby came up the stairs with a plate carefully covered to keep it warm and insisted on watching over her while she ate. How could she refuse to do so like some fine lady in a fit of pique when he had taken so much trouble to look after her? Luckily he was also old and wise enough to know she didn't want to talk about what was upsetting her, but a little later Hal and Josh tapped on her door and sidled in, looking as if they thought it was their fault she was blue-devilled.

It was no good, she decided with despair eating even deeper into her than it had before. She couldn't do it. Not even for the sake of loving Lord Mantaigne as she so badly wanted him to let her love him could she cut herself off from her brothers. Since her stepmother had died when Josh was a baby, Polly had tried to fill the gaping holes in his little life as best she could. Then there was her usually serious and studious middle brother, who sometimes lost himself in a book as determinedly as Lord Mantaigne did in his life of hedonistic pleasure.

Did Hal hide the same sort of sensitivity behind a front of self-sufficiency as his lordship did then? Unlikely, Polly decided as Hal's own character trumped the fear he was deeply damaged by the loss of parents he barely remembered. Her Hal was a natural scholar, a thinker who would find a comfortable corner of life somehow and settle into it with a genuine pleasure few outside his own world would ever understand. Worry as she might about Toby and his adventurous spirit and Josh's sometimes wild imagination, she knew Hal would be happy as long as he was able to keep following clues and trails only he could read in some dusty old tome.

So now she could worry about Toby instead. He knew how it felt to have two loving parents and a comfortable life because he'd been eight years old when his whole world fell apart. Those first years were nothing like the past seven had been and now she thought she could rob him of the small security he had with Lady Wakebourne and all their other friends and fellow travellers? No, not even for Lord Mantaigne. There wasn't a man on earth she could love enough to risk throwing away her brothers' happiness for.

So, that was that. She would do whatever it took to keep these boys as happy and secure as they could be without a penny to their names but what she could earn or accept from a man who felt guilty about them for some reason. Once upon a time she had been too proud to accept charity, but could any woman who stared destitution in the face afford pride? It might be charity, but it would do. They would go to the Dower House of Spring Magna Manor House when it was ready if Lord Mantaigne offered it to them. The man had houses enough to quarter an army in and was hardly likely to miss one he admitted he'd forgotten about until he stumbled on it on one of his lone rides and asked who owned it.

If he intended to salve his conscience by allowing her and her friends to live in the Dower House, then so be it. She would watch that fine and suitable marchioness of his playing lady bountiful in the villages and smile. Polly might hate the pity and puzzlement in such a fine lady's eyes whenever she encountered the oddest of her husband's dependents, but she would be polite and deferential to the devil himself if it kept her brothers safe and happy.

'I know you don't want to hear it, but I do love you all, you know?' she said and watched them roll their eyes at each other and pretend to be sick with a feeling her real world had just slotted back into place.

Anything else was only a dream, yet wasn't the pain supposed to stop if you told it not to be real? How could something as insubstantial as a dream still hurt as if part of her had fallen off a cliff and been bruised and battered half to death?

'We know, and we do you too,' Toby said as if to get it out of the way in as few words as he could on behalf of all of them.

'We decided to show you our secret to make you feel better about whatever it is you feel miserable about, Poll,' Hal informed her solemnly, and the parent she had tried to be for the past seven years pricked up her ears and worried about what that might be. 'It's all right, it's nothing bad. We didn't want to tell anyone about it, but since a man's going to come and set the castle right very soon, or at least so Lord Mantaigne says, you might as well know about it before everyone else does.'

'I agree,' Josh said solemnly, and Polly wondered if letting them sleep in the men's quarters in the ancient castle keep had been such a good idea after all. It might have made them more independent, but apparently it had also left them free to wander about the rest of the empty and maybe dangerous old house whenever they felt like it.

'Where is it then?' she asked warily.

'We'll have to show you or you won't understand properly,' Hal said with a look that said it wouldn't be much of a surprise if they told her where it was and Polly concluded her middle brother could sometimes be a bit too clever for his own good.

'Come on, Poll, the doors will be locked and everyone supposed to be in bed if we don't hurry and we need to know what to do about it anyway,' Josh said with a defiant look for his bigger brother as if that was an argument they had long been having with each other.

'Very well,' she said, for they might as well get it out of the way so she could tell Mr Peters who would inform his employer about whatever small niche the two of them had found in this once-great fortress.

'It's as well you aren't wearing skirts tonight,' Hal said with an approving glance at the breeches and jacket she'd put back on for some obscure reason even she couldn't understand when she came up here to brood alone over what was and what ought to be and wasn't.

'Most brothers would be glad to see their sister ape the lady.'

'We're not most brothers and you're not most sisters,' Hal said, and Josh just looked puzzled by the whole idea she could be anything else but what she was—their big sister.

Chapter Thirteen

'Got them at last,' Peters murmured as soon as he caught the sound of a latch snick very softly into place somewhere on the other side of the wide hall he might have admitted finding echoing and ghostly in the last dying rays of daylight under threat of torture.

'Quiet,' Tom cautioned him and went back to waiting for whoever was haunting his dusty mansion to walk into his trap. 'What the devil?' he muttered a few moments later when unexpectedly light footsteps walked down the hallway as if they had no great need to hide their presence and a right to be here.

'Who goes there?' Peters allowed himself to challenge them as some boyhood part of him must have longed to all his life.

'We do,' Josh Trethayne's voice sang happily back at them, 'and what are you doing sitting here in the dark all alone like Polly was until we went and got her, Mr Peters?' he asked as brightly as if they'd met at a summer picnic.

'Confound it,' Tom cursed quietly to Peters because it was either that or bellow at them like a choleric squire. 'Why the devil must they choose tonight to roam about my house in the dark?' he added and opened up the shutter on his dark lantern to light up the three young Trethaynes nearest to them, then raised it to inspect their sister by directing the beam of candle on her unconventional breeches and spencer jacket.

'Lost something?' he drawled as if he had the right, but how could she simply stroll in here with her little brothers in tow as if that fiasco his first night here had never happened?

'No, have you?' she asked with a dignified lift of her chin Peters seemed to admire rather more than he did just at the moment.

'My patience,' Tom muttered under his breath, racking his brains for a way of getting them back into the older and safer part of the castle without giving away the fact he and Peters were here for a purpose. 'But it's getting darker by the minute and surely those two urchins of yours ought to be in bed by now?' he made himself say as lightly as if they had met in the everyday rooms as a matter of course. He'd never thought himself much of an actor until that moment and was even quite proud of his unexpected skill, until she sniffed as if to inform him she wasn't a fool and anyway, she was the one who decided when and where her brothers went and not him.

'We've come to show Polly the secret room to cheer her up,' Josh said happily.

'What secret room?' Tom made himself ask casually.

'Unfair, my lord,' Polly Trethayne rebuked him, 'Josh is seven years old and not yet up to playing your games.'

'Yes, I am, Poll, and anyway I'm nearly eight.'

'Do you think you could postpone this particular argument until another day or take it somewhere else?' Peters asked wearily, nodding at the uncovered window of the lantern to remind Tom they were lying in wait for villains, not four people they already knew were at Dayspring and probably knew it better than either of them.

'Aye, will you please return to your part of the castle if I promise to tell you exactly what happens here afterwards?' he heard himself plead and wondered where the occasionally haughty Marquis of Mantaigne had disappeared to for a fleeting moment, then found he didn't much regret him.

'No,' all four Trethaynes replied at the same time.

'Then we must abandon the hunt, Peters,' he said, straightening up and scowling at Peters as if it was his fault, since he could hardly take his fury out on three boys and a militantly oblivious female, however richly they deserved it.

'That you must not,' Polly said with an offended glare he ought to have learnt to expect by now. 'Hal will make sure Josh keeps quiet and Toby and I can mind our own tongues, thank you very much,' she told him and folded her arms across her chest to make it doubly clear to him she wasn't going anywhere.

Tom bit back a full-blooded curse for the benefit of her brothers rather than Polly Trethayne and let himself admit he admired her daring nearly as much as he wanted to curse her for putting so much as a hair on her head in danger. How the devil had that happened? He eyed her through the gloom and ran a series of images of her through his head, from the moment he first looked up to see her looming in the stable-doorway to the delicious, delirious experience of kissing her with every inch of him one long agonised scream of frustrated arousal this afternoon.

Was it even possible Thomas Banburgh had fallen in love? And with possibly the least suitable potential marchioness he could find in the entire kingdom while he was about it? Clearly it was impossible, yet somehow or another there it still was, as real and alive as if he'd written it all over the walls of his own castle and advertised it in the Strand.

Stunned by the certainty that if he never set eyes on her again after today his life would be lived in twilight, he felt as if he was floundering in the face of the storm of powerful emotions running through him like a natural disaster. He loved her? Yes, he did love her. Tom Banburgh, who didn't want to either love or be loved, loved Polly Trethayne with all the hope and joy he hadn't dared feel so fully since he was a boy surging through him like a spring tide.

What was more, he loved a magnificent, delightful, grumpy and unconventional female who would never bore him or make him wish for his clubs or the sophisticated lovers he'd enjoyed before he met her. She was glaring back at him now; daring him to treat her like some delicate little gently bred female and send her back to her bed to cower there in safety. It would be a wild ride, loving her for the rest of his life, he decided with a hot look for her at the thought of starting it.

Meeting it seemed to make her forget her impression of an angry goddess confronted by a human she intended turning into a toad. Seeing puzzlement and a fine seasoning of curiosity in her gaze, he felt even more tempted to kiss that lush, doubtful mouth of hers. He'd better provoke her back into a fury before he lost all credibility with her and her brothers and Peters for life by kissing her in front of them and blurting out his shocked feelings.

'There's no excuse for putting your brothers in danger, even if you're reckless enough to forget how much they depend on you for love and support, and put yourself in danger,' he said in the hope she might be persuaded to worry about her brothers' safety as she didn't seem ready to about her own.

It occurred to Tom that one of the hardest parts of loving this woman might be enduring fear for her when she didn't seem to have any for herself.

'You were right, then, Hal, there really are pirates looking for our treasure here at night?' Josh asked wide-eyed and ready to believe almost anything. Tom could almost feel his sister being torn between a need to take her littlest brother out of here and a belief he would immediately find a way back, or make such a noise the intruders might be scared into shooting someone out of sheer shock.

'This isn't the Spanish Main, Josh, and I think we'd best get you to bed after all,' she said softly, then froze in her tracks as that soft thud she had puzzled over before silenced them all.

As if Tom had said what he was thinking, that she should give up trying to find out who was breaking in herself, she shook her head emphatically at him and glared as if he'd told her to go and drown some kittens. He supposed she knew her brothers a lot better than he did and waved a resigned hand as if to concede they probably had a right to know who was coming in and out of here at will as well. He resolved to put a stop to the whole business if there was even the sniff of real danger, but for now he'd just have to trust his own judgement that Grably's nephew and his partner in crime were neither habitual criminals nor natural murderers.

'You four can have the cupboard over there and Peters and I will watch the door from the basement, then,' he told her with what he hoped was steely enough purpose to tell her she had others to care about her even if she was thinking of rushing headfirst into action. 'It's not too late for us to make so much noise they will run off and never come back,' he added as the only threat he could think of to make them agree to stay out of the line of fire.

'Josh, are you sure you can keep quiet and not get hurt if the men have to fight?' Polly asked as if her littlest brother was at least ten years older.

'I'm very good at not getting hurt when the others fight,' he said matter-of-factly, and his sister nodded an admissions he was right.

'You are that, so pray continue to be so and promise me you'll run and get help if it looks as if we're going to be outnumbered?'

'I promise,' Josh said and crossed his heart for good measure.

Tom felt as proud of the boy as if he'd been his own little brother, or even his son, and the very thought of the tribe of potential giants he and Polly Trethayne might make one day threatened to turn his brain to a mush of besotted daydreams.

'You're all as mad as each other,' Peters muttered as if he thought Tom the worst lunatic of all for not abandoning their attempt to trap the intruders on the spot, or somehow make the rackety Trethayne family leave them to spring it alone. He clearly didn't know any of them as well as Tom did, then, or he wouldn't even consider it a real possibility.

'Maybe, but at least in there they'll be relatively safe,' Tom whispered so low so that the intrepid quartet now piling into the broom cupboard as if it was the only place they would dream of being on a June night wouldn't hear him.

He wanted to laugh at the same time as he felt oddly proud of them for being who they were. He also longed to get Polly alone so he could persuade her to trust herself and them to him for as long as they might need him. There was no question of him ever not needing her now, but one day her brothers would want to live their own lives. Until then they would be his as truly as if they really did carry Banburgh blood in their veins instead of the unique Trethayne kind he was longing to see zing through his own children mingled with his.

He half-believed they'd made enough noise and fuss to warn anyone within half a mile, but a mechanism behind the panelling in the room that had once been used as a butler's pantry clicked and opened even as he drew breath to call the whole thing off. He scented something he remembered from long ago on the air with a real sense of dread and wished too late he'd managed to send them away. Of course they would then lay in wait farther away from him and be at even more risk, so he stopped cursing himself for a dozen different sorts of a fool and listened for what came next with a fast beating heart instead.

'I told you we shouldn't come back here no more,' a half-familiar voice whispered as he followed a dimly lit and burlier figure into the hall.

'Stow your rattle,' the one he recalled a little too well from that first night here ordered impatiently, and Tom heard the smoothed-out tones of an educated man and raised his eyebrows in the darkness of their hiding place.

'If we can't find it after all these months, it ain't here to be found, Ollie.'

'Hold your tongue, you fool, of course it is.'

So what the devil was Grably's nephew doing back at Dayspring? Searching for something his lunatic uncle left behind when he was carted off to the private asylum by his embarrassed brother-in-law all those years ago, Tom supposed, hearing the two men argue about where they had left to look. Was this the moment to let them know they'd been discovered and it was time this wild goose chase came to an end? Probably, but the fools were between him and the Trethaynes' hiding place and he didn't trust Polly or her little brothers not to leap out and put themselves in danger just because it was there.

'He said there was a priceless treasure hidden between the moon and the earth and in the same part of the castle as he lived in when he ruled it and that idiot of a boy was kept in his proper place,' the nephew said with the same fixed stubbornness Tom recalled hearing in his guardian's voice all those years ago and only just managed to suppress a shudder.

He ran over their clue to the hiding place of whatever it was again in his head and this time had to bite back a laugh. There was an ancient carving of the moon and the sun orbiting the earth in a mantelpiece in one of the bedchambers Tom decided now had been reused from one of the older parts of the castle when the new wing was built. It must have seemed a shame to waste even such a quaint old masterpiece on a servant and so the fireplace had been moved. The fools had probably walked past it dozens of times and not even realised what they sought was right under their noses, but why they would be looking for it in the first place was beyond him.

Still, he heard a muffled grunt from the cupboard and shrugged in the darkness as he resigned himself to springing his trap a little before time. He hadn't much stomach for hearing more and at least they'd given any accomplices time to crawl out of whatever worm-hole they used to enter the castle without being seen. These two were alone and he doubted very much they would put up much of a fight.

'You've been deceived,' he drawled as he stood upright.

Two more dark lanterns were hastily added to the total as the intruders felt the need to find out who was challenging them. Tom hoped the Trethaynes would realise the Mantons in his and Peters's hands were primed and loaded and have the sense to stay where they were.

'Mantaigne, what the hell are you doing here?' the taller of the two asked as if he was the one with every right to ask questions.

'Funnily enough, I thought I owned the place,' Tom said lightly, circling the petrified figures to put himself between them and Polly, who saw what he was about and emerged from her hiding place to startle the intruders into stunned silence.

'He does,' she said with an emphatic nod that defied anyone to argue.

'I heard about a giant doxy in breeches who lived here behind Mantaigne's back, but I never thought you'd stay and warm his bed for him now he's found courage to come back after all these years of cowering away in town.'

'You take that back, she's my sister and she's not a doxy,' Henry Trethayne ordered, in a fine brotherly fury Tom hadn't thought the scholarly boy had in him.

'Ladies don't wear breeches or carry pistols,' the nephew pointed out with a sneer, and Tom wondered if *he* had found some courage over the past two decades, until he reminded himself the fool probably didn't believe she would actually shoot him, his mistake.

'Yet still I have the pistol and you have a great deal

of explaining to do,' she said as coolly as most ladies of Tom's acquaintance might if they were wielding a teapot and asking if an unwanted visitor would like more tea rather than brandishing a pistol he hadn't even known she possessed.

'I suggest you start now before one of us decides to shoot you for the hell of it,' he said coolly, despite this mad impulse to grin like a fool because he'd suddenly realised exactly how complex and how simple his life was going to be from now on.

Arrogant of him to believe he would win her when Polly was about as predictable as the north wind, but something told him the chance was right here, ready to be seized and gloated over, and he really didn't intend to waste it.

'I, for one, am getting very bored,' Peters said laconically and Tom had never liked the fellow better.

'And I just wish someone would let me have a go,' Hal said with an aggrieved look at his sister, who narrowed her incredible eyes and straightened her arm as if getting ready to pick which bit of villain to shoot first.

'All right,' the smaller of the two men said with a look of terror on his face. 'I'll tell you everything if you all promise not to shoot.'

'I'm not set on it, at least not in your case,' Tom said reasonably enough to his way of thinking.

'I really don't like the idea of them invading your house whenever they feel like it,' Polly said calmly, and Peters just grinned and cocked his pistol as if he didn't have to dislike a man to take a potshot at him.

'Our house,' Tom corrected as patiently as he could manage.

It was possibly the oddest proposal ever made, but she read it for what it was and let her gun arm waver for a breath-stealing moment. It was as well Peters seemed so deadly calm neither man moved an inch as he watched them with chilling indifference, since Tom was more interested in her response than their unwanted visitors.

'Do you remember all those seaman's knots Sam Barker has been teaching you to tie, Hal?' Peters asked casually.

'Of course I do. I'm not dexterous like Toby, but once I learn something I don't forget it.'

'Then tie one or two in these and make sure neither can get free. There's a good chap.'

'I can help,' Josh said crossly, for being seven was clearly no excuse for missing out on anything interesting for the Trethayne clan.

'You can keep your sister's gun steady on the fat one, my friend,' Peters said as if he didn't think so either. 'And I truly hope the sight of Josh Trethayne with a gun terrifies you as deeply as it does me, whoever you are,' Peters said as he held his own aim rock steady and made sure neither man had any thoughts about seizing Hal and using him as a hostage against their own escape.

Luckily it seemed to do so and they kept still as statues. Tom and Polly were far too preoccupied with not looking at each other to be much use, although Tom always swore afterwards if he hadn't had such an able pack of helpers he might have taken a much more active role in subduing the prisoners himself.

'Deal with them, would you, Peters?' he said absently as he took his eyes off Polly long enough to nod sagely at the others and let them leave without him.

'Will they be all right?' Polly asked as if she only had half her mind on the supposed business of the night as well.

'I should imagine so. I know your pistol wasn't loaded, even if Josh and that poor man he's driving along like a cow to market have no idea,' Tom replied.

'What do you mean "ours"?' she demanded in the semi-darkness from the single lantern the others had left them to light up a whole cavernous hallway and half an empty house.

'I mean marry me, live with me, love me,' Tom said a little desperately, for suddenly it didn't seem quite so certain she would believe him after that ridiculous scene this morning when he made it very plain he wasn't going to ask her to be anything in his life.

'Why?'

'Because I want you to?'

'Not enough.'

'Then do it because I think you the most extraordinary woman I ever met, because I can't imagine how tedious my life would be without you and your brothers and your oddly assorted band of friends and because I love you more than I thought I had it in me to love anyone. Be everything to me that I always thought I couldn't have, Paulina Trethayne. Please? Before I beg and embarrass us both.'

'I can't be meek and conventional and there's no point trying to make me into a proper marchioness. I'm more suited to be your mistress, but I can't do it. I can't abandon my family.'

'And if anything happened to me you would fight the devil himself back into hell to see that our whelps were safe. If I'm ever to have a wife and gamble on making children with her, she will just have to be you. I couldn't dare the fates and risk making them with anyone else, Polly. No other woman on God's earth has your courage and loyalty and that lioness's heart of yours and at last I've had the good sense to realise I don't want to live without you.'

So far they had faced each other like adversaries, but now he moved closer. She eyed him sceptically and he could sense her going through his list of reasons with a fine-toothed comb, but they had been enchanted on a more sensual level from the very first moment they set eyes on each other and he intended to take advantage of the fact right now.

'And you're sure you love me? It seems to have come upon you suddenly, considering you rejected me earlier today.'

'It crept up on me inch by inch from the first day on, but having the sense to know it did ambush me tonight. Now I wonder it took me so long to realise why I felt as if I was living in the wrong skin, why I lay awake in the middle of a howling gale, in the barest and most draughty room I've slept in since I was eight years old, night after night and longed for you to be lying in that bed next to me, even if you were fast asleep. If you'll promise to lie by my side for the rest of our lives, I'll put up with living in this old wreck while it's made fit for a marchioness to live in once again. If you tell me you can't endure the idea, I don't think I shall even be able to come back to Dayspring again, however, for I truly couldn't endure it without you now, Polly. I can't stand the thought of anything much about my life without you in it now I've come to see sense at last.'

'Put like that, I almost believe you mean it,' she allowed, and neither of them took much notice when the pallid light suddenly went out, as if the candle had been snuffed by some mischievous ghost.

'Believe it, my darling Amazon,' he whispered and the darkness seemed to unleash everything they felt together this morning and something more as well.

'Convince me,' she breathed as his eager hands reached for her and found no resistance at all, so he did so as thoroughly and emphatically as he could at such short notice.

Hours later Polly lay at her lover's side in that draughty bedchamber he'd complained about earlier and watched the moon set as he slept. She treasured every snuffle and snort as he lay there prone and deeply asleep, without any of the barriers my Lord Mantaigne usually put between himself and the rest of the world. Speaking for herself, she felt too energised, too loved and needed to sleep. A smile of remembered satisfaction curled her lips in a smile that felt as if it might never leave her lips, and she rolled over onto her front so she could watch him even more closely.

She had no doubt Tom was a peerless lover of beautiful women and part of her might thank some of them for teaching him how to rouse and then satisfy a woman until every inch and sense she had sang; on the other hand she might not, since they were so beautiful and had been so satisfied.

With awe and wonder and a residual heat she should probably be ashamed of, she recalled how it felt to be taken over by love, washed under by it, carried along yet robustly active in the timeless dance of lovers she had only just learned so it itched against her fingertips to start up all over again. She couldn't resist smoothing a hand down her bare thigh in a sensuous line of pleasures beyond her wildest dreams until today, couldn't repress a wriggle of delight against the fine linen sheets his finicky valet insisted my lord had on his bed, even if everything else about his makeshift chamber was beneath the dignity of a marquis and lowered the consequence of his personal servant.

'It's like sleeping with an eel,' Tom murmured a sleepy protest, and she reached out and traced his smile with an exploring finger, because she couldn't resist knowing she had the right, or almost had it until they were wed and she was sure of it. Here was everything she had never thought to have with any man, let alone this one, and how terrible it would have been never to feel even a shadow of such glory.

'You will have to get used to it then, my lord,' she murmured as another of those delight-soaked quivers shot through her body, but this time a little less lazy appreciation and a lot more eagerness for more shot through her in its wake.

'I dare say I might, although it's obviously going to be a sacrifice,' he said and promptly went from sleepy to demanding between one breath and the next.

'I admire a man willing to make those for the sake of the woman he loves,' she joked, still hardly able to believe it could be her.

'You are worth it, my Polly, worth every last long, elegant inch of sacrifice I'm making by sharing this very hard and narrow bed with you. You do know that you're perfectly designed to fulfil a man's wildest fantasies, don't you? I don't think I ever saw such long and lovely legs or felt the way I feel about you, here, and here and especially…here,' he whispered into the sensitised curve of her kiss-swollen lower lip and played with it between his own. 'Then there's all the way down here,' he husked as he ran kisses down her throat in a long and lovely line of hot licks that made her pulse race and her insides hot and wet and ready for him all over again.

She writhed under him as he reared up to appreciate that curve fully, then track even more intimately down and cup her waiting breast for them both to marvel at. She looked down and saw what she already knew. Fire stirred ever hotter in her belly as she craned her neck back to watch him nuzzle at the frantic nub of one of her tightly needy nipples, then seize it in his mouth to drive her nigh mad with clenched need. Even after he'd taken her so gently earlier tonight that they soared into an awesome new world she hadn't let herself believe in even in her wildest dreams until then, she couldn't quite believe even he could satiate the heavy need burning and demanding at her most intimate core right now.

He raised his head and sucked in a deep breath, seemed to draw in gentlemanly good manners along with the cool pre-dawn air, and tried to shift her so he could give her almost heaven with his gentle yet wickedly knowing touch alone.

'No, you or nothing,' she argued boldly.

'You will be sore, love, and I might get you with child,' he murmured a protest back. How could she not love him when he looked by the tight expression on his dear face in the last glance of moonlight as if his good manners were costing him dearer than even she knew?

'Since you might have done that already, and even you have to admit it takes two people to make one of those, you had best marry me out of hand then, my lord,' she told him, smoothing one of her unsteady hands over his set mouth to make him loosen the hold he had himself under so determinedly it was eating her up inside.

'It will take three days, according to Peters, who seems to know more than most about hasty marriages. I'm not risking a long courtship or a seven-month child with you, love, since you'd never let me hear the last of it if we happen to set the world by the ears in nine months' time.'

'I wouldn't dare reproach you, since it would be half my fault, but I want to be your wife, Tom, more than I've wanted anything in my life until today.'

'As far as I'm concerned you already are, but we'd best get the formalities out of the way as soon as can be,' he said and since he had been caressing her so intimately she had to pinch herself to realise this was really happening to her, Polly Trethayne of nowhere, then she writhed under his inflammatory touch, demand in every inch of her body as she wound as much of it as she could against as much of him as she could reach.

'Love me all the way through, then,' she whispered and ran a fingertip down his supple backbone and felt him quiver like a greyhound with sensual excitement. 'I need you far too much,' she added huskily.

'No,' he argued fiercely with her, 'you need me just enough. Enough to meet the desperation I have for you, the ache in my gut I've lived with since the first time I set eyes on you and wanted you so badly it felt as if I was being ripped apart by it at times. I thought I could never have you lie like this, feel you take me inside you like this...' He paused, and she opened to him, felt him drive within the slick, hot tightness of her most intimate core and shivered with sheer joy and exultation. 'I thought I could never rock and ride with you all the way to the heart of the sun,' he gasped as he took up the race again, and now she had the measure of it she felt the drive into something wonderful as well, as he rode hard and high inside her, and she wrapped her long and slender legs about his neat buttocks and rode with him.

She felt hot and greedy for everything he had to give her and deep and generous with all she had to offer in return. She wound her ankles together over his striving thighs and felt his whole body gasp at the feel of her wholly with him, completely engaged in the lovely flight into somewhere nobody else could ever go but them, together. Now the race was frantic and even more intense than it had been last time. She felt almost as if the full force of Mother Nature herself flowed through her as she threw back her head and felt the life of it shoot through her until even her toes and fingertips seemed to glow with it. 'Oh, my love,' she gasped as she writhed against him, and his thrusts deepened and seemed to take her even further away from her day-to-day self. There was that forlorn moment of wondering if the journey was all there was and their destination just tantalisingly out of reach and then they were there and how could she have doubted they would be?

'I love, love, love you,' she murmured on a keening whisper that turned into a satiated sigh that deferred to the fact her brothers were asleep only a floor below with the windows open.

Still their bodies soared together and the climax of that frantic ride seemed to promise eternity as they lay locked and mindless and yet so deeply mindful of each other all at the same time. Polly felt quivers of ecstasy rock her all the way down to her toes and wondered how rapidly he'd made her proud of her lanky inches instead of always half-ashamed to be so tall and supposedly unfeminine.

'Aren't you glad you came?' she asked innocently as the fire finally sank to a dearly remembered spark and the odd magical shiver of ecstasy still shook her.

To her surprise he seemed to find that comment irresistibly amusing and buried a bark of male laughter against her hair, where it spilled in a wild silky cloud against the down pillows of my lord's makeshift bed.

'What?' she demanded, almost managing to feel cross with the great puzzle of a man as he groaned with suppressed laughter, then finally made himself disengage from her sated body as reluctantly as she made herself admit it was near dawn and about time she resorted to her own part of the castle.

'I'm delighted I came back to my own and to you this spring, my love. Even more delighted that the next fool on my beloved godmother's list can now take over his part in her Machiavellian schemes and deliriously happy that I'll very shortly be marrying a marchioness after all my protests that I never would. Will that do?'

'Possibly, but why were you laughing at me so hard you nearly gave us both away just now?'

'I will tell you another time.'

'Will you now?' she asked as if she had the least intention of staying out of his bed anytime it could be avoided for the next forty or fifty years.

'It will give you something to look forward to,' he teased her with a wicked glint in his eyes and since she was beginning to be able to see the colour of them as the sun thought hard about rising on a fine June morning, she shot him a challenging look before she sprang out of bed and began to resume her scandalous breeches and best coat.

'Maybe, but today I'm looking forward to the boys showing us this phantom treasure that sounds like the little details of your mother's life nobody seemed to recall seeing for the past two decades. Then you should probably show me the lord and lady's private quarters of your soon-to-be-refurbished mansion, my lord,' she said with a jaunty smile and saw shadows steal into his gaze as he contemplated whether he could live with her in that part of the house after all.

She held her breath even as she pretended to be serenely convinced there was nothing out of the way in her plans for their morning and reached for my lord's fine set of hair brushes to smooth the tumbling mass of her hair into her usual plait to at least start the day halfway to being tame. 'My valet will be as shocked as a maiden lady if he comes in and catches you sitting on the end of my bed combing out your witchy hair for my very personal delight,' he warned her lazily.

'He'd better learn to live with me or find another job, because I'm not going to spend any more nights in my room across the courtyard to save his blushes or anyone else's,' she warned.

Chapter Fourteen

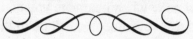

'Ah, Farenze, can't say I expected you to come since you're supposed to be busy with that ramshackle old place you bought off your brother-in-law. Is this your viscountess? Good evening, my dear. Delighted you could join us after all the invitations your husband has refused on your behalf. I dare say he wanted to keep you to himself.' The Earl of Trethayne bowed to the mystery lady the *ton* had been so eager to meet all Season and preened himself that they'd had to wait until his granddaughter's ball to do it.

The latest Trethayne chit and this grand waste of money his daughter-in-law had forced on him would be the talk of the town after tonight and for once he didn't begrudge the money all this show and frivolity was costing him. His gaze drifted onward to gauge what effect this social triumph was having on whoever was next in the receiving line, then sharpened abruptly, as if he'd been replaced by a statue of a grumpy old cheese-paring aristocrat instead of the real thing.

'The chit must know she ain't welcome here, I told

her last time she was here never to bother me or mine again,' he managed to stutter out between stiff lips as the statuesque lady dressed in the first stare of fashion reached him and looked as if she wasn't quite sure why she had bothered.

'I'm not a chit any longer, if I ever was, and I don't know why you imagine I need your welcome now, sir—I found none when I came to you and begged for help when I was seventeen and alone in the world but for three little brothers.'

'French whelps,' he almost spat at her as if she had suggested he helped her to look after a litter of unwanted puppies rather than three then very small children.

'Half-French,' the stripling at her side informed him with nearly as much brass-faced impudence as his sister.

'I can assure you the other half is pure Trethayne,' the next gentleman in line said with his usual casual impudence and Earl of Trethayne frowned at the Marquis of Mantaigne and wondered why he'd never told the idle fool exactly what he thought of him before tonight.

'What the devil do they have to do with you or the Farenze connection?'

'Lord Farenze and I were brought up together, so we share a lot of family feeling, Trethayne. I'm sure you know the ones I mean—love, loyalty and caring for the welfare of others even when you don't always want to? I hope you don't expect Lord Farenze and I to ignore each other as our wives make their first forays into the *ton* tonight. That would be downright unnatural for such close connections, don't you think?' Tom asked silkily.

His host paled and flashed a glance from one to the other of the striking group taking up so much of his guests' attention there was near silence in the overcrowded ballroom. For a moment he seemed about to admit that the unlikely group of people in front of him were indeed connected in some way he didn't understand, then he gathered his senses and his long-standing conviction he was right and they were all wrong and fought back.

'What's that sentimental rigmarole got to do with them?' he said with a dismissive wave of his hand at Polly and Toby Trethayne, who stood surveying the glittering ballroom as if they were far more interested in the spectacle of the *ton* at play than anything their reluctant host might have to say about them.

'Firstly there is the fact we all value the company of your great-niece and great-nephew and would not go anywhere they are not welcomed. Secondly—'

'Thank you, my lord, but we are quite capable of speaking for ourselves, are we not, Tobias?' His bean-pole of a great-niece had the effrontery to interrupt an even more important nobleman than his lordship knew himself to be. 'Pray don't splutter like that, sir, it isn't becoming and since we're related it won't reflect well on us for it to be known our great-uncle cannot string two words together without recourse to cursing or roaring and ranting like a lunatic.'

'I don't know how you got in here…'

'No, I'm quite sure you don't, since you have done your best to make sure we all went straight to the devil. I may have begged you for help and been turned away time after time seven years ago, but I didn't have to walk here with a babe in arms and two little brothers at my heels this time. Nor do I need to plead with you to help me put food in their bellies, because I have somehow managed to do that myself for the past seven years, since you threw us out of your house as if we carried plague. You don't need to worry, my lord, we're not here to beg for help you have no intention of giving us tonight. I know from past experience it would not be forthcoming.'

Now the silence that had greeted the delightful surprise of Lady Farenze making her first public appearance at this débutante ball was giving way to a flurry of delighted speculation, and Lord Trethayne didn't have to turn round to know whispers that he'd let such youthful members of his own family all but starve were sweeping about the ballroom as the witch paused for a moment, as if selecting the best spot to slip in the killing knife blow.

'What do you want?' he managed to grab enough presence of mind to ask, before any further revelations could fall from the giant female's mouth and ruin the night he'd paid out so much to bring about.

'An apology would do nicely to begin with,' she told him softly. By now his guests were straining so hard to hear her he was surprised they didn't just pitch up and form a circle.

'I'm sorry,' he murmured with a furious glance at his open-mouthed daughter-in-law and that wispy little chit he'd gone to so much trouble to get off their hands.

'I didn't quite catch that, Trethayne,' Mantaigne very

nearly bellowed with that almost-an-idiot grin of his that Lord Trethayne suddenly realised he'd always found so damnably irritating.

'Sorry,' he barked more loudly.

'Such a gracious manner as you've always had with us, don't you agree, Tobias?' the woman murmured and had a dowager or two reaching for their ear trumpets.

'I remember,' the boy said, and Lord Trethayne could see he did from the hot glitter in those green-and-blue Trethayne eyes he'd managed not to notice when he scouted the French hussy's brats out of his house and slammed the door behind them for the last time.

'I very much wish you could not, but how could a boy of eight forget such a harsh dismissal from this very house and the life of beggary you condemned us all to seven years ago?' his sister said as if all this was for the boy's sake and not her own.

'Come to force me to frank a Season for you, have you, m'dear?' he made himself ask as if he was a genial uncle to a niece whom the very idea of a Season and presentation at court would make a hardened match-maker blench. Make a joke out of the girl and the polite world would laugh with him and forget he'd rid himself of her so hastily last time she dared darken his doors.

'I wouldn't dream of asking you for anything, but my friends and my husband requested my company, so I agreed to come here tonight very much against my better judgement,' Paulina the Pauper had the brass-faced cheek to drawl as if she'd been taking lessons in being elegantly annoying from Mantaigne.

'Ah, so you persuaded some fool to wed a girl who

will always make a fool out of him by overtopping him at every turn, have you?' He forgot his audience long enough to gloat. If the awkward filly was already wed, there was nothing for him to do but shrug and make it obvious he pitied the poor idiot his mistake.

'No, I laid siege so determinedly that in the end Miss Trethayne gave in and agreed to wed me out of sheer boredom at having to say me nay one more time,' Tom lied with a smile for his gallant love that ignored the apoplectic-looking peer and everyone else in the room but her and their friends and family.

'You?' the old fool barked out at the top of his voice.

'Me,' Tom replied with infinite satisfaction and a long, hot look for his bride that made her blush delightfully, despite the presence of her brother and the small matter of around three hundred of his lordship's closest acquaintances.

'She's a marchioness?'

'My wife is a marchioness, something I expect she will forgive me for one day if we both live long enough. That's what happens when a woman weds a marquis, you know, Trethayne? Whether she wants to or not, she becomes his marchioness.'

'Wants to? Of course she wanted to, that's why she married you, isn't it? Can't think any sane female would want to unless you had some strawberry leaves on your coronet.'

'I do have one or two more of them than you, though, don't I? Ah, well, never mind, I'm sure my lady will resign herself to them in time.'

A titter or two greeted that outrageous piece of play-acting, except Tom knew they were wrong and he meant it. Had he been a commoner it would have been a lot easier to persuade Polly to marry him, then come to London and grasp her right to a certain position in the social world, if only for the sake of the boys. As he was thinking of that, his eyes hardened on the steely old bruiser in front of him.

'My friend here acts for me on matters of delicate family business. You might have done well to employ him in your long and frustrating search for your nephews and niece after you let them think you would not help them upon their father's death, Trethayne. I hate to imagine how hard you must have looked for them after Tobias's godfather died and left most of his fortune to the boy, with you to hold it all in trust until he came of age. One can only imagine how ill at ease you must have felt at knowing you let them leave after one of those heated family arguments we've all heard so much about once you held such a fortune in hand for them and no heir anywhere in sight. Not being able to track them down to explain their abrupt change of fortunes must have galled you to your very soul.'

'Er...yes, distraught, weren't we, Robina?' the old fox picked up his cue as Tom fixed him with a cold stare that dared him to refute Polly or Toby again.

'I have often heard you speak of it with great sorrow for your loss of temper, Papa-in-law. Such a shame Miss Trethayne took your hasty words so much to heart that she and her brothers were gone before you could calm down and tell her you didn't mean them,' the lady said smoothly enough, but something about the glint in her eye told Tom a corner had been turned in her relationship with the miserly old hypocrite as well and he would not dominate the rest of his family so easily from now on.

'Knowing you as we all do, I'm sure you will have taken the utmost care of Tobias's fortune, Trethayne. Peters here will be visiting you tomorrow to discuss all the wise investments I'm sure you've made on the boy's behalf while he was too young to manage his fortune for himself.'

'That will be delightful, but tonight I'm sure you came here to renew your connections with your family, then dance and enjoy being with us on such a joyous occasion, Cousin Paulina?' Lady Robina said with a lot more conviction than accuracy, and Tom stepped back and let his wife meet the woman on her own terms.

It was how she lived her life after all, and she had done such a fine job of it up to now he didn't see any need to interfere, even if she would let him.

Chapter Fifteen

Tom watched and assisted his wife and brother-in-law whenever they needed it for the rest of the hour they had agreed to spend at the Trethayne ball before going on to another society ball to show the world they had come to town to do more than just challenge the old vulture at the head of his wife's family tree on his home ground.

'My thanks, Lady Chloe, Winterley,' he said as soon as he'd handed his lady up into the vast old town chariot Virginia had insisted was far more comfortable than more modern and less accommodating vehicles.

'Not at all. It was far better entertainment than I expected of my first appearance in London society,' Chloe Winterley said, 'and now I'm no longer the prime target of all the gossips. I swear I would like you for that, Polly, even if I didn't love you already for marrying Tom and preventing my lord here from worrying himself to flinders about his well-being and peace of mind when I would far rather he was intent on mine instead.'

'Then I'm pleased to have been of service,' his Polly

said lightly enough, but Tom knew she was a lot less relaxed than she was so gallantly pretending to be all the same.

'I wonder who the next one is,' he remarked to divert their attention from the strains of taking on the Earl of Trethayne and the most conservative part of polite society all in one evening.

'What next one?' Toby piped up, and Tom felt Polly's interest stir despite her weariness with this whole wretched business of claiming back Toby's fortune from the money-grabbing old villain who'd appropriated it as his own and blessed the topic of conversation he'd found so appallingly unamusing at the outset of his season at Virginia's beck and call.

Satisfied? he asked silently, as if his godmother could somehow hear him.

You'll do now seemed to come back to him as if she'd whispered it in his ear, but the laughter and satisfaction in it felt so much like her that his breath caught with love and loss. It was almost easy when you got the hang of it, this love business, and he realised he'd had a flying start at it by being taken in and loved despite himself by Virgil and Virginia all those years ago.

'My godmother's next victim,' he explained with an apologetic nod at the corner of the carriage he knew very well only held Toby and a silk cushion, even if it had been her favourite seat when she was alive.

'Victim?' Toby asked sleepily, and Tom wondered if they really needed to drag him across London for another interminable party, but Luke and Peters had insisted and he suspected they knew more about staying on the right side of the dowagers than he did.

'My great-aunt, being a great deal more fun and loving us as dearly as your own great-uncle clearly only loves himself, decreed four of her closest relatives and friends spend a quarter each of the year after her death carrying out errands on her behalf. This quarter was Tom's and the next... Well, only my darling wife and Peters' senior partner know who the next one on her list is and they are not telling us.'

'First I had to inform the person who will be expected to carry out her wishes, Luke,' Chloe told him, and Tom thought he knew what his friend had meant at the beginning of all this about enjoying watching the next on the list dance about at Virginia's bidding because he knew his task was safely over.

He felt Polly next to him and the enormity of the changes in his own life caught him up in wonder, that he should be so other than how he had thought he was back then and that Polly should love him anyway.

'So who is he?'

'That is not for me to reveal.'

'Me,' Peters's voice rasped from his own dark corner of the vast old vehicle as it rumbled to a stop, and the flares and noise of another great rout spilled out on to the streets around it. 'Confound it, but she picked me for some reason best known to herself.'

'I'm quite sure she had a good one,' Chloe said soothingly, and Tom felt his Polly lean forward to ask more and ran a distracting hand over her pert *derrière* now shadows and the flurry of disembarking covered up his need to touch her as often as he could get away with it.

'Enough, love, it's his job to work through the next few months as best he can. We have our own lives to work on for our next fifty or sixty years together.'

'True, but I can never thank your godmama enough for sending you back to Dayspring Castle this spring, Tom,' Polly said with such certainty in her voice he had to swallow back an unmanly lump in his throat.

She had done so much damage to the Marquis of Mantaigne's light-hearted indifference to the rest of the world he hardly recognised himself in Polly Trethayne's besotted husband, but the very thought of having missed out on this new life of theirs made him realise how deeply indebted he was to Virginia for making him return to the castle he'd sworn never to set foot in again as long as he lived.

'True, and if I hadn't loved her before I would have to now, love, for she's turned all I ever swore not to do on its head. If only I'd come back when I came of age instead of ordering the place to fall down without me, we could have been happy for years by now.'

'If you hadn't left Dayspring empty, we would never have gone to live there in your absence, you idiot,' his loving wife chided as Tom sprang out of the carriage to hand down his lady before any other rogue could do it for him.

'There you are, you see, Peters? I have a lifetime of scolds and humility to look forward to,' he said smugly as he stood back for Luke to echo his own determination not to let any other man lay a hand on his wife tonight and hand Chloe down from the grand old coach.

'I look forward to observing it from afar, my lord,' the supposedly quiet young lawyer told him solemnly.

'If you think you can get away from Farenze that easily you're about to discover your error. Fellow's like a limpet. Polly and I will call our first son after you, then you won't be able to deny our acquaintance either.'

'Frederick, wasn't it?' Polly asked, looking as if she was trying hard to like the idea, and Tom considered the notion with apparent seriousness.

'Peter?' he suggested, thinking that sounded a fair enough name for a future marquis and the son he'd once sworn never to have. He caressed Polly's long fingers as they walked up the steps to the next grand town house on their list unashamedly hand-locked. 'It would keep the boy's feet on the ground to have a good solid name to remind him he's not one of the lords of Creation.'

'He will have me for that,' Polly reminded him with a radiant smile as they joined the tail of guests waiting to be introduced to their host and hostess for the next hour or so and yet another blushing daughter recently launched on the marriage mart.

'How true,' Tom replied with a mock grimace at the idea of being humbled for his own good for the next fifty years or so. 'Perhaps we'd best call him after a great warrior after all then. It sounds as if the poor lad could need encouragement.'

'Even if I thought you were serious, my lord, there's no need to do either on my account,' Peters told him with an uncomfortable glance around another glittering ballroom that told Tom he would rather be almost anywhere else, but he'd been drawn into that Farenze Connection old Trethayne had referred to so scornfully against his will and felt some sort of obligation to support the rest of them tonight. 'Those are not my real names,' he added as drily as if discussing some obscure point of law with his fellow lawyers.

'An alias?' Tom asked with raised eyebrows and tried to ignore his wife's frown and shushing gesture as he challenged his latest brother-in-arms.

'We all sail under false colours in some ways, don't you agree, my lord?' the man challenged him back, and Tom looked at himself at the beginning of his quest and decided the man was right.

'Perhaps, but some of us not quite as deliberately as others. Are you the black sheep of the family then, cast adrift for some youthful sin I'm quite certain you won't tell us about?'

'I could be,' not-Peters said tightly as they approached the head of the receiving line, and delighted whispers began to break out in another overcrowded ballroom like ripe corn chattering together on a stir of summer hot air. 'I could be their worst nightmare,' he added so low nobody else but Tom and Polly could hear.

'Or their favourite dream,' Polly argued. 'You never know what the next three months might bring you, but I'm very glad Tom's brought him to me. Perhaps you should go back to them and find out if they really think themselves better off without you rather than deciding for them?'

'And perhaps I should do the decent thing and stay

away,' he replied with a bleak certainty even Tom found rather chilling for a man he'd come to respect and like, if he could get through the rigid self-control Peters used to fend off the world.

'Whatever you should or shouldn't do, you're at Virginia's mercy for the next season and I wish you joy of it,' Luke put in with a grin after they had got through the surprised greetings and hasty congratulations of their hosts and moved out into the ballroom beyond. 'I certainly intend to enjoy the fruits of my labours to the full,' he added with a wicked smile at Chloe.

'Cocksure braggart,' she chided softly enough so only they could hear her, despite the stars in her eyes.

'Guilty,' he admitted brazenly and whisked her into the next dance to show the polite world he only had eyes for his wife and intended to ignore all those dreadful rumours that the Farenze curse had struck again.

Dark and dangerous Lord Farenze himself had been captured and spellbound beyond diversion and now, horror of horrors, there was a rumour going about the ballroom that the Marquis of Mantaigne had wed the magnificent creature he refused to let go long enough to even be introduced. Society, or at least the young and hopeful female part of it, let out a long sigh of disappointment and readjusted its expectations of making a brilliant marriage or taking a dazzlingly handsome lover with that particular gentleman.

'So you see, Peters, for I don't imagine you're about to gift us with the use of your real name, you are in danger of being made happy despite your best intentions to be miserable,' Tom told him and dragged his own lady onto the dance-floor in his friend's wake before Polly could protest at leaving her brother to be guided through the avidly curious throng by Virginia's next hero.

'He'll guard your eldest lamb as if he's the only heir to a kingdom, never fear, love,' Tom whispered as Polly watched her eldest brother grin at the neatly dressed lawyer and follow him to the groaning refreshment table.

'I don't. Mr Peters has a very safe pair of hands and Toby is far more grown up than any of the pampered sons and heirs these people are accustomed to. If they try to pump him for details, he'll very likely to tell them some wild and improbable story just for the fun of it.'

'Aye, and I can't help liking him for it.'

'Neither can I,' Polly admitted with a chuckle that did something very drastic indeed to Tom's heart and sent him into a state of complete desire between one second and the next.

'I much prefer his big sister though,' he admitted huskily as they came back together for the next part of the dance and even a brisk measure with a very disapproving matron hadn't been enough to restore him to a fit state to inhabit a lady's ballroom. 'You couldn't manage a bit of a stumble, or perhaps even a faint, could you, love? I want to bed you even more urgently than I did this afternoon and I don't think there's any way I can conceal the fact from the rest of the world for much longer.'

'It would take half a dozen footmen to carry me out,' she said with a wry smile and a huff of laughter as she looked down at the evidence of his rampant need for her. 'Hmm, I do see what you mean, though,' she added with a delighted smile that only made it worse.

'I won't have you traduce yourself, or me for that matter, my love. You are just as tall as you need to be and I wouldn't have you even half an inch less and at least if I'm carrying you I can hide behind your skirts, for once.'

'You couldn't,' she gasped a little less certainly as the music finally wound down, and she looked as if she felt ready to melt from the inside out as well.

'I'm impressive, Polly, my darling, but not even I am too huge not to be able to hide what you do to me behind that delightful but highly unnecessary wisp of silk and nonsense,' he said with a dismissive glance at the finest gown in a whole wardrobe of them that the Bond Street modiste had rushed through her workroom in time for Lady Mantaigne to make her début in polite society at the advanced age of four and twenty.

'It is very necessary,' she argued absent-mindedly as she flitted through scenarios for getting out of this ballroom in double-quick time and without her lord making a scandal of them both mere days into their marriage.

'Not as far as I'm concerned it's not,' he argued as his intensely blue eyes met hers with a wealth of hot promises that made her shiver with anticipation. 'I want you in it, out of it and any other way I can have you, my lovely witchy Polly. From the first moment I laid eyes on you I've been racked with need and I don't intend either of us to be denied satiating that need again for much longer.'

'We sated it all afternoon, Tom,' she protested half-heartedly, but there was as much heat in her grey-green-blue eyes as in his, and her breath was coming so short his fascinated gaze was fixed on her décolletage as her breasts rose magnificently, begging for his attentions as soon as possible under the promise of all he'd taught her to expect these past few days since they married in haste. 'I suppose I am very hot,' she managed to say rather breathily.

'You most certainly are,' he drawled, with the Tom-cat smile that had once made her hackles rise and hot shivers of desire plague her dreams and now made her long to share them with him even more than she had a second ago.

'I love you, Tom,' she breathed, and to the devil with anyone who might be listening.

'And I love you, my darling, but any minute now I might have to beg you to get us out of here, because I can't seem to string two thoughts together than aren't of making love to you as soon and as long as I can find an excuse to.'

'Oh, very well then,' she said with a tight little sigh that told him more than a hundred words of how much she loved and wanted him back, because she obligingly drooped as if quite overcome by the heat and excitement of her first night amongst the *ton* and trusted him absolutely to catch her and get them out of here as fast as he could order his host to lend them the nearest carriage and throw guineas at the coachman to get them back to Mantaigne House faster than he could say knife.

* * *

Polly stayed totally limp against him for a long moment, savouring the mighty strength of her lover and revelling in being needed and wanted by the man she wanted and needed so desperately back.

'I never dreamed I would marry at all, you know?' she whispered as he held her even closer to shield her from the rocking carriage as it swept across Mayfair.

'I know it,' he said rather grimly, considering he had interrupted kissing his way up her throat to do so. 'I deplore it and yet… Oh, love, I'm so glad you were safe at Dayspring and away from the wolves all the time I was strutting about the *ton* pretending I didn't care a damn for anyone. I have no right to be so proud to be your first lover, but I am and fully intend to be your last as well, if God will grant us the time to glory in each other like this for life.'

'Idiot,' she muttered on a blissful haze of joy that almost went beyond words. 'Of course I'm glad it was only ever you and always will be. There's nothing wrong with being all in all to each other, nothing wrong with being glad we love and live and want each other so immoderately. Do you truly think Toby will be all right with Mr Peters, though?' she added as remembrance of the rest of her family impinged on the desire he was feeding so shamelessly she wondered if they would make it home and into his splendid marquis's bed before they fell on each other like ravenous tigers.

'Why else to you think the man agreed to come with us tonight?' Tom said and gasped in a huge breath as the brush of her thigh against his mightily aroused manhood made him grip his fists tight in his determination not to make love to his marchioness in a stranger's carriage. 'He's no fool and knew neither we nor Luke and Chloe would be able to keep cool in the company of our lovers. I dare say he would rather have teeth pulled than enter a Mayfair ballroom of his own accord.'

'Then he's a good man,' she said with a nod that said it confirmed her conclusions about her new husband's lawyer and perhaps friend. 'I hope your godmother hasn't bitten off more than she could chew this time, though, for I would dearly like to see your Mr Peters happy.'

'He's neither mine nor Mr Peters, love, but I have learnt to have even more faith in Virginia over the past three months than I had before, so I expect he'll end up wherever it is he thinks he has no right to be. However, my interest in the man is lukewarm at best when I have my Lady Mantaigne available to distract me with her many and varied charms,' he said as the carriage finally lurched to its destination.

'No,' she ordered him brusquely as he jumped out of the carriage and turned to lift her in his arms again. 'You will just have to carry this,' she declared, handing him her cloak as a mask for the state they had done nothing to diminish during the drive. 'I refuse to have you winded and exhausted when we finally manage to get ourselves upstairs,' she added with a haughty sniff as he eyed her with lordly determination and made a grab for her.

'She-wolf,' he accused as she dodged him and reminded him he'd agreed to pay the coachman another two guineas if he got them here before the clock finished chiming midnight.

'Tomcat,' she shot back over her shoulder as she gathered up her silken skirts and frothy petticoats in one hand and ran up the steps as if the devil was on her heels.

'Hand over the keys to the wine-cellar, marry him to your eldest daughter or just pay the man for me, would you?' Tom asked his butler distractedly before he set off up the steps to his once-stately and echoing mansion without a second thought for his lost reputation as an elegantly bored and sophisticated man about town.

'Yes, my lord,' the butler said with a glare for the grinning coachman. 'Breathe a word of this and I'll make sure you ain't up to marrying any man's daughter, let alone mine,' he threatened the man as he handed over the extortionate fee his master had promised him.

'Even the nobs will know by now he can't keep his hands off her, cocky, so that's a horse as has already bolted,' the man said cheerfully and went off to tell his tale to whoever was the most eager to listen to it.

'And ain't that just how it ought to be between a man and his wife?' the butler asked the sparkling June night, lit by stars so bright they even managed to outshine the man-made glitter of Mayfair in full fig.

'Hurry,' Tom gritted between clenched teeth as Polly streaked up the stairs ahead of him and he could see enough of her slender legs and the long, sleek lines of her hips and bottom outlined by that wicked provocation of a gown to drive him nigh demented. 'I hope your maid isn't waiting up,' he managed as she got to the door only one step ahead of him and fumbled it open before turning to snap a hasty denial.

'Of course not. Jane has far more sense,' she told him as if he was an idiot to even mention it.

'Silly me,' he said with a predator's grin and shut the door behind them with a contented sigh. 'Alone at last, my love,' he whispered and set about the laces of her gown with hands clumsy with too much haste even as he devoured her temptation of a mouth with a driven groan.

'Ah, love, quiet,' she soothed even as her still slightly calloused fingers raced to undo as much of Lord Mantaigne as she could while he was doing the same for Lady Mantaigne in his ham-fisted fashion. 'We have all night,' she promised even as she hastily shrugged out of her loosened gown and gave a crow of triumph as she pushed his roughly unbuttoned waistcoat and tightly fitting evening coat off his shoulders.

He dipped his head to feast on her roused nipples even as she moaned with pent-up need and haste and caressed his wildly disordered locks with such tenderness he raised his head and snatched another of those hasty, open-mouthed kisses before pulling far enough away to fumble off his cravat and tug his shirt over his head. Any last trace of ladylike restraint vanished as she eyed his hard-muscled torso and lean waist with a heavy-eyed smile.

'Evening breeches are a cursed nuisance,' she informed him as he bent to unbutton them at the knee and heel off his elegant shoes before impatiently stripping away his stockings.

'Oh, I don't know, they have their uses,' he said huskily as she attacked the buttons at his waist with more haste than skill.

'Not for hiding this,' she told him with would-be severity, but her eyes glittered hotly in the light of the candle Jane had left on the nightstand, so they might at least try not to ruin another set of expensive raiment and cause her and his lordship's valet even more trouble.

'Did you want to?' he asked with a wicked grin.

'Not from us, from all those other women,' she admitted rather painfully.

'None of them matter. I didn't love anyone until I met you, remember?'

'Oh, you man, you. You have always had it there deep within you, Tom, but you wouldn't let yourself know it. How else could you have made a family of the heart when your real one faded? How did you win a legion of friends and lovers who put you at the centre of their circle and had the sense to know you made them more than they were without you? You are so much more than you ever let yourself know, but what if you learn that for yourself one day and don't need me any more?'

'Now who's the idiot?' he asked with a catch in his deep voice. 'I will never not need you, Polly. I found pleasure with other women before I met you and if that makes you sad and uncertain of me, I'm sorry for it and wish it otherwise, but it was nothing like this. I've never needed to make love to another woman so desperately it feels as if I might expire of sheer need without you. Does it look as if I could ever stop wanting you, my love? Because if it does, I think we'd better get you fitted for some eyeglasses as soon as the spectacle makers are open in the morning.'

'I don't think there's anything wrong with my eyesight,' she said with a hiccup of laughter as she let her gaze linger on the very evident need he had of her. 'You're beautiful,' she told him, quite forgetting to be insecure at the sight of him so openly and proudly wanting her to the finest fibre of his being.

'Ah, love, come here and let me show you how breathtakingly lovely you are,' he said in reply and he actually blushed at her wide-eyed appreciation of his muscular body and rampantly aroused manhood. 'I love you, Polly Trethayne,' he told her as he held her eyes and parted her legs so he could thrust into the hot wet heat of her and unite them once more.

'Polly Banburgh,' she corrected breathlessly and opened wholeheartedly to him, sparing a moment to marvel anew that Polly Trethayne had found herself a husband, and such a fine and rampant husband as the Marquis of Mantaigne as well. 'I love you, Tom. With every last inconvenient inch of me, I love you.'

'Every last magnificent and delightful inch of you I hope you mean. Every bit of you is precious to me,' he said as he met her dazed eyes with his blazing hot, blue gaze so full of conviction she had to believe him. 'I wouldn't have you an inch less, my Polly, and don't let anyone make you feel awkward or overgrown ever again.'

'Very well, I won't,' she said meekly and let her inner muscles ripple around his hard member in delighted encouragement. 'There are so many parts of me in need of reassurance that you love right now, husband,' she murmured with wanton encouragement as she sneaked a suggestive hand over her own hard-peaked nipples and down the smooth line of her narrow waist and the curve of her hips before she reached their joined bodies and found his more fascinating than her own.

'Oh, I love you all right, so get ready to be reassured to your heart's content, Lady Mantaigne,' he said huskily as he silenced her with a long, hard kiss as if they'd been parted for weeks instead of hours and proceeded to show his wife he loved and appreciated and wanted every last fine inch of silky skin and every hair on her head.

* * * * *

Join Britain's BIGGEST Romance Book Club

- **EXCLUSIVE** offers every month

- **FREE** delivery direct to your door

- **NEVER MISS** a title

- **EARN** Bonus Book points

Call Customer Services
0844 844 1358*

or visit
millsandboon.co.uk/subscriptions

* This call will cost you 7 pence per minute plus your phone company's price per minute access charge.

BKCB3